Midnight Desires

"Serena . . ." Gage's voice whispered hotly in her ear. "Do you want this?" He pulled her back enough to look at her squarely, leaving no room for hesitation. "Do you want me?"

"Yes," she told him, drawing him close again. "Only this. Only you."

Gage wanted to believe her, wanted to believe she did want him—not merely need him. But he couldn't afford to want, to need. It would only end like it had every other time—him walking away empty, leaving behind a piece of himself and taking nothing with him.

With a wrenching effort, Gage jerked himself out of Serena's embrace. "I'm sorry," Gage said softly. "I can't give you what you want. Not now. Maybe not ever."

Very slowly, Serena lifted her eyes to his. "What do you want? What can I give you?" When he stayed silent, she shook her head impatiently. "You can't answer because you don't know. You never take anything for yourself, so you don't know." Drawing in a shaky breath she swiped a tear from her cheek before staring him straight in the eye. "Let me tell you what I know. I know we belong together, Gage Tanner."

* * *

"Courageous heroine and tragic hero find love in this pleasurable read."

—Bobbi Smith

TODAY'S HOTTEST READS
ARE TOMORROW'S SUPERSTARS

VICTORY'S WOMAN   (4484, $4.50)
by Gretchen Genet
Andrew—the carefree soldier who sought glory on the battlefield,
and returned a shattered man . . . Niall—the legandary frontiers-
man and a former Shawnee captive, tormented by his past . . .
Roger—the troubled youth, who would rise up to claim a shocking legacy . . . and Clarice—the passionate beauty bound by one
man, and hopelessly in love with another. Set against the backdrop of the American revolution, three men fight for their
heritage—and one woman is destined to change all their lives forever!

FORBIDDEN   (4488, $4.99)
by Jo Beverley
While fleeing from her brothers, who are attempting to sell her
into a loveless marriage, Serena Riverton accepts a carriage ride
from a stranger—who is the handsomest man she has ever seen.
Lord Middlethorpe, himself, is actually contemplating marriage
to a dull daughter of the aristocracy, when he encounters the
breathtaking Serena. She arouses him as no woman ever has. And
after a night of thrilling intimacy—a forbidden liaison—Serena
must choose between a lady's place and a woman's passion!

WINDS OF DESTINY   (4489, $4.99)
by Victoria Thompson
Becky Tate is a half-breed outcast—branded by her Comanche
heritage. Then she meets a rugged stranger who awakens her
heart to the magic and mystery of passion. Hiding a desperate
past, Texas Ranger Clint Masterson has ridden into cattle country
to bring peace to a divided land. But a greater battle rages inside
him when he dares to desire the beautiful Becky!

WILDEST HEART   (4456, $4.99)
by Virginia Brown
Maggie Malone had come to cattle country to forge her future as
a healer. Now she was faced by Devon Conrad, an outlaw
wounded body and soul by his shadowy past . . . whose eyes
blazed with fury even as his burning caress sent her spiraling with
desire. They came together in a Texas town about to explode in sin
and scandal. Danger was their destiny—and there was nothing
they wouldn't dare for love!

*Available wherever paperbacks are sold, or order direct from the
Publisher. Send cover price plus 50¢ per copy for mailing and
handling to Penguin USA, P.O. Box 999, c/o Dept. 17109,
Bergenfield, NJ 07621. Residents of New York and Tennessee
must include sales tax. DO NOT SEND CASH.*

DANETTE CHARTIER

MIDNIGHT PROMISES

ZEBRA BOOKS
KENSINGTON PUBLISHING CORP.

To Bobbi Smith
Friend and Mentor

ZEBRA BOOKS are published by

Kensington Publishing Corp.
850 Third Avenue
New York, NY 10022

First Printing: July, 1994

Printed in the United States of America

Prologue

Arizona Territory, 1888

Standing a few feet from the hanging tree, a gaunt shadow in the pre-dawn darkness, Moroni watched as one of his men put the rope around the old man's neck. A quick snap of wind flattened his black calf-length duster against his lean frame, shifting the curled haze of smoke at his feet, but he stayed still, his face expressionless. Only his eyes, dark and hollow, betrayed any feeling. They glinted with hatred, devoid of mercy or pity.

"Where is Tanner?"

The old man squinted at him with his one good eye. He stood slumped-shouldered, his body slouched in resignation, beaten by the horrors he'd been forced to witness. "Don't know," he said, his thin shoulders lifting in a shrug. "And I ain't likely to tell you if I did. None of the rest would tell you, now would they?"

"And they're all dead. All except Tanner. I want him."

"Cain't tell you what I don't know."

For an instant, Moroni considered killing the old man with his bare hands. His fingers clenched into a fist and he flexed them several times, his own flesh biting into itself, before he could speak with his usual cold self-possession. "Then you will die with them."

"Best get it over with then," the old man said, only a slight tremble in his graveled voice betraying his fear.

Moroni stared at him a moment longer, frustration and loathing burning through him. In the fading hours of the night, the wind cried through the empty ranch buildings, kicking up flurries of dust from the desert floor. Flickers from the dying fires made small points of wavering light against blackened timber skeletons, the acrid smell of smoke and blood still heavy in the air.

Finally, Moroni made to raise his hand to signal the man holding the rope. But before he could give the silent command, a shout came from one of his men along with a snarling growl. From a corner of the courtyard, the ragged, lumbering shape of a large dog came hurtling through the sand in Moroni's direction.

"Joe!"

The old man's anguished cry caused the dog to pause. Seizing the advantage, Moroni slid his revolver out of his holster, aimed, and fired in one fluid motion. With a howl of pain, the dog staggered and fell.

His face set in the same flat, hard lines, Moroni gave a sharp gesture. The men hoisting the rope tugged at it until the old man's feet left the ground.

Moroni glanced briefly at the old man's terror-stricken expression, at the gnarled hands scrabbling at the thick rope, then turned and strode toward the open gates that protected the ranch house.

One of his men followed, looking back at the dangling figure, blurring then vanishing behind the thick swirls of dust. "What do we do now, Moroni? Tanner isn't here—"

"He will be." Stepping over the lifeless body of one of the ranch hands, Moroni shielded his eyes with the sleeve of his coat and headed toward the fence where he'd tethered his horse. He'd waited too long for the opportunity to regain the ranch. Tanner had no right to it, nor did anyone else, Mormon or gentile. It belonged to him. Fools—blind fools who refused to see his vision for the ranch and its priceless natural water supply—had taken it from him.

But he would take it back. He had never conceded anything he knew as rightfully his. And he would destroy anyone who opposed him.

"We will wait for Tanner to return," he finally told the man at his side. "He will come back."

"We can't stay here," the man said, faltering back when Moroni whirled on him, stopping him in mid-stride.

"No?"

"S-surely you know . . . every lawman and bounty hunter in the territory is looking for us. If we stay, they'll know we're responsible for—this." The man swept a hand behind him.

"We won't stay here. There are other ways of watching and waiting." Turning back, Moroni walked up to his horse and gathered up the reins, pulling himself into the saddle. "I'll see Gage Tanner dead." He had to shout to be heard over the fury of the dust devil. "And I will get back what is mine. Everything that is mine."

Sending the man to call his group together, Moroni waited while they mounted their horses and grouped behind him. They then moved almost as one, riding out across the plain, through the storm of wind and dirt.

None of them spared a backward glance for the old man.

Struggling against the choke-hold of the noose, he managed an agonized look at the still form of his dog. "Joe," he croaked out on a harsh rasp of breath. "Devils. Not angels. Devils."

Chapter One

Arizona Territory, March 2, 1888

The feel of trouble shot cold and fast up Gage Tanner's neck. He turned to the man riding beside him, shifting uneasily in the saddle, the leather creaking with his weight. "Something's wrong."

Ross Brady sat deathly silent, suddenly stiff with tension. "Ahead or behind?"

"At the ranch." Hunting with his senses, listening to his instincts, Gage tried to narrow down the source of his nameless apprehension. The wind brushed the whiskey-colored hair that curled into his shirt collar against his skin, intensifying the quicksilver feeling. His hand itched to reach for the butt of the revolver on his hip, but the sling that held his wounded shoulder in place stopped him short. Cursing the injury, he fixed his clear green eyes on the landscape in front of him. Even though the shape of the ranch house and outbuildings were just gray smudges on the far edge of the plain, the feeling that something unspeakable had happened there in his absence was as clear to him as the turquoise sky above. At times like this he almost damned the uncanny accuracy of his intuition; he always smelled death before he saw it.

Tugging his broad hat a little lower on his face, Ross glanced around them. The shadow of the hat, and his long untamed beard and shoulder-length hair, obscured his expression, but didn't hide the tautness in his low, rumbling voice. "No one's been trailin' us . . ."

"That's because they made it to the ranch before we did," Gage said grimly, then kicked his horse into a gallop, leaving Ross to follow in the dusty wake.

As he drew nearer, he quickly scanned the stables and sheds at the back of the sprawling property. The smell of smoke lingered in the drifts of dust and wind, strong enough to be scarcely an hour old. Silence hung heavily in the sharp morning air, the only sound breaking the eerie quiet was the knock of the door to the sheep stable against weathered planks. It swung wide open freely, dangling on one hinge. Gage pulled in the reins and jerked his newly broken stallion around.

To the south, the split-rail corral that ought to have held half a dozen mustangs stood empty, the gate ajar, several rails ripped away. At the far edge of the row of outbuildings, the charred remains of the toolshed lay in a smoldering heap, a black haze still spiraling from the ashes.

Ross caught up to him just as Gage whirled his horse away from the outbuildings toward the two-story stone ranch house. "Whoever it was must've been here durin' the night," he said, giving the damage a quick appraisal. "That fire's still got life to it."

Gage yanked his rifle out of its saddle sheath, his face hard. "It's not the fire I'm worried about."

"Libby and the boys are locked in," Ross said, pulling out his own rifle and following Gage toward the walled ranch house that looked more like a fortress than a home. "No one can get through that gate."

As they circled around from the rear, the ranch house

gave Gage no clue as to the truth of Ross's claim. Logic told him his friend was right. A huge rectangular building, it was constructed to fend off intruders in blocks of solid stone, without windows or doors on any side, the only openings in the walls the rifle slits, placed strategically all around. From the top of the walls those inside could look down and control who would and would not be allowed to enter. The only way in or out of the huge house and its central courtyard was at either end through massive sets of oak gates.

And only he and Libby had keys.

With the gates locked, Gage doubted anything short of cannon fire would open them to intruders. But he didn't doubt there were those who would try even that. For the thick walls protected a commodity more precious than gold in the harsh Arizona strip country. Water. An oasis, fed by an underground spring, centered in the courtyard between the two wings of the ranch house. And here, whoever controlled water, controlled a big chunk of the territory.

His uneasiness growing stronger by the second, Gage rounded the corner to face the gates—and the dread he had tried to reason away hit him straight between the eyes.

The gates gaped open, framing the bodies of two of his ranch hands. One glance was enough for him to see they were long past breathing.

With scarcely a moment's hesitation over the men, Gage urged his stallion around them and into the courtyard. He started to turn the horse to the side of the oasis when a slight motion caught his attention. A gaunt figure dangled from the branch of one of the cottonwoods that bent over the spring-fed pool. Directly beneath lay a large, scruffy dog, its rear leg twisted and bloody.

"My God—Pete!" Gage jerked his mount to a pawing

halt near the pool, sliding down before the horse came to a full stop, and pulling a knife from his boot with the swiftness of a predator. One swift swipe across the rope, and the unconscious body fell limply into his arms.

Ross came up behind him just as Gage gently lowered Pete to the ground, bending an ear to his chest. "He's still alive."

"I can't say the same for Mac and Riley," Ross said. "I thought I had the stomach for most kinds of death. But this . . ." He shook his head. "The bodies are still warm. We couldn't have missed the killin' by more'n an hour or so."

"Pete wouldn't have lasted if it had been much longer."

"After that much time with a rope around his neck, he ain't ever gonna be the same, that's for sure," Ross said, kneeling down beside Gage to get a closer look at the old man.

Gage felt his apprehensions hit full force again, side by side with a slow burning anger that started to take on a strength of its own inside him. "Take him," he told Ross. "I have to find Libby and the boys."

Sweeping the courtyard in long strides, Gage nearly stumbled over another of the hands, sprawled at an unnatural angle at one end of the yard behind a barrel he must have been using for cover. His hand tightened on his rifle and he ran upstairs, taking the steps two at a time, to scout through the second-story rooms. Finding nothing but the destruction of a recent rampage, he hurried back down to the courtyard.

Ross, busy wrapping a dampened bandanna around Pete's neck, looked up at the sound of Gage's footsteps. "Find anything?"

"They're not there," Gage said, his voice tight. "I'm going to check the stables."

"If they're gone—" Ross pushed his hat back, looking Gage straight in the face. "Might've been Apache. Geronimo's renegades know you helped lead the cavalry to him. There's still a handful of 'em runnin' around these parts. Could be they decided to take their revenge. If it was . . ." He let the sentence die.

"Then they took Libby, her sister, and the boys," Gage finished for him. "Apache never kill what they can use or trade. You don't have to say it. It looks like their way of killing. Except for Pete. A hanging doesn't make sense."

"No rule says it has to, friend."

Gage picked up the reins of his horse in his left hand and threw a leg over the saddle. "Maybe," he muttered, then wheeled his horse around and rode out into the front yard, in the direction of the corral. On the short path leading to it the churning in his stomach grew stronger. He knew a second before he got there what waited for him.

At the far edge of the fence, he found Libby's sister, her arms crossed over her face, palms up, as if protecting herself from a blow. Giving her a quick, despairing glance, Gage headed straight for the stable.

The smell of blood and dust met him at the stable doors. Setting his jaw, he slid out of the saddle, his rifle feeling awkward in his left hand, and stepped inside.

He didn't have to look far. In the first stall, crumpled in the crimson-stained hay, lay the still bodies of his adopted family.

For a moment, he could only stand and stare, the emotion shocked out of his mind and heart, leaving him numb. He dropped to his knees beside them, the rifle slipping out of his hand.

"No . . ." With his good arm he reached down and curled a hand around the slender shoulder of his best friend's widow, gently turning her face upward. He felt the deceptive warmth of her, but no life. And there was no life in either of the two small boys sprawled at her side. "I promised Jon I'd take care of you," he whispered. "All of you."

Lost in a storm of grief that left him blind and deaf, he didn't realize Ross had followed him to the stable until the other man laid a hand on his shoulder. "There's nothin' you could have done, friend."

"I could have been here." Gage reached out and touched a finger to a strand of one boy's lank blond hair. "His daddy was the closest thing I ever had to a brother. We tracked Geronimo side by side for the cavalry until. . . . When he lay there with an arrow in his chest, he asked me to keep his family safe. I gave him my word . . ."

"You couldn't have predicted this. The cattle were prime. You had to drive them in or you'd have lost your price. Jon would have done the same thing."

"I should've been back a week ago. I would have been here." His voice fell flat. "If only I hadn't taken extra time on the way back here to try to chase down those ponies on the north rim."

"You wanted those ponies for the boys. Chances are, if your own horse hadn't slipped on that hillside when the boulder shifted and thrown you, you'd a' been here, lyin' there with 'em. Was a shame we had to shoot him. But the extra time it took to break Gusano so you could ride him back here probably saved your life. The only thing to do now is telegraph the marshall, try to find out who—"

Gage shot Ross a hard stare. "I don't need the marshall. Pete can tell me who. That's all I need." Turning back once more, he brushed a hand over Libby's eyes,

closing them. Then, with a last look at the pale, innocent faces, he forced himself to his feet.

"Pete ain't gonna be much help," Ross said as they
walked out of the stable. "I asked him every question I
could think of, but he ain't right in his mind. He was
strung up too long."

Gage shook his head. "I'll make him right." Turning
away, he strode out of the corral, back across the stretch
of yard, and through the open gates to where Ross had
left Pete hunched against the hanging tree that almost
took his life, cradling the still-bleeding dog in his arms.
At Gage's approach, the old man looked up, his eyes
wide and glazed, one wandering independently of the
other, his neck marred with an ugly purple ring. Bending down, Gage took him by the shoulders, forcing him
to look up. "Who did this? Tell me."

Pete's head bobbed in erratic movements. "It was
devils."

"Names, Pete. For God's sake, try and remember."

"Devils in the trees. Shadows. Tree devils." The old
man's whispered horror chilled the sun-scorched morning air. "They were lookin' for Tanner! You! Tanner—
they wanted Tanner!"

"Me . . . who was? You have to tell me—" Frustration mounting by the minute, Gage gave the old man a
shake. "What did they want? Pete—"

"You're not doin' him or yourself any good," Ross
intervened. He stepped to Pete's side and eased the
wounded dog away. "Best let him get some rest. Maybe
he'll remember somethin' later."

"Don't count on it," Gage said, helping Ross get Pete
to his feet and carry him into one of the downstairs
rooms. He put a torn-apart bed back together well
enough to lay him down on, then pulled a blanket over
the thin, shivering figure. "After what I've seen, I can't

say I blame him." Straightening, he looked toward the courtyard, his expression grim, his eyes hot with anger. "And whether he remembers or not, I'm going to find out who's did this if it takes me this lifetime and most of the next. But right now—" He looked toward the open gates. "I'm going out to look for tracks."

"You know as well as I do, the way the wind was blowin' on our way in, the dirt don't have no story to tell."

"I don't know anything for certain until I see it with my own eyes." Gage mounted and searched the yard and beyond on all sides of the ranch, but as Ross had predicted, the dirt lay in wind tossed ripples, hiding secrets he'd never uncover. Anger, frustration, and the pain of loss raging in his gut, he forced himself to turn back and face the grim task of burying his adopted family.

Ross met him on the slope behind the ranch. "Let's get it done," he said under his breath.

The sun was high by the time they'd found the rest of the bodies of the ranch hands and dug the nine graves on the slope behind the corral. Lost in separate thoughts, they'd scarcely spoken during the bleak task. Now, finishing the last mound, Gage unbent and wiped the sweat from his face.

"Birk Reed's had an eye on this place since he showed up in the territory. Might have been his gang," Ross said, breaking the long silence.

"I thought about that. But if he wanted to take the ranch, he'd have moved in while I was away. Why kill everyone, then leave his prize?"

"Hard to say. He might've got scared and left it."

"Maybe. Except Libby would never have let anyone she didn't trust through those gates. Especially at night."

"Well, somebody got inside." Ross jammed the blade

of his shovel into the hard earth, leaning against the handle. "And it's a sure bet they're still lookin' for you. Best thing to do is wire for the marshall and let him deal with it."

"No."

Ross started back, raising a brow. "You're not thinkin'—"

"They were looking for me. Now I'm looking for them."

"You and who else? You can see plain as I can, it took more than a man or two to do this much damage. I ain't exactly sayin' I won't help you track 'em down, but as long as there's a chance there's a helluva lot more of them than there is of us, I ain't riding out after 'em, askin' to be shot full of holes. Besides, right now with that bad shoulder, you don't even have a decent shootin' arm. We ain't got no tracks to follow, and by the time you're healed they could be anywhere."

Gage's hand clenched at his side, his need for revenge stronger than his need to breathe. "Then I'll just have to bring them back. Pete said they want me. If they know I'm here, they'll come back."

"Only if they're as crazy as that old man. I mean, would you come back after you'd left the place wrecked and innocent folks dead? Especially when the man you'd come for never even show'd up? Hell, Gage, they'll know you're here waitin' for them. And they'll figure you got the law and plenty of backup on your side too. They ain't comin' back here any time soon. And if we'd a' caught em, I'd wager those two fine mustangs from the north rim on it."

"If you're saying you want to walk away—"

A thoughtful expression came into Ross' eyes. "No . . . I'm just thinkin' you should even the odds. I get around to most of the ranches in the territory at one time or another. If I spread the word yours was attacked by Apache and only a half-witted old man survived—"

"—then whoever did this will figure the Apache got the revenge they came for. They'll think I'm dead and the ranch is theirs for the taking?" Gage finished, quickly realizing his friend's plan. And, despite the driving urge to hunt down the killers then and there, no matter what the odds, grudgingly, he had to admit the wisdom of it.

"You'll have a better chance of catchin' 'em off their guard. And when they come, you can be ready and waitin' with the marshall."

"I'll be waiting all right," Gage ground out. "Without a lawman to stop me from dealing with them my way." He picked up his shovel and shoved it into the ground again.

"It's all over, friend," Ross said quietly. "We're finished here."

"Not quite. I've got one more grave to dig." Gage tossed aside another shovelful of rock and dirt with a vicious thrust.

"Mine."

March 17, 1888

A chill wind slashed rock and barren trees, echoing in a desolate keening against the stone walls of the ranch house. It plucked at the edges of the girl's tattered skirt, flicked her skin with a whip of sand and dust.

Serena Lark slid off the weary horse she'd stolen and stumbled to the foot of the gates. Leaning a hand against the wall, exhaustion kept her from indulging the annoyance she felt at finding the gates locked. She supposed she should have expected it, arriving in the middle of the night, unannounced and probably unwelcome.

But after three days of headlong flight, of riding and hiding and the perpetual gnawing fear of being caught, her utter relief at reaching her old home blotted out every other emotion. Though the Mormon settlement at Kanab from which she'd fled lay just on the other side of the Utah border, the ride down to Pipe Springs had taken a much greater toll on her than it ought to have for the short distance she'd traveled.

If only she hadn't found the stable locked! As it was, only a couple of aging animals were left outside in the corral. She'd taken the best of the sad lot, but he'd proved exasperatingly slow. Even so, she might have made the journey in a day if she hadn't been forced to rest every few hours. She damned her body's frailty. She'd lost precious time and ground because of it.

Summoning the last of her strength, Serena pulled a rifle from the bundle tied to the back of her saddle and pounded repeatedly at the heavy wooden gates with its butt.

"I know it's the middle of the night but someone should hear me," she muttered to herself. "Wake up!"

Her voice, reflecting bewildered irritation, bounced back at her a hundredfold. Elder Caltrop had left the ranch in the care of a man called Tanner, who had planned to raise cattle and had promised to continue to provide shelter for those Mormons courageous or devout enough to continue the pilgrimages to the Utah territory.

But there were no pilgrims, no families here now. The barns, the outbuildings, the corrals and stables, all looked deserted. It even smelled deserted, as if the scent of rock and sand and grass had vanquished any human essence. Somewhere in the distance, a door creaked to and fro to the cadence of the wind.

Nothing. No one. Only Serena Lark. Serena who ran from her past and found no future.

Anger and self pity welled up in her, and Serena swiped at blurred eyes. She couldn't go back now, even if she were weak or foolish enough to admit defeat. Her capricious actions had banished her.

She could almost see the stern, towering image of Elder Caltrop, chiding her in his grim, sonorous voice. *You are ungovernable, Serena. You are a spoiled, willful child, always demanding what you have not earned as your right. You have never grown up, and I fear you will never truly be a part of us, a part of anyone.*

Well, so be it! Fierce determination overcame her tears. She didn't need any of them and she certainly couldn't abide the things they wanted her to meekly accept. And she absolutely would not become Jerel Webster's wife, with his ruthless determination to possess her.

She would get what *she* wanted, starting with a way inside this gate!

"There has to be someone here," she muttered, anger fueling her shaking arms. Again she beat the gun against the heavy doors, two-men tall and barred with metal slats, then kicked at the thick, unrelenting wood in frustration, wincing as the blow reached through the worn leather of her boots to her tender skin.

Where is this Mister Tanner?

He wouldn't have just abandoned the ranch without getting word to Elder Caltrop. She'd often heard him praise Gage Tanner as a friend—a hard, driven man, but one capable of compassion, an upright man whose word was as good as a kept promise. When Elder Caltrop said Mister Tanner had even taken in a widow and her family when her husband was killed, Serena knew she'd finally found her rescuer.

A man like that surely wouldn't just up and leave. A man like that would have to take pity on her and help her gain her freedom. She had gambled on Gage Tanner living up to his glorious reputation, hoping he would understand her plight and give her refuge.

Serena glanced up and down the imposing walls, not holding much hope of getting inside by wit or will. The stone house had been built as a stronghold against attack. There were no windows or doors facing outside, only the gates.

It was almost enough to make her turn back. Almost. If they didn't hear her knock, they might hear her shout. . . . She walked a short distance to where she saw a slit had been left without a stone as a lookout. Leaning her rifle against the wall, she strained up on her tiptoes, pressed her face into the opening in the wall, and yelled at the top of her lungs, "Will you please wake up and let me inside!"

Setting her jaw, Serena sat back on her heels and waited for a minute, then started to make her way to the back of the house to shout through another of the openings. But as she turned toward the horizon, she froze in place, held motionless by the image before her.

Outlined in an argent moonlit mist, the towering shadow of a man in a wide-brimmed hat and ankle-length duster stood several yards away, watching her. They stared at each other, silent and still, lost alone together in a moment of night.

Serena stayed poised, breathless, for timeless seconds, possessed by a sense of a powerful presence, captivated by the enigmatic midnight vision. Was he real?

She didn't dare move until the sudden groaning protest of wood and metal nearby startled her from the odd spell. Swiftly glancing behind her, she snapped her gaze back. The stranger had vanished. "But . . ."

Taking a step forward, Serena held out a hand, as if she could recall him with a touch. She started forward; the gate hinges creaked, calling her back. The wooden doors began to swing open, so gradually it seemed an eternity before they parted.

The muzzle of a rifle thrust out between them. It wavered uncertainly in Serena's direction.

She hesitated, waiting for the owner of the gun to make an appearance. Long moments trudged by and finally, exasperated, she finally called out, "Who is it?"

"Are you a tree devil?" a graveled voice whispered.

"Am I a *what?*"

"A tree devil." An unseen hand jerked the rifle muzzle at her. "Tell me quick."

"Please—don't shoot," Serena said warily. "I'm alone. I'm Serena Lark. I used to live here. Are you Mister Tanner?"

The gates opened a little wider and a scrawny, wizened man, barely above her own height, edged out, still brandishing the rifle. His hair, white wisps of cottony fluff, stood on end at odd angles. His shirt collar gaped open, revealing a wide ring of blue-green bruises. As he squinted at her, his head cocked to one side, Serena was disconcerted by the strange slant of his gaze. One of his watery blue eyes wandered, independent of the other.

Serena flung a hand back at the horizon. "There's a man out there. Is he—?"

"So. You seen him." The man bobbed his head several times. "Only at dawn. And at dusk. Some says they's seen him at noon time, but that's pure bunk. He don't like the light."

"I beg your pardon?"

"He don't like the light," the man repeated, raising

his voice and slowly pronouncing each word as if she were a near-deaf, slightly afflicted child. "Cause he's dead, I reckon."

"Dead?" Serena mimicked the word blankly. She looked back at the night-dark landscape. "But he was there . . ."

"Course he was. Even the tree devils know that." With a disgusted snort, the man shook his head and stumped back inside the gates, making to close them behind him.

"Wait!" She scrambled to follow him, her legs quivering with the effort. "Wait. Who are you? Where is Mister Tanner?"

The man stopped so quickly, Serena nearly stumbled into him. He glared at her, suspicion narrowing his eyes. "Tanner?"

"The man that lives here. He's a cattle rancher . . ." Serena let the sentence die, not liking the sudden gleam that sprang in the man's eyes.

"So—are you one of them?"

"Them? Who?"

"The devils," he said hoarsely, darting a look above them as if he expected his devils to materialize from the sky. "The devils in the trees."

He leaned toward her, peering at her with one eye and Serena took a faltering step backward. "I-I told you, I'm Serena Lark." Impatience erased her momentary fear and she demanded, "Where is Mister Tanner? You must know."

The man squinted at her. "You might be her. The widow. 'Cept you got too much spit and fire in you. Not like her." He reached out a quivering hand and, ignoring Serena's startled recoil, gently touched her lank hair. "Chestnuts afire, that's what he used to say. She was an angel. Maybe you're an angel, too. An angel sent by her. 'Cause she's gone." His shoulders slumped and a queer light came into his eyes. "They're dead. All of 'em. Gage Tanner. The widow, her sister, the boys. Killed. Everyone from these parts knows that. More'n two weeks past now. Maybe he's sorry 'cause he didn't stop it. Maybe he's waitin' for the tree devils. He said he'd find 'em, for what they did. And Gage Tanner's word was as bindin' as a hangman's knot."

"You mean . . . they're dead, Mister Tanner, the family he took in?" Serena stared at him, appalled. "But— but who killed them?"

"Apache. Or outlaws. That's how the story goes. Course, you cain't always believe a tall tale, now cin you? Especially when the devils are tellin' it. They're as shy of the truth as a goat is of feathers."

He looked hard at her as if he expected her to contradict him. Serena, completely nonplussed, shook her head, feeling dazed. "Well—I'm not a devil nor an angel. I'm just very tired, very hungry, and absolutely filthy. I've come a long way."

"That so? Well, then you should've heard the story by now. It's goin' 'round the whole territory. Be a legend someday." He said it with a pleased pride in his voice. "No one likes to come 'round much 'cause of it. They're afeared they'll see him. The Spirit in the Wind. I reckon they don't like bein' shot at neither," he added, nodding at his rifle.

"Spirit in the Wind . . ." A strange uneasiness shivered up her spine.

"Whiskey Pete." The man shoved a hand at her, smiling a broad, ragged-toothed grin as he pumped her small hand with his leathery one. "That's all that's left here now. Me and my friends. Deacon Mather and Lucky Joe and ole' Last Chance. Friends thick as seven men sleepin' on a cot, we are. The Spirit in the Wind lets us stay." He bent forward and added in a confidential whisper, "We give him a hand now and again, Lucky Joe and me."

Raising a finger to his lips, he winked and started back inside the gates.

"But that's just nonsense—" Serena began, before realizing she spoke to empty air. "Wait a minute," she called, chasing after him. "You can't just walk off and leave me here!"

Whiskey Pete turned his head to one side. "Why not?"

"Because—because I'm moving in here." Her mouth set in a stubborn line. "I've traveled weeks to get here and I'm not leaving."

"Don't matter by me," Whiskey Pete said with a shrug. "Long as it's okay with Lucky Joe. You can ask him."

"But—"

"Come on. This way."

Abandoning any attempt to reason with the addled mind of Whiskey Pete, Serena hurriedly retrieved her own rifle, scooped up her quilt and ragged bundle of belongings and followed him inside the gates to the central courtyard she remembered as her playground. He closed the gates behind her, and then headed into one of a long row of narrow doorways.

Crossing to a table, he lit a lantern, holding it up to stare at her. "Got this room back the way it oughta be. It's all me 'n Joe need." He pulled a full bottle of whiskey from a shelf and took a long pull.

As her eyes adjusted to the dim glow, Serena glanced around in mild surprise. The room was rustic, but neat enough. A stack of rough woolen blankets lay folded on a cot in the corner; battered pots and crockery evenly lined a rude shelf; the table and single chair sat near the fireplace. The smell of a wood fire mingled with the welcome scent of coffee and beans, Whiskey Pete's staples, she guessed.

"Lucky Joe don't like visitors," Whiskey Pete said at last. "I reckon you best make friends with him as soon as you can. You talk to him. I'll make coffee this time. Go on," he prodded as Serena hesitated in the doorway. "He's under the bed, like always since the devils come."

"Under the bed? Never mind." Goaded to look, Serena sat her belongings down and knelt on the floor beside the bed. A low growl greeted her. Jumping backward, she slipped, landing square on her bottom on the dirt floor. "It's a dog," she said, glaring at Whiskey Pete. "Lucky Joe is a dog."

"Did I say he weren't?"

Grunting and wheezing, Lucky Joe deigned to emerge from under the bed. Serena wrinkled her nose in disgust. Large, ungainly, Lucky Joe was a mangy yellow beast, a gnarled stick tied to the place where his left hind leg should have been. He looked both ridiculous and pitiful at the same time.

"The devils did that," Whiskey Pete said, nodding at the stick. "His leg. I gave him the stick. Sure have a time keepin' him from chewin' it up though. Stupid Lucky Joe, chewing his leg off and me havin' to always go and fetch another stick. He's trouble, Lucky is."

"And I suppose Deacon Mather is your cat." Serena picked herself up off the floor, dusting the sand from her worn skirts. Taking a chair at the table, she rested a cheek on her hand, watching Whiskey Pete make coffee. "Aren't there any *people* here? You can't possibly run this entire ranch alone."

"Not much to run. Deacon Mather, he keeps after the few cows that's left—he ain't no cat, by the way—I tend to the chickens, Lucky Joe watches out for the tree devils, and once every bit or so Last Chance takes us to town."

"That's all?"

"Well—what else is there?" Whiskey Pete shook his head as he poured out muddy-looking coffee into two tin cups. "There's nothin' else. Not since the tree devils."

"And who—or what—are tree devils?" Serena asked, exasperated with the repeated reference, not sure she even wanted to hear the answer. "I've never heard of such a silly thing in my life!"

"Shush!" Whiskey Pete's face closed up, the burning fear in his eyes the only sign of emotion. "Don't you ask 'bout 'em. Don't you ask. They don't like it."

Serena rolled her eyes, throwing up a hand. "Fine."

Sighing, she sat quietly for a moment, sipping at the bitter brew in her cup. Five years ago, when the Mormons had taken her from here, it had been a thriving cattle ranch and a sanctuary for the faithful. Even when the Mormon clans left, driven out by fear and hatred, Elder Caltrop had confidently put the ranch in the care of Gage Tanner.

She'd never heard him say anything about an attack on the ranch, certainly nothing about tree devils or the haunting spirits of dead men.

Spirit in the wind. . . . She thought of the man she'd saw, there and then vanished, and a quiver of superstitious fear rippled through her. How much of Whiskey Pete's ramblings were true? *Don't be stupid.* But she couldn't quite rid herself of it. Here, she was cut off, alone, hunted by the living; would she also be prey to the dead?

Shoving her cup away, Serena got to her feet. "Tomorrow I want to see the rest of the ranch."

Whiskey Pete looked at her with his one good eye,

closing the other. "Well ... I s'ppose. Ain't much to see, though. Hope you got somethin' else to do."

"Right now all I want to do is rinse a layer of this dirt off my skin and sleep until the sun is high."

Grunting a reply, Whiskey Pete led her to a second-story room that looked as if a wild beast had been let loose in it. They managed to put it in order enough for her to spend the night, but long after Pete had gone back to his room, Serena lay awake tossing and turning, feeling so sore and hot and caked with dirt she couldn't find a position comfortable enough to lure her to sleep. She rose and opened her door. Above the walls of the ranch house, the black sky was alive with a million tiny sliver twinkles.

Glancing around, her eyes were drawn to the oasis below. The unexpected, deep pool, sheltered by the spindly embrace of cottonwoods and poplars, tempted her, beckoning her with memories of a soothing balm. Serena swiped at the gritty sheen of sweat on her forehead.

Briefly, she squeezed her tired, burning eyes shut, and almost immediately, vivid images of her treacherous journey, the fate she'd risked her life to escape, assaulted her mind. It didn't matter she'd been branded a fugitive and an outcast, that she'd abandoned her prized safety and security for a reckless journey to the unknown. She'd racked her mind for months to find another way out. But in the end her only choice was to flee. No one was going to force her to submit to marriage, and certainly not as anyone's fifth wife. She had to put herself first, had to escape, regardless of the consequences she left behind. She would be free of them, of *him,* whatever the cost, and damn them all.

The night air of the high desert lightly brushed her skin, but the heat of a fire seemed steeped in her blood.

She craved relief, and looked to the oasis again. Clear, cold spring water sang a siren's song. Pete had drunk nearly a full bottle of whiskey in the short time they'd spoken. That alone was enough to make a man sleep for hours, and shs suspected by the insanity of his conversation, he'd drank a good deal more earlier that night, before her furious pounding and shouting roused him.

Her legs made her decision, taking her down the stairs and into the courtyard, before her mind could reason her out of it. Dropping to her knees on the earthen bank near the oasis, she drew in a long breath before slowly sliding her hands into the water.

The first touch made her tense as a shudder of awareness shot up her arms. But the cooling lap of water relaxed her and she sat back on her heels, reveling as the icy shiver on her flesh coupled with the heat pulsing fast and furious under her skin.

Cupping the water between her hands, Serena brought it to her face and let it spill through her splayed fingers, over her cheeks, in rivulets down her arched throat. The moonlight through the shadows of the trees turned the water pure silver against the velvet darkness. She tasted its clean sweetness on her lips, let slow, drizzling drops chase each other down her spine and between her breasts.

Serena loosed the bodice of her dress, boldly slipping the thin material off her shoulders, feeling hidden in the secret sanctuary of the night. She smoothed the wetness over her bared skin, trembling a little at its caress.

There was nothing to hear, no sound but the rush and splash of water as she scooped it between her hands and let it slide against her body. Even the wind fell silent.

No noise to warn her before a reflection melted with hers in the silver pool. The image of her midnight stranger.

Chapter Two

He appeared with the eerie hush of a dream walker. Tall, powerfully built, no hint of softness in his body or expression, with a rough beard, his over-long hair looked dark gold in the silver moonlight, the rest of him a primitive painting of gray and black. From his poised stillness, the essence of savage, untamed spirit he brought with him into the serenity of the oasis, he seemed more wild animal than human. His eyes watched her as if he lay beneath the smooth surface of the water. Serena sucked in a breath. She slowly turned and looked up.

His eyes, hollow and haunted, looked back.

Countless moments they held each other captive, gazing as though hypnotized by some unseen force that ruled the night. The world around them ceased, all other sensations succumbing to the need to absorb what each could from the other: she falling deathly still beneath the strange power he wielded like an invisible sword in the dark, subduing her against her will; he paralyzed, a prisoner to the phantom exposed under the faint hint or morning light edging the dark desert sky.

He didn't breathe. He didn't dare move. Because if he did either, the image of her might break and shatter into

a thousand fleeting pieces, the vision of beauty before
him become his nightmare again, taunting him, feeding
his guilt, reminding him of how he had failed her. Left
her to die.

She stared until her eyes begged to close and leave
her blind to the sight before her. Her emotions, her
thoughts a wild tumult, Serena decided he must be a
spirit to hold her in bondage without so much as a touch
of his hand. She tried to move; her body failed her.
Bared before his searing gaze, her dress fallen and
clinging damply at her waist, she stayed kneeling by the
pool's edge, helpless, waiting, praying he would vanish
as quickly as he had appeared.

"Libby?" Hidden beneath his beard, his lips formed
the word without sound.

She stared at him, her eyes wide with fear and fascination in equal measure. The night turned her hair to eb-
ony; but he knew how it would look in the sun.
Chestnuts afire. Her skin golden, her breasts, cloaked
now only in shadow, full and sweet with promise, her
eyes dark and depthless. More beautiful than he recalled, as if his memory had perfected her.

Serena felt his touch at her cheeks, on the hollow of
her neck, brushing her breasts, as surely as if his hands
had passed there, leaving her skin burning in their wake.
The realization that she was naked to the waist only
then seeped through her dulled senses like water
through a crack in rock.

Then slowly, ever so slowly, she began to emerge
from the trance he'd cast over her. Blindly, she groped
at her dress and slipped it back up over her breasts and
shoulders. A vague notion that she ought to feel shame
or embarrassment at her state of undress passed briefly
through her mind. But it disappeared unheeded, seeming

foolish when dealing with a spirit who saw what he would regardless of the trappings of the flesh.

He took in each languorous movement, enthralled. Libby had never moved so gracefully, so sensuously. In death, she had become the seductress she could not be in life. A flood of confused memories swarmed through is anguished mind. All of these nights, he had haunted the ranch, looking for answers from the grave. He vowed to keep coming back until he found them. But maybe tonight had been once too often. Now Libby had come to haunt him.

"Are you real?"

Her soft voice met his ears barely above a whisper. Except it didn't sound as he remembered. There was no gentle, coaxing lilt about it. It was stronger, more fire and spice in the honey. As she slowly rose to her feet he noticed she held herself differently too, more confidently, not flustered by the still provocative droop of her dress.

He stared, saying nothing, giving nothing of himself.

She tipped her head, studying him. "Are you alive?"

He heard the challenge pierce the tremble in her voice, but offered only the silent narrowing of his gaze in response.

She reached out a hand that quivered close to his face, then dropped away before it touched. The damp, warm, musky scent of her lingered on a breath of wind. "I know. You aren't dead. I just don't believe it."

Something in the stubborn tip of her chin, the little upturn at the corner of her full mouth stirred an echo of lost feeling in him. A glimmer of amusement at her bravado, a goad of irritation at her childish certainty. "Libby . . ." the name slipped from his lips to drift away on the breeze.

"What? You said a name. I heard it. I know I did.

Libby? You called me Libby." She waited for either confirmation or denial, as long as she could stand the silence. But after several moments, when he offered neither, she went on without his encouragement. "Well, I'm not Libby. I'm Serena. Serena Lark."

He slowly stepped back, the name was like a curse on his guilty soul. *She's come back to torment me, because I didn't protect them.*

"Talk to me! I know you said that name!"

The sharp edge of her tone cut through his haunted imaginings as clearly as the blade of a knife. Libby never spoke to him like that. His eyes focused with new intensity on her face.

Serena returned the probing look. "You don't frighten me, you know," she said, knowing it was a lie. He did frighten her, but not with his presence. With the confusion of feeling he roused in her. "How did you get in here? The gates—" She glanced over his shoulder.

The gates were closed, looking exactly as they had when Whiskey Pete had locked them for the night.

Her gaze snapped back to him.

He took a step closer.

With more courage than she felt, Serena faced him squarely, not faltering. "Come on ahead, I don't scare that easily," she said, steadying the quiver in her voice. All the while, at the back of her mind, a niggle of caution warned her against confronting him. Yet his obvious desire to frighten her riled her, aggravation stampeding over her uneasiness. "I don't know who you are, or what you're trying to do with your strange comings and goings, or how you got inside, but you might as well know that I don't believe in ghosts. You can't make me leave. Whether you like it or not, I do intend to make this my home. I've come too far to turn back now."

Gage almost laughed aloud at her bold address, and yet at the same time, he wanted simply to dismiss her as an annoyance, a disturbing mirage, another fleeting image born of isolation and loneliness. But part of him instinctively rose to test the strength of her defiance. Glad to have his gun arm back in working order, he eased his hand to his holster, testing the limits of her brave facade.

Tension knotted in Serena's stomach, but she struggled to deny that it was born of fear. "So, the ghost carries a gun?" she taunted.

He stood his ground, unflinching.

She matched him in stance, refusing to budge.

But before she could challenge him further, he suddenly turned from her and slipped backward away from the oasis into the midnight shadows and disappeared.

Left alone with the darkness once more, Serena stood transfixed for a timeless span, unsure what to feel or how to react, wondering whether she was slowly going mad, or if her imagination had conjured up the otherworldly conversation. It belatedly occurred to her she should try and follow him, find out how he managed to walk through gates and walls that would take an army and several cannons to penetrate. instead she stayed by the oasis pool, unable to either advance or retreat.

He was real. He had to be real. And yet. . . . There seemed no comforting explanation of how he had gotten inside the locked gates and, more disturbing, no way to exorcise his memory from her mind.

This time the fear welled up and crashed over her. Dashing back to her room, slamming the door, she leaned against it, breathing hard, one question continuing to torment her. How had he gotten inside? Only the whisper of the wind and the sharp cry of a night bird answered her.

Serena rubbed her fingers against her temple, feeling the dull ache of exhaustion in her head and behind her eyes. The overwhelming tiredness she'd somehow suppressed until that moment suddenly consumed her and she dropped down on her borrowed bed. Hugging a scant sheet close, she lay perfectly still, curled in a tight ball, listening in the waning hours of fading darkness for any sign or sound of him, until finally sleep turned her blind and deaf to everything but her troubled dreams.

Miles away over the rolling sagebrush and scrub pine hills, sheltered by the domineering walls of the canyons and hidden in the depths of the night, the smoke of a secret fire swirled and dipped, partnering with a ring of bare-footed dancers. Behind them, Gage Tanner sat cross-legged, watching, listening to a single drum beat out a low, throbbing song. It was the song of the Paiute, a message of communion with the spirits of their dead. Though he knew their language he needn't have; he understood the song with his soul.

Buckskin slapped bare brown thighs, sinuous bodies pulsating in union to the hypnotic rhythm. Their feet seemed one with the dusty earth beneath, their steps tapped out messages, sending words and thoughts to each other, to lives past, below, beyond. It was the song of the ghost dance.

Gage had come tonight after the disquieting encounter at the oasis. Until tonight, he'd lived in absolute solitude since Libby's death. But this evening was too much; his mind must now be as sick as his soul.

Dead to the world, he had nowhere to turn for help, no one to trust but the Paiute. He longed for the relief they found through this holy dance, to be grafted into the privileges of their sacred religion, spirited away to a place beyond sorrow, far away from the ghosts of his past that now possessed his future.

Beside him, an ancient man sat gripping a large woven basket in his lean, brown hands. Flickers of light from the huge flames nearby illuminated the countless scars on his leathery skin. His hands were gnarled and battered, the result of the years his tribe had been forced to scavenge for food through thorns and rock, forced off their lands by the increasing numbers of settlers.

Gage glanced at Kwion, the eldest of the Paiute tribe. The still proud leader wore his tattered blanket about his shoulders like a king's mantle. His silver-white hair lay in long, thick strands against the black wool. Dark eyes, as fathomless and fearsome as two unprobed caves searched Gage's face as if intent on knowing his thoughts.

"Welcome back to us, White Brother," Kwion said at last, speaking the tribe's dialect, his voice as rich and expressive as the night.

"I've missed you these months," Gage answered in the same tongue. From his lifetime on the strip country where the Paiute migrated, he had come to understand and speak Paiute well, though at times the sound of the words still struck him as odd and atonal, uncomfortable to form on his lips.

"What brings you here to us once more after so long a time? You were long weeks away. And when you returned, it is said you died with those you cared for as your own. I did not believe it. I knew you still breathed."

Gage drew in a long breath, slowly released it. "Something happened tonight. Jon's wife returned to haunt the ranch. I saw her, by the oasis. Except—" He struggled to find words for alien feelings. "Except she's different, stronger, more fearless. Bold enough to hand out any revenge she chooses."

"Revenge?"

"I left her, the boys, all of them, alone, to die," Gage said, his voice a broken whisper. "I swore I'd keep them safe. I broke that pledge."

Kwion studied him, expressionless. After a long silence, he handed Gage the basket, saying quietly, "Perhaps she comes not to punish you, but to warn you. Perhaps she can help you find the true murderers. For I know, my son, you did nothing to harm her or her children. What happened could not have been stopped. All that is left to her now is justice."

"Maybe." Gage fingered the rough basket, uncomfortable with the need to talk. Picking up several of the leaves, he tasted their bitter essence.

"You always shared with us what you were able," Kwion persisted. "On the ranch, you allowed us to take freely of the water, you gave us land and cattle. Now, we offer you our help."

Gage shook his head, not willing to tell his friend that only the cold satisfaction of revenge could help him now.

He made to hand the basket back to Kwion, but the old man held up a palm in protest. "Tonight it is for you."

Nodding his thanks, Gage chewed several more of the leaves. The effect of the peyote and his long pent-up anger and anguish at last loosened his tongue. "You've already done much for me, too. Libby—she learned a great deal from your women. And your children were the boys' only playmates."

"You cared for them as your own family," Kwion said softly.

"I promised Jon before he died that if anything happened I would look after his family. It seemed a small thing to do considering the debt I owed him. He was beside me all those years I spent in the Cavalry, tracking down outlaws and Apache, Geronimo himself. He saved my life, more times than I can count. After Geronimo's band was through with him . . ." Gage rubbed a hand over his eyes, shutting out the vision of his friend as he lay dying, a renegade Apache's arrow in his chest.

Kwion laid a hand on Gage's shoulder. "Use the leaves to help you see. And hear. Listen to her speak to you, to what truths—or warnings she brings. You have done no wrong. There is no need to fear what she tells you."

Reaching into the basket again, Gage sought, if not peace, escape, a brief time when he didn't have to feel anything. He stared blankly at the dancers until their shapes melded into a red, orange, and brown blur on a black canvas. With clouded vision, he turned to Kwion. The old man's image wavered, then transformed before him. First to an antelope. Then an elk. A jackrabbit, a hawk, then back to Kwion, ancient beyond time. The familiar face became sharp again, the features hollowed and creased below his heavily boned brow.

In front of him, the liquid flame darted and flirted with the desert sky, mocking his struggle to understand. It seemed to breathe and dance, hiding the answers he had to find.

Gage blinked and scrubbed at his eyes. His head felt like lead. He didn't realize he was swaying. When he closed his eyes again, he saw her. Libby. Her ghost, dancing with the fire, swirling atop a midnight pool.

Libby? So familiar the slim lines of the bewitching form. Yet the way she stood, proud and defiant, her smile daring him . . . no. Not Libby. Gage shook his head, trying to clear it. Libby had never been like that.

Eyes closed, Gage plunged his hand into the basket again. It wasn't working. He still felt the pain and the regret. After nearly two years of living side by side at the ranch, Libby and he might have exchanged fleeting moments of a desire born of loneliness, but Gage had never succumbed; he would always see her as his best friend's wife, and she had buried her heart with Jon.

But tonight he had felt something different seeing her, the woman at the oasis. A primitive ache, long suppressed; a need that didn't seem wrong or forbidden.

He put his hands to his temples, trying to shut out the vision.

Was it Libby at the pool? It couldn't have been. But then who? And why did she insist on staying?

"She speaks to you?" Kwion's voice stirred Gage from his stupor.

"Your leaves speak to me, brother," Gage answered with a faint, rueful smile. "I should know better than to dabble with your magic plants."

"It is good." Kwion nodded. "You will know the meaning when it is right. But take care, my son, that you do not linger too long in the land of the ghost dance."

Gage got to his feet, fighting the unsteadiness in his legs. "Once I have my revenge, I don't plan on staying anywhere too long again.'"

Kwion's eyes half-closed. He stared at the waning fire as if he had not heard Gage's last words. "It is said that there is a land where the ghosts dance around a fire. It is said one should never follow the dead to that place or he too will become a ghost, never to find his way back to the living." He looked up and almost smiled. "Rest now. Stay with us tonight. Lehi will lie with you."

Gage mulled over the idea of riding the long, winding trail back into the canyons to the cliff that concealed his makeshift home. But the savage Arizona wilderness wasn't a place to travel by night with a sick belly and a pounding dull-headedness that rendered his brain useless on his shoulders. After months spent alone with the black night for a companion and a musty wool blanket for a bed, the thought of Lehi's warm, willing body wrapped around his settled the question.

Until tonight, the notion of a woman's comfort had scarcely crossed his mind. Revenge, cold and hard, had been his only companion.

Now, the vision of the woman at the oasis visited him again, stirring a primal, nearly forgotten hunger deep inside him. He didn't even know he'd lost his desire until he saw her bathing in the moonlight.

Now, suddenly, he realized he was starving.

Outside Serena's room, the wind whipped up to a brisk tempo, sending sagebrush skittering across the flat expanses of rock and sand. She tried to clutch at sleep by pulling the thin sheet over her head, but the stream of salmon light flooding the window facing the courtyard won the fight. Yawning a little, she sat up, scrubbing at her eyes. Every muscle responded slowly, stiff from her troubled sleep and the days on horseback.

After her eerie encounter with the phantom of a man at the oasis, even the promise of a new day didn't banish the haunted feeling he gave her. She dreaded facing the deserted loneliness of the ranch, but forced herself to turn out of her bed and struggle to her feet, and toss on a worn cotton skirt and blouse.

She stepped out on the balcony, held fast to the railing, and peered out over the top of it, her dark eyes shadowed as cherished remembrances of nearly five years past clashed with the harsh vision of the present. Breathing in the sweet pine scent of the early air, she found her memory had gilded the savage beauty of the inhospitable strip country, the vivid pinks, golds, and reds of the desert in bloom, with the colors and sounds of summer, the warmth of sharing it all with an adoring family.

Now reality stripped the cherished memory to its essence and the land stretched on endlessly before her, rugged, wild, unforgiving to the weak and fearful.

The only softness in the palette of the landscape was cloistered behind the wall around her—the oasis, the pool embraced by pale, sage-shaded cottonwoods and silver-leafed poplars, bringing life to flower in the desolation. But beyond the deep silver waters of the pool, beyond the stone fortress that guarded it, the flat sprawl of belly-deep grasses, scattered with squat juniper and pinon trees, panned out in a vista of strong greens and browns and grays. The crags and edges of the Vermillion Cliffs hovered over the ranch from behind, jutting into the sky, hued in scarlet, pink, white, and chocolate. In front, in the far distance, only one sheer plateau, black and sharp, sliced into the unrelenting landscape.

As she looked out over the untamed land, she felt the strange apprehension again, this time more strongly as it slithered cold and quick up her spine. Serena shifted to look away. And then stared, blinked. Again. And again, certain she must be dreaming or crazy.

The red fire of the sunrise drew a thin line on the horizon, casting a hesitant light, leaving shadows and uncertain shapes, the familiar alien and undefined.

Except for him.

Suddenly there. Etched in black, he stood motionless on the precipice of the plateau, the silhouette of a horse beside him. A faint haze curled at his feet, yet only touched, not softened his hard edges.

A trick of the light, a figment of her weary mind, his figure could have been any of those.

Yet Serena knew he wasn't.

It was him. Her spirit of the oasis. His image brought an eerie sense of presence among the empty stone buildings, a voice to the wail and whisper of the wind. Her skin quivered from an unseen touch. Slowly, she rubbed her hands up and down her arms, knowing, without seeing his face, that he watched her.

He was too far for her to give him any features, a specter of a man, only an outline of a sloped hat, wide shoulders, the flap of his duster against long legs.

She took a step forward.

The rising sun dazzled her vision for a moment. She brushed a hand over her face, then focused again on the plateau.

It was empty.

"He was there . . ." she murmured, her eyes searching the plateau in vain.

Below, the gates creaked open and Whiskey Pete ambled in, a bucket dangling from his fingers. "You still here?" he called up, squinting at her with his one good eye.

"Of course I am," she snapped back, gathering up her skirts to go downstairs. She was being foolish, imagining all sorts of things. If she didn't regain her wits, she'd soon be as addled as Whiskey Pete.

Pete was dipping the bucket into the oasis when she stepped into the courtyard. "Well, then, come on. If you're so set on seein' things, it best be now."

Biting back a sarcastic retort, Serena followed him outside the gates, waited while he locked them, then continued with him down the path to a ramshackle, half-

mended corral, stables, and a row of smaller stone outbuildings. All of them showed signs of battering, some
from age, others from deliberate abuse. A heap of black
debris lay where she assumed a small shed once was.
The other outbuildings they explored were cluttered
with the remnants of a blacksmith's tools and the as-
sorted tubs and implements once used for cheese-
making.

"Are the cattle out to pasture?" she demanded when
Whiskey Pete presented her to the few scruffy hay-fed
cows and calves inside a rudely built corral. "Where are
the horses?"

"There ain't no cattle and there ain't no horses. Just
Last Chance and what you see. 'Cept for Deacon
Mather—and he ain't a cat by the way—see?" Opening
up one of the doors of the stalls, he gestured at the
large, reddish-brown bulk inside.

Serena peered around the corner and as she did, a
long-faced bull stuck its nose near hers, eyeing her dis-
dainfully with the one eye it did have. The other was
blind, and the bull's face was mottled with black
blotches, giving him the appearance of wearing a mask.

"Deacon Mather was gonna be a Sunday dinner 'fore
I offered to buy him," Whiskey Pete said. "Now he
keeps my ladies happy."

"I hope you got a bargain," Serena muttered under
her breath.

"He didn't have no home. Just like Lucky Joe. Just
like me."

"You have a home, here."

"It ain't no home." Whiskey Pete leaned on the rail
of Deacon Mather's stall, staring down at the floor. He
scuffed at the dirt with the toe of his boot. "It's a place
for folks with no place and no one to go back to. So we
just stay. Like you, I s'ppose."

"No, not like me!" The words came tumbling out. "I had a home! But I chose to leave. I had to—to come here." Furious at him, at herself, Serena whirled about and stalked out of the stall.

She stood in the open rocky stretch between the house and corral, balling her fists to keep back angry tears. Damn that crazy old man, and damn Gage Tanner for getting himself killed! It wasn't fair. Nothing was working the way she wanted it to. No one was ever there for her when she needed them most. They always, always left her alone.

"Well, hell." Whiskey Pete stumped up behind her, taking hold of her arm and tugging her toward the house. "Come on, come on."

Serena dug in her heels and pulled him to a stop. "What's the matter now?"

"They're comin'," he said, wagging a finger toward the open expanse of grassland. "And I can tell you now, they ain't ever in the mood to be neighborly."

Chapter Three

Shading her eyes against the brilliance of the new sun, Serena picked out three riders moving toward them in a whirl of dust. Her heart skittered painfully as both fear and nervous excitement shot through her. "Who are they? Tree devils?" she added with a twist of sarcasm to hide her own worry.

Whiskey Pete shot her a vexed glance. "You don't know nothin' 'bout tree devils. Now them—" He stabbed at the riders with his forefinger. "Them will ask questions, try to get inside the gates. Didn't take 'em long to start pesterin' me. Just won't stay away, no matter how many times I shoot at 'em." He shook his head. "Don't seem fair, but there it is."

"Where do they come from?"

"Vulture Creek. Tree devils don't live in Vulture Creek," he added, cocking his head at her and peering at her with his one good eye. "Not much does. It's just a spit in the road. They don't live there neither. They're cattlemen. Got their own spreads here and around the canyons."

Trying to pry some reasonable piece of information from the old man, Serena prodded, "But what do they want?"

"The usual thing. The water. Ain't much else to want."

"The water . . . the oasis. Of course." The one thing that drew first Indians, and then the Mormons to build the ranch on the uncompromising borderland between the Arizona and Utah territories. The underground spring that ran beneath the ranch house, burbling up inside the courtyard to form an oasis pool now protected by thick stone walls and locked gates—a treasure richer than gold in the arid strip country.

"Everyone wants the water," Whiskey Pete lamented, "else they'd leave us be. Humph . . . well, you best git inside. They'll ask questions."

The last thing Serena wanted was anyone asking questions about where she came from and who she was. She could hide, but chances were they had already seen her and the idea of skulking behind locked gates didn't appeal to her. Her face wrinkled in concentration as she seized and discarded several ideas before brightening as inspiration struck. "I'm your niece," she tossed at Pete, startling him back a step. "Your sister's girl."

"I ain't got no sister."

"That doesn't matter! It's just what we'll tell them. I'm your niece staying with you, helping to get the ranch back in shape." She grimaced at the charred and broken buildings around them, then at him. "Everyone will believe that."

"I ain't got no niece neither."

Serena gave his arm a sharp shake. "Yes, you do. Me. Your sister, um—Hetty. Your sister Hetty's girl."

Whiskey Pete appeared to mull it over, then looked back at her with a grin. "Course. Hetty." He frowned a little. "You don't look like her, though."

Serena sighed. "Neither do you."

"Strange thing." Pete shook his head and started back toward the ranch house.

Inside, Serena waited while he retrieved his rifle and a lackluster Lucky Joe. He left the dog flopped on its side by the gates, then started up the stairs leading to the second-story balcony of the north wing. "What are you doing?" she demanded as Whiskey Pete stopped near the top of the stairs, hunching low near a small, narrow opening in the wall.

"It's a good place to shoot. They cain't see well enough to shoot back."

"Don't you ever just talk to them?" Serena asked, crouching down beside him.

"No reason to. They ain't the talkin' kind. Meaner'n a rattlesnake on a hot skillet, most of 'em." As the riders neared the ranch, he lifted the rifle to his shoulder, poking the muzzle through the small opening, his finger trembling on the trigger.

The moment the riders pulled up a few feet from the ranch house, Pete fired a shot, kicking up a puff of dust in front of the trio, frightening the horses into a nervous dance.

One of the riders, a square dark man, jerked back the reins of his jittery Appaloosa, bringing the stallion to a stop. "Your aim's a bit off this mornin', old man," he called up, his voice low and dragging. Pushing back his hat, he squinted up at the wall. "We know you got company. What're ya hidin' up there? Another bunch of your pilgrims?"

"I'm not hiding," Serena muttered. Before Whiskey Pete could protest, she snatched up the rifle from his hand, stood up and climbed to the top of the stairs where the edge of the balcony ran even with the top of the wall. Slinging a leg over the railing, she inched toward the edge of the stones and stood tall, legs splayed, the butt of the gun firmly against her shoulder. "My aim's a little better," she said loudly, her finger caressing the hot metal of the trigger.

"Well, well." The square man flung a smirk over his shoulder at his two companions, then nudged his horse a few paces forward. "I don't recall meetin' a Mormon woman as brazen as you."

"I'm not a Mormon. I'm Pete's niece. And I'm not impressed by the neighborly welcome."

"Forgive me, ma'am." The man pulled off his hat and made her a mocking half-bow. "Birk Reed. Funny, the old man never mentioned no family before."

"Since you don't seem like a friend, I can imagine why." Serena shouldered the rifle a little firmer against her body. "What do you want?"

"The question is what do you want? This ain't exactly the place for a holiday. Unless you're a pilgrim," he added, a brush of menace in his tone.

"Shoot 'em," Whiskey Pete hissed, still bent low behind the wall. "Shoot 'em quick!"

Serena shot him a scowl. "I told you. I'm not Mormon. I'm here to help my uncle rebuild the ranch. We're taking over from Gage Tanner."

"Is that right?" Birk Reed eyed her up and down with the expression of a cowboy appraising a lame horse. He slid a large hand over his wind-ruffled hair. "I got a hard time believin' even Mormons would leave this spread to a skinny girl and a crazy old man, and I doubt Tanner left it to the old man. He didn't have the time."

"I couldn't care less what you believe, Mister Reed."

"You might," he drawled. "I got a notion the Mormons still have a claim on this place. If that's so, then you'd be breakin' the law by stayin' on. Some folks 'round here have never believed Gage Tanner owned this ranch. They think maybe he was hidin' the fact he was managin' Mormon land to keep it from bein' seized. Makes sense. No one ever heard of it bein' up for sale or I'd of been the first to put in a bid. Did give him a fine place to put down roots, while the Mormons kept the ranch in case things changed back to where they could live here again." Birk's eyes narrowed. "But it also made Tanner an outlaw. A dead outlaw. Damned shame what happened to him and his friends, wouldn't you say?"

Serena bristled, her finger itching to pull the trigger. "If you're threatening me—"

"Just offering a bit of advice," Birk said, his face hardening. "There's a bad feeling about this place. Was there even before Tanner and his group got themselves killed. Folks don't stay here long. 'Specially pilgrims that like breathin'."

"Maybe some folks. I intend to stay for a long time." Her lips curved upward, the fire in her eyes belaying any notion of sweetness in her smile. "Thank you for stopping by. Perhaps we'll meet again—in Vulture Creek. I'm sure I'll be doing business there."

Birk yanked his hat back low of his brow. "Count on that. But don't get too used to bein' here. That rifle and the old man's ghost stories won't keep those gates locked forever."

He wheeled his horse about and kicked it into a gallop, followed by his two companions. Serena didn't lower the rifle until their figures were blurs in the distance. "We'll see about that," she spat, anger surging over her. "The damned insolence—"

"Told you," Whiskey Pete said. He took the gun and started back down the stairs. Midway he glanced back at her, shaking his head. "You should've shot 'em."

* * *

A lone lamp burned against the blanket of darkness wrapped around the ranch. Serena sat on the narrow bed in her second floor room. It was in shambles now, with furniture, clothing, blankets strewn everywhere, nevertheless, Serena knew it had been *her* room. Libby's. The woman the Spirit in the Wind could not forget.

Everything in this room spoke of her; her clothes, simple cotton dresses, spilling from the open chest at the foot of the bed, her silver-backed hairbrush tossed from the vanity to the floor, her lilac-scented soap in the cracked wash basin atop the dresser. A single, empty rocking chair. It was almost as if she could return tonight to put her home back in order, to resume her life with Gage Tanner, whatever that might have been . . .

Serena felt a strange sense of relief at the realization that the room held no sense of *him*. In the musty silence, Serena neither saw nor felt anything of Gage Tanner, no clothing, no personal belongings, no masculine scent; even the bed seemed meant for one person. He'd obviously cared deeply for her, but had he spent his nights here with her?

"I'm being stupid," Serena said aloud to the room. What did it matter anyway? The past was the past; they were dead and it was no use speculating or wondering about them any more. She jumped up and began pacing the small area, feeling restless.

It shouldn't matter. But she couldn't shake the image of the strange encounter at the oasis, the black image of the man on the plateau. Was it Gage Tanner? How could it be? Whiskey Pete, even Birk Reed and his bunch, believed he was dead. Yet she couldn't believe she'd met an ethereal spirit at the oasis. There had been something too imposing, too powerful about his presence for him to be a midnight vision. Except what other explanation could there be?

Trying to shake off her uneasiness, the sense of unreality pervading the room, Serena stopped to finger the soft, pale yellow calico of a discarded dress. "Why not?"

She was dirty and tired and her only other dress was nothing near this fine. Libby certainly didn't need it any more. And Serena did.

An hour later, with both the room's appearance and her own greatly improved, Serena sat clad in the loose-fitting frock, she sat a little ways from the fireplace, finger-combing her damp hair into gentle waves of autumn brown, the flames discovering licks of burnt-red highlights. A piece of wood in the fire snapped, sending out a tiny ember. It brushed against her skin and Serena jerked back, feeling the edginess crawl over her again.

Would she always feel like this, never secure, always wondering if someone—if Jerel Webster—waited just outside the gates, ready to snatch away her freedom?

The fire cracked again, and she scrambled to her feet. She squeezed her eyes tightly shut. Her thin hands clenched into fists, flexing open and closed at her sides.

From the time she was old enough to understand, her parents had taught her to think only of herself, to survive any way she could. She had listened and believed, and she had heeded her father's last urgent command and fled when Indians had attacked their wagon caravan, killing everyone but eleven-year-old Serena Lark. And she had ran again when Jerel demanded she be his wife. She had saved herself. She was always running.

It was the only way she would survive. The only way she would be safe. Then. Now.

Jumping up, Serena rushed outside to the balcony railing. Leaning over it, she sucked in deep draughts of cool night air. The blood thundered in her ears; flames danced in front of her eyes, tormenting, refusing her peace.

She stayed there, bent double over the rail, the dull pain of the wood cutting into her belly gradually forcing away the surge of panic inside her. Concentrating on the quiet around her, Serena eased up, her hands still gripped around the rail. She made herself listen to the far-off bay of a lone coyote, the only thread of sound in the black tapestry of the silence.

Long after the fire in her room finally sputtered and died to embers, she finally returned to her bed, curling up in a tight ball under the thin blanket, letting sleep blot out the memories.

Lehi eased her smooth brown thigh over the back of Gage's knee. He shrugged away. For the second night in a row, she'd done her best to exhaust him into sleep, but the peaceful state eluded him. Restless, waiting for dawn's light to appear in the opening above him in the wickiup, Gage finally gave up on finding the elusive state.

He eased Lehi's arm from his chest and slid out from under the hides and into his clothes. Intending to head back to the abandoned cliff dwelling he now called home, he swung himself up onto Gusano, giving the stallion his head. But within two hundred yards of the canyon, Gusano changed direction of his own accord. The stallion turned toward the road that led to the ranch instead of veering off toward the cliffs.

"You know my mind better than I do," Gage murmured, patting the horse's neck. Since the day he had returned too late to prevent tragedy, Gage had vowed never to spend a restful night at the ranch again. He hovered, waiting, these past weeks, in the shadow of his past. Always waiting. He couldn't go back and he couldn't move forward until he had found the people responsible for the massacre and wrought his revenge.

Especially after last night. Even with a clearer head, the vision—woman or mirage—refused to leave him alone. A part of him wanted to believe Libby had returned to tell him the truth, to end his obsession for finding it. But reason—what reason he could muster in the middle of the night—told him that idea had sprung from his own damning guilt. If he couldn't stop the guilt, at least he could dole out the same fate to whoever had murdered Libby and her children and eight of the ranch hands without mercy or remorse.

Maybe Kwion was right. Maybe the woman knew something. Maybe she knew everything. Gage dug his heels into Gusano's flanks. The stallion reared back then rushed forward in a headlong gallop toward the woman who could give him the answers.

The anguished creak of the gates followed by a wail of wind brought Serena out of her dreams and upright in bed in one dizzying motion. It sounded as if someone had opened the gates and was inside the courtyard. But she had locked the gates—hadn't she? She must have been dreaming. Whiskey Pete had told her that once locked, the gates would resist any would-be intruder.

Only a dead man could walk through locked gates and stone walls.

The thought came unbidden. Serena rubbed her hands over her arms, feeling an icy shiver. "That's crazy," she muttered, rolling her sore body to her feet. "I'm crazy." She groped in the darkness for the lamp, her vision blurred with sleep.

Before she could lay her hand to it, the door to her room slammed open.

Serena froze. She swallowed hard and glanced to where she knew the double-barreled shotgun leaned in the corner near the door. Where was Pete now? Hadn't he heard?

"Who is it?" she said at last, speaking to the darkness, her voice sounding small and tremulous. "Pete, if that's you—"

"I should have known you'd take this room."

The voice from the oasis, now hard and angry, rode the night wind, chilling Serena through her rumpled dress straight to her soul.

As her eyes adjusted to the faint light, she recognized the shape and stance of the man of her midnight encounter. "Gage Tanner," she whispered. "It has to be."

"Don't be so sure," he answered.

Serena supposed raw fear and plain good judgment ought to drive her to back away, slam and bolt the door in his face, or at the very least to scream for Whiskey Pete. Lacking a healthy sense of either, she instead made a lunge for the shotgun. She never heard him move, but suddenly behind her the slight click of a pistol's hammer sounded close to her ear.

"You said you weren't real." Shutting her ears to the danger, she reached out and snatched up the shotgun just as the cold metal butt of his pistol touched the bare skin of her shoulder from the back.

"Is this real enough for you?"

She couldn't see him, but she felt him, large, looming, powerful. Her legs threatened to weaken. Not from fear, but from a racing, tremulous feeling she couldn't define. No ghost smelled of leather and fire, of sage and wind and earth. Her hand tightened around the cold gun as his breath came hot against her neck. "You bastard," she said low and fast. "You won't frighten me away."

"You must have a death wish, woman," he muttered close to her ear.

"Not if it means joining you in hell, Mister Tanner." The muzzle of his gun prodded her back. She sucked in a breath. "If you're going to shoot me, then you best do it fast. Because if you keep pushing me, I'll shoot and I won't stop until I see your face hit the dust. We'll see how dead you are then."

A humorless rumble of mocking laughter answered her.

The sound provoked Serena's temper. Jerking away from him, she made a quick twist to the side. In the next instant, she found herself backed into a corner of the room, the hard butt of the gun pressed into her shoulder, the muzzle pointed directly at his heart.

Gage didn't flinch. Instead, he holstered his pistol and took two long strides toward her, barring her escape, challenging her courage with the sheer force of his presence. "You can't kill a dead man. Though from what I've seen of you, I don't doubt you'd try."

Feeling terribly small and definitely disadvantaged, Serena forced herself to keep her eyes leveled on his. He was close, too close. Only the length of the shotgun separated them. The moonlight fell softly on half his face, giving her a hint of hard, rugged features. But opposed by the midnight darkness and the low slope of his hat, the dim light concealed more than it revealed, leaving him an enigma.

Serena struggled to swallow the tremble that started in her chest and worked its way up her throat. "You're damned right, mister. So you better explain what you're doing here, or I swear I'll find out once and for all just how mortal you are."

"And you? Trespassing?" He looked her up and down, a hint of dry amusement in his tone. "I didn't know you'd been invited to stay."

The dark edge to his voice sent a shiver up Serena's spine, but she refused to cower. "How would you know? You don't live here any more." She leveled the gun barrel in the direction of his chin. "I want you out of my room."

"Before you go blasting my head off, I suggest you hear me out. This is a dangerous place to be."

"So I've noticed."

"A lot of people died here not long before you showed up. Just because you're behind locked gates, doesn't mean you're safe."

A phantom of secret anguish haunted his words and for a moment, Serena felt her guard slipping away. In the next breath, she yanked it firmly around her. The mystery of him intrigued her; the pain she glimpsed found an empathetic softness in her heart. But she couldn't afford to feel anything for him, not if she wanted to save herself. "I'd like to know how you managed to get inside those gates."

"I'm a ghost, remember?" Gage casually flipped.

"Don't insult me," she said, unable to muster a full measure of anger and annoyance with the sad resonance hanging in the air around them.

He said nothing, letting the silence linger between them for long moments. The wood and metal of the shotgun became slick with the sweat of her palms, sliding in her grip. She heard her own breath, shallow and fast, felt her blood racing through her veins. He was so still, so quiet, if she closed her eyes she might imagine he wasn't there . . .

"If you're not going to talk to me, then get out," Serena spat out suddenly, unnerved by her own thoughts.

"You aren't going to frighten me away and I don't need to hear any of your warnings. I don't believe in ghosts and I don't—" Her sentence snapped and broke as he lifted a hand toward her face.

He moved so slowly, with mesmerizing intent, his eyes followed the motion of his fingers, that Serena fell captive to the moment, unable to draw back. She watched his hand draw nearer and nearer, transfixed, until the warmth of him whispered against her skin.

"Don't . . ." The trembling plea in her voice surprised her and stopped him. Suddenly, with him so close, solid and real, she felt afraid. Not of him, but of the feelings that jumped inside her when she knew he intended to touch her. Strange, dark, liquid feelings that tried to seduce her into letting down her defenses. The barrel of the gun dipped downward, threatening to slid out of her hands. "Don't come any closer," she said more firmly, praying her voice wasn't shaking the way her hands were. She brought the gun up again. "I'll shoot. I swear it."

Gage drew in a long breath. His hand fell back to his side. "Put the gun down. I just wanted—"

"Wanted what?"

To her astonishment, he shifted uncomfortably, for the first time glancing away from her. "I wanted to see how it felt to touch you, if your hair smelled like . . . hers."

Like Libby's. "Well, does it?"

His eyes snapped back to hers. "No."

The mingled twinge of regret and jealousy she felt at his response bewildered her. "What does it smell like then?" the question spilled out before she could check it.

"Wild flowers. The kind that bloom at dawn."

The satisfaction she felt was so sweet she didn't trust

in it. Angry at herself, her brazen confidence shaken, she let the muzzle of the gun drop a few inches.

"Go on. Put it down. I'll keep my distance." She sensed rather than saw his half smile. "I promise." With his words, he took several steps backward, taking with him the warm shelter of his presence against the chilled pre-dawn air.

"I'm supposed to take your word? I've heard the dead lie."

Gage stiffened, his tenseness crackling between them. "I can't lay claim to many virtues, but I keep my word." He went on before she could think of a reply, "And you have it wrong. The dead never lie. We don't have any reason left to lie. Now put the gun down." He motioned to the wavering shotgun with a nod.

Why she obeyed him when for the better part of her life, every command had been an invitation to disobey, Serena didn't understand. His strange, larger-than-life aura frightened her, and at the same time, something about him tugged at her deep inside, drawing her to him, making her wonder what lay beneath his harsh veneer.

She wanted to see his face clearly. The yearning stabbed at her, as powerful at that moment as the need to breathe. Yet in the shadows of starlight filtering through the open doorway, all she saw was the image of strength and animal grace she'd first glimpsed in the midnight pool of the oasis.

"Maybe now you can listen instead of trying to decide where best to put a hole in me," Gage said, startling her out of her scrutiny.

Ignoring him, Serena blurted out the first question that came to her mind. "Why did you want to know if I was like her, like Libby? Do I look like her?"

The answer came after a pause of seconds. "At a glance."

Serena felt his gaze rove over her in the quiet that followed, and it roused in her the same hot, anxious sensation it had when he watched her at the oasis. She sensed an immovable strength in him, a power she might match, but never weaken or break, and it both intrigued and frustrated her. With her own boldness, she'd either infuriated the men she knew, or bent them to her will. Yet he seemed moved neither by anger nor by her defiance. He only watched her, waiting, silent.

She wanted to demand he look away. But instead she stood, momentarily speechless.

"You're about the same size, and it's her dress," Gage said finally. "But you don't look like her. And you definitely don't have her temperament."

"Really?" Were his eyes as deep and rich and mesmerizing as the sound of his voice. "I don't think that's a compliment. And if you mean she meekly let you tell her what to do and when to do it, then you're right, I'm nothing like her."

"She knew how to hold her tongue. How to listen."

Serena bristled. "I've heard all I ever intend to hear about keeping quiet, and letting anyone who cares to tell me how to think and act, Mister Tanner. And if you have something to say, get it over with. Otherwise, get out."

Instead of backing down at her sharp tone, he seemed amused. "You don't have much patience."

"I like to have things done and over with."

"Bossy is more like it."

"Is that all you have to say?" Serena asked, resisting the temptation to bring the gun up again. "Because if it is—"

"There are people around here who want the ranch,"

he said, overriding her protest. "They aren't above killing to get it."

"I've had a visit from them," she told him, thinking
he meant Birk Reed and his companions.

She saw him give a small jerk backward, as if she'd
said the unexpected. His abrupt tension cracked like
lightning. "What do you know about them?"

"Why would you think I know about them?" she said,
fighting back an irrational surge of fear. "I only just
came here. I've never even been to Vulture Creek."

"Vulture Creek?" Gage paused, and she could almost
hear him assessing what she had said, weighing it
against what he knew. "It's interesting," he said at last,
his tone thoughtful. "The ranch has only been vacant a
few weeks. Not long enough for too many folks beyond
Vulture Creek to know about it. And then you turn up,
from nowhere, expecting to move in, just days after the
killings."

"I didn't know about the massacre. I—I thought the
people living here would be . . ." How could she hide
what she knew about him? If what Birk Reed said was
true, and he really was only a superintendent for the
Mormons, a renegade in the eyes of the law, then he
was more dangerous than the specter she imagined him
to be. "I thought they would be friendly," she finished
vaguely, inwardly wincing at her weak explanation.

"Friendly?" he jeered. "You're either more naive or
more bullheaded than I took you for. No one here is
friendly. They're interested in surviving. Whatever way
they can."

"Just like you," she shot back. "If that's so, why are
you so obsessed with scaring me away? Why do you
care what happens to me? You don't live here any more.
I do."

"No. You don't."

"I do, and you haven't answered my question. And you haven't bothered to tell me who these mysterious people are who would kill to take over this place."

"If I knew that, I wouldn't be here."

"And where would you be, oh Spirit in the Wind?" she asked, lightly mocking.

"Gone."

His voice was a hollow echo. He sounded as though inside, he had already vanished to a place where only he existed. Only his body, empty of spirit and soul, remained to carry out his revenge for the deaths of the people he had cared for.

A draft of wind sang mournfully through the small room, and Serena shivered. But it was the chill of his emptiness that made her feel the cold and pricked at her heart. "Look," she said, pointing behind him to the first rose blush of morning that brushed the sky. "You've managed to keep me up all night."

Gage whipped around to stare at the faint light. Without a word, he strode out of the room and disappeared. Caught off guard, Serena gaped at the empty place he left behind for a few startled seconds before dashing out after him.

She reached the center of the courtyard a few steps behind him, noticing that somehow, the gates now gaped open. "You're leaving? Just like that? You don't even have a horse. You can't walk off into the desert, alone. No one can survive that."

A faint smile touched his mouth, but he said nothing.

"Besides," Serena forged on, feverishly trying to cover her uneasiness at his odd behavior, "you haven't answered my questions. You can't just . . . just vanish."

"Why not?"

Serena recoiled a step at his blunt retort. "Because— because I want . . ." She wanted him to stay. The answer, formed suddenly in her mind, felt right. He irritated her, disturbed her, stirred her temper. Yet, at odds with it all, she felt safe with him, protected somehow by a man she only knew as a shadow in the darkness. "I want you to stay," she said at last. "I want to talk to you."

"Spend your time packing," Gage said, walking toward the open gates. "You may not get a second chance. Life means nothing here. The dead know that." Without giving her time to answer, he stepped outside the sanctuary of walls and gates, vanishing into the misty grayness with a the swift fluid grace of a dream-walker.

He left Serena standing alone in the courtyard, furious, frightened, fascinated, but with a new resolution to stay and discover just why Gage Tanner wanted to be dead.

"That's right," she whispered after him. "I may not get a second chance. But I will survive, Mister Tanner. I always have. No matter what the cost."

Chapter Four

"How many wagons, Pete? Can you tell from there?" Looking up the second-story stairs from the middle of the courtyard, Serena shielded her eyes from the brilliant morning sun. Just a few hours past dawn, it already mercilessly beat on the reddish-gray stones of the ranch house, scorching the unrelenting vista of rippling silver grasses and barren rock.

Whiskey Pete, crouched by the small slitted opening near the railing, squinted through the narrow hole at the brown swirl of dust in the distance. "Looks like two. And headin' this way, no doubt about it."

"That's all we need now." Serena scrubbed at her bleary eyes, annoyed at having to deal with more unwanted visitors. Couldn't they just leave her alone? Restless, disturbed and frustrated by her strange night encounters with Gage Tanner, she had lain awake long after he disappeared. Then, no sooner had she drifted into an uneasy sleep, than Whiskey Pete's furious pounding at the door jerked her awake again. "Go and get the shotgun," she told him, irritation in her voice. "We'll probably need it."

"I'll get it," Whiskey Pete said, stumping down the stairs. "But I won't be usin' it."

Serena stared. "What do you mean? You're the one who's always telling me to shoot at them. Why is this time different? Do you know these people?"

"Nope." He turned and started to walk toward his room.

"Wait a minute!" She reached out and snagged his bony arm. "That's not an answer."

"It isn't?" Scratching at his ear, Pete cocked his head to one side, giving her a questioning glance with his good eye. "Sure sounded like one to me."

"It's not! Why aren't you ready to shoot at those wagons? They're headed straight for the ranch and you always want to shoot at anything else that moves this direction." Serena stomped her foot in frustration. "Tell me why!"

Whiskey Pete shrugged. "Neither ranchers like Reed and his boys, nor tree devils ever come here in wagons. Why should I be shootin' at 'em? You sure got some funny ideas 'bout who gits shot at. Yer finger got a trigger itch, or what?"

Exasperated, Serena slapped her hands to her hips. "You're the one who's always saying everyone's out to get this place."

"Don't recall sayin' that." He shook his head, frowning. Then his face cleared. "C'mon Lucky Joe," he called to the dog. Stretched out by the gate in a patch of morning sun, Lucky Joe raised his head a few inches and gave Pete a bored glance. "Well, come on. You done bit yer leg off again and I've got t' fetch you a new one. Cain't do it with you lyin' around like a piece o' leftover hide."

Serena took a step after him, then stopped. What was the use? In minutes the wagons would be at the gates and Pete obviously wasn't going to be any help. She'd have to deal with them herself. As always, she ended up with only herself to rely on for help.

Ever since her parents' deaths, when it came to making crucial decisions, she'd depended on her own instincts. No one else would act in her best interests after all. Her kind Mormon sisters always sacrificed their own wishes and wills to the wishes of their fathers and husbands, or to the betterment of the family as a whole. But Serena found early on after they adopted her that it was not, and never would be, in her nature to be so acquiescent or selfless.

With her parents' encouragement, she'd learned from her early childhood on to think for herself. They'd taught her that in the dangerous life they led traveling through the rugged western territories, her self-confidence, her wits, and an independent spirit might mean life or death to her in the event of an Indian or outlaw raid.

Their tragic fate had proved them right, and Serena would never, never forget it. Her independence and the ability to think and act fast had saved her life once. No matter what else she might sacrifice to survive, she would never surrender her will.

Cursing under her breath, she hiked up her skirts and climbed the stairs to peer out the tiny opening in the wall. Through the brownish haze, she could just trace the shapes of people in the wagon: two men driving the first, a man and a woman on the front seat of the second. The wagons swaled and rattled over the rough terrain, lugged along by their teams of dirt-coated horses. Serena watched as they slowed, then stopped a few yards from the front gates.

The man in the first wagon, lean, his wispy iron-gray hair lifted by the slight wind, glanced up. Sunk into dark pouches, his eyes seemed black and expressionless.

"Hello," he called. "Is anyone inside? We're looking for Gage Tanner."

Serena hesitated. After the welcome she'd received from the denizens of Vulture Creek and the Spirit in the Wind himself, she wasn't going to open the doors to more trouble. And she certainly didn't intend to wait hand and foot on uninvited visitors.

But, just as she opened her mouth to send them away, for an instant her eyes lit on the young woman seated in the lead wagon. In the slender, drooping figure she saw a vision of herself, many years past, sitting next to her father, travel weary, thirsty, excited by the sight of the promise of a real bed and a meal not cooked over a campfire.

More times than she could recall growing up, Preacher Lark and his wife and daughter had been welcomed in by families along their trek from Oklahoma to Utah, families who generously offered food, warmth, and kindness to the itinerant minister and his small family. Families who, if only for a few hours, let Serena share in the security of having a real home instead of a space in the back of a wandering wagon.

"What do you want?" she finally answered.

The man stared up curiously in the direction of her voice. "I am Elder Uriel Welby. We are seeking shelter for the day and night. Are you missus Tanner?" His graveled tone held doubt.

Am I? Serena struggled with the decision. Mormons. And obviously they hadn't heard of the fate of the ranch, Gage Tanner, or the family he had taken under his wing. And if the church elders in Utah didn't know . . . it could be the best stroke of luck to come her way in a long time.

Unless they discovered she was the errant Serena Lark.

A familiar surge of resentment welled up in her. For five years, her Mormon father and the more forceful among his wives had dictated to her, tried to mold her into a meek, spiritless woman who would accept anything told her without question. Now if she didn't do something to protect herself from recognition, they would try to take her back to the life she'd risked her life to flee.

"Yes. I'm Missus Tanner," she said firmly. Even as the name left her lips, she regretted saying it. A slash of wind whipped across her face, hot and gritty. Almost unwillingly, her gaze slid toward the plateau. It was just beyond her vision, but she still felt him there. He was watching her, his eyes as hard and flat as the sheer face of the plateau. A lone figure created from the shimmer of heat on the horizon, the force and wail of a sirocco, the stony, impenetrable facade of the cliffs. And perhaps, in part by her own need.

Or her own madness. Despite the heat, Serena shivered with a chill of superstitious fear. It was as if the Spirit in the Wind had heard her lie and waited, somewhere beyond the walls of her sanctuary, to expose the truth.

The voice of Uriel Welby cut into her momentary daze, dispelling the eerie feeling of unreality. "It is a pleasure to meet you. Elder Caltrop told us of the many kindnesses your people here have shown to the pilgrims that pass this way. We are looking for shelter," he repeated, this time with more emphasis on the request.

"Yes, yes, of course." Serena ran down the stairs to open the gates, the response almost involuntary after her years of being forced to yield to the stern dictates of the Mormon elders she had found shelter among. She felt the same fire of rebellion she had felt all those years, but was still able to hide it when it benefited her. "Welcome," she said as the heavy door swung open to reveal the little group. "You can stable your horses there——" She pointed in the direction of the furthest corral. "Then I'll find rooms for you."

"Thank you, Missus Tanner." Uriel looked her up and down, a slight frown between his eyes as he took in the loosely-fitting blue frock Serena had carelessly pulled on after being so rudely roused by Whiskey Pete. One sleeve had slipped partway down her bare shoulder; she'd scorned putting on any tight-fitting chemises or petticoats in the scorching heat and left her shoes behind in the hurry.

Serena tugged up the shoulder of the dress, resisting the urge to smooth her tumbled hair, aware she must appear the furthest thing from a gentle, conservative rancher's wife. "I'm happy to have guests," she said with as much warmth as she could manage. "But I have to apologize for the state of the rooms. I've——been sorting and cleaning, and I'm afraid you've caught me at an awkward time. I'll have your rooms back in order in no time, though," she said with false assurance.

"Yes, well——allow me to introduce my wife . . ." He nodded to the plain, smooth-faced woman who climbed out of the back of the first wagon, shaking out her gray skirts. "Nora, and my daughter Sarah." The young woman still seated on the driver's bench bowed her head in greeting. "And this is Elder Levi Goddard and his son Nathaniel." Climbing down from their seat, the two men from the second wagon stepped forward, giving her a brief nod.

Serena gestured to the corral again and as the men started to lead the wagons and horses away, she guided the women inside the gates.

"It seems very deserted here," Nora commented,

glancing around at the dust and silence of the courtyard. "Surely you aren't here alone."

"I—of course not." Serena silently cursed herself for ever beginning this charade. She'd have to be careful, much more careful with every word she spoke to avoid arousing suspicion. If they discovered who she really was, what she was running from. . . . "I have one hand here. The others are all with my husband, helping him pasture the cattle near the north rim of the canyon."

Nora raised a brow. "At this time of year? It seems odd."

Damn. Another pitfall. When did the darned cattle go to pasture? Why did it matter? Concealing her growing frustration, she answered with what she hoped was a casual shrug. "My husband knows his business."

"I'm sure he does. But what about the children? And the other women? Where are they?"

Women? Children? Frantically scouring her mind, Serena finally recalled Whiskey Pete's vague reference to the women and boys killed in his tree devil massacre. She felt a sick, sinking feeling low in her belly. She didn't even know all of their names.

"They've all gone into town for supplies," she said, aware of Nora's eyes on her, questioning. "They have friends they plan to visit a short while, that's why I'm taking advantage of the time to do some rearranging and cleaning here."

"I see," Nora said, although it didn't sound as if she did. "I suppose that's why it's so quiet here." She looked around them again. "When we first saw the ranch my husband commented on how deserted it looked. Like a ghost ranch . . ." She trailed off, giving a nervous little giggle.

Her stomach flip-flopping, Serena forced a laugh of

her own. "I suppose it may seem like that, here so far from everything, with everyone away."

Leading the two women up to the second-floor rooms, Serena glanced back at the harsh landscape framed between the open gates, silently willing the Spirit in the Wind away from his haunt tonight.

With a considerable amount of wheedling, demanding and out-and-out insisting, Serena badgered Whiskey Pete into helping her clean up a few of the second-story rooms and scrounging enough supplies from the depleted pantry and cellar for an adequate supper. Muttering something about too much fuss and noise, Pete then retreated to his own room with Lucky Joe, leaving Serena alone to entertain their guests.

As the sun sank to an orange-red sliver on the deep violet expanse of sky, they all gathered at the long rough pine table in the largest downstairs room, filling tin plates with the slices of smoked ham, beans, cornbread, and dried apple cobbler Serena had served up. While they ate, Serena, dressed more decorously in a high-necked, pale green cotton dress, her hair trussed in a neat braid, plied them with questions to avoid answering any herself. She discovered their journey through the Arizona territory into Utah country had been largely prompted by Levi's desire to live in a Mormon community and by Sarah's impending marriage.

"You and Nathaniel seem well suited, Sarah," Serena commented, when Uriel told her about his daughter's betrothal, smiling from the lanky, dark-haired youth seated across from her to the delicate blonde girl. "When is your marriage to be sanctified?"

Nathaniel looked uncomfortable, Sarah's eyes flew wide and a furious blush reddened her sallow skin. Nora dropped her eyes, fidgeting with her napkin, and the two older men both frowned at Serena, sitting straight-backed and stern in their chairs.

Serena watched Sarah's gaze flick almost involuntarily to the handsome young man seated across from her. She and Nathaniel exchanged a lingering, intent glance before both snatched their eyes from each other to the half-cleared plates in front of them.

Levi finally spoke, breaking the awkward silence. "I am Sarah's betrothed, not my son. Nathaniel chose to come to the Utah territory with me after his mother's death."

Serena stiffened. "I see." She deliberately glanced at Sarah, pale and silent. "I'm sorry."

"My daughter is fortunate to be the betrothed of a man of Elder Goddard's stature," Uriel said, looking hard at Serena. "And she will have four other sisters in the house as part of her new family."

"Very fortunate," Serena said, unable to keep a touch of derision from her voice. She had fled the Utah territory for the very same reason. While there were many Mormon traditions she admired, others she had bit her tongue and abided. She had never respected the marriage traditions. She wanted a man to love her as her father had adored her mother and her, with a singular, consuming, possessive emotion that offered everything and demanded nothing.

It provoked her to know Sarah had little choice in the matter. Yet Sarah would submit. Serena had run.

"We realize a Gentile like yourself isn't accustomed to our ways," Nora said softly, her expression an appeal for understanding. "But Elder Caltrop said your husband has always been in sympathy with us. Surely you share his convictions."

"You must," Levi said, bitterness edging his words.

"Else you would not offer us shelter. The Arizona territory isn't known for its welcome to our brethren. The
people here have done their best to purge us from the
land."

"If Elder Caltrop hadn't been able to trust Gage Tanner with this place, the church would have lost it also,"
Uriel added. "When the government joined the persecu-
tion against us, seizing our properties, our only hope
was to allow Gentiles to manage them, to convince everyone they were the true owners. Your husband has
risked much for us, knowing as he does the consequences of anyone discovering he is not the true owner
of this land."

Memories of hurried packing and a rushed journey
out of the territory revisited Serena. As a child, alone
and stranded by tragedy, she'd stayed here over a year
with her Mormon benefactors before moving with them
to Utah, and now she realized, in part, the reason for
their sudden departure.

And she understood how the Spirit in the Wind came
to make a home at an isolated Mormon sanctuary. And
how much he risked to stay.

Was that the reason for the massacre? Had Gage Tanner's determination to aid the Mormons cost his family
their lives?

The idea both chilled and evoked in her a strange empathy for his resolution and the loneliness he imposed
on himself.

Suddenly aware of several curious gazes provoked by
her silence, Serena tried to smooth over her lapse. "My
husband does respect your beliefs. And you've always
treated us with generosity and kindness," she said, hoping it was the truth and anxious to cover her anger and
apprehension at her own plight. "I know it appears the
ranch has been neglected, but it's only because my hus-

band is away. We were short-handed and he couldn't spare the men to stay here and help. Once he's back, things will be in order again."

I'll make sure of it. He'll have to help me. He's the only one who can help me. They can't ever know I'm not Missus Tanner.

"My husband has given his life to this ranch," she added. Or given his life for it. She didn't know which. But she intended to find out, this time for certain.

Next time we meet, I'll find out just how real you are, Gage Tanner.

"Elder Caltrop will be pleased to hear that," Uriel said carefully. "He and Mister Tanner have had a long friendship."

Serena fixed a wide smile on her face. "Well, it certainly seems the ideal arrangement for the moment, doesn't it? You and your brethren have a sanctuary when you need it and I—" She smiled more broadly and waved a hand around the room. "I finally have the perfect home."

The rumble of thunder, low and ominous, just at the edge of her hearing, woke Serena from her light, uneasy sleep. She pried open her eyes, listening in the depthless midnight darkness. It came again, the sound shivering the air around her.

Shoving back the worn cotton sheet, Serena tumbled out of the narrow bed. It was he. Gage Tanner. The Spirit in the Wind. She knew it as surely as the quickened pulse of her heart. His presence, always there even when he was beyond her sight, had infected her blood like a fever, roused each time she sensed his return under the silent canopy of starlight.

Not bothering to take the time even to pull a wrap

over her thin night dress, she ran out of the room and down the stairs, her bare feet silent on the dirt and rough wood. At the bottom of the stairs she started toward the oasis . . . and froze in mid-step.

Both gates gaped open, creaking to the slight brush of the wind's hand.

She whirled around. In the center of the courtyard, illuminated by a shaft of argent moonlight, Gage Tanner stood silent and unmoving.

Time suspended for the eternity of a moment; they stared at each other. The wind's whisper died on a sigh, leaving behind a perfect, fathomless quiet. Silver starlight spilled into the courtyard, lending a surreal air to the shapes and shadows surrounding them.

Serena caught her breath, an unexpected emotion trembling through her, something warm and deep and compelling. All of it seemed unreal, more a dream than not. Yet it stirred a strange awareness inside her, as if in a hidden place in her heart, she knew where they would end even before they began.

They stayed motionless, snared in a silken web of silver light and silent dark, until a sudden gust of wind blew through the gates, shattering the fragile enchantment. Serena, suddenly realizing the danger, found her wits and her voice.

"Are you crazy?" she hissed, her voice an angry whisper. Striding a few paces forward, she stopped within a few feet of him, craning her neck to glare up at his shadowed face. "There are people here—upstairs sleeping, I hope." She glanced up to the closed doors, breathed a hesitant sigh of relief, then turned back to Gage. "Mormons. If they find you here—"

"Then they will have to admit they've seen a ghost," he said, his voice low and hard.

"They don't know about the wretched ghost! They'll

just think you're back from your cattle drive and they'll expect to meet you and your adopted family and all the so-called ranch hands!" Serena snapped. "You're going to ruin everything with this stupid charade of yours."

Gage stared at her, then with a quick motion, moved with unmistakable intent toward her. Taken aback by his unexpected action, Serena's brash courage wavered. Suddenly he was too real, a treacherous flesh and blood manifestation of the faraway spirit on the plateau.

He stopped an arm's length from her and she breathed in the essence of him, not something ethereal and elusive, but a blending of sweat and leather, wind and danger. "What have you told them?"

"I told them I was your wife," Serena answered brazenly, refusing to let him intimidate her.

The word made Gage flinch. "Why did you lie to them?"

"It shouldn't matter to you. You're dead." Serena took a step nearer, her eyes narrowed. Her lip curled in challenge. "Aren't you?"

Gage stood his ground though she moved close enough for the wind to catch her scent and draw it against him. The diaphanous cotton of her shift clung to her slender body, caressing each hollow and curve, and her hair rioted over her neck and shoulders in an undisciplined tumble. She might have called herself his wife to the visitors, but Libby, the woman he once considered asking to fill that role, had never been this wantonly bold, this daring. Libby had been the first tentative softness of spring, bending to the harsh will of the elements. Serena Lark was like lightning, the sudden clash and conflict of a summer storm, untamed and brazen.

He'd thought he could frighten or bully her into leaving. Most women he'd known would have yielded like a willow in the wind to threats or warnings. Not her.

She was so stubborn Gage doubted she'd give him standing room in Hell if he begged for it.

"It should be easy enough to prove," she murmured, her voice pushing its way into his thoughts. "This time I'm going to make sure."

She took another step closer and he abruptly realized she intended to touch him. He could see it in the obstinate lift of her chin, the spit and fire in her eyes.

It galled him to retreat.

And she knew it.

Serena sensed his uneasiness, his struggle to decide. Giddy with an elixir of triumph and determination, she stretched out a hand. Gage moved backward, but before he could escape, she lunged forward and slapped her hands flat against his chest.

His heart, her conquest, beat a ragged rhythm, strong and fast, under her palms.

The sensation of life unexpectedly startled her. Surprise rippled through her at the feel of rough cotton and the heat of him, even as she called herself a fool for ever thinking he might not be real. "You're remarkably solid for a ghost," she said, splaying her fingers over hard muscle, abruptly aware how much she liked the feel of him. A different kind of sensation, akin to wonder, keen and disturbing, poured over her like the first shock of rain after a long, hot afternoon.

Instinctively, Gage reached up and shackled her wrists in one hand. He intended to push her away, but the rub of her skin against his stopped him. He'd spent so much time playing the role of a dead man, living on the edge of life, that the feel of her, warm and fiery and alive, startled him with its intensity.

His grip unconsciously tightened and Serena winced at the bite of pain. "Let me go," she said, twisting and tugging to free her wrists as her temper flared.

"No."

The stunned look on her face was almost funny. She gaped up at him, for once speechless.

"Hasn't anyone ever told you that before?" Gage mocked. "You were eager enough to touch me before."

"I only wanted to prove you were real so you would stop pretending you weren't."

"What makes you think I am real?"

"I felt your heart beat. I felt you breathe," she whispered, her own breath failing her. She struggled to settle her emotions beneath the set of her mind. "I need your help," she told him with as much force as she could muster, her fingers still tingling from their brush against him. "This place is practically in ruins."

Gage held her easily, frustrating her attempts to wriggle away. "Why do you care?"

"I told you I'm here to stay."

"No," he ground out. "You're not. I made that clear before."

"And how do you intend to stop me?" Serena demanded. "If you try, I'll tell everyone you're not a ghost. That's what you're afraid of, isn't it?"

His face hardened and his fingers bit into her tender skin. Serena felt the harsh rasp of his breath on her face, sensed the anger in him running deep and strong. Emotion cracked between them like lightning, jolting the stillness of the night. More powerful than fear, hotter than fury.

"And what are you afraid of?" Gage asked. "Why are you so set on hiding here?"

"I'm not hiding!"

"You've been here before," he went on as if she'd never spoken. "You know the danger. Indians, the ranchers who want to oust the Mormons—all kinds of outlaws."

"So I've noticed," Serena returned smartly. "And I don't care about any of them. I'm not a part of their battles over sheep and cattle and land and water. I'm here because I want to be and that's reason enough. I'm going to stay and make this a home with or without you. Now let me go!"

"Not until you tell me why you came here. You're not Mormon."

"Not if my other choice was being damned to Hell." Catching the flicker of surprise in his eyes, Serena plunged ahead, venting some of her fury and frustration. "I know you're their devoted friend, but I can understand why the ranchers are so anxious to be rid of them."

"Can you? Somehow I don't think your reasons for despising them are the same as the ranchers. Cattlemen despise them for claiming the best lands and waters, then letting their sheep graze until the land is stripped and useless. You aren't here to try to lay claim to the same lands and waters the Mormons and ranchers are at war over, are you?"

"In a way, yes, I suppose I am. But I didn't leave them over land or water. I left after living with them for five years, to put an end to being told what to do, how to act, how to think. My parents taught me all of that. I kept telling my Mormon father and the others that no one would ever change my beliefs or take away my free will. But they wouldn't listen to me!"

She paused, sucking in a breath, expecting him to say something, to refute her, to chastise her. Something! Instead, his expression had turned thoughtful, his eyes abstracted as if he were lost in his own thoughts.

"You aren't listening to me either!" she snapped, jiggling her wrists to catch his attention. "If you don't want to know the answers, then stop asking me stupid questions and let me go."

Slowly, Gage's eyes focused on her again. A frown crept between his eyes and he shook his head slightly. "Then you were here before—"

"The massacre?" she finished.

"What do you know about it?"

The quick blend of suspicion and menace that sprang to his face unsettled Serena, cooling her hot temper. "I—I don't know anything. Only what Whiskey Pete told me. He said they all died, even you." She paused. "Is that the reason you want to stay dead? Because of them? Or because you're afraid everyone will find out you don't really own the ranch? Is that it?"

"I am dead," he said harshly. "And I intend to make sure anyone responsible for those killings is the same."

"You think I know something, don't you?" she said slowly, not liking the iron glint in his eyes, the grip of his fingers around her wrists. "How could I?"

"You tell me. It's strange, a woman alone, showing up in the middle of nowhere, without an explanation. You've no love lost for the Mormons. You obviously don't want them to know you're here. You're running. From what?"

"I'm not—" Serena began hotly. Gage's sudden tensing cut her short. Something was wrong. She glanced around them, uneasy without knowing why. "What is it?"

Gage hushed her with a quick, savage wrench of his hand. In one swift motion, he loosed her wrists and spun her around, flattening her backward against his body with his arm. His free hand snapped to the gun on his hip.

The awareness of danger came without warning. His years as a Cavalry scout, tracking renegade Indians and outlaws through the rugged Arizona and New Mexico territories, had honed his instincts to a fine edge. He relied on them more than he did a gun or a knife, relied on them then as he did now to search out the presence he sensed on the balcony above them.

Using his body to shield Serena, Gage looked back over his shoulder, his eyes hunting the darkness. There was nothing.

And then, for an instant, a light flickered in one of the upstairs rooms.

Serena wanted to turn with him, to make him tell her what threatened them. The alert rigidity of his body warned her from it. She felt every muscle flex, all his attention fixed on whatever—or whoever—was the menace, his breath light and fast. That alone should have kept her from moving.

But it was the surety of being protected that held her quiet. His arm wrapped around her, pressing her hard against him, sheltering her with his strength and his life. For the first time in what seemed an eternity, she felt safe, secure, in a place she had longed to find and never wanted to leave.

Focused on the danger, Gage nearly forgot the woman bound to him, but as the presence above faded, his thoughts and senses gradually returned to her. Slight and small compared to his sinuous height, the feel of her found a softness in him he never wanted to know. He could feel himself drawn to protect her, to help her, to fill the emptiness inside him with her needs, her desires.

He'd felt the same before, the urge to take on someone else's problems and wants as his own. Except this time, something warned him this woman would take more from him than he could afford to leave behind.

"Did someone see us?" Serena whispered, the words breathed into the hollow of his throat.

"Yes." Gage abruptly dropped his arm and turned away from her, striding out of the courtyard, into the darkness outside.

"Wait!" Serena raced after him, breathless with the rapid rush of events. Stunned by his swift withdrawal, her heart pounded furiously in her chest as she watched him slowly pause to glance back at her. "If someone did see us, what am I supposed to tell them? I can hardly repeat your ghost story. They won't believe it."

Gage shrugged. "Lie. You seem to be good at that."

"You can't just leave me here like this! Not again!"

No, I can't. But I have to. He looked at her, feeling tugged between two opposing desires. One sane, driven by his vow of revenge; one a completely alien longing that unnerved him with its force. "It's nearly dawn," he said at last, uncomfortable with feeling anything at all.

Serena glanced to the horizon, seeing the first tinge of light fade the black to a smudged gray. "What does it matter?" she wanted him to stay, *needed* him to stay. But she didn't know how to tell him, to convince him to bend to her will.

For the first time, a hint of humor softened the edge of his mouth. "I don't like the light. Remember?" With a tug of his hat, Gage walked away from her, the blackness quickly swallowing his figure until he and the night became one.

Serena stared after him, rushing to the gates to lock them again. Before she shoved the bolt she glared out into the night, bemused by his ability to vanish into the desert with the ease of the wind. How could he just leave her? Especially now, when one of her guests might have overseen them and recognized him as Gage Tanner. What if they realized she wasn't his wife and discovered she was instead the errant betrothed bride of Jerel Webster? She shuddered as an image of Jerel rose before her, the arrogant ruthlessness of his smile, his voice, when he decided he wanted something for himself. When he'd decided he wanted her.

Heat flooded her skin. She'd glimpsed a ruthlessness in Gage, too, when he'd questioned her about the massacre. Except in him it was a grim determination to avenge the deaths of his family and friends.

Serena looked out into the unrelenting panorama of black, feeling his presence even though he was no longer near. There were times, seduced by the unreality wrought by the night and her own confused emotions, she believed he might truly be a spirit on the horizon, come to torment her.

At other times she sensed only his heart was dead.

His scent lingered on her skin, her shift, and the embrace of it started the fever inside her once more. Wanting to douse it, Serena wandered back to the oasis and dropped to her knees at the edge of the pool. She bathed her heated face and arms in the cool water, letting the silvery trickle pour over her again and again.

The coolness soothed, but it also reminded her of Gage, of the first time she glimpsed his reflection in the pool. There had to be a way to make him help her transform the ranch into an inviolate sanctuary, a place she could escape the past pursuing her. She had to find a way to conquer Gage Tanner. Before it was too late.

Comforted by her own resolve, Serena lay down under the embrace of the cottonwoods, wrapped in the blanket of darkness, studying the bright diamond points of the stars through the branches of the trees until the desert's song lulled her eyes closed. She drifted into a numbing sleep, her dreams haunted by the vision of a restless spirit who called to her heart . . .

* * *

"Missus Tanner!"

The voice, sharp and insistent, seemed to come from far away. It called her, but with a name that didn't fit. Serena stirred a little, her head heavy from her fitful rest. It couldn't be real. Nothing seemed real to her except her midnight dreams.

The voice came again, this time accompanied by an urgent shake of her shoulder. "Missus Tanner, are you all right?"

Reluctantly, Serena pried her eyes open. She looked up into the strained face of Levi Goddard. "Of course I'm all right," she began crossly, breaking off when she abruptly realized she was still lying beside the oasis, clad only in the meager cover of her thin cotton shift.

Levi towered over her, staring down as though she were the epitome of all that was sinful—and mad in the bargain. "What are you doing here?," he asked. "Are you ill?"

"Ill . . ." Serena seized on the suggestion. "Yes—no . . . I-I felt a fever in the night. I came out to cool myself and I—I must have fallen asleep." She struggled to her feet, not even attempting to explain her state of undress or to make herself look more respectable, knowing it was useless.

"Do you need assistance? Nora is somewhat skilled at healing—" He stopped, looking at her with an expression of growing doubt.

"No—no. I'm sorry for disturbing you," Serena said, edging her way in the direction of the gates. "I didn't realize you would be up so early. I should see to breakfast. Just let me freshen up a little and I'll see you in the kitchen."

She managed to take several steps toward the stairs

when Levi said suddenly, "I thought I heard voices last night. Quite late."

"Voices?" Serena forced innocence into her voice. "Surely not."

Levi looked hard at her. "It is dangerous ever to open the gates at night. Anyone might come in. And there are those who would welcome the opportunity. The walls of this house were built as a sanctuary against those who would steal our water supply. Surely you know that."

"Of course," Serena returned, barely keeping irritation from sharpening her words. "And I apologize for disturbing you. It must have been me you heard down here, trying to douse the fever." She lowered her eyes, aware the rebellion she felt glittered there, betraying her demure attitude.

"Perhaps the heat has affected us all," Levi said. When Serena glanced up in surprise, he shook his head, his mouth drawn in a disapproving line. "Sarah is convinced she saw a horse and rider on the plateau at dawn. She said she watched him for a moment and in the next instant he vanished. Like a ghost."

Serena's breath caught in her throat. "A ghost? Surely, she must—maybe it was only a trick of the light and the heat, as you said. It must have been," she said more firmly.

"It must have been," Levi echoed, his eyes drawn for a moment to the plateau.

Serena turned with him, thinking of Gage Tanner. Of the Spirit in the Wind who visited her at midnight. *Which was he?* Levi's voice gave her no time to decide. "I hope you are feeling well again."

"Perfectly. I'm fine. I know you're anxious to continue your journey. I'll dress and see to breakfast."

"Yes, we would like to reach Kanab no later than tomorrow."

Serena's stomach lurched. "Kanab?" she muttered accidentally. The settlement she'd fled only a short time ago, now seemed so far away. But in reality she knew how close it was, how close Jerel was. "Will you be staying there long?" She tried to bury the fear welling up in her.

Levi frowned slightly. "No. One night, two at most. Why do you ask?"

"Oh, I was just thinking of what you might need in the way of supplies and water for your journey."

"That is kind of you."

"Not at all," she said, backing away. Before he could reply, Serena ran up the stairs to her room, feeling his eyes on her all the way. She knew he had doubts, but there was nothing she could say to him he would believe. Nothing but the truth she refused to tell.

Dressing quickly, she hoped she could send them on their way after breakfast. Once gone, maybe their journey and Sarah and Levi's impending wedding would fade the memories of the ranch and her odd behavior.

Even as she said it to herself, Serena realized the gamble she took. She had nothing in her hand to bluff with. All her aces were in Gage Tanner's pocket.

And somehow, spirit or not, she had to persuade him to join her game.

Chapter Five

It took Serena the better part of the morning—and the cooler part of the day—to feed and pack her unwanted guests back onto their journey up the honeymoon trail into Utah.

She'd hoped to set out for the trading post before the sun was high. But the visitors dallied and talked away the morning, asking uncomfortable questions about Gage and the others. She only hoped she'd answered vaguely enough to assuage their obvious suspicions, yet not betray herself by giving them specifics they might be able to check on.

But even now, after a two-hour ride in the cart under the broiling mid-day sun, with Whiskey Pete babbling all the way about his tree devils and her fortune in not having seen them, the uneasiness that twisted in her stomach as she watched the Mormons' wagon rattle over the plain hadn't abated one bit.

They don't believe I belong here.

And if they didn't, if they passed on their suspicions to Elder Caltrop, or worse, if Jerel Webster guessed the truth. . . . She quickly shut off her thoughts, focusing on the landscape. It wouldn't do any good to panic. Not now. Chances were they would never cross paths with any of the Mormons who knew her. And if things weren't exactly working out the way she'd intended, they could. They had to.

Ahead a low, flat-roofed adobe building appeared through waves of rippling heat with the shimmer of a mirage. Serena blinked and rubbed her eyes, before accepting what they told her. In the desert things often weren't what they seemed. But the structure remained, yet blended so well with the brown and gray and muted gold vista surrounding it, that it melted away before her eyes into the haze of dust, then crystallized again and again, until they drew near enough for her to make out the firm outline of it.

There was little else in Vulture Creek from what she could see. Beyond the trading post hunched a half-timbered building identified as a stable and blacksmith's shop by the lettering over the door. Two other nondescript shacks hung on at the end of the wide, well-beaten path running alongside it all.

Whiskey Pete pulled Last Chance to a jolting stop in front of the trading post, and Serena glanced to the sign hanging above the door, its letters sand-scuffed and faded. Dalton's Trading Post and Saloon she read, and took a deep breath. Who should she be to the people inside?

"So—who you think' of bein' this time?" Whiskey Pete startled her, echoing her thoughts precisely. "You see t' got more names than a cat's got hairs. You gonna be Hetty's girl again, or you got somebody else you wanna be?"

Serena might have bristled if not for the complete lack of sarcasm in Whiskey Pete's question. From his seat beside her on the bench, he eyed her with skew-eyed interest, a ready accomplice to whatever deception she chose to employ.

"Well," she turned again to wonder at the building, "that depends on who we might meet inside. Do any Mormons get their supplies here?"

"Not no more they don't. Used to, they'd come over from as far east as Jacob Lake and down from Navajo Wells and Fredonia. Now, though, since they been run back up over the border into Kanab, they don't do no tradin' here."

"Who does then?"

"Trappers, folks from surrounding towns. Ranchers. Indians. Never know who'll you see 'round here. Anybody travelin' through the strip country askin' for supplies'll end up here. Miss Amanda's got the best whiskey this side of the north rim, and just 'bout anything else you got yer mind set on, or she can lay a hand to it given the time."

"In that case," Serena said, "I think I'd better be your niece again." She hesitated, then asked, "Did people around here know Gage Tanner and the family he took in well?"

"Well 'nough. Mister Tanner used t' pack up the wagon once every month or so and bring Libby, her sister, and the boys down this way." Pete's clouded eyes smiled with the memories. "You shoulda seen them boys on those days. Why we'd be still near a mile off and they'd both be jumpin' up and down, upsettin' Last Chance somethin' awful with their whoopin' and shoutin' and runnin' off to pester Miss Amanda into takin' out her secret store of peppermints and honey candy fer them to choose from." He shook his head. "Mister Tanner always gave into them easy as a kitten hoppin' over a caterpillar. They'd have their pockets overflowin' in no time."

Serena tried to imagine her Spirit in the Wind as a kind of doting uncle, but somehow the image refused to form in her mind. It didn't match with the eerie midnight encounters she'd had with him. "And Libby? Was he the same with her?"

Scratching at his grizzled jaw, Pete appeared to mull over the question. "Cain't say as I remember her ever askin' fer nothin' fer herself. But I do recall him tryin' to buy her a new bonnet once."

"Trying?"

"Yep. She'd have nothin' to do with it. Said it were a waste of money for a woman past dressin' up in silly fineries. Funny thing," he said. "He held tight to that hat for a long spell, just starin' at it. Then finally, he set it back on the shelf like it were somethin' he was afeared of breakin', instead of a bit of fancy cloth." Climbing down from his seat, heading for the front of the cart, he added, "S'ppose it's true what they say. You cain't turn a woman no mor'n you cin a runaway hog."

Serena sat a moment longer, wondering why the pictures Pete painted of Gage Tanner seemed to show another side of the man entirely. A man capable of feeling, caring, even of tenderness. It was an intriguing contrast to the hardened, enigmatic man of silences who paid her nighttime visits. Perhaps he truly was dead inside, his heart buried in the past.

The wind gusted, the sudden wail of it stirring the uneasiness in her that lay coiled like a snake in a dark corner, ready to strike. She glanced around her, half-expecting to see the image of the Spirit on the Wind appear on the edge of the plain or the precipice of a cliff.

"You're being stupid," she told herself sharply. Shaking off the feeling as well as she could, Serena hiked up her sand-salted skirts and climbed off of the cart. Pete, finishing unhitching Last Chance, started tugging the mule toward the water trough while Serena gathered her courage and her wits to go inside.

She needn't have bothered. A moment later the front door swung open and a man fairly flew out, landing face down in the dust. "I told you Verge Willet, you ain't gonna get one more drop of whiskey from me unless Birk comes with you. Now go on home and sleep it off."

Her eyes wide, Serena stared at the woman who had followed the hapless Verge outside. Dressed like a man and sounding like one in every respect but the timbre of her voice, she stood over his prone body glaring at him, a shotgun slung on her hip.

His face and body plated with sand, Verge squinted up at his opponent, a look of dumb incomprehension on his narrow face.

"Did you hear me?" The woman sounded more irritated than furious, as though she dealt with a foolish child rather than a drunken cowhand. She poked Verge's shoulder with the tip of the gun. "Get up and go on home to Mae."

As soon as Verge reluctantly dragged to his feet, Whiskey Pete turned to pull Last Chance to the trough. "C'mon, show's over," he muttered to the mule.

"Pete! Why, you're as welcome a sight as a pat straight flush! I sure am glad to see you out among the livin' again." The woman turned to Serena. "If your comin' here to visit your uncle is what got him off that godforsaken ghost ranch after all these months, then I'm just as glad to see you."

Serena couldn't hide her start of surprise. "You know who I am?"

"'Course I do. We don't get much news up here, so when we do it travels faster than forked lightnin'. Besides—" She gave Serena a wink. "Birk Reed did nothin' but curse you from here to Hell the day he paid you a visit. Name's Sarah, right?"

"Serena," she answered tentatively, trying to assess the other woman's face against the sun's glare. "Serena Lark."

"Amanda Dalton, but everyone around here calls me Mandy, so you take your pick." She thrust out a hand. "Welcome to Vulture Creek."

Stunned to hear kind words in a place she'd given up for completely hostile, Serena fumbled a moment for words. "Thank you," she blurted out at last.

Amanda eyed her curiously. "Been a long ride in this ugly heat. Come on inside and let me fix you somethin' tall and cool. You too Pete, soon as you get your friend squared away."

"Whiskey'll be fine fer me," Pete told her.

"It'll be waitin'," Amanda said with a smile, then led Serena into the building.

The store seemed as gloomy as a cave after so long beneath the sun's glare. Serena, finding herself temporarily blinded, accidentally bumped into a stack of crates piled by the door.

"Careful there," Amanda called over her shoulder. "Ain't had time to unpack those yet. Pack train unloaded them two days ago, but I ain't had a chance to get at 'em."

When her eyes adjusted at last, Serena followed Amanda through the only pathway down the center of the crowded store. The room pulsed with the thick smells of earth and animals. As she followed behind the other woman, Serena took stock of the rows and rows of shelves packed with goods: sacks of flour, bags of wool, canned goods, coffee, ammunition, cooking utensils, fabric, and blankets lined the exposed adobe walls.

In one corner two Indians passed a package of tobacco back and forth between them, inhaling and speaking to each other in low, muffled tones. Serena tensed. Their dark skin and black hair, the bands of sliver at their wrists catching what little light filtered into the room, their strange language, and somber, fathomless eyes—she could never feel safe near them. The memory of their attack on her family still ripped at her mind and heart as though it happened yesterday.

They were savages! Serena didn't care how many laws supposedly were going to keep them under control, she would never trust them.

Averting her eyes, she glanced away. The low ceiling drew her attention up to the thick log beams stretched side by side along the length of it. They were strung with smoked hams and sausages and the pelts of bears, deer, and rabbits. She took note, thinking ahead to winter, knowing she'd need heavy gloves to haul logs morning and night to the fireplaces and stove. For an instant she missed the ease of having men around to take on some of the heavier chores. *A man, yes; a master, no.* The sobering thought was enough to kill any fantasies.

"You all take your time lookin'." Amanda directed the comment to a stout woman who stood in front of the candy jars, two little girls and an older boy clutching at her skirts, palms outstretched, pleading for this sweet and that. "I'll be in the saloon when you decide what you need."

As Amanda moved to the back of the room, Serena noticed her turn slightly and flash a brief smile at a burly man leaning at the far end of the counter. A large, wide-brimmed hat, nearly the size of a sombrero, drooped low over his brow, shielding the better part of his face. In fact all Serena could make out of his appearance other than his massive build, was a heavily bearded square jaw, and dark brown waves of hair streaked with gray hanging loose well below his shoulders.

At the far end of the store, a doorway and two steps down led into a large rectangular saloon. Several small tables crowded the space, and a group of men sat at one of them near the bar, dealing out a poker hand. Square, grimy windows along one wall let enough light in to allow Serena to get a better look at her hostess.

"Take any seat you like," Amanda was saying as she rounded the back of the counter to take three glasses off of the shelf. Serena watched her, wondering what sort of woman ran a trading post and a saloon in a harsh, unforgiving country like this, apparently by herself.

Either a brave or a crazy one, she decided. Yet, even in the men's shirts and pants, Amanda's figure managed to look womanly. Her hips were smoothly rounded below the silver and leather belt that defined the curve of her waist, her legs long and slender. Her fair hair hung in a single waist-length braid tied Indian fashion, with intertwining leather strips, and her ears were ornamented with dangling silver earrings that bore the same etchings as the conchos on her belt.

Sleeves rolled up past her elbows revealed unusually muscular arms, though, and the hands now reaching for glasses looked leathery, rough as any man's. She was tall, gawky actually, Serena decided, big boned, yet somehow not ungraceful in her movements. There was an air of authority about her that her size only enhanced; her strength, like that of a lioness enhanced rather than overwhelmed her unusual brand of femininity.

Amanda turned, and Serena averted her eyes. "It feels wonderful to sit on something other than that bouncing bench in Pete's cart."

Amanda cocked her head and looked baffled.

"Did I say something wrong?" Serena asked, her eyes flicking around her and back to Amanda.

"No. It's what you didn't say." Amanda shrugged. "S'ppose I just imagined you'd call him uncle, that's all."

Serena would have slapped herself if she could have. "I suppose it's unusual, but I haven't seen much of Uncle Pete," she nearly choked on the words, "since I was born. It's—easier for me to call him just Pete."

"Makes sense," Amanda said, pouring out a tall glass of tea. "Here you are." She slid the glass across the bar and it stopped exactly in front of Serena's waiting fingertips.

She grabbed the glass and gulped it down greedily. Her parched tongue softened, savoring each sweet drop. Forgetting any pretense of manners, she licked her lips. "You can't imagine how wonderful that tasted!"

Amanda shook her head. "Oh, I think I can." Then, leaning over the counter, "Whoa girl, didn't you wear a hat? The sun's hot enough to scorch a cub bear's butt out there today, and it looks like it's done your face the same favor."

"I—I wore a bonnet this morning, but it blew off in a gust."

"A bonnet?" Amanda laughed outright. "Where you been hidin'? I don't know where you come from, but you ain't gonna last one week out here unless you buy a decent hat. You may as well toss those bonnets of yours to the vultures."

Amanda turned to tend to a woman who'd come into the bar asking for pickled peaches and Serena let go the breath she'd sucked in at Amanda's mention of the past, relieved she hadn't pushed the subject. "Hiding" skimmed way too close to the truth for her comfort. Living with the Mormons, she felt she had been hidden away, designated mainly to indoor chores because of the occasional bouts of weakness and dizziness she suffered when she over-exerted both her body and her temper in tandem.

So she worked alongside the women in the house, cleaning and cooking out of the heat of the day. She missed playing outdoors with the other children, watching them revel in the sun, riding the horses, skipping rope, playing hide and seek, missed being a part of a loving, close-knit family, the center of the attention and love her own parents had lavished on her.

Her one solace had been cooking. Finding new ways to combine flavors, experimenting with spices and sauces that made the men marvel and praise her, while the women huddled to puzzle out her secrets, was a source of pride and entertainment that helped pass the otherwise endless days.

Serena couldn't deny the kindness Elder Caltrop's Mormon clan had shown her by taking her in and giving her a home. But, accustomed to having her own way, to speaking her mind, she had never learned to submit with grace to their ordered way of life. It had helped them to survive prejudice and banishment, to hold fast to their deeply-rooted beliefs. It made her forever an outsider.

When night finally came, she would often sneak out alone to savor the cool air, the sounds drowned out by incessant human voices during the day; the hoots of the owls, the howls of the coyotes, lonesome creatures, she imagined, crying out in the night, like herself.

She blinked, not realizing how far away she had drifted, and found Amanda staring at her, one brow raised. "Maybe someday you'll tell me where you just came back from." A kind, almost maternal smile touched her lips. "And where you been."

The gesture softened the otherwise prematurely harsh

lines at the corners of her mouth. She couldn't have been more than five or six years her senior, Serena thought, yet she had the look of having lived a lifetime in those years. Her skin, meant to be fair by the color of her hair, had weathered from sun and sand. Her gray eyes, sharp and keen, were not without kindness. But what had they seen?

More than the Mormon women she'd grown up with were ever allowed, no doubt. And the "sealed" wives, one of whom Serena would have been numbered among, saw even less of the living world. Rebellion flared in Serena. "I'll have a shot of whiskey in the next glass." The surprised look on Amanda's face waned her bravado. "Please?" she added, more quietly.

Amanda laughed aloud. "If I do, I'll bet your uncle's mule it'll be your first."

"No, of course not," Serena lied. Badly. She longed to feel alive—in control of her own destiny, not dominated and deprived of—of anything! Yet in the same instant she thought of life, she thought of *him*. The Spirit in the Wind. Even here, far from the ranch, it felt as if he watched her, his eyes learning her from outside to the deepest reaches of her soul.

"That fer me?" The saloon door banged shut and Serena jumped. Giving her a curious glance, Whiskey Pete climbed up on a stool next to her, his eyes riveting on the bottle and shot glass set on the counter there.

"All yours, Pete, unless your niece beats you to it."

Pete shot Serena a horrified stare and snatched up the bottle close to his chest.

"Now, don't you worry about it, Pete. After what you've been through at that blasted ranch these past months, I'd say you deserve a bottle or two. Wouldn't you, Serena?"

"Yes, of course," Serena said quickly. "From what I

know about the whole horrible incident that is." She shrugged slightly, and nodded toward Pete who was carefully pouring out his second shot.

"Well, we all got our stories t' tell," Amanda said softly. Then in a louder voice she asked Pete, "Now you don't mind if I take your niece away from you for a spell while you finish that off, do you? She looks like she caught the fire."

"Fire?" Serena asked.

Pete bobbed his head, tipping the bottle to the glass again. "When yer skin and eyes are so hot that if you died an' went to hell, you'd feel like wirin' home fer a couple blankets."

The image made her shudder. "Come to think of it," Serena mumbled, touching her cheek gingerly with the tip of her finger, "it does feel strangely cool inside here; my face is burning but I feel cold."

"Come on. I just got me in a case of witch hazel and one of talcum powder. Won't make it go away, but it'll help take the burn out of it."

Whiskey Pete managed a wave of his hand as Amanda rounded the end of the long polished bar and lifted a section of it by hinges. Serena swallowed the last of her drink and slid down from her stool to follow her back to the store. But as they passed the table of card players, one of the men leaned his chair back on two legs, reached out and slapped Serena soundly on her bottom.

Serena yelped, her face flushing hotter than before. Amidst the instant roar of laughter that followed from the rest of the men, she reacted instinctively, returning the slap with double force across the man's bristled jaw.

The grungy-faced fortyish man shot to his feet and grabbed her by one arm. He glared down into her face, baring tobacco-stained teeth, the stench of stale whiskey

making her wince. "'Bout time somebody showed you
how to respect a man," he muttered, yanking her closer.

Amid the escalating whoops and hollers of the other
men, Serena struggled and tried to kick at his ankles,
but he held her fast.

"Why Birk ought to be right proud of you when he
hears how you roped and tied this little filly all by yourself, Zeke," Amanda's sarcasm cut a sharper swath
through him than the dagger dangling at her fingertips
would have. Deflated by her insinuation and by the re-
newed hoots of mockery and laughter from his companions, his grip on Serena's arms slackened and she
wriggled free.

"Yep, better not rumple that one's petticoats Zeke,"
one of the other men called out. "Birk says if you give
her half a chance, she'll blow yer pants right off yer butt
'fore you know what hit you."

Another round of drunken glee followed, bringing the
wild-looking beast-man to the doorway between the
store and the bar. Standing rather than slumping over
the counter as he had when Serena had first brushed
past, he now looked enormous. The breadth and height
of him shrunk the doorway. His hand rested at his thigh,
atop a leather-sheathed knife. Silent, he lifted his chin
enough for his mysterious, hooded eyes to glance about
the room from beneath his wide-brimmed hat.

"You boys enjoin' your game?" he asked smoothly.

Zeke slumped back into his chair, a defeated hunch to
his shoulders.

Serena's eyes moved from one face to another. Someone else spoke for Zeke. "No harm in a friendly game
of cards, Ross."

"None at all," the bear of a man said, his baritone re-
verberating throughout the room. He glanced to
Amanda, who was shoving her knife back into the

sheath looped at her belt. As she nodded back to him, Serena noticed their daggers had the same carved ivory and brass handles. "You give Reed my regards, now won't you Zeke? I don't believe I'm gonna get by his place this time around."

Zeke grumbled something indiscernible in response and Ross, followed by Amanda and Serena, gave a tug to his hat and stepped back up into the store.

"Thank you," Serena told Amanda when her heart slowed its ragged pounding.

"You were doin' fine by yourself," Amanda said, leading her to a chair and putting her in it. "Just outnumbered, that's all. You got pluck. I like that."

Somehow it satisfied Serena very much that Amanda thought she had pluck, and she smiled her appreciation. "Who is that—that man? The other one? Over there. The one who has the same knife as you." Serena nodded to Ross, who now stood at the counter talking in low tones with the two Indian men who had been looking over the tobacco earlier.

"And observant too, aren't you? I see I'll have to keep my eye on you or you'll be findin' out all my secrets," Amanda teased, starting to dab witch hazel on Serena's burned face and neck. "His name is Ross Brady. He's a trapper. Knows everyone around these parts. And everyone knows him."

Inwardly, Serena cringed. Did he remember Elder Caltrop and his clan? Did he know Gage and his family? How to broach the subject . . . ? "He must be well respected."

"That he is."

"I understand Gage Tanner also had a good reputation," she prodded, the taste of his name on her lips a strange blend of wild and sweet.

"Gage? God rest his soul. He was one of the finest

men I ever met. Rough around the edges and hard as a whetstone when he set his mind to somethin'. But I never knew a man who was more of a squareshooter. 'Course your uncle would have told you all about Gage and the woman he took in after her husband died. Was his best friend who got killed I heard, and Gage adopted his wife, her boys, and her sister just like they were kin."

"No, actually he hasn't. You see, he's—well he talks crazy most of the time. I can't make much sense of what he tells me. I don't really know what happened at the ranch." She hesitated. "Do you?"

Amanda sighed. She pulled out her knife and ripped open a wood crate. After taking out one of a number of containers marked "Talcum Powder" and opening it, she nodded. "Much as anyone does."

"I'd like to know," Serena said, hoping she didn't sound too eager. "I need to know so I can protect myself. And my uncle, of course."

Rubbing the powder over Serena's neck, Amanda seemed to weigh the request in her mind. Then, in a low, expressionless voice, she told Serena the story of a man who cared for a dead friend's family as his own, then lost all that he loved in this world in a bloody massacre, who, it was said, unable to find peace in death, roamed in between the living and the dead, haunting his ranch from afar, watching as though waiting for his dead to come home. "It's just all tall tale, mind you. But—"

"Spirit in the Wind," a sound too deep and sonorous to be human seemed to permeate the room from nowhere and everywhere.

Serena's gaze shot from Amanda to the trio of huge, dark men now lurking over her shoulder. The two Indians flanked Ross Brady like centurions to a pagan king.

They were staring at her, all three of them; they the predators, she the prey. Wide-eyed, she shrank back against the pine planks of her chair.

Following her frightened gaze, Amanda craned around, patting Serena's shoulder. "Don't let Ross try and scare you with his campfire stories. Everyone 'round here's heard that ghost tale from him, and some folks are now sayin' they've the spirit out there on the plateau. Probably after a whiskey shot too many."

"Have you seen The Spirit in the Wind, Miss Lark?" Ross asked, his voice a deep rumble.

Serena froze. "Me? I-I've only been here a short time. And I've had so much to do, I haven't paid any attention to stories. And I certainly haven't seen any ghosts. Only Pete, and Bird Reed and some of his men came out to the ranch once. To try to scare me off," she added her mouth twisting.

"Figures," Amanda spat.

The Indians' black eyes remained riveted in silence upon Serena as though the other two people didn't exist, making her squirm inside.

"I—I really should head back," she faltered. "Or Pete will drink himself into a night on your floor."

"Be still now," Amanda protested when Serena made to stand. "You ain't leaving until I finish dressing these burns."

"Mandy," Ross dipped his hat back down over his eyes. "Running Buffalo and Shunab left a ring and moccasins at the end of the counter for their purchases. They're a fair trade."

"I never doubt it," Amanda answered with a soft lilt Serena hadn't heard before painting her words with affection.

Slanting a glance from one to the other, Serena wondered at their relationship, her thoughts winding their way around it as the Indians followed Ross out.

Thanking Amanda for her impromptu nursing, Serena followed her around the store, gathering up food stores and other items to tide her and Pete over for several weeks.

She paid Amanda with the only thing of value she had, a small gold child's bracelet she'd been wearing the day her parents' were killed. Her father had it engraved for her before their journey west, and even after she'd outgrown it, she'd kept it hidden safely away from everyone. It was the keeper of her memories, the image of a perfect childhood past, and the only hope left of a future.

"This is all I have," she said dropping the bracelet in Amanda's hand. "Will it be enough?"

With a critical eye, Amanda looked the bracelet over. "Serena Marie Lark," she read out the engraving. She hefted it in her palm, then shook her head.

Serena's heart sank. "If I could just have a little time—"

"I can't take this."

"But it is gold—truly—"

Amanda laughed. "I know that. And worth ten times what you're puttin' in the cart today. But I got a feeling it's got a value that can't be measured in blankets and coffee. That's why I can't take it from you. You're just too—young."

"Young?" Serena screwed up her face. "You can't be much older than I am. That doesn't matter. Please—it means more to me now in blankets and coffee, and if I can buy extra with it later, all the better. Just until I can get something worth selling out of the ranch."

"Well, I can see you're determined enough," Amanda said with a sigh. "Tell you what, you go and take that

hat off the wall, the one with the big brim, and I'll keep your bracelet. And it'll be here waitin' when you can buy it back. Sound fair?"

"Oh, better than that!" Serena moved swiftly to the wall and reached for the brown leather man's hat. But her fingers somehow drifted to the hat on the shelf below. It was a bonnet. A beautiful yellow calico with crisp, white lace at the edges. Fit for the first Sunday in April. Fancier than she'd ever seen. Finer than she'd ever need. Forcing her hand back up, she pulled the leather one down off its hook.

Slapping it on her head, she smiled at Amanda's grin of approval and turned to find Pete and load up the cart.

"Mama, my tummy's hungry."

The small voice, the voice of a little girl, reached Serena's ears like a ghost of herself before her own mother died. She turned abruptly. Instead of an imagining, or a little, fair-haired child that she might have expected Amanda to have, a delicate black-eyed, raven-haired beauty clung to Amanda's waist, staring at Serena with wide, curious eyes.

"All right, Tallie. Mommy'll have your dinner fixed in no time," Amanda said softly, lifting the Indian child in her arms and kissing her cheek.

Seeing Amanda, the tough almost invincible woman, her new friend, suddenly so tender and maternal, cradling a child who stared, like the others, the Indians in the store, the ones who killed her parents.... Serena rushed to the door, yanking it open. Heat washed over her in a blistering wave. It was so hot, so strange, she had to get out, away, back to the ranch and lock the gates behind her—to be safe again.

She rushed out into the dust and heat, not looking back.

* * *

"Pete! Pete! Come on now, don't fall asleep on me," Serena punched her "uncle" in the ribs to keep him from dropping into her lap.

Beside her in the cart, Whiskey Pete wavered, the reins dangling from his fingertips with less control over each long, hot mile. "I ain't sleepin'," he protested with a jerk of his head that Serena knew was as much to assure himself as her.

Last Chance trudged on at a steady snail's pace, his hooves floundering with each step in the deep, sinking sand. From time to time a light draft of warm breeze at least broke the intensity of the temperature that had scarcely dropped despite the sun's decline to the lowest edge of the sunset-flushed cliffs in front of them. Serena, glad for the protection of her new hat, still found herself rubbing her aching eyes against other desert elements as the breeze fast picked up to a wind, whipping sand up in every swipe it took at the ground.

"Dust devil," Pete muttered. Nodding toward a spiral of dust gathering and swirling toward them from the north, he yawned and swayed dangerously close to the edge of the cart bench. "Not a tree devil, though. Different, not as mean."

"Get back over here," Serena snapped, her patience at an end. "Give me those reins before you drop them. You might as well lie down in the back, you're useless at driving that mule." She grabbed the reins from his hands.

Pete yawned. "Well, s'ppose I could use a little nap."

"Oh, just go on." Serena fairly shoved him into the back with the goods they'd bought and took the center of the bench. She snapped the leathers against Last

Chance's back. "Hurry up. I don't want to be out here after dark you stupid animal."

Last Chance's ears perked. But instead of hurrying he stopped cold. The dust devil picked up speed and sand, whirling and spinning like a dancer without a partner straight for them. Sand flew at Serena's eyes and mouth, forcing her to shift the reins into one hand to vainly try to brush it away. Sensing her hesitation, the mule seized the chance to take his head and suddenly lurched forward. Nearly blinded by the swirling wind and sand, Serena cried out in anger and a sudden, gripping fear.

The wind ripped the words from her and flung them to infinity. She no longer saw the dust devil in the distance. It had found her. She saw nothing but a brown blur that grated at her eyes, and scratched and pricked her skin with twigs and stickers and tiny rocks it had lifted from the earth in its path.

"Pete! Help me!"

If he answered, she couldn't hear him above the wail of the tempest.

"The reins! Where are the reins!" Her hands were empty. Somehow, she'd lost the leathers when Last Chance lunged forward. Her eyes sealed against the sand, she groped like a blind woman at her skirts, the bench. Nothing but sand, covering everything.

The cart fell still again.

"Last Chance—" Wind bit into her voice, dirt into her mouth.

The mule brayed loudly, and the cart jerked ahead, slowly this time, moving by inches. Serena grabbed the broad bench to brace herself against the animal's whims. She heard the trudge of hooves through the sand. It sounded different. Not one mule. More. She strained to hear. A horse whinnied and she tried to open her eyes, but found them glued shut with tears and dirt and sand.

"Who's there? Tell me!" Last Chance continued his plodding into the storm, taking her to a place she couldn't see. "Tell me!"

It's him, she thought wildly. *The Spirit in the Wind. He's here. I know he's here.*

He, Last Chance, the wind, led her somewhere, a silent, guiding force. Serena trembled, shouted, swore. Nothing. Nothing but dust and wind and heat.

It lasted ten minutes, an hour, forever, she didn't know. Finally, the mule slowed, then stopped. The wind eased and died on a mournful lament. And the sand battering her face stopped. The whole world seemed to fall into a black silence, like the dead of night.

Serena waited, listening for the whinny and thought she heard the sound of sand shifting beneath hooves, moving further and further from her ears. She pressed anxious palms to her eyes.

But before she opened them, another sound, more terrifying than the mere sound of a strange horse's whinny, caught the breeze and drifted closer and closer to her ears.

Kosi wumbindoma,
Kosi wumbindoma,
Kosi wumbindoma.
Kai ua wumbindoma,
Kai ua wumbindoma,
Kai ua wumbindoma.

Strange words, chants, crept along an invisible path to haunt her mind. Deep and whispered, the voices grew louder, closer until she could bear the suspense no longer. Against all the grit grinding at her eyelids, she forced them open.

Then wished she hadn't.

What she saw before her, around her on every side terrified her so she ground her lids shut again.

Indians! She'd die before she reached the ranch, though she could see it just past the next ridge. Perhaps they were a mirage that would dissipate when she again found the courage to open her eyes. But the singing went on . . .

Through pained tears she faced her tormentors, glaring from one pair of dark eyes to another. There had to be at least a dozen of them on horseback encircling the cart. Desperately she scoured the plateaus for some sign of help.

Not far off, she knew he watched her. The Spirit in the Wind on the horizon, half-hidden in twilight's dusky haze. But he was there. Unmoving.

Serena gritted her teeth and reached back to punch Whiskey Pete. He groaned and mumbled an unintelligible word or two. Realizing he was useless, she fought back the terror, the paroxysm of fear holding her tongue captive. She was trapped; she had to run. Like an animal awakened by the barrel of a gun, she froze, her heart throbbing wildly in her breast. *Be strong, save yourself* . . .

"We mean you no harm," one of the dark faces spoke, in English, his voice deep and rich.

Serena stared. He looked older than time. The reins. Where were the damned reins? She leaned forward, searching, until at last, she spied the two strips of leather, not wound in Last Chance's legs as she'd feared, but stretched out in front of the mule, as though someone leading him had dropped them then vanished . . .

Again she glanced at the horizon. And saw only sky and earth.

"We sing only of the whirlwind, and the dust. It is a

song of our people, our religion, don't be frightened. We come in peace."

"Peace!" Serena pent-up anguish and fury rose unbridled, infusing her with a boldness that trampled her terror. "Then why are you keeping me here?"

"We are a desperate people. The oasis is now yours. Gage Tanner shared his water with us. But now, you come to claim the land, the water. We ask your kindness to trade water for skins and grains and animals, as we traded with Gage."

Shocked by the gentle sound of the request, Serena was taken aback. And yet the fears, the mistrust, the instinct to preserve her safety washed over her in great powerful waves fighting to silence the whisper of compassion in her shielded heart. She dug for reason, for memories.

"We are a dying people."

"No!" She saw their weapons at their waists and backs. They might kill her now. Later. Take the ranch. Her sanctuary. Her life. She must appear strong, in control. "No! Find water somewhere else. Stay away from my ranch."

"There is no where else."

Knees shaking, heart weak and throbbing, Serena jumped down from the cart and seized their reins. "Just go away!" she cried, climbing back onto the bench. As she slapped them against Last Chance's back, the Indians parted for her to pass.

The mule moved past them, trotting in the direction of the ranch. Serena hurried him, desperate to escape.

But she couldn't escape the mournful chants that followed her on the wings of the wind until at last, inside the gates, she dropped, exhausted, to douse her face in the cool water of the oasis.

"Finally," she breathed. "I'm alone."

Her instincts defied her mind. She found herself searching the horizon before night engulfed it, where the barest trace of a shadow of a man hovered.

Watching.

Chapter Six

Serena squinted up at the roof of the horse stable, shading her eyes from the dazzling glare of the late afternoon sun. It looked like half a day's work at least. The weathered red and gray stone foundation and lower walls had stood up to the harsh beating inflicted by the elements, but the wooden roof.... Serena shook her head. Peeled and cracked layers of shingles wavered and blurred; she knuckled her eyes, trying to clear her vision.

"Don't know why yer set on tryin' to fix it," Whiskey Pete observed, his good eye flitting from the battered roof to Serena. He leaned back against a post of the corral fence and scratched at his grizzled jaw. "Be about as easy as findin' hair on a frog, I'd say."

"I don't care," Serena snapped, her temper frayed to the breaking point from endless burning days of loneliness and emotional strife coupled with the scant two hours of sleep she'd had last night. But she refused to let the ranch wither and die with a whimper just because Gage Tanner wanted to play dead. If she had to replace every stone and board herself, she'd restore the ranch and create the sanctuary she sought the day she fled a fate she could not bear.

She'd spent the entire morning hammering at the rickety gates and loose boards in the barn stalls. The next item on her list of repairs was the roof of the stable. The job hadn't looked so threatening yesterday, but now, exhausted from the heat and the effort of her labors, the pounding in her chest told her she'd be as crazy as Pete to tackle it alone.

"But if it isn't fixed, it won't stand the winter," she mused aloud. "The thing leaks like a sieve if it even smells like rain. One good snow will cave it in."

Whiskey Pete shrugged. "Last Chance don't pay it no mind."

"I don't doubt it." Letting loose a gusty sigh, Serena bent to pick up the hammer and pouch of nails at her feet. As she did, her breath caught in her chest causing her heart to give an agitated flutter. Slowly she straightened, sucking in a deep breath of hot, dusty air, willing away the insidious weakness. "I don't have time for this," she muttered.

"Then why're you messin' with it?" Pete asked her, his head cocked to one side. "Ain't nobody around to care."

"I care! I'm going to get things fixed up around here with or without your help." *But Gage Tanner's help I could use* . . . she added silently. She had hoped he might come around today and, however reluctantly, come to her aid. More likely, though, he merely planned to make his usual starlight appearance.

She didn't have the patience to wait for him. If he didn't think of helping her, then she'd have to go out and demand it! She already possessed some of the skills necessary to put the ranch back together on her own, and what she lacked she'd beg, borrow, or steal if it meant making a safe, secure home away from Jerel

Webster. Gage Tanner was out there somewhere, watching her struggle alone.

If he wasn't gentleman enough to come to her aid, she'd just have to ride out and find him. "Go bring me my horse," Serena ordered Whiskey Pete. "I need help, and Gage Tanner is going to give it to me whether he likes it or not."

"Wouldn't count on it." Whiskey Pete shook his head doubtfully, but turned and obeyed.

While he went to the stable, Serena went inside the ranch house to fetch a canteen. A few minutes later, outside the gates, she warned him to lock up as soon as she turned away. "I have the key, so you just stay inside until I get back. Hear me?"

"You're more thick-headed than Last Chance," Pete said. "Things sure was quiet 'round here 'fore you came along stirrin' 'em up."

"It's what I do best," Serena shot back, turning her stolen mount toward the plateau. "I know he's just a little ways out there. He must be. He sees everything that goes on here." She brushed the back of her hand across her forehead, irritated at the tremble in her fingers. "I'm going to find him and finish this job before dark," she told him sternly, then jerked her reluctant mount toward the horizon.

The sun burned its hottest, beating down on her head as she rode off. The tremor in her hand caused the reins to slip between her fingers, but she refused to give in to her body's warnings, and instead pressed on in the direction she'd so often seen him appear. When she thought she ought to be nearing the place he stood, keeping watch, she began to call out for him.

Her only response was the silent, dead heat engulfing her, she rode a little further and called again. Beneath her, the old, brittle animal began a jerky descent along a rocky path through a shallow canyon. She grasped at the sweat-slicked reins, but the motion made her head spin and her stomach lurch. Hot and cold chills chased up and down her spine; her heart started thundering in a rapid, racing rhythm.

Cursing, Serena knew she was falling into the throws of one of her spells again. She tried to ignore it, but her aggravation with her own failings only shortened her breath and worsened the dizziness. She closed her eyes to it, riding out the surge of nausea and faintness until she could focus enough to try to halt the animal and climb down.

The ground below seemed to shift and sway, the rocks and bushes blurring into shapeless figures. The old horse protested again and again, louder with each whinny, but she couldn't hear him over the pulsing roar in her ears.

Wanting to push it away, Serena raised a hand to swipe at the air near her head. The movement cost her precarious balance. She swayed to one side, the reins falling from her fingers; she clutched desperately at empty space.

Serena fell sideways, sky and cliffs whirling together in a maelstrom of red, gray, vivid blue, and brilliant gold fire. She felt a *whoosh* of warm air, heard the cry of her own voice, before a sharp burst of pain tore through her head, burying her in blackness.

Night time's cooling caress stroked away the day's scorching heat, coaxing the creatures of the dark from their daytime lairs. The air, still with numbing heat during the light, became subtly alive as twilight fell, carrying with it the sounds and smells of the predators—coyotes, mountain lions, wolves—the rustles and songs of night birds; the gentle hushed echo of the wind weaving through the cliffs and canyons.

Gage rode out over the rugged stretch of grass and sage toward the ranch, letting Gusano linger in a lazy canter, hearing but not listening to the familiar chorus.

He was crazy to go back. He had told himself again and again, to no avail. Somehow he'd made a habit of returning each evening, drawn by a longing he didn't want to define. And this time, he had good reason for coming back. Despite his warnings, he'd failed to convince Serena Lark to leave the ranch. Never again would he so much as claim even the half-night's sleep he'd grown thankful for, if he didn't at least succeed at that.

Tonight, though, something even stronger than habit or honor drew him to the ranch. Alone in the daylight hours in the isolation of the canyons, burning heat and stillness his only companions, a restless feeling of unease plagued him like a sickness. His instincts, whetted and honed to sense the nuances in the air itself, told him something was wrong. He felt it, grappled with it all day.

He knew it when the sad excuse for a horse of Serena's turned up loose. He found it wandering through the last canyon he crossed every day before climbing the steep hill to his post on the plateau near the ranch.

Sliding off Gusano he grabbed the horse's reins and searched the area. The darkness swallowed him, leaving him blind, forced to rely on touch and smell and sound and his awareness of her to guide him. The night around him crawled with a thousand different sensations, testing his focus. Yet his senses found her a heartbeat before his eyes traced the slight, crumpled bundle a few hundred feet away.

"Serena?" Her name, spoken aloud for the first time,

tasted bittersweet, felt strange coming from his mouth. Dropping to his knees beside her, Gage hesitated, not wanting to touch her anywhere, afraid of inflicting more hurt than good. Finally, he skidded his fingertips against her throat, searching for a throb of life. Weak and erratic, her heartbeat pulsed under his touch and he let go the breath he'd unconsciously been holding in a long rush.

"Damn it, woman, what have you gone and done now?" he muttered, not hesitating this time as he quickly ran his hands over her neck, her shoulders, down her arms and ribs, then her legs, deftly probing tender skin and soft flesh for broken bones or bleeding. Satisfied she'd survived at least that, he debated with himself for a moment before carefully gathering her limp body in his arms. She felt small and light cradled against his chest, drained of all the vibrant energy that brought her to life. Her endless chatter and demands annoyed him, but as he carefully lifted her, her stillness left him feeling strangely awkward and uncertain.

Gage stopped. What to do with her? They were closer to his hideout than the ranch, and the ride to the ranch was all uphill from here. The way to his makeshift home was rocky but more or less level. But if she discovered where he spent his days, his secret for disappearing, she could expose his ruse and ruin his plan for revenge. Exposure too, might mean those looking for someone to blame for the massacre might take a notion to consider him a likely suspect, considering the months he'd shunned the living.

He'd have a better chance of keeping his neck out of a noose and his identity safe if he took her back to the ranch and left her with Pete. "Hell, Gusano," he muttered under his breath. "You won't make it with the two of us. And she'll fall off that sad excuse for a beast of burden of Pete's. Come on. Let's take her back to the cave."

Gage tied the reluctant horse to his saddle then shifted the unconscious woman to hold her with one arm and pulled them both onto his mount. Had he not found her to weigh little more than an adolescent girl, he still might have turned and attempted to climb back up the canyon to the ranch. For he knew that unless she woke up, once they reached the cliff dwelling he called home, he'd have to toss her over his shoulder and tote her up the ladder, step by cautious step. Gusano lurched a little, snorting and chewing at the bit, as if sensing the danger he carried.

His jaw set in a hard line, Gage looked down at Serena's face, pale and fragile in the misty starlight. The sight of her, quiet and limp, stirred something both fierce and tremulous inside him. Slowly, moving in a dream, he raised a hand and touched her cheek. Her skin felt damp and warm, her breath a trembling sigh, coaxing his calloused touch to gentle into a caress. A dark tendril clung to her face and he brushed it away, wondering at the feeling. His hand smoothed her lank hair, lightly fingering the thick braid, then fell away.

Left with the memory of her branded on his skin, Gage gripped the reins in his free hand and wheeled Gusano about in a spray of dust and pebbles, urging the stallion into a gallop toward the black, impenetrable walls of the cliffs.

The sound of drums, low and pulsing in her ears, called Serena out of the dark. She drifted into a gray mist where shadows leapt and danced on the vast stone above her. A strange scent, sweet and hot, curled into the haze, making the shapes around her blur and spin.

Feeling oddly divorced from everything around her, Serena tried to remember where she was. The roof, riding out into the canyons, she'd felt hot, so hot then . . . fallen? Her fingers twitched, touching smooth hair. It seemed somehow wrong, but she couldn't focus enough of her thoughts to recall why. She wanted to move, to see clearly. Everything around her felt soft and undefined, as unreal as the stuff of dreams. Scraping up the last dregs of her strength, Serena turned her head a little to the side.

And found herself staring into fire.

"No," she moaned, seeing the past, suddenly afraid of being doomed to relive it all again. "Don't let them burn. Please . . . not again." At the sound of her own voice, faint and fearful, the image of a man's face blocked out her vision of the flames.

The glow of the fire rose up behind the man, casting his severe, wrinkled face in darkness, burning a red halo on his long white hair. Slowly, he reached out a gnarled leathery hand to her. In a faraway place in her mind, an old fear screamed for her to run, to protect herself from the people who had slaughtered her parents with cold, savage cruelty. But she could only mutely stare at him, unable to summon the power to move or speak.

A throbbing pain washed through her when his long fingers touched. She moaned again and closed her eyes to it. The red glow burned hotly behind her eyes though her body felt cold and remote. She tried to focus again, vaguely surprised at how much it hurt.

"Don't try to move. It won't last long."

The voice, *his* voice, was dark and hard, yet soft at the edges. Serena looked up into Gage's eyes, sure she conjured him from her midnight illusions. "I thought . . . someone else—he was here . . ."

On one knee beside her, Gage shook his head. "You should sleep."

"I have been sleeping. Haven't I?" Moving without feeling, Serena stretched out a hand and brushed the soft cotton of his shirtsleeve, then his bared forearm. The warmth, the rough and smooth feel of him seemed real. She frowned as her eyes focused on the long, ragged pale streaks etched on his skin, unable to recall whether or not she'd seen them before. "I don't know," she whispered, the mist coming between them. "I can't remember."

"It doesn't matter," he said quietly. "Close your eyes."

Serena let him fade from her vision, lulled back into the comfort of the darkness by the dream of Gage's fingers gently touching her face, her hair, his hands wrapping her in a cocoon of safety and warmth. She took him with her as she sank into it, leaving behind the pain and fear, certain none of it was real.

Gage finished tucking the thin blankets around Serena's thin shoulders, touching her as little as possible. Awake, alive, her boldness and impetuous courage, her irritating demands and impatience with everything and everyone created a vivid impression of strength and life. Now, lying silent and pale, she looked so small and fragile compared to him that he felt even e touch might hurt her.

"Sleep will heal her." Kwion's low voice slipped into the firelit darkness of the cliff dwelling.

Turning from Serena, Gage looked over the fire between them to the old Indian. "Thank you for coming. I know the danger—"

"The danger is to you," Kwion answered slowly. "You risk much. This woman will return you to the place of the living."

"I'll return her to the ranch as soon as she's mended. After your magic medicines, she won't remember the way here, or anything about this place." Gage stood up, stretching the stiffness from his legs. He prowled the confines of the stone walls, trying to ease the tension in his muscles. "You're the only one who could ever find your way here alone."

Gage expected some reply to his assurances. Instead Kwion stayed silent, his dark eyes studying, searching, flames reflected in their depths. Tossing another branch onto the fire, Gage sat back down on the hard sandy floor, watching embers dance and swirl upward, listening to their crack and snap.

"She will find her way back," Kwion said at last, "because you will bring her with you."

"Not likely."

"You will. It is the way with you to give of yourself—even when it would be better to give nothing."

"You're saying I'm a fool for a hard luck tale," Gage said with a wry grimace.

Kwion gave a slight wave of his withered hand. "Some might call it that. But I see you choose the paths of others because you have not yet chosen the path for yourself. That is the danger."

Gage shrugged, poking at the fire with a splintered piece of pine. "The only danger I face from her—" he jerked his head back toward Serena, "—is being talked to death."

"So you say." Kwion paused, gazing steadily into the center of the flames. "There is a story told once to me of two spirits who searched for a heart. Yet when destiny brought them together, they could not see what they searched for even when their hearts were placed in each other's hands. They carried them for a long journey, still searching, but haunted by a feeling so strong it compelled them to return to each other again and again until finally both could see what had been lost and gained."

"I only brought her here to heal," Gage said lightly. "It's hardly destiny."

"Destiny chooses its own. It is timeless, without knowledge of what can and cannot be." Slowly rising, Kwion settled his tattered robe around him and gave one last look at the woman sleeping at Gage's side. "A day, maybe two, she will be well again."

"Then I'll take her back."

"Yes," Kwion said. "But it will not end there. You told me you have promised to help again." He nodded at Gage's silence, accepting it for what it was. "Bring her among us when you are able. Maybe it will take away some of her fears." Not waiting for an answer, the old man slipped out of the cave.

Gage scarcely heard the whisper of his clothing and his footsteps as he climbed down the sheer face of the canyon wall on the narrow ladder. He got to his feet and, crossing into the next room, walked to the edge of the dwelling, waiting until Kwion reached the bottom before hauling the ladder back up into the room.

Back inside the protective walls of the cliff dwelling, Gage stirred up the fire again, staring into it for a long moment. Then, slowly, he turned and looked down at Serena.

As if sensing his presence, she shifted restlessly against the deerskin pallet, moaning softly. Gage knelt down beside her and without thinking, laid his palm on the curve of her cheek. His touch seemed to soothe her. She turned her face into the flat of his hand, whispering his name on a lingering sigh.

The gentle sound stirred a hesitant tenderness in him, like the first brush of sunlight at dawn. It was an emotion he didn't need or want. Accustomed to being alone,

even among others, he'd grown comfortable with solitude, the freedom of not having to own up to his own
fears or failures. Yet from the first moment he'd seen
her, bathing in the moonlit pool of the oasis, this new
feeling had dogged him like a relentless nemesis.

Uncomfortable with it, Gage slipped his hand away
and started to turn back to the fire. As he did, a shudder
ran over Serena. She curled up on her side under the
blankets, legs tucked up against her chest, obviously
chilled despite the heat of the fire.

Weighing his own reluctance against her need, Gage
barely paused in pushing aside his uneasiness and moving to lie down beside her on the narrow pallet. He
curved his arm around her, drawing her against his
warmth, offering her shelter. She grasped it, burrowing
close to his chest, quieted by his protective strength.

Gage wished he could find the same peace in so simple a gesture. Instead, he lay awake at her side far into
the night, listening to the sound of her even breathing
mingle with the hiss and spit of the fire and the wind
song in the canyons, until finally he drifted into a restless, dreamless sleep.

In the first misty moment of dawn, Serena woke,
vaguely wondering why her bed felt so strange. She
wriggled her toes, frowning as they curled into the sleek
hair of an animal skin instead of rumpled cotton. That
was wrong. But she felt so wonderfully warm and comfortable, she almost overlooked the oddity to relish the
pure sensual luxury. Almost. Until she started to stretch
out and her arms and her fingers met the hard chest and
shoulder of the man sharing her bed.

Pain shot through her head when her eyes jolted
open. Astonishment blinded her to it. In the murky early

morning light, she didn't recognize anything of the place he'd brought her to. But she didn't need light to know Gage Tanner.

She knew the shape of him; knew his scent, the earthly blending of leather and the elements. Without thinking, she reached up to where her eyes touched, glancing over his face with her fingertips, tracing the strong, hard features, the errant lock of dark blond hair that fell over his forehead, the lines of stoic endurance around his eyes and mouth, the rough springiness of his beard. Each new sensation fascinated her, made her greedy for more. Her fingers slid lower to swan the hollow of his throat. As she did, his arm around her shoulders tensed.

Serena looked up and found him watching her.

"You must be feeling better," Gage said, his voice low and rough.

"I . . . I am," she faltered, oddly unsure of herself. For the first time, she realized his eyes were a deep, clear green, like an emerald hidden from the light. "You brought me here. Why? Did I—?"

"I found you in a canyon, unconscious, waiting to be dinner to the first hungry wolf who sniffed you out."

His bluntness roused her flagging spirit. "And that was you?"

A wry smile crossed Gage's lips. "Could have been. You've been sleeping so soundly, you'll never know whether I had a taste of you or not."

Serena scrunched her nose at him. "You didn't take advantage of me. I know it."

"Is that disappointment I hear in your voice?"

She moved to a more comfortable angle. "Yes. But save your vanity for someone else. I'm disappointed because I had to go out searching for you to help me! That ranch is a disaster. I'm doing all I can, with Whiskey

Pete's reluctant help. But I needed you to fix the stable roof. I just couldn't—"

Serena killed her sentence in mid-word. Flushing, she averted her eyes. She refused to reveal her weakness to him, to anyone. It was the one thing she hated about herself.

Gage studied her, his curiosity piqued at her sudden reticence. Usually she talked so fast you could smell sulphur. Now she looked almost vulnerable.

"Stop staring at me," she muttered, both annoyed and disconcerted by his silence. "It's bad enough you don't listen to me, you don't have to look at me as if I were something you'd like to throw out with the wash water." Serena's dark eyes flashed to his. "I wish you would pay attention to what I have to say. Maybe then I wouldn't have . . ." The look in his eyes stole her frustration and left her without a voice.

Intent, searching, the expression on his face made her catch her breath.

A feeling both powerful and overwhelming hit Gage with the force of a two-fisted blow. He'd never felt this kind of tenderness for a woman before, this longing to be both gentle and, at the same time, consume her with all the swift fierceness of a hungry wolf. It left him off balance and uneasy; he wondered if she felt anything close to the same as he watched surprise wash from her face, replaced by something deep-running and needy.

Serena waited, for the first time hesitant to demand what she wanted from him. The moment seemed as fragile and ethereal as a dream, her own emotions too strong and sure to be true.

Gage bent to her, slowly, his eyes never leaving hers. The world narrowed to the moments before he touched her, bittersweet and strong, heady with promise. And when he brushed her mouth with his, nothing was real but that first taste, the impossible feeling that this was all that mattered or could ever matter on earth or in heaven.

Slipping his hand against the curve of her throat, his thumb idly stroking her face, Gage let gentleness crumble to the surging strength of passion. Master of and slave to it, he lost himself to her. He deepened his kiss until his mouth mated to hers and she yielded, the feeling sweet and wild. It flowed into the deadness inside of him, taking root and spreading outward like a morning blossom until it became an ache too poignant to bear, threatening to bring a change that could never be undone.

Serena felt his withdrawal before his mouth left hers. She wanted to clutch at him, to keep him near her. At the same time, the intensity of her feelings frightened her. She wanted his protection. Yet secure in his arms she felt more exposed, more at risk than she had during all of the long days alone in the desert.

Looking down at her, Gage watched the flicker of confused emotion in her eyes. Her gaze didn't falter under his, but he sensed her growing agitation in the twitch of her body under his hands. Her feelings echoed his own. Sliding his arm out from under her shoulder, he got to his feet in one fluid motion, turning away from her to regain some solid sense of himself again.

He didn't know what to say to her, how to explain. She saved him the effort—

"Do you have any coffee? It's freezing in here."

At the commonplace question, the familiar confidence in her voice, reality reasserted itself. Gage turned back to her, flicking her a brief, wry smile. "You must be feeling better. You're making demands again."

Serena shrugged. Sitting on the deerskin pallet, her knees curled to her chest, she tugged the blankets more tightly around her shoulders to stop her trembling. "I'm cold. And I don't know where anything is in this . . . this cave, or wherever we are." She glanced around. "Just where are we anyhow?"

"In the canyons," he answered. Rerolling his shirt-sleeves to the elbows, he knelt down and poked at the fire until it flared into new flames.

"Canyons? What canyons? In the cliffs behind the ranch?"

"More or less."

"That's no answer! Do you live here? In a cave? At least—" She scrunched her nose, glancing at the stone walls, mottled in shades from black to light sand. "I suppose it's a cave." For the first time, Serena took notice of the low-ceilinged room. There was little in it but the pallet she lay on and the fire pit. In one corner, Gage had carelessly tossed his duster, hat, and holster. A battered lantern sat next to the far wall near a rounded opening that appeared to lead into another chamber.

Serena pressed fingers to her forehead, trying to dredge up a memory of how she'd gotten here. All she could remember was a brief flash of color and pain as she fell from the horse, then vague, dream-like images of fire and an ancient Indian face and a leathery hand evoking pain where it touched.

"I had the strangest dream . . ."

"That's not surprising." Gage mumbled nonchalantly as he reappeared through an opening between the darkened cave chambers, holding up two tin cups, a coffee-pot, and a plate of biscuits. "I won't guarantee the quality. But at least it'll be hot."

"What's on the other side?" Serena demanded unnerved he could slip in and out so silently she never noticed. "You haven't answered my questions. I can't imagine why you'd want to live in a cave. You could just as easily stay at the ranch."

Gage settled the coffeepot onto the fire. "It isn't a cave. It's a cliff dwelling. There are hundreds of them in the canyons. The Indians who lived here abandoned them years ago."

"And this is where you disappear to during the day? But I've seen you on the plateau. There can't be any canyons out there. And what about your horse?" Serena flung up a hand. "You don't keep him here too, do you? None of this makes any sense. And I still don't understand why you brought me here. You could have just as easily—" She broke off, abruptly realizing Gage's attention was focused on moving the coffeepot away from the flames and pouring the murky brew into the cups. Heaving a sigh, Serena flung the blankets off her shoulders and plopped her chin on her knees in exasperation.

Gage glanced up at her, his gaze questioning. "I could have easily what?"

She twisted her head to look at him, startled. "You were listening," she said slowly.

"Isn't that what you wanted? Here—" He walked up to her, stretching out a hand to offer her a cup of steaming coffee and two of the biscuits.

As he did, Serena noticed pale slashes branded on his forearm from the back of his hand to his elbow. The sight evoked a hazy memory of him bathed in firelight, swaddling her in warmth, easing her pain with his cool touch. "What happened to your arm?" she asked, nodding at the scars as she took her breakfast from him.

"Cougar," he said, moving back to the fire to get his own cup.

Serena rolled her eyes at the laconic reply. "You certainly will bore me to death with your talent for long-winded explanations."

Gage shifted his shoulders in a brief, upward jerk. He didn't have a talent or a taste for idle conversation, but it didn't seem like something he could explain to her. "How's your headache?" he asked instead.

"Fine," she snapped, turning deliberately to her breakfast, welcoming the sharp bite of the hot coffee as she nibbled at the cold biscuits. Finally, irritation exhausting her limited store of patience, she blurted out, "Don't you ever have anything to say about yourself? I've asked you a hundred questions—"

"So I've noticed."

"—and either you avoid answering or you don't say anything at all. Maybe you really are a ghost." A dull pain had started between her eyes and she rubbed at it with her fingertips, feeling suddenly drained. "You don't seem to have any past, present or future."

"You should rest." Moving to her side, Gage took the cup from her hand and waited until she slid down under the blankets again. He pulled them to her chin, gently tucking them around her.

Serena wanted to badger him with a hundred more questions, to demand answers this time, to know all there was to know about Gage Tanner. Instead, she fell almost instantly asleep with them whirling in her mind, manifested as dancers without partners, waltzing alone on the edge of a black plateau.

The next time she awoke it was night again; the fire still blazed in the pit. He sat a little apart from her, near the fire, his attention focused on the knife in his hand.

Curled on her side, Serena lay for a few minutes watching him, trying to figure out what he was doing. The firelight glinted gold off the steel blade of a knife as his large hands deftly manipulated it in short, stroking motions. The smooth rhythm held her enthralled, leading her eyes each time he drew the steel down slowly against the object cradled in his hand.

He paused, holding the small figure to the light, scrutinizing it with a slight frown. Gage's concentration broke as he sensed her eyes on him, and he glanced her direction. "How are you feeling?"

"Hungry. What is that?" Serena poked her head a little further out of the blankets for a better look.

Without answering Gage stood up and handed her the figure. "I'll get you something to eat."

He disappeared into another portion of the cave through a narrow opening, leaving Serena to look in wonder at the object he'd handed her. Slightly rough, still smelling of pine, it was a miniature carving of a cougar, nearly complete save for the slight arc of its tail. Picturing him sitting here, sculpting tiny creatures from wood, seems so at odds with the portrait she had of a haunted desert wanderer.

She handed it back to him when he brought her the tin plate of beans and cold biscuits and a cup of warm liquid, putting it in his hand with an almost reverent touch. "It's beautiful," she murmured.

"Do you think so?" Gage held it up again, studying it with dispassionate interest. "They never come close enough to the originals for me." He shrugged, laying the tiny cougar aside as he picked up his own plate and sat down again by the fire.

They ate in silence, Serena's mind busy with unanswered questions, unresolved contradictions in his personality. It wasn't until she picked up her cup and brought the rim to her lips that she realized the brew wasn't the expected coffee. It smelled slightly bitter and spicy. "It tastes like the chamomile tea my mother used to make for me when I had a stomachache," she said, taking an experimental sip. "What is it?"

"It'll help your headache," Gage said, not looking at her.

"Really?" She took a larger drink, growing more used to the odd flavor. It slid down her throat, warm and soft, settling gently in her stomach. "I won't say much for your cooking," Serena said, "but this is soothing. Better than your coffee."

"Thanks," Gage said with a rueful grimace. "I'm not used to company."

"That's obvious." Serena stifled a yawn with the back of her hand. The fire, Gage, the room around her blurred, the edges growing fuzzy, all the sharpness of reality melting into misty shades of fiery red and gold, muted blacks and grays, and the smoky green of Gage's gaze. "How long have you been living here?"

Gage stiffened, staring away from her. "I exist here. It was a place to go—after."

The massacre. He didn't say it, but Serena heard the words, and his flat, expressionless tone caused a quiver of uneasiness in some faraway part of her mind.

But she felt too remote from it all, too relaxed to try to understand it. The warmth spread over her, making her feel languorous and pleasantly drowsy. "It's nice," she murmured, finishing the drink. Putting the cup down, Serena stretched back against the deerskin, smiling sweetly at Gage's wavering image. "It's very nice. I don't have a headache at all."

"Glad to hear it. Then it's time for me to take you back to the ranch."

"But—"

"You're going to be very sleepy soon, and I don't intend to cart you down that ladder and all the way back on Gusano again," he said, lifting her to her feet.

She resisted, complaining all the way, but he managed to help her carefully step back down the ladder. At the bottom of the cliff he wrapped her in a blanket and made her wait while he retrieved their horses from a place blocked to her eyes by the rolling hills that sat at the foot of the cliff.

Securing her on Last Chance, he took the reins and tugged the horse behind his mount. She held on to the saddle horn, feeling pleasantly relaxed and safe traveling so close beside him. How long and which way they rode seemed absolutely unimportant. She could hear herself chattering to him, but for once she didn't mind a bit that he gave her no more response than a disinterested grunt from time to time. It was enough to be with him.

Her last vision of him was of a dark figure, lifting her off of the horse and into his arms, watching her from some place where she couldn't reach him.

Harsh, late-morning sun, streaming through her open door, burning against her eyes, broke the spell of sleep she'd dissolved into in the odd safety of Gage's secret cave. Disoriented, she looked wildly around her, realizing after a moment she was back in her room at the ranch. Could it be she'd never left it? She put a hand to her head. Her mind was clear, only slightly befuddled with the last vestiges of sleep. Probing at her temple, she gently touched the bruise there, still tender from her fall.

That, at least, she hadn't imagined. But the rest? In the clear light, it felt more like a dream than ever. Had she ever been away, had Gage taken her to his cliff dwelling in the canyons, or had she made it all up in a feverish delirium?

Serena struggled to sit up, determined to ask Whiskey Pete how she'd gotten to her bed, but a wooden point prodded her palm, distracting her. Pulling herself upright, she slowly opened her curled fingers. In her hand lay a tiny pine carving of a cougar, finished to the last detail.

She stared at it, then flung aside the covers, carrying it with her as she groped her way outside, stumbling bare-footed down the stairs and out the open gates to the horse corral. Whiskey Pete was leading Last Chance into the largest pen as Serena stopped, breathless, in front of the stable.

"Nice job, that," Pete said, nodding at the newly-repaired roof. "Last Chance sure don't miss the leaks."

As he led the horse toward the watering trough he left Serena gaping up at the roof. She looked at it, then back to the carving clutched in her hand, astonished and completely confused at the gifts left her by the Spirit in the Wind.

Chapter Seven

Swiping the sheen of sweat from her forehead with one hand, Serena gave the bubbling stew on the stove in front of her a final stir. She despised the oppressive heat of the small kitchen area, but she vowed she wouldn't eat one more serving of Whiskey Pete's beans and salt pork if the alternative was starving to death. Forced to fend for herself, she decided to put her culinary skills to some use.

Carefully ladling a generous portion of the hot, spicy stew into a bowl, Serena carried it to the long pine table and set the dish in front of Pete. She waited impatiently while he gingerly jabbed a spoon into the center of it, then stuck his face close to the concoction of vegetables and chicken, sniffing at it.

Finally, after Serena rolled her eyes and heaved a sigh, he raised his spoon and took a tentative taste. He considered the flavor for a moment, then a grin creased his face. "Ain't bad."

"That's all you can say?" Serena demanded.

Whiskey Pete, digging his spoon back into the bowl, gave a shrug. "From the looks of it afore, I was thinkin' you was makin' a son-of-bitch stew."

Serena scowled, shaking her head. "Making what?"

"You know, the kind where you throw in everythin' but the hide, horns, an' holler, and it comes out so tough you have t' sharpen yer knife to cut the gravy." He nodded approvingly at the bowl. "This ain't that kind."

"So glad to hear it," Serena muttered, moving back to the stove to fetch her own bowl. She glanced to the corner of the room, to where Lucky Joe hunched over a dish of his own, devouring his portion. Whiskey Pete always insisted the mongrel dog eat with them, no matter if they dined on Pete's beans or Serena's more imaginative fare. Serena, quickly realizing the futility of objecting, finally resigned herself to having a three-legged dog as a dinner companion. "Lucky Joe doesn't seem to mind it."

"Hmmph," Pete snorted. "Joe'd eat soup made outta dirty socks if you gived it to him. He don't know dung from wild honey."

Serena sat down at one end of the long table, taking a small bite of her stew. "He doesn't seem too smart. He keeps chewing off that stick you tie on for a leg. I don't know why you bother."

"'Cause if I don't he'll—" Whiskey Pete broke off, tipping his head to one side, his good eye flicking independently of his other to the door they'd left open to invite the cooler evening air inside the stuffy room. Lucky Joe left his bowl and limped to Whiskey Pete's side, ears perked, teeth bared.

"What is it?" Serena asked, setting down her own spoon. She looked the same direction, seeing nothing.

"Riders." Pushing back his chair, Pete hauled himself to his feet, reaching for the rifle he'd left propped by the door.

"Riders? How do you know that?"

"I cin hear 'em."

Serena looked unconvinced. "Why would anyone be

coming at this time of day? Unless they're Mormons." After the last visit, she didn't welcome the thought.

"They's probably from the post." He shook his head in disgust. "That bunch is as mean as a naggin' woman and about as stubborn," he said, slanting a quick look at Serena. "Never willin' t' just let things be."

"Maybe they're tree devils," Serena muttered as she grabbed her rifle from the corner of the room and rushed past him to hurry outside to the stairs so she could see out the narrow slot in the wall.

Whiskey Pete, Lucky Joe at his heels, clomped up the stairs behind her, squinting over her shoulder at the limited view through the small opening. "It's just Birk Reed and his bunch," he said a moment before Serena recognized Birk's Appaloosa. "And he's brought that damned Zeke along. Never have been able to git a clean shot at him. Now this time—" He shouldered the rifle, carefully poking the tip through the slot. "This time, you best let me shoot at 'em, else we'll never be rid of 'em tonight and I'll never get bedded down. They way you been roustin' me up afore dawn near every mornin', I need the shut eye."

"We're not—" Serena jerked the muzzle out of the opening. "—going to shoot at them. Not yet," she added under her breath.

"Yer not gonna talk to 'em again, are you?" Pete asked, looking at her in dismay. " 'Cause if you are, I'm goin' to bed. Once you git talkin', you could argue a gopher into climbin' a tree just to git you to stop."

"And you'd better be glad of it. It's my talking that's kept them and those Indians out of this ranch and away from our waters since I got here." Serena checked her gun. Loaded and ready, if they left her no other choice. "You cover me from below. I'm going to try and find out what they want this time."

"I cin tell you that in one word, but you never listen to me. And she says I'm crazy," Pete muttered, reaching down to pat Lucky Joe on the head. "C'mon, go on and git yer leg and bring it here. I'll fix you up case we gotta run outta here fast."

The dog limped away, Serena's skirts swishing past as she strode further up the stairs. She marched up to the point where the balcony's edge met the wall and stood with one foot propped on the wall, the gun steady in her hands. Birk Reed led several of his men straight to the gates of the ranch house. They pulled their horses to a dusty stop and Birk, leading the pack, looked up at her, mockingly tipping his hat.

Serena clutched her rifle, readying to square it and shoot if he pushed her too far. Lurking in Birk's shadow, she caught sight of Zeke, his thick lips peeled back in a scowl, baring tobacco-stained teeth. Her stomach lurched at the memory of that filthy face pressed to hers.

"What is it this time Mister Reed?" She held her voice low and level.

Birk leaned back in his saddle and scratched his forehead under his hat. "I came here today 'cause I heard one of my boys, Zeke here, done took liberties with you down at the post."

"Is that so? Well somebody else must have told you if you heard it that way, because every one of your *boys* seemed to think Zeke had a right to manhandle me."

"Matter of fact, it was the trapper I trade with, Ross Brady, who told me what Zeke done." Reed craned around in his saddle to where his men waited just behind him. "Keep yer hands off this one, all of you, she ain't no whore," he ordered.

Serena heard no trace of mockery in his voice, so she waited, somewhat perplexed. He turned back to her.

"There now. Far as my boys go, you're as safe as you are with your Uncle Pete. They won't disobey me. Not more'n once anyhow."

"Good," Serena said uncertainly. What was he up to? Surely he didn't expect this little ploy to inspire her trust. "If that's all you wanted, then you can be on your way."

"I'd do just that, but to my recollection we ain't finished the little talk we started last time I came callin'."

"So, we're down to the real reason you came out here today. I told you—"

"I remember what you told me. But I got a few questions that ain't been answered yet, a few problems you and me better work out lady, or one of us ain't gonna be around to fight about it no more."

"You're wasting your breath threatening me, Birk."

"It ain't no threat. Way I see it, it's fact. We're gonna have to work somethin' out, or you're gonna have to kill me to keep me away from that water you're hoardin' inside those walls. You got the guts to kill a man, little girl?"

"Try me," Serena said through gritted teeth. "The water is inside the ranch and the ranch is mine. Mine and my uncle's. Gage Tanner left this place to him. Plain and simple."

Birk shifted in his saddle; behind him restless horses snorted and pawed at the dust, their riders muttering amongst themselves. "You got papers to prove that?"

Serena's stomach clenched. *Papers? There must be a legal document somewhere. But it would be a rental agreement with the Church or the like, not a deed....* "In the strong box," she lied.

"I'd like to see 'em, wouldn't you boys?"

His cohorts rumbled back in agreement. Serena stuck her chin in the air, mustering all the bravado she could.

"You're not the law. I don't have to show you anything. My uncle's word is good enough."

"Your uncle ain't been sober long enough to promise nothin' to no one since Gage Tanner and his lot were killed and you know it," Birk said with a derisive snort. "And no, I ain't the law. But if I have to call the marshall in here to make you prove ownership, I got a hunch you're gonna wish you dealt with me instead of him."

"I doubt that."

"If you can't prove Gage Tanner owned this place, lady, Mormon or not, you're gonna find yourself hangin' from a tree. If you're that lucky. Way we look at, if you're managin' this place, and it belongs to the damned Mormons, then you're breakin' the law. And if it means my herd will get water, I'll do anything I got to do to prove it."

Serena weighed his words carefully. Was he bluffing? How much did he really know about the ranch and its connection to the church? "If you don't have water, then how can you have a herd?" she asked, trying to force the truth and divert the conversation.

Birk's brows drew together. "I did have water when I come out here from Virginia. That is, I found water and built my herd around it. Damned desert took every cent I'd saved to come out west. Took the boy I brought with me." He paused. "Took everything." Staring off blankly for a long moment, he returned his focus to Serena. "But I done it. I got my thirty thousand on the hoof. Then the main watering hole ran dry. Nesters stole others. My crops died out. Then my cattle started dyin' off, one by one. I only got enough of my herd left to keep the creditors away. For now. Been buyin' water rights here and there where I can, and searchin' for new holes. Always lookin', ain't we boys?"

Again the other riders grunted their agreement.

Despite her wish to deplore the man, Serena couldn't help but feel a twinge of pity for him. He'd given his all to the new territory, and it had scorned him. He was only trying to survive. The same way she was. She wrestled against herself, considering his plight, fearful of her own. How could she afford to share the water? What if her own spring dried up?

"I'm sorry for your trouble, but I can't give you my water. I have my own herd to think of."

At that Reeds' men burst into unbridled laughter.

"Watch out Birk or you'll make all six of 'em stampede."

Serena searched the men for the smart mouth. The smirk on Zeke's face answered her question.

"Shut your mouth Zeke, before I shut it for you," Birk growled. He glared back at Serena. "You got somethin' sides that lame mule of yours hidin' somewhere?"

"That's my business."

"Might be interestin' to find out who you're doing business with. Might be you have friends—or kin—who need a place to graze their cattle. Or damned sheep. Although, come to think of it, no one seems to know where you come from."

His insinuation was plain. He meant Mormon friends or relatives. Serena stopped to think before answering. Better to dispel Birk's imaginings with partial truths than to leave his mind free to fill with suspicions. "You don't listen very well. I told you I'm not a Mormon. In fact, my daddy was a good Christian preacher. I've lived in the territory since I was a child. This is the only land I know."

"You told me a lot of things. I ain't seen proof of nothin' yet. All I know for certain is that the Mormons built this place around the only strong water supply in the area." He waved a hand toward the walled enclosure. "They hoarded that spring and locked it up inside those walls so none of the rest of us could get it to when our own springs ran dry."

"Maybe they thought their spring might run dry if they let every rancher and Indian with a bad temper use it," she said sweetly, bringing the color up in Birk's face.

"Tanner let the Paiute use it anytime they damned well wanted to. And it ain't seemed to hurt the supply none."

"And did he share it with you too?"

Birk straightened. "Never asked. Had my own water then. Ain't never asked no one for charity. And I ain't askin' you now. But I'm tellin' you I ain't satisfied you got any more right to that spring than I do."

"Your peace of mind isn't my concern. I'm just trying to survive here, same as you are."

"That so?" He glared up at her.

Serena clutched her gun tighter and straightened her shoulders. "Yes. It is. I'm putting down roots here on this property, the land Gage Tanner left to my uncle, whether you like it or not."

Reed's men grumbled and a few cursed her, low and nasty. "Now you listen up lady, 'cause I'm only gonna say this once," Birk snapped. "Water's scarce enough around these parts, and now with so much of the grasslands gone to over-grazing," he shook his head, "plain stripped down to dust by the damned sheep, some folks are crazy or stupid enough to try and run. There ain't hardly no land left for cattle. That's what makes this place like gold to me. You got water and you got pasture." He paused, his eyes hot and angry. "You got what I need, lady."

Serena felt her courage flagging, but she didn't dare show it now. She gulped down the fear welling in her dry throat. Staring directly up into his eyes, she said, "Well Mister Reed, I need it too. This is all I have. So you may as well take your men and start looking elsewhere for what you need."

Birk hunched over the saddle horn and heaved a long, deep sigh. "There ain't no where else."

"I can't change that."

"Well I sure as hell can!" Zeke blurted out.

At that Birk's gang hooted and cheered, several of them tossing their hats and catching them, restless and ready for a brawl. A sideways glance from their boss quieted them.

"See," Birk turned back to Serena, "I've had my eye on this place ever since the last of the Mormons left to where the whole filthy lot of 'em belong. With their own kind. Then right about the time I was ready to make my offer on this place, Tanner moved that widow and her family in and took over 'fore I even knew the place was up for sale. Mighty strange the way this place changed hands. No one heard nothin' 'bout it 'til it was said and done. Ain't right, with that telegraph in there, them Mormons sent word out and got it back 'fore the rest of us knew anything about it. Now, how do I know you ain't gettin' messages regular from them even now?"

A telegraph? Where? Not that I'd know how to use it if I did find it. But it could come in handy . . .

"I don't know anything about that," she said, a little too quickly.

"She's lyin' boss!" Zeke put in. "She's a goddamned Mormon lover, just like Tanner was, I'm tellin' you!"

Inwardly Serena cringed, but made certain that to Birk's eyes, she didn't so much as flinch.

"Zeke's right," another said. "Tanner let 'em stop in here many a time and she has too."

"You know it and we know it," a third chimed in, feeding Serena's uneasiness. They were itching for a fight. Or worse. She began to think less highly of her decision to face them without the full protection of the wall. If even one of them pulled a gun on her now, she might not have the time to back down behind the wall. She eased her foot back onto the landing so that only her shoulders and head were still exposed.

Pete you'd better be covering me. She wished she had eyes in the back of her head to assure herself he hadn't dozed off. He was about as reliable as a stray tom cat after midnight.

"I say Tanner was a snake-tongued liar!" Zeke called out. "My guess is he was a Mormon and so's she. Why them Mormons likely thought they done fooled everyone into thinkin' they'd sold off the ranch to some gentile, then thinkin' it was safe, went on ahead and sent her down to be his wife!"

"Makes sense," another man seconded. "Look at her. Ain't nothin' 'bout her looks like her *uncle,* is there?"

Serena tried to protest the ridiculous assumption, but the shouts of the other men drowned her out. Their horses, sensing tension and excitement in the air, whinnied low and scraped restlessly at the hard earth that cracked beneath their weight like china plates.

The men's grumbling and bellowing escalated; Serena's heart thumped hard against her breast. *Is this how it happened before? Had they cornered Libby and her family, riling themselves into a bloodthirsty frenzy?*

Her head throbbed as they pressed closer together, milling around the front yard, egging each other on, a slap on the back, a punch in the ribs, prodded by the shared conviction of their conjectures.

Leading the pack, Zeke rode out in front of Birk, the others following, to circle, closer, tighter, to the wall. Serena fought back a strong, hard jolt of fear. What if they somehow managed to get inside?

She shouldered her rifle and pointed it straight at Zeke's smirking face, then glared at Birk, who sat still and silent in his saddle. "Call them off, Birk, or I swear I'll blow them off my land."

The men laughed and hooted wildly. A bullet suddenly ripped close by her face and Serena scrambled down behind the wall, breathing hard. Pete was nowhere in sight.

"I don't think you'll git the chance." She recognized Zeke's raspy voice without having to see his ugly face.

Serena's blood went to ice. The taunts grew louder and ruder; the men hovered outside like starving scavengers ready to feast on her.

Looking out one of the openings in the wall, she saw Birk casually take out a cheroot, ignite a sulphur match with a single flick of his thumbnail and light it. He took a deep draw and seemed to stare right at her. His eyes went hard.

She thought of Libby Tanner, of her children, of their terror. She could feel it, taste it, hear it thundering in her ears. The pitch of the men's rantings raked across her ears and nerves.

"You won't get inside the gates," she yelled out at Birk, wishing she felt the confidence of her words. "There's nothing you can do. Call them off."

Birk ground the cheroot between his teeth then slowly drew a double action Colt from its rig. With a bored look on his face and a dull droop to his eyes, he lifted it into the air.

But before his finger ever touched the trigger, a hail of shots thundered out into the yard. The horses milled around, lurching forward or sideways, some rearing back, as their riders scrambled to control them.

Serena whipped around, certain it had to be Pete. But she was alone at her post. Still she seized the moment of distraction. "That's my uncle!" she shouted. "Unless you leave now, he'll start shooting and once he gets started he won't stop!"

Instead of heeding her trembling threat, the air around them fell deathly silent, save for the echo of the gunshots. All the men seemed to be looking off in separate directions, over each other's shoulders, some toward Birk, some toward the ranch house, some to the horizon. Serena peered between them at Birk and found him frowning at his gun. He glanced up, not to one of the lookouts in the ranch as she expected, but off into the distance, toward the cliffs and canyons beyond.

The fading thunder resounded again and again off of the towering red rocks and deep canyon walls. The last trace of it died along with the attack.

A confused sense of dread and relief flooded Serena in equal measure. She looked at Birk and saw his look of confusion.

"If that wasn't you, Birk, who was it?" Zeke asked.

Serena thought fast. "My uncle. And you know as well as I do, he isn't right in the head. You're lucky to have gotten one warning from him."

Birk's eyes narrowed. "That old man ain't hit nothin' yet. And I ain't sure those shots came from inside those walls." He stared off toward the plateau again, abruptly stiffening.

Serena followed his gaze, her eyes flying wide when she saw what caused the blank expression of disbelief on his face.

A long row of men on horseback, nearly double the number of Birk's group, lined the flat rock shelf, their images shimmering in the searing heat. Serena instantly recognized them.

"Apache!" Zeke jerked his horse around hard.

"Now, wait a minute—" Birk started.

"I'm gettin' the hell out of here," Zeke said, not giving him time to finish. Several of the men had already turned their horses and kicked them into a gallop toward the plain leading away from the plateau. "Let her fight with 'em. We ain't got the ammunition to tangle with no Apache."

Another round of shots boomed out overhead and this time Serena knew they came from the plateau.

So did Birk and his men. Firing a few haphazard shots in the direction of the Indians, the remainder of them bolted out over the plain.

As soon as they'd gone, the sound of gunfire suddenly ceased. Serena waited a few minutes, then peered back out of the opening in the wall, her heart in her throat. Reed and his men had vanished. And so had her unlikely rescuers.

She blinked, certain her eyes deceived her. But they had disappeared as quickly as they had come.

Slumping down against the wall, Serena stayed there a long while, listening to the gradually slowing pace of her heart and the receding echo of her fear and their hatred, wondering at the strange help that had come from and gone to nowhere.

"Oh, I'll never make this thing work," Serena spat, slamming an instruction book against the desk. She'd spent the entire afternoon wrestling with the telegraph she'd found tucked away in a dusty corner of one of the upstairs rooms after a lengthy search of the entire ranch house. The discovery offered her a welcome escape from the frightening episode Birk Reed and his gang had stirred up that morning, and the completely unexpected part the Indians had played in the entire incident.

For hours, while her fingers wrestled with the stubborn machine, her thoughts warred over Birk's threats, his sideways appeal to her sympathy. In many ways, though his tactics were vile, she had to admit his plight mirrored that of the Paiute who confronted her. They all wanted the oasis, the water—her water—to save their animals and lands. To survive.

That much she understood. So far the Paiute at least had come to her in peace, but desperation could push them to violence. Had it already? Were they responsible for the massacre? Could it have been other Indians like the Apache Zeke had mentioned? Then why hadn't they attacked today when given the chance? Or was it Reed himself and his men, determined to take what they wanted? If so, why hadn't they seized the ranch right after the massacre?

Had Gage's return surprised the killers, forcing them to another plan? No, if that were true, then they would have murdered him as well. Did the killers realize the Spirit in the Wind was neither ghost nor legend but a flesh and blood man ready to wreak his revenge? Even so, it was one man against many. Wasn't it?

Things just didn't add up.

The frustrating puzzle in her mind mirrored the one at her fingertips. In the same way, all of the instructions for the telegraph made sense one by one, but when she put them together, the stupid machine plain just didn't work.

"You'll have to go to school to learn how to operate that thing. Like Libby did."

Serena jerked around to answer the deep, familiar voice. But the sight of him left her momentarily speechless. He leaned on the open door frame, arms crossed insolently over his chest, his rigging slung low across his slim hips, the brass head of his pistol gleaming like burnished gold in the waning sun.

"I wish you'd just stop . . ." She started to say, before a glint in his eyes caught the words in her throat.

He settled back against the wide oak frame, crossed his arms over his chest, then casually kicked up one black boot against the opposite frame, where it rested, effectively stopping any ideas Serena might dream up about running for the door.

"You wish I'd stop doing what?" he murmured, soft and low, with a touch of sarcasm she hardly knew him to be capable of.

Serena searched for her voice, but discovered it somehow had given way to her senses. She inhaled him visually, staring unabashedly over every perfect inch of him from his long lean legs to his broad shoulders to his beautiful, haunted eyes. Whiskey-colored swipes of unruly hair curled below the collar of his dust-stained shirt. It hung open nearly to his waist, baring deep golden skin and a matt of gold-brown hair that looked soft enough to rub her cheek against.

When he caught her eye, a hint of a mocking smile flickered at the corners of his lips, and the light caught a glimmer of emerald in his eyes. Anybody that gorgeous had to be either an angel or a devil. Or all man.

"I—I wish you'd stop appearing and disappearing," she stammered at last, "like a—"

"Ghost?"

"That's not funny."

"It wasn't intended to be. But you seem glad enough to see me."

"Why, you arrogant bastard! No, I am not glad to see you. I wish you would go away and leave me alone and stop showing up at all hours and not letting me sleep and taking me to strange dark places, and where the hell are you when I need you anyway?"

"Whoa! One at a time."

She heard him, but the tumult of confusion assaulting her mind and the urges clamoring to control her body drowned him out. "I have questions for you, Gage Tanner, and this time you aren't leaving this house until I'm satisfied with your answers."

"How do you intend to stop me?"

"I—I . . ." Serena stomped her foot in frustration. "Why can't you just talk to me for once?"

Gage held up his hands in a gesture of surrender. "Fair enough." In two long strides he was inside facing her. He pulled up a chair, turned it around backward less than a foot from hers, spread his legs and planted himself backward in the seat. He rested his muscular forearms on the top of the ladder back. "As long as you satisfy me as well."

Serena's skin tingled icy cold then scorching hot. What the devil did he mean by that? Had more happened that night after her fall from the barn than she remembered. What she did recall, the warmth of his body close to hers, the brush of his lips to her face, his hands caressing, was enough to torment her constantly already. Was there more? Had he taken advantage of her illness? If so, she should feel outraged.

Shouldn't I?

She searched for any vestige of affront, and instead discovered a longing that felt like an ache, as if she were possessed by some strange, relentless sickness.

Deciding to ignore his innuendo, she plunged in to the issue at hand. "The killers must have been Birk Reed and his gang. They're uncivilized and bloodthirsty, and he holds the only bridle on them. I know you were there today. Watching. You must have brought the Indians. You understand what I'm talking about, don't you?"

"Yes."

Serena waited for him to offer more, opinions, information, something! But he gave her nothing more. "So? Why not go after Reed? You've as much as admitted you think he was responsible."

"It's one possibility."

"So, do something!"

"I am. I'm waiting."

"Waiting! For what? For the killers to send out an announcement inviting you to loop a noose around their necks?"

The barest hint of a smile touched his lips. "No. I'm waiting for you to get scared enough to get the hell out of here and go back to your family."

"What do you know about my family?"

"So you do have one."

Serena scowled. He'd trapped her, damn him. "I did." She stopped, stubbornly refusing to say more. Two could play his game.

"I see."

She wondered if he did. Had she already admitted too much? "My parents are dead," she said, trying to lead his thoughts away from any connection to Mormons.

"I'm sorry."

"It was a long time ago," she muttered, then rose and turned her back to him. Reaching into her pocket, she drew out a sulphur match and lit the candelabrum on the desk. All the while she felt his eyes on her, memorizing her every movement. The sensation both unnerved her and gave her a chill that wasn't entirely unpleasant. As she touched the small flame to the last candle, her shaking hand accidently knocked one of the tapers onto the pile of papers on the desk.

They flared wildly up toward her face. Paralyzed by irrational fear, she stood mute, staring like an animal facing death.

Something hard bit into her stomach and she felt herself being pulled to the side like a rag doll. Dumb and helpless, she hung limply on Gage's arm while he beat out the flames with his hat.

"You almost lost that mane of yours," he said, sitting her back on her feet when he'd doused the flames. "Are you all right?" He eyed her curiously, looking her up and down.

Serena shoved her trembling hands behind her back. "Just taken a little off guard, that's all," she lied. The last thing she wanted to do was to incite his unwanted interest in her or her past. "I'm fine. Thank you."

Gage shook off his hat, secured the candles and sat back down. Serena brushed her skirts out and sank into her chair.

"We were talking about your parents' death," he said too pointedly for her comfort.

She felt her blood drain to her feet. "They're gone. There's nothing more to be said about it," she managed, her words tremulous. "Anyhow, they say time lets you forget."

"Does it? Somehow you don't seem as if you have."

Tempted to tell him he was one to talk, she bit her tongue. His hurts were much too deep, and too recent. Better to avoid personal conversation altogether, she decided. He had a way of getting her to say more than she intended to. She chose to change the course of their discussion altogether, to lead him back to the pressing matters at hand, far away from her.

"Reed, and the Paiute, and Heaven knows who else,

they all want my water. Who knows what they'll do—
what they've done—to get to it."

Gage raised a brow. "Your water?"

"Yes," Serena said, lifting her chin. "I control it
now."

"Do you?"

"Yes!"

"Wasn't this morning enough to convince you that
you don't? Why are you so damned determined to stay,
especially now?"

Glancing down, Serena plucked at her skirt, not quite
sure how to answer. "I—I feel safe here."

"Safe?" He shook his head. "You've got a funny idea
of what's safe."

"If they would just find water elsewhere I wouldn't
have these problems," Serena snapped back, her eyes
flashing to his.

"Water means life here. And death. That's why I let
the Paiute use the oasis. It was theirs first. The first settlers took it from them."

"And Reed? You're so charitable, why didn't you
share with him too?"

"He had his own watering holes, then. Besides, he's
a settler, he only deserves what he's bought. Which is
plenty, considering the way he did it."

"What do you mean?"

"It's not an uncommon practice," Gage said with a
shrug. "Just not exactly legal. He bought the 160 acres
allotted him by the government, then hired ranch hands
to lay claim to 160 more acres each. After six months
or so, they deeded their portions over to him in exchange for his promise to keep them on the payroll.
That's the only way some ranchers out here survive.
Once land is stripped it's useless. Unless a man's got
enough water to keep his herd going."

"With all of that land, didn't he have several watering holes?"

"At first, but nesters stole several for their homesteads, some dried up, and some got taken over by other ranchers. There aren't any fences long enough to corral a man's holdings out here."

"It's every man for himself then."

"Or woman."

She looked at him with sharp eyes. "Precisely."

"Serena . . ." For the first time, he looked uncomfortable. Shifting in his seat he glanced away, then back at her again. "Birk Reed's got no claim to the water, but the Paiute do. And they're a dying people."

"And what if my water runs dry?"

"It's a risk worth taking."

"In your opinion, maybe. But if everybody was of that mind, there would be no new west. If I were to share the water, I might die with them. You have to be selfish to survive."

"Maybe. And maybe white men never should have pushed out this far, at least not like this. Not by killing innocents for it."

"I don't see you pulling up and moving out."

"I've got something to finish here," Gage said, his face hardening. "Then I intend to do just that."

His words hit her like stones. "Why did you ever settle here if you didn't mean to stay? You knew the risks, didn't you?"

"After living in near every corner of this territory at one time or another, I knew plenty. The only thing I didn't know was how bad it hurts when something happens to someone you're supposed to be taking care of."

"Supposed to?" Serena mimicked his words unconsciously, the context striking her as odd. In the same instant, the idea of being taken care of, protected by him, sounded like an answer to a prayer.

Living among the Mormons, she had never known a man who roused any more than a fleeting infatuation. As a girl, she'd been too bold, too outspoken, too eager to explore the depth and breadth of every new emotion and feeling, that she either intimidated or repelled the boys who paid her any interest. When she grew older, she'd liked several of the men well enough, might have even come to care for one of them in time. But she could never reconcile herself to sharing a life mate with anyone else. For her, there was no sense of security in that, no feeling of true intimacy.

She had known it long before Jerel Webster decided he wanted her for his wife. She had been certain when he arrogantly told her she would be his. None of the other Mormon men ever pressured her to accept their way of life. Jerel, who believed it was his right to have what he wanted, never offered her a choice. Her stubborn refusals had only inflamed his ego and made him more determined to have her.

But she had stood firm, despite his vow to make her life hell if she defied him. She would wait, until she met a man who could give her what she wanted, a love that was everything between two people, body and soul, all encompassing.

Yet she had never met a man that made her feel the way Gage Tanner could with just one long, slow glance. Wild and reckless, sweet and yearning. A man with a strength and will that was more than a match for her own, and a straightforwardness that made her trust him without having reason.

If she could convince him to stay, just long enough to be certain Jerel would forget her, let her live in peace . . .

She searched his eyes for some sign of caring, some

signal he might be willing to give her the safety she craved, if only for a little while. She found only fathomless depths that told her nothing, but took her to somewhere beyond the present, beyond tragedy and pain, somewhere between heaven and earth.

They sat inches apart, locked in silent communion, both needing so much from each other, unable to ask.

Help, security, yes she needed those desperately. But more, so much more even than these; he made her want something unspeakable, something intense and intimate. With him the emptiness of her losses vanished. Though everything about him spoke of strength, power, even danger, her fears melted away when he drew near.

Near her, the loneliness ended. Gage struggled to stay focused on his purpose. He had an idea, a bargain to strike with her, and he needed her help. But all he could think of in that instant was how sweet she smelled, how remarkably the waves of her hair glowed in the soft light, how lightly her breath had touched his face the time she'd slept in his arms.

He had cared for her less than one night, for a few stolen hours he'd watched her sleep, quieted her cries, stroked her arms and face and hair to calm her. How could so short a time with a woman change a man? He'd wrestled with the question since the morning he laid her back in her own bed, finding no answer, but that something inside him would never be the same again.

They'd scarcely touched, yet she left her imprint on him as surely as a brand on his soul.

Even his makeshift house still bore traces of her presence. The stone was imbued with the jasmine scent of her; his blankets burned his body where she had lain. His secret refuge, once less than a home, had been enough. Until she slept there. Now those dark, hollow walls that shielded him from the land of the living cursed his solitary existence. She left the emptiness of the cave like the emptiness in his heart—exposed.

Serena broke the spell of their gaze, shifting her chair around to sit perfectly opposite him. "It was you, wasn't it? You came. You brought them."

"Yes."

They spoke without explanations.

She knew he'd orchestrated the appearance of the Indians that had scattered Reed's men; he felt her appreciation, warm and welcome as a fire on a cold night.

"Why?" she whispered.

"You needed my help."

"Now you need mine."

"Yes." He reached over and hesitatingly lifted a single tendril of her hair, touching it as though the slightest pressure would damage or destroy it. For one brief moment, her breath had breathed new life into him, leaving him desperate for more. "I do need you."

His voice had rough edges, and for a moment the hardness in him faltered. It might as well have been her heart breaking for him. Serena reached out and stroked his cheek with the back of her hand. "And I need you, Gage Tanner."

Chapter Eight

Serena stood in the slender shadows of the poplars, watching the first stars emerge from the night sky. For three nights, she'd waited by the oasis for Gage to appear; for three nights she'd waited in vain. Part of her seethed with anger and resentment that he'd so callously abandoned her. Obviously, he intended to settle his wretched vendetta his own way. The promise they'd exchanged to help each other meant nothing to him!

At the same time, side by side with her angry disappointment, she couldn't banish the strange, unsettling restlessness inside her, the feeling she was missing a vital part of herself. It was as if he'd taken something from her and in its place left only a cold, cavernous void as empty as the canyons beyond, as dry as desolate as the desert itself.

Tonight it seemed especially bad. *It's got to be the heat,* she told herself, thinking the ever-escalating temperature must be magnifying her tension, setting her frustration aflame. For the past two days, the heat had pressed in with a heavy, oppressive stillness. She couldn't escape it, lived day and night with the sweat and the hot prickling at her skin. How she longed for even one moment's respite from the fever steeped in her blood.

"He's not coming," she whispered, the darkness absorbing the sound. She raised a hand and brushed away the damp strands of hair clinging to her forehead. Looking down at the still waters, she saw nothing but the twilight muted reflection of branches and leaves. Why did she think, feel, that tonight he would come? "Why should he?" she berated herself, kicking at the rocks near her feet. "He doesn't really need anyone but himself."

Finally, Serena gave in to her annoyance and turned to retreat to her room. But as she did, though she tried not to look, the silver gleam of the oasis pool caught her eye. Tonight, she felt reckless, rebellious, in the mood to indulge herself in the delicious cool bath.

Giving into the feeling, she quickly shed her clothing and, drawing in a long breath, stepped into the pool.

As the cool water lapped in smooth waves around her ankles, her calves, caressed her thighs, closing around her body like a living hand, her rapture escaped on a sigh of pure pleasure. Sunk to her shoulders in the pool, Serena leaned back and let her hair scatter on the surface, looking up to the canopy of starlight above.

It felt so good, so sinfully sensuous and soothing. Closing her eyes, she immersed herself completely in the water. Slowly surfacing, relishing each lick of coolness on her skin, she smoothed her hair back, opening her eyes.

And found the ripple of her reflection coupled in the pool with Gage Tanner's image.

Her eyes shot upward. Motionless, he stood at the pool's edge, staring down at her. He towered over her, still to the point of lifelessness, bathed in an aura of surreal starlight, like a powerful force from another realm, as frightening and as mesmerizing as the first night she'd laid eyes on him.

But this time she felt no shame, no surprise. Only desire.

"Some day," she said softly, "I'm going to figure out how you manage to get inside those gates without any sound or warning. Because at times like these I believe you are a spirit in the wind."

Her light, fearless tone left Gage without a reply. He wanted to tell her he'd only come back to say their bargain had been a mistake, to warn her away again, this time for good. He wanted to tell her that seeing her tonight, like the first time, made her move inside him again, stealing his sense of himself. Instead he said nothing.

"I wondered if you'd come back. I nearly convinced myself you wouldn't." A sprinkling of mischief wove into her voice. "I don't suppose you came to fix the fences, though."

"What are you doing?" Gage said at last, roughly, without a hint of gentleness. "It's dangerous, out here alone."

"Is it?" Slowly, Serena started moving through the water, back toward the pool's edge. "There's only you and me." She felt no hesitation, but instead savored the power she had to hold his eyes on her. She wanted to unnerve him, to bend him to her will, to make him want to stay and nothing else. But when the water slipped from her shoulders and she met his unwavering gaze, the power suddenly became his in equal measure.

Gage refused to back down. It would be wiser to walk away, not to give in to what she wanted. He'd done it so often before, ignored his needs in favor of another's best interest, that it came almost as easily as breathing. Except this time, he wanted to take from her as much as she demanded from him.

He let his eyes follow the patterns of moonlight on her skin, from the shadows against her throat, to the mantle of ivory on her shoulders, to where the silver water scarcely covered the curve of her breasts. Images like this had danced in his head for days. But each time he tried to banish them, they refused to leave, finally driving him back to the ranch.

The air stretched taut between them. Every nerve jumped in response. Gage flexed a hand at his side, feeling the tension snap and crack like lightning, his sense of right and wrong diffuse like candlelight.

Serena said nothing, could do nothing but watch him in return. The cool water felt cold, the desert air hotter than the hottest afternoon of summer. A warm breeze scuttled through the trees; as it touched her she shivered.

The slight movement loosed the tension between them enough for Gage to take a few steps backward from the pool. "Get dressed," he said. "You're going to catch cold, and I don't want to play nurse maid again." He turned his back to her, fixing his stare on the black shadows of the cliffs towering above the walls.

His tone made her feel suddenly ashamed of her brazen attempt to seduce him and she rushed to climb out of the pool then hurried into her clothes, running shaking fingers through her damp hair. She paused a moment, then walked to stand beside him, a little ways apart, looking beyond the oasis to see what held his eyes. "They look so imposing at night," she said. The fine tremble in her voice betrayed her attempt to hide her embarrassment. "In the day, I can hardly believe anyone travels through them. But at night, I'm convinced only a true spirit could go further than the plain."

"I remember the first time I rode through the canyons at night," Gage said slowly, glad for the change of topic. He shifted a little, not looking at her. "In the daylight, it can knock the breath out of you, there's so much of it. Higher and deeper and farther than anywhere else you could be. At night . . . the darkness makes you blind. But you have the chance to smell it and taste it and listen to it. I learned more about them in one night than I did in a month of days."

His halting description sang like poetry inside Serena. "I wish I could see it," she said. "I traveled through a little of it, but I never had time enough to just look at it all. I was too concerned with simply staying alive. I wish I could see it through your eyes."

"I could show you." Gage said the words before he had time to regret them. Except when he thought them over, he couldn't retract them.

Serena glanced at him, not bothering to hide her astonishment. "You—"

"Tonight." He turned to her, holding out his hand.

She had no reason to trust him, less to take his offer at face value. The thoughts flashed through her mind even as she put her palm flat on his, and his fingers curled warm and strong around hers.

He started walking away from the oasis to the gates, guiding Serena with him. She followed, the grasses brushing her calves, cushioning her bare feet. They walked outside and she took the key from her dress pocket and locked up behind them. She moved in silence at his side until the ranch melted from view and all Serena could see around her was the gently swaying grass, washed white by the moon; the sky, spread with a banquet of stars; and Gage, painted in the colors of the night. The wind made quiet music. It all felt unreal to her, like walking through a dream.

The plain stopped at the edge of the cliffs, and in a sparse grove of pinon trees, Serena saw his horse. It lifted its head as they approached, nickering softly in recognition. "So this is where you hide it. I knew you had to have your horse out here somewhere."

Gage let go of her hand to rub the pale jagged streak on its forehead, the only spot of color on the stallion's black coat. "This is my companion of the night," he said. "My spirit steed."

Serena ignored the mocking comment as she reached up to touch the stallion's soft nose. "What's his name?"

"Gusano." A note of laughter ran through his voice, "Because of this," he ran a finger down the tallow-colored streak, "Worm. He'll take us both."

"Worm?" She waited for further explanation.

"That's his name," was all he offered, before turning her to face him with a touch to her shoulder. He then lifted her sideways onto the saddle, waiting until Serena slid her leg over to straddle the hard leather before pulling himself up behind her.

He fit against her easily, his arm settled in the curve between her waist and hip as he gathered the reins in one hand and turned Gusano toward the canyons. With her skirt bunched above her knees, the bared skin of her calves and thighs brushed his legs, grazing rough cotton and flexing muscle in rhythm with the horse's steady gait. Serena held to the pommel, her body swaying in rhythm with the back and forth motion, warming to the steady rasp of his breath on her neck.

Between the walls of the canyon, the black rock blotted out the moon and the fullness of the night unfurled around them. Serena trembled a little. Gage was right. There was nothing to see; everything to hear, to smell and taste and feel.

"Afraid?" he asked.

"No . . ." It was true. He protected her from the fear, leaving her senses free to wander. "I understand what you meant before, about being here at night. I see why you live here. It's like stepping into a different life. You can forget there is another world except this."

Gage shifted in the saddle, making no reply. Her nearness had taken the edge from his sense of the cliffs around them, leaving him vulnerable to her. Tonight, she had appeared again to him like a dream, without warning or reason. And he was lost, drowning in a river of deep-running feelings that kept drawing them back together despite all that ought to keep them apart.

They rode in silence for a time until a sudden drawn-out cry, somewhere between a howl and a snarl, tensed Serena against him.

She leaned closer to his chest. "What is it?"

"Cougar. Not far, but far enough not to give us trouble." He listened, testing the air. "It's hunting, for deer—or someone's cattle, maybe sheep."

"How can you be so certain?" Serena asked, curious, feeling a rare urge to listen, rather than talk. It was a strangely invigorating sensation. The notion struck her that with a man like Gage, so private and reclusive, perhaps she might gain more by listening than demanding. "You belong here, even at night," she said, hoping to lead him to tell her why that was so.

"On the ranch I grew up on, just outside Albuquerque, there was a hand, half-Navajo. He used to take me into the mountains and the forests. To hunt, and sometimes just to watch and listen." She felt him shrug, as if uncomfortable with hearing too much of his own voice. "He gave me a respect for the wilderness and he taught me how to survive in it. It stood me well, later, when I was scouting for the cavalry."

"Scouting? Here?"

"A little of everywhere, here, New Mexico, Texas, a little into the Utah territory and farther west. Wherever they sent me, or I ended up."

"Didn't you ever want to stay anywhere? My father was a preacher and I always wanted him to stop and stay somewhere, anywhere. I was born in Oklahoma, and three days later we were in Kansas. It was always like that. Didn't you ever want to go back to Albuquerque, put down roots?"

"No." He said it flatly, without room for regret.

Serena waited for him to say more, and when he didn't, she craned her neck a little to look back at him. "Why?"

"Don't you ever run out of questions?" Gage sighed, knowing it was useless. "My mother died having me, and my father killed himself with a bottle sixteen years later. I never had any place to go back to. So I just kept going."

"I'm sorry," she said softly. His only response was a slight tensing of the arm next to her side. Determined to talk him out of his usual silence, she reached up and trailed gentle fingers over the hand that held the reins, feeling the trace of the scars on his skin. "How did that happen?"

"I was scouting the cliffs, on the Utah side. I got between a cougar and a man." He paused. "He thanked me by giving me charge of the ranch."

For the first time, a threat to her tenuous security permeated the surrounding darkness. "He was Mormon?"

"Yes. Silas Caltrop, an elder." Gage said the name slowly and deliberately, gauging her reaction. She moved forward in the saddle, distancing herself from him. He could taste her fear, sense it in the tensing of her back and shoulders. "He and I became friends. He, the Mormons, gave me a chance to settle somewhere when I needed a place to stop a while."

"How generous." A mix of disquiet and bitterness flattened her tone.

"Yes." Gage paused. "Do you know him?"

"No! No, I—of course not. Why should I?"

"I don't know. Why are you afraid of the Mormons?"

"I'm not afraid!" His perceptiveness startled her, stripped her defenses and bared her feelings. She closed her eyes, sucking in a long breath, and said the words as quickly as she could, trying to outrun the pain. "My parents were killed in an Indian raid. I ran. My father told me to run and hide, to save myself, and I did. I left my mother and father, knowing I'd never see them again. Knowing they were already dead." Her stomach knotted with guilty pain. She had to stop.

"Your father was right. You have to realize that now."

Serena braced herself. Ignoring his comment, she forced herself to continue. "The Mormons took me in. I . . . I'm grateful to them. They were kind and generous in many ways. They gave me food and shelter and a place in a family."

"Then why do you fear them?"

"Because they thought they could make me one of them. They were always trying to change me, to turn me to their ways. I didn't mind working, doing my part to help with the family. Like I said, I was thankful, indebted to them. But I could never renounce my father's teachings to accept theirs. I'm not one of them and never will be. I couldn't bring myself to accept their faith. So I left and . . . and I came here to make my own home."

Gage said nothing fo a long time, and Serena wondered what he was thinking about her story—if he was thinking about it at all. Maybe he hadn't even been listening, or maybe he just hadn't heard what he expected to hear. Maybe he didn't like it. Obviously, he had a different view of the Mormons; he hadn't been forced into running from them. Either way, it seemed he had no reply to make. She was about to push him into some kind of response when she realized they had started up a steep trail. The darkness eased under the soft ivory light of the full moon.

"Where are we?"

"A place I come once in a while. The Paiute showed it to me."

He said nothing else, and this time Serena left him to his silence. As Gusano carried them up the slanted path, she was jostled backward into Gage. His right arm still fit to her, he wrapped his left around her waist, steadying her, drawing her close to his chest, so near she could feel each breath he took.

The trail led to a towering rock formation at the peak of one of the cliffs. Rain and wind and time had shaped the rock so it stood like two massive pillars topped by a huge slab; in the center of it was a roughly heart-shaped opening. A series of jagged rock ledges led to the edge of the opening.

Serena couldn't take her eyes from it. Gage guided Gusano to a stop near the bottommost ledge, then he swung down. He reached up and she forced herself to look away only when his hands touched her waist.

"I've never seen anything like it," she whispered almost reverently as he took her hand and began leading her up the staircase of ledges to the heart of the stone.

"It's called Heaven's Window," Gage said softly. "The Paiute say if your heart is pure, you can look through it at night and see beyond time, to the truth."

They took the last step to the opening and Serena slowly reached out to brush her fingers over the inside of the hollow. Then, anticipation shooting over her, she looked through Heaven's Window to what lay beyond. At the first glance, her breath caught in her throat in an astonished gasp.

A black to ivory vista of canyons and cliffs, awesome in their size and grandeur, stretched out as far as she could see. Above them, the sky glittered with infinite starlight. Looking at it, Serena felt dizzy; her footing on solid earth melted into the cushion of an invisible cloud.

In that moment, she knew freedom. From the past, the present, the uncertainty of the future. She was looking through a window to forever. And the window was open wide. How long she stared, absorbing the splendor, the power, the sheer magnitude of it all, letting the view transcend every earthly problem and fear, she didn't know. Until the rough, warm clasp of Gage's hand around hers narrowed the universe to a single, simple, intimate embrace.

Gage moved a step closer. "I know how you feel," he said quietly.

His gentle voice soothed her. "Do you?"

"Yes. I never have words to describe it. But coming here, it makes things—clearer."

"Yes . . . clearer. You don't need words to describe it." Serena looked up at him. "You do understand," she murmured.

Side by side, they stood looking through Heaven's Window, content in the silence. Then, very slowly, Gage moved behind her and slipped his arms around her waist, drawing her against him to share the view. He nodded to the sky. "The Paiute call it *tu-omp-pi-av*. They said it's an inverted world, full of *poot-see*, living stars that travel around until they've made trails all over the sky."

"Restless, always searching for something," Serena

whispered. Her senses were full of him, of his voice, and his touch.

"That one . . . there—" Gage pointed to the brightest star in the sky. "It's called *Oui-am-i Wintook,* the North Star. The Paiute say he can't travel because there's no place for him to go."

"Tell me," Serena asked him, glancing up. "Why can't he go any further?"

"I'm no storyteller—" he started in protest.

"I want to hear you tell it. I'll understand when you do." Wrapping her arms around his, locking them together, she waited, listening.

He hesitated, then he told her, his voice deep, a little rough at the edges, stronger than the darkness. "There was *na-gah,* a mountain sheep on *tu-weap,* the earth, and he was always climbing the roughest and highest mountains. Until he found a peak reaching into the sky. So steep, he couldn't see the top.

"He climbed, up through darkness, into danger, until he came to a place higher than any other." With gentle hands, Gage turned Serena in his arms until they faced each other. In the moonlight, he touched the face that had haunted his dreams.

"Once he was there, he could never come down. He couldn't travel any further because there was no place for him to go, no higher peak for him to reach." He swanned his fingertips over her cheek in a curious, lingering caress. "So he stood still. Finally and always."

Thunder rumbled in the distance, trembling through Serena, into his hand. In the darkness, alone together, in the world under the midnight sky, Serena didn't know where she ended and Gage began. They had ceased to be each other, and instead were something new together, something greater and more infinite than they could ever be apart.

Gage felt the night dissolving around him. Here, nothing mattered but her. Seeing her, touching her, holding her. Because away from here, in the light, he couldn't do any of this. They were different, wanted different things: she absorbed with building a life for herself, determined to stay in one place; he drifting in and out of other lives, determined to keep moving. He couldn't allow himself to feel anything but the dull, empty ache and the cold resolve that had driven him to dig his own grave.

Slowly, savoring each moment, Gage slid one arm around her and his hand into the damp hair at her nape, bringing her against him, her mouth to his.

The first lightning shot across the horizon and the air smelled and tasted of rain. She tasted of an echo of smoke from the fire within her.

Serena held tightly to him, lost and found. With him she felt safe, at peace, and yet more thirsty for life, to learn and experience it with him, through him, than she had ever thought possible. Strong and protective one moment, in the next he grew tender and insightful. It was as though he'd always known her and she him. She never wanted this night to end.

His fingers sifted through her hair, exploring, demanding she came closer. His tongue mated with hers, probing, taking, promising, giving. He consumed her senses. How she'd hungered for this: the hard muscles of his shoulders gripped in her hands, the rasp of his beard on her skin, the smell of fire and wind and leather, his breath in her ear, whispering on her throat.

When the kiss melted to an embrace, Gage brushed his mouth to her temple, gathering her to his chest. He held her, and she him, forever, suspended in a timeless moment where being together seemed right and possible. The force driving them together rivaled the view from Heaven's Window.

A loud clash of thunder and lightning, the harbinger of the imminent storm, shook the earth beneath their feet, shocking them apart. Silently wondering why, they stood staring, a sudden distance that could have been miles between them, a thousand feelings left unsaid. Crying through the canyons, the wind rushed over the peak on a long gust bringing the first mist of rain.

Gage smoothed slashes of hair from Serena's face with his fingertips. "You can't stay here."

She nodded, understanding, but not willing to let go. Here, wrapped in protective isolation, safe in his embrace, here she wanted to stay. "I wish—"

"I'll take you back," he said abruptly, pulling back his hand.

They said nothing during the long ride to the ranch. Serena rested in the circle of Gage's arms, greedily hoarding a last lingering taste of safety and peace, knowing it vanish with him as soon as they reached their destination.

Gage stopped Gusano at the gates. He lifted Serena from the saddle, holding her with a light touch for a long moment before letting his hands fall away. "It's nearly dawn, and the storm's coming in," he said quietly. A whip of wind punctuated his words. "Go back inside."

"Will you come back?" Serena asked, afraid to ask the question; afraid to leave it unspoken. She unlocked the gate and walked partway inside then turned back. "Tomorrow night?"

"Looking down at her, Gage nearly told her no. Instead, he took all his chances and bent and grazed a gentle kiss on her soft mouth, stealing the tremble and fire from her lips. "Tomorrow night."

Without waiting for her to reply, he stepped backward, swiftly mounting Gusano, disappearing into the night.

Serena watched him silently vanish, any sound of his departure flung into the chorus of the burgeoning storm. Standing under the cottonwood near the pool's edge, in the same place she'd waited for him an eternity ago, she wondered if he truly was a spirit, and all of the night a dream.

Except the essence of him branded on her mouth and skin, on her heart, left her believing their midnight meetings, truth or illusion, were more real than anything she could see or touch in the light of day.

Standing on the precipice of the sheer cliff overlooking his makeshift home, Gage watched several jagged arms of forked lightning strike at the crags and peaks. The storm had turned the late afternoon sky to violet-blue twilight, slashed with gray and black. Apart from a brief shower an hour before dawn, it hadn't rained for the whole of the day. But the air tasted and smelled of it, and he expected a violent downpour at any moment.

He'd spent most of the day atop the cliffs, watching and thinking about the hours with Serena. It didn't do a damned bit of good, but he'd given up trying to put her out of his head. He'd let himself get pulled into someone else's life again, except this time he was being tracked by a new and dangerous urge; he wanted to be a part of it, for the first time, and not for her, but for himself.

Before he had loved and cared because he was needed, but Serena Lark's needs were only an excuse. An excuse to be near her, to talk and to listen to her, to smell and hold and kiss her. An excuse to let her make him whole.

A gust of wind threw a fistful of rain at him, dredging him out of his thoughts. He wasn't in the mood to get caught in a deluge, not now. Dusting his hat against his pants' leg, he shoved it back on his head and started down the cliff path, stopping midway when he caught a glimpse of the horse and rider. Gage's hand slid instinctively to the gun on his hip a second before he recognized the bald-faced palomino and the wide-brimmed hat of his rider.

It was Ross. Normally his friend was a welcome sight, except at this time of day, chased by a storm, his arrival could only mean trouble.

Moving quickly, Gage got to the edge of the cliff dwelling just in time to toss the ladder down to Ross.

"Not the best time to be rock climbing," Gage commented as Ross hefted himself up the last rungs of the ladder onto the stone floor.

"You and your cave are gonna be the death of me yet," Ross grunted. Pushing himself through the narrow opening leading into the room with the fire pit, he eased himself down on the blanket beside the embers of last night's flames, breathing heavily.

"What kind of trouble? The ranch?" Gage asked, leaning his back to the wall.

"I figured you'd guess this wasn't a social call. And I don't know if there's trouble yet. Let's just say I'm bein' cautious. If I'm gonna get hit with it, I'd rather take it in the front than in the back." The corner of his mouth twisted up. "It looks better."

"What is it?"

"Another group of pilgrims rode in today. Passed through Mandy's place on the way to the ranch." Ross pushed his hat back a few inches, giving Gage a straight stare. "Maybe it's nothin', but I don't like the way Birk Reed's boys been talkin' lately. There's enough hot blood among the ranchers in these parts over rumors of Mormons holdin' tight to the best water in the strip that it wouldn't take much for it all to boil over. They're already wonderin' about Miss Lark and her crazy so-called uncle." He paused deliberately, then said slowly, "Some people around here don't believe the Mormons ever gave up ownin' the ranch. They think the Mormons are there now . . . and were then."

"Then?" Gage's eyes narrowed as he caught Ross' meaning. Tension slipped up his spine, tightening every muscle as he straightened. "You think someone hated Mormons enough to massacre nine people—" He stopped, the words as sharp as ground glass on his tongue. "You believe the killers thought I was Mormon?"

Ross shrugged. "Don't know. Hatin' is easy when you're looking for someone to blame for your troubles." Getting to his feet, he tugged his hat back down low over his face. "I figured you ought to know, seein' as you've been keepin' such a close eye on the ranch."

"Yeah. The ranch," Gage muttered. He pushed away from the wall, his jaw set. "I warned that damned woman it was dangerous. But she wouldn't listen. She doesn't have the sense to see trouble when it's staring her in the face."

"Well, friend, there's two theories to arguin' with a woman," Ross said as he started back down the ladder. "Neither of 'em works."

Serena leaned on her rifle, watching the wagon through the slot in the ranch wall as it trudged slowly through the light mist of rain toward the ranch. Mormons. It had to be more Mormons. "Damn it, not now," she said under her breath. She'd had more than a fair share of trouble with Birk and his cowboys, and inviting new Mormon pilgrims inside the gates only begged for more.

But stronger than her irritation at the intrusion, or her uneasiness caused by the frightening suspicions among the strip ranchers, was the echo of Gage's voice in her head. Twilight was passing with each moment; in no time the sky would be black again, and she couldn't forget his midnight promise to return tonight.

She'd relived their ride through the canyon a thousand times, thought of him in the storm-tossed heat of the sleepless early morning darkness, in the dusty dawn light as she lay among the twisted sheets, damp and spent from her tormenting memories.

"How many of 'em?" Whiskey Pete asked, coming up behind her. "Sounds like a herd."

"A small herd. Just one wagon."

Pete bent to peer over her shoulder. "One? Cain't be?"

"Look for yourself," Serena said, gesturing to the slot. She sat back on the stairs to let him squint at the wagon with his one good eye.

"Humph . . . that ain't all. There's more of 'em comin'."

Serena sighed, picking up the rifle and starting down the stairs to open the gates. "Then they must be more spirits in the wind. All I can see is one wagon. And whoever they are, I hope they don't plan on staying long."

"You ain't gonna open the gates, are you?"

She turned in mid-step. "What?"

Whiskey Pete hung back by the stairs, shaking his head back and forth. "It ain't a good idea."

"Why? They're just more pilgrims. Or do you think they're tree devils this time?" she added mockingly.

Looking out the opening, then back at her, Pete stumped down the stairs and across the courtyard, stopping at the door of his room. "Used to feel sure they'd never come in wagons. But s'pposin' they's tryin' to trick us. . . . Just cain't tell," he said before he closed the door to her. "Now can you?"

"No, you can't because you're crazy," she muttered, throwing a glare at the closed door before turning to unlock one of the gates. Still, she carried the rifle with her as she stepped outside. Pete might be crazy, but the hollowness in his eyes and voice every time his tree devils were mentioned was enough to cause her a shiver of superstitious fear. Surrounded by isolation and heat it was easy to believe in devils. Or ghosts.

The wagon clattered over the last few years of rough grassy plain, stopping a few feet from the front gates. Two bearded, somber-eyed men in dusty brown climbed down from the bench seat, nodding a greeting as they neared.

"Are you the widow Gage Tanner took in?" the elder of the two asked, glancing at the rifle in Serena's hand.

"No. I am his new wife. The widow and her family are in Vulture Creek with friends for a time." The lie slipped easily from her lips. "Are you pilgrims?"

"Yes. I am Elder Aaron Beeman. And this is Elder Ephraim Gardner. We are seeking shelter for two, perhaps three days' time. My son, his wife, and a sister's child they are caring for also." He spread a hand to the couple emerging from the back of the wagon, a gawky youth and a woman Serena guessed to be a few years older then herself, both fair and squarely built. "If we could stable our horses in your corral—"

"You shouldn't stay," Serena blurted out.

A look of astonishment creased Aaron's stony facade. "I don't understand. This has always been a shelter for those of us making a journey to the Utah territory." He frowned a little. "What is wrong?"

"It's dangerous," Serena said, knowing it was dangerous for her to refuse them shelter, but for some reason possessed by a stubborn urge to keep them from invading her sanctuary tonight. Maybe it was Whiskey Pete's odd warning words, or the trouble she sensed brewing among the ranchers. Maybe it was Gage Tanner. Although she knew he wouldn't approve. He seemed only too willing to help everyone and anyone.

"Dangerous?"

"The ranchers here don't like Mormons—"

"That has been the way of it for many years," Ephraim said, his mouth twisting slightly. "You know it is why Elder Caltrop decided your husband should manage this place for us."

"Yes, but it's growing worse. They want the water. I'm worried some of them are frustrated to the point that they might resort to violence to drive the Mormons—and me—away for good. They suspect I'm either Mormon or I'm breaking the law by pretending to own the ranch to hide that the Mormons still have it."

Aaron eyed her curiously. "You? And what does your husband say of this? Surely, he is here . . ."

"No—no, he's not." Serena cursed herself for ever giving into the urge to sending them packing in the first place. She'd dug herself in deeper than she'd anticipated. "He and—most of the hands are hunting. The pelts bring a fine price at the trading post, and we need to store the meat for winter," she finished, pleased at her creative explanation. At the same time, she realized it was getting harder with each pilgrimage that passed through to explain Gage's absence. Sooner or later they would discover her lies. And then Jerel Webster would discover them.

"We are aware of the tensions in the territory, and we accept the risks, or we should have stayed in Missouri and not made the journey at all," Aaron said firmly. "But if you are no longer willing to offer us shelter—"

"No!" Serena said quickly. "No, that isn't it at all. I—" She paused to draw in a slow breath, to ease the unnatural hammering of her heart. Sweat beaded on her forehead, trickling in a cold line down the sides of her face, between her shoulder blades and down the curve of her back. "Of course we will continue to offer you shelter," she said, forcing away the surging desire to bolt back inside the gates. "I only meant to warn you of the danger."

"We are grateful for your concern," Aaron said, his tone as expressionless as his face. "Now, if you will allow us, we will stable the horses. We are all in need of rest and water and it is growing dark. I am certain you do not want to be outside the gates any longer than necessary."

Serena nodded and he turned to his companions to motion them to lead the wagon to the corral. Gripping the rifle at her side, she took a step toward the younger Beemans, intending to invite them inside the walls.

Her foot touched the hard earth an instant before the air exploded with a flurry of gunshots. One of the shots screamed by her ear and she felt a kiss of hot wind on her cheek. She dropped to a crouch, slamming the butt of her rifle into her shoulder.

The pair of horses harnessed to the wagon reared up, knocked Ephraim backward. Another barrage of shots hailed down on them. Somewhere near the back of the wagon, the woman screamed.

Serena tried to look everywhere at once, the rifle

trembling in her hands. The encroaching darkness hid their attackers. But if she could fire in the direction of the sounds— She raised the gun, her finger trembling on the trigger.

The next shot kicked up the dirt a few inches from her side. Grit and rock bit into her skin. Serena swiped a hand over her eyes, trying to clear the gray web obscuring her vision. Her finger slid against the curved metal, slick with sweat.

But before she could fire, the body of Aaron Beeman fell at her feet, his dead eyes staring into her face.

Chapter Nine

"No!" Serena wailed, falling to her knees beside him. "Not again. No more killing!" She pressed her ear to his chest, praying, searching desperately for a sign of life.

Ephraim rushed to the fallen man's side and bent over him. "Aaron, brother . . ." His eyes closed and Serena saw his lips move in silent prayer. A tear slid down his face.

"He's dead!" she shouted over the turmoil, shaking his arm. When he opened his eyes, staring at her with a mixture of bleakness and reproach, Serena tightened her grip. "I'm sorry. But there's nothing we can do for him and we have to hurry and get the others inside the walls. There's no time!"

Her urgency seemed to penetrate his momentary withdrawal. As more and more shots cracked the air close to them, Ephraim swiped the dampness from his cheek. He gripped Serena painfully by her shoulders and stared squarely at her. "I will cover you. Lead them in."

Serena nodded and shoved her rifle in Ephraim's hands, watching while he crawled behind a stack of pine fencing to take aim at their attackers.

The onslaught of gunfire rained hot and furious, coming from everywhere. She tried to make out the figures of the people she'd seen near the rear of the wagon. Sulfur smoke and dust blurred her vision. A woman's shrill scream pierced the blood-red twilight haze. Shouts from the rampaging riders excited both terror and fury in Serena. And guilt thrust a painful dagger.

If I had let them inside instead of trying to protect myself, my sanctuary. . . . How could anyone kill so savagely? These people are innocent!

All at once the chaos raging around her fell silent for a heartbeat's span of time. Except for the single sound of an infant's terrified shriek, piercing and alone.

"My God . . . !" Serena listened less than a moment. Before she could give herself time to think, she plunged beneath the wagon, crawling, scraping her way between the wheels, along the brush and rocky ground toward the back of it.

Briefly, she glanced out from underneath her shelter, desperately trying to make out a familiar horse, a face, a hat, anything to prove the identity of the attackers. But with the sun's crimson rays fading beyond the horizon leaving only traces of muted light muddied with the flurries of dust from the horses circling wildly around the wagon, kicking dirt in her eyes, she saw nothing and no one she recognized. Only black. Was it the black of the coming night or the black of the horses or the black shirt of a rider?

Her hand brushed skin. She clutched at it, felt for a pulse of life. Fought back her own tears when she felt nothing.

Like thick ebon fog, the darkness engulfed her, obscuring her sketchy view through the wagon spokes. The baby's cries came louder, shrill with panic. Darkness spread around her until she had no vision. Only hearing. Only the child.

She tasted fear, sharp and cold, smelled the blood and dust. It recalled past horrors—her parents' deaths, the graves behind the corral. And she heard her father's voice, calling out, pleading with her from a dark place in her mind.

Save yourself Serena! For God's sake, child, save your own life!

"No, Papa!" Serena shoved aside the words, the memories. "Not again," she spat muddy words into the earth. *It's no good to live while others die. I have to get there in time. I have to.*

Her skirts bunched and caught, slowing her, frustrating her to the brink of insanity. Beside her a horse reared and snorted; his hooves fell to the ground inches from her fingers, trembling the earth beneath her. She could no longer pick out the answering fire of Ephraim's rifle from the rage of gunfire.

Serena's nails bit into the ground as she pulled herself along like a dying animal toward the back of the wagon. There she could climb up and call to the people inside. At last she reached a spot under the belly of the wagon where she could grip the back end and hoist herself up enough to peer into it.

Eyes burning with sand and tears, she heard one bullet after another rip through the canvas above her. She spat onto her sleeve and rubbed at her eyes furiously. Shouts and cries, more like those of wild animals than humans slashed at her ears. Serena's stomach clenched in fists and knots.

She crawled up enough to call out. "Hurry," she panted. "You have to follow me under the wagon. We have to get back inside the walls."

Nothing but the baby's hysterical cries answered. She strained to see them. But she only saw the dark.

She called out again, louder, then finally, frantic, she

heaved herself inside. A warm wetness met her hands, and everywhere the pungent, sour smell of blood assaulted her senses. Her stomach lurched. She scavenged through the wagon toward the sound of the infant.

Her fingers grazed a limp arm, a warm cheek. Her head spun and her legs began to shake so violently she feared she would faint. But when her hand at last brushed the soft skin of an animal, then a woolen blanket and finally a baby's flailing fingers, a new surge of strength rushed through her.

She lunged out for the tiny, screaming person, snatched the infant up in her arms and backed out of the wagon. Only when her feet hit the ground behind her did she realize all the gunfire had stopped. Silence, a long, deadly silence took its place.

Serena didn't take time to look. She rushed headlong for the gates, the nearly weightless infant clutched to her chest.

"Pete! Pete!" she shouted, not realizing how faintly her plea rang out. Reaching the gates, she flung one look at where Ephraim had taken cover, long enough to see he was beyond needing the sanctuary of the gates. The horror of the killings nearly overwhelming her, she tugged at the door, desperate to pry it open.

Before she could move it, an arm caught her around the waist, capturing her in an iron grip.

"No!" Serena held the child tighter, her eyes closed against the horror she expected. "No, please. This child is innocent!"

"Serena! It's all right. It's me." His voice came to her, flooding her with relief so heady her legs buckled.

"Gage," she whispered. "You came back." Her eyes flew open in terror. "They're here again! They've killed—I can't ... I can't, not again."

"I know," Gage said, holding her, rocking her in his

embrace. "I know. They're gone now. You and the baby are safe."

"But—" Serena looked wildly around the yard. "There were so many. How could you . . . ?"

"I had a little help," he said, and Serena's thoughts flashed to the morning the Indians had appeared on the plateau, at the time she most needed rescuers.

"Pete?" she asked suddenly. "Where's Pete? And the others . . ."

"Pete's inside. The others—" He spared a grim glance at the chaotic scene behind them, then focused his attention back on her. "Let me help you. You're shaking so hard, you're going to drop him." Gently, he pried her fingers from her helpless bundle, cradling the infant with one arm while sweeping her against him with the other, half carrying her inside the ranch walls.

Whiskey Pete met them at the gates, Lucky Joe at his heels. "Git on in here, hurry now," he urged them, craning his neck to throw worried glances behind them. "I told you openin' the gates weren't a good idea, now didn't I? You never know when the tree devils are there. I cin feel 'em now, sure as I feel the cold air settlin' in fer the night."

Serena saw Gage cast him an odd look. But she was too tired and horror-stricken to attempt to interpret it. She slumped against him as he led her to the kitchen and carefully lowered her into a chair.

When she was settled, he lifted the child in his arms for a better look. "Either your ma or your pa must have had the biggest blue eyes on earth, that's for certain," he murmured softly to the whimpering infant. "What are you, besides soaking wet? Boy or girl?" He unwrapped the bundle down to its soggy diaper, then spread a blanket on the table top to lay the baby on.

"A boy," Serena said under her breath as she watched

him. "Six, maybe seven months. Still suckling his mama, I'd guess."

Gage cocked his head and stared openly at Serena.

Serena crossed her arms over her breasts. "Don't look at me!"

"Well, I sure as hell can't feed it."

Uncomfortable, not knowing where else to turn, they both stared at Whiskey Pete. Hovering at their side, Lucky Joe panting at his knee, he stared back, first at Serena, then at Gate. "Now wait just one fine minute, both of you. Why are the pair of you lookin' at me? I ain't no wet nurse!"

Serena managed a weak laugh. "No, but that's what we need. I don't think this one's even old enough to eat gruel. And he's probably nursing several times a day. We've got to think of something or he won't last long, not long enough to find a wet nurse out here."

Gage took the baby's tiny hand between his forefinger and thumb. "I'm sure one of the Paiute women would nurse him, but we can't risk taking him to the camp tonight."

"I'll see what I can fix up," Serena said, gripping the edges of the table for support as she struggled to stand on wobbly legs. "Will you watch him?"

Gage looked from the child to her. "You sit here with him and I'll do it. Tell me what to do."

Serena felt uncomfortable. Babies had always made her anxious. They were so helpless, so utterly dependent, so needy. And though she desperately wanted this one to survive, she couldn't imagine herself caring for it day and night. She had so many other things to do—the ranch, her future. . . . The baby began to sniffle, then cry again, this time without the hysteria; a sad, lonely cry.

Before she realized what she was doing, she found herself whispering softly to him, leaning over to brush his cheek, pushing aside the wet diaper. "Pete, bring me something, a soft cloth to replace this, will you?" she asked, handing him the dirty diaper.

Whiskey Pete held it by two fingers as far as possible from his nose. "C'mon boy," he said to Lucky Joe. "Let's burn this thing."

"No!" Serena and Gage said in unison. They glanced to each other.

"Just soak it," Serena said. "We'll be needing it. And lots more of them. Tonight."

"Last thing we'll be needin', or that youngin' either, I'd say," Whiskey Pete grumbled as he stumped out of the kitchen.

"What now?" Gage asked, moving to the stove.

"Well, let's try boiling some milk with a few spoonfuls of cornmeal and a little sugar in it. When it cools, then we can try forcing it through some cheesecloth." She pressed the baby to her breast and patted his back. He cried still, but it was a plea, too weak to be a demand. "I saw one of the Mormon women do that once with an elderly man who was too ill to eat. Maybe this little one will be hungry enough to try to eat any way he can. Let's just hope he's old enough to catch on."

Nodding, Gage fetched milk from the spring house, and added meal and sugar according to Serena's directions. As he stirred the concoction, he watched her pace the kitchen, talking softly, soothing the orphaned boy.

Libby's boys were long past babyhood by the time he'd taken responsibility for her and her family. He'd missed that stage entirely. And gratefully, he'd thought, until this very moment. But as he watched Serena, her whole body seemed to wrap around the child, protectively, her hair falling from one shoulder, then the other as she bent to press her face to his, her voice soft and melodious as a spring wind; this was all that was female, all that was grace and beauty and woman, wrapped in one simple exchange of love; one selfless embrace.

Gage's heart clenched, aching with the pain of longing, of deprivation, of that love he'd never known, the sense of family he'd only tasted. And all he could do was stare.

Sensing his eyes on her, Serena looked up from the child to Gage. How good it felt to see him there watching her this way. Despite the horrors of the past hours, days, years, she felt safe with him near. Whether fighting off her attackers, pursuing justice for a family that was never his, or taking on so simple a task as stirring meal and milk for an orphaned child, he did it with a strength and conviction that never faltered. He gave without question, unselfishly. It was a trait she once would have scorned as foolish, a hindrance to surviving the cruel realities of life. Now, it was a part of what made Gage Tanner both a temptation and a desire.

With him here, the stark little kitchen no longer felt cold and empty. It felt warm. It smelled like milk and babies. It felt like a home. And the three of them, in that odd, tragic moment, seemed to make a family.

"What're you tryin' to do now?" Whiskey Pete's graveled voice came between them as he clomped back into the room, straight to the stove. "Burn the place down so they don't have t' shoot us out?"

"What?" Gage stared dumbly at him, then to the pan on the stove. "The milk. I—I forgot."

Serena glanced down to the baby's creamy, round face. "He's fallen asleep. Let's let him rest a while then we'll try."

"If you say so." Gage took the pan off the burner.

"We should call him something," Serena mused, tenderly rocking the infant back and forth. When Gage raised a brow, she added defensively, "Well, we can't just keep saying him or it."

"Why not?" Pete asked, his head cocked to one side. "You know somethin' better?"

Thinking it over for a moment, Serena looked up at Gage. "Nathan."

"Nathan?"

"My father told me once, it means gift." She glanced back down at the baby, then to him again. "I think it's appropriate."

"In more ways than one," Gage agreed. "Nathan. It's a good, strong name. All right, Nathan it is."

Serena smiled at him and received a brief twist of his mouth in return.

"I'll leave you to it," he said. "I'm going out front. I want to take a look around. Pete, get the shovels." His voice became leaden. "We've got graves to dig."

"Do you have to—now?" Serena said, searching his eyes for some hint of his feelings. "It won't be easy, after . . ."

"Nothing is out here," Gage said roughly. "It has to be done."

"But . . . what if they're still out there? Waiting? They could get inside—"

"They won't. They're gone. For now."

Serena shivered a little. "It must have been Birk or at least some of his men. They were like that—before. Ruthless. Ready to kill."

Gage said nothing, his face expressionless.

"Who else could it be?" she persisted, not understanding his reluctance to condemn the ranchers. "They hate Mormons. Who has a better reason to attack us?"

"I don't know."

Whiskey Pete shook his head. "Devils. They're the ones that has done it. Come and go like the night."

Gage stopped midway in his stride toward the door-way. "Did you see them?"

"Sure I did. Same as before. Devils of darkness."

Serena rolled her eyes. But Gage didn't share her annoyance. He was looking at Pete intently, one hand flexing and unflexing at his side. "Go on. What did you see?"

"Up in the trees," Whiskey Pete said, his voice drop-ping to nearly a whisper. He shot a wide-eyed glance around the room. "They watch, they watch 'til they know you ain't lookin', then they come down like a hawk after a rabbit."

"And then they disappear like a spirit in the wind." Serena shook her head. "I for one have had enough for tonight. I'm going to find something to use for a crib." She stopped abruptly. "You won't leave us to go after them, will you?"

"Try one of the dresser drawers," Gage said, not looking at her. "No. I won't leave you tonight. I—can't chance leaving you two." Moving swiftly, he and Pete walked out.

Serena took his suggestion and tucked the exhausted baby into a drawer atop a cushion of clean sheets, tuck-ing a thick woolen blanket around his tiny form. For some time she sat at his side, watching him sleep, checking anxiously every few minutes for a heart-beat, for breath. She'd never realized babies slept so soundly. All she recalled of infants from her years with the Mormons was noise, noise, and more noise. This was a different side. A disconcertingly pleasant side.

She pressed a hand to her face. Lord, what could she be thinking! Just keeping herself alive was a challenging enough task without the added burden of a helpless child to worry over. She needed help badly enough al-ready. A small sound came from the innocent face at her fingertips as Nathan squirmed a little to his side, sucking at his fist.

Then again, she mused, with a child, Gage couldn't turn down her request for help. Could he? He hadn't turned Libby away. He had never turned away those in need. And, after all, what could be more needy than a woman and child alone against a hostile land?

She cared for him, with a depth and breadth she had only begun to explore. His strength and instinct to protect and defend, his unwavering sense of justice, the passion she felt in him when he looked at her, touched her, the tenderness she glimpsed when he held Nathan—they made the idea of making him part of her life the only answer, the right answer to her questions. And the only answer to the emptiness in her heart.

Besides, she reasoned, reaching for logic to defend the choices her heart wanted to make, the child needed a mother. What if the Paiute refused him because he was white? She couldn't believe they had any love for the race that took their land, why should they come to the aid of an enemy?

And, stronger than any other logic she could muster, was the haunting feeling she owed this child her protection, a home. Her selfish refusal to let his Mormon family inside the gates immediately had cost their lives and very nearly his. Gage's help or not, she felt an obligation to care for Nathan, to make sure he survived. That had to be her gift to him.

Serena mulled over her plan while the infant slept. A few hours later it awoke with a squall, and she tried feeding him the thin gruel, using the cheesecloth as a makeshift nipple. It was messy and Nathan spit out all but a few bites she managed to coax between his pursed lips when he opened them to scream at her. After an exhausting hour's attempt to feed him more than a dozen mouthfuls, he drifted off again, his face scrunched in a fretful sleep.

This time Serena, after tucking him in, found she felt suffocated by his demands, frustrated by her failure to meet them. And she couldn't wrest her thoughts from Gage, digging new graves beside those of his family, alone with his tormented thoughts and feelings. Certain the baby was safe and secure in his makeshift crib, she crept outside the gates, locking them behind her to check on Whiskey Pete and Gage.

She found them behind the horse corral, digging the last of the graves. "I'll help Gage with this if you'll go in and stay with Nathan for a little while," Serena told Pete. "Don't worry about falling sleep. He'll wake you when he's ready, believe me."

"Go back inside, Serena," Gage said tersely, tossing a shovelful of hard earth aside. "You don't belong here."

"My back is achin' a little—" Whiskey Pete put in.

"You mean your throat."

"Well, now that you say it, I bin at this for a long spell. I'm feelin' a bit dry."

"It's all right," Serena said, touching a hand to Gage's shoulder. "I need to be here. With you. Just for a short time."

Gage stared at her a long moment, then nodded at Pete. "Don't leave that baby or you'll have me to answer to."

"No sir, I won't," Pete said with undisguised glee, and handed the shovel to Serena. "I won't do that. I'll be layin' right next to the youngin'. Long as it takes. You just take yer time."

With shaky hands Serena took the shovel from him. "I'll go back in and check on him soon," she said as Pete loped off toward the ranch house. "I need a little air, that's all."

Gage wiped his face with a rumpled bandanna, shooting her a mocking glance. "I don't think digging graves is going to leave you very refreshed."

"I suppose not," she said quietly, reaching out to gently grasp his arm. "But I wanted to be here with you. This must hurt, to do it again, so soon after—"

He stared off into the distant night, his face a model of stone. "After burying Libby, her sister, and the boys. It never ends. I've done this a thousand times in my dreams."

Serena stayed quiet, not knowing what to say, respecting his silence. Finally, gathering her courage, she gave his arm a final squeeze, then gripped the shovel and plunged it into the ground. "Well, we should finish this. Maybe then at least part of this nightmare will be over."

They worked side by side beneath the shelter of trees that surrounded the site, the only light to guide their work a sketchy scattering of starlight filtering through the branches above.

When they were done, Serena set her shovel against a tree and looked at the newly turned earth, and the graves Gage had dug only weeks past. Thirteen of them, only twelve sheltering the dead. She shivered, suddenly cold. "This is where you buried yourself."

Tossing his shovel aside, Gage looked down at the graves. "When I first found them all I wanted was to chase down the damned bastards who killed them. I looked for evidence then, like I did tonight while you were with Nathan, anything I could follow. But in the dark, I only found that they scattered in all directions. The day Libby died, the killers' tracks were erased by a dust storm. My death was the only way to lure them back here to finish what they started. With me."

"I understand now why you had to 'die.' I felt—I

should have been dead too when my parents died," Serena confessed haltingly. "I wished over and over and over I hadn't run. Then today, when . . . when it all started and I could have run. . . . I felt like I'd been given another chance."

"What do you mean?"

Serena turned from him and wandered a few feet away. "I mean I didn't want to run away. To save myself. When I heard that baby cry—" Tears stung her eyes. "I felt that if I survived and he died, nothing would have any meaning. I just wanted him to live."

Gage strode over to her, lifting her chin with his fingertips, gently raising her face to his. "Now you know how I feel. I didn't save them. They would be alive today, if I hadn't—"

A fierce, unexpected anger swelled up from deep inside Serena. She took his face between her hands, forcing him to see the fire in her eyes. "No, it's not the same! You came back too late. There was nothing you could have done. I could have stayed. I saw the whole thing, I could have stayed. But I ran to save myself. You would never do that. Never!"

"You were a child, Serena. What could you have done? You did the right thing then; you saved a life."

She fell against his chest, burying her face in his soft shirt. "My life. And if it was so right, then why doesn't it *feel* right? I'll never forgive myself. Especially now."

Gage wrapped his arms around her and rocked her against him. "Now? That baby is alive because of you. You risked your life for him."

"If I hadn't lied about who I was, if I had told the truth about the massacre of your family, those pilgrims might not have come here today. Someone might have warned them. If I had just let them in the gates and not stood outside trying to 'send them away. I was afraid, afraid of not being safe any more . . ."

"Serena, they've known about the danger for months. Murders aren't uncommon in this territory. And they know the law, they know the settlers here are trying to purge Arizona of Mormons. You can't take the blame for what happened."

Serena pulled back and looked up at him. Gage brushed the tears from her eyes with his thumb, a softness in his eyes she hadn't seen before. "You do. All of your what ifs and I should haves that might have saved your adopted family. What if the same killers shot those people today. Is that any different?"

"Maybe." He let go a long breath. "If only I'd seen them today. I was in the hills beyond the canyon nearest the ranch with Kwion. I found a new cluster of bushes he uses in his medicines, and I was just showing him where they were when I heard gunfire . . . By the time I got to the ranch, it was too late. Again. They'd come and gone with no traces but the blood of innocent pilgrims."

The hollow timbre of his voice made Serena cling to him, desperately, furiously, pulling closer, tighter, taking, giving all she could from the emotions they shared. No other man, no one else could ever fill the dark places inside her with warmth and light the way he could. She felt lost without him, always afraid, never whole. "Neither can I," she whispered. "I need you. I need you to be with me."

"Serena . . ." Gage brushed a kiss across her brow. She looked at him, all of the losses they'd shared written in her sad eyes, and he kissed her, long and deep and slow. It was a caress, a healing balm; she melted into him, became part of him, matching his hunger, his longing, the aching want in him.

"Stay with me," she moaned softly. "Please don't leave me."

Gage swept her closer still, kissing her cheeks, her neck, her shoulders, tasting the sweet escape of her. Her indomitable will, her spirit, the soft surrender of her body chipped at his resolve to stay aloof, never to care. "I don't want to leave you."

"Then stay. It's so simple. This is right." She returned his kisses, almost frantic in her need to make him believe. "This is right. We need each other. I can help you. I want to help you find them. I want the killing to stop. Now it's my revenge too. You can't tell me it isn't."

"No . . ." Gage rubbed his hands over her back, pausing to caress the small cleft at the base of her spine with his fingertips. "But you're asking me to—" He broke away and paced a few feet from her. "You're alone," he said, more to himself than to her. "With a child to care for. You won't be able to keep up the ranch. It won't work. I can't—"

"I can," Serena said firmly. "I won't leave. We can help each other or I'll do it myself."

Raking a hand through his hair, Gage turned on her with a mixed expression of irritation and admiration. "Has anyone ever told you how damned stubborn you are, woman?"

Serena walked over to him and, standing on her tiptoes, brushed a kiss on his lips. "You. A thousand times. And besides, where else would I go that could be safer? You came to my rescue again tonight, I know you did. You always come back for me."

"Against my better judgment," Gage growled low. "And there isn't anywhere I can send you that would be safer. Not a woman and baby alone. You wouldn't last a week."

"Exactly."

"Then—"

"—we're in this together, like it or not."

"I don't."

"You will," Serena said softly, wrapping her arms around him again, bringing him to her, oblivious to all but the fever of their mutual need, the giddy triumph she felt in having kept him near. For now, at least for now.

She heard leaves rustle overhead in a wisp of breeze, but discounted the noise as common. Until the sound of the wind became rhythmic, discordant, but somehow musical. And she opened her eyes.

A group of men on foot encircled them. Serena's heart gave a painful leap. "They're . . . they're—"

"Paiute," Gage finished for her, his voice strangely calm.

"But—what do they want?" She passed a hand over her eyes, wondering if she were imagining it all. It seemed too unreal, too impossible to be anything other than a midnight vision. Except Gage treated it as if it were nothing more unusual than the stars overhead. "Why are they here?" she asked, trying to ignore the strange, haunting song they chanted in unison.

"They've been here all along. They helped me even the odds earlier. And now—they've stayed to share our sorrow. To help our dead pass to the next world."

In a far corner of her mind, Serena recognized the ageless face of one of the men from the night she'd spent in Gage's cliff dwelling. He made his way to the center of the circle around them, moving with the slowness of time. In his left hand he held an eagle feather, in his right a white cloth. The others closed in around the three in the center, beginning to pound out a dance around them, singing in time with each step, their

MORE PASSION AND ADVENTURE AWAIT... YOUR TRIP TO A BIG ADVENTUROUS WORLD BEGINS WHEN YOU ACCEPT YOUR FIRST 4 NOVELS ABSOLUTELY *FREE* (AN $18.00 VALUE)

Accept your Free gift and start to experience more of the passion and adventure you like in a historical romance novel. Each Zebra novel is filled with proud men, spirited women and tempestuous love that you'll remember long after you turn the last page.

Zebra Historical Romances are the finest novels of their kind. They are written by authors who really know how to weave tales of romance and adventure in the historical settings you love. You'll feel like you've actually gone back in time with the thrilling stories that each Zebra novel offers.

GET YOUR FREE GIFT WITH THE START OF YOUR HOME SUBSCRIPTION

Our readers tell us that these books sell out very fast in book stores and often they miss the newest titles. So Zebra has made arrangements for you to receive the four newest novels published each month.

You'll be guaranteed that you'll never miss a title, and home delivery is so convenient. And to show you just how easy it is to get Zebra Historical Romances, we'll send you your first 4 books absolutely FREE! Our gift to you just for trying our home subscription service.

BIG SAVINGS AND FREE HOME DELIVERY

Each month, you'll receive the four newest titles as soon as they are published. You'll probably receive them even before the bookstores do. What's more, you may preview these exciting novels free for 10 days. If you like them as much as we think you will, just pay the low preferred subscriber's price of just $3.75 each. *You'll save $3.00 each month off the publisher's price.* AND, your savings are even greater because there are never any shipping, handling or other hidden charges—FREE Home Delivery. Of course you can return any shipment within 10 days for full credit, no questions asked. There is no minimum number of books you must buy.

4 FREE BOOKS

TO GET YOUR 4 FREE BOOKS WORTH $18.00 — MAIL IN THE FREE BOOK CERTIFICATE T O D A Y

Fill in the Free Book Certificate below, and we'll send your FREE BOOKS to you as soon as we receive it.

If the certificate is missing below, write to: Zebra Home Subscription Service, Inc., P.O. Box 5214, 120 Brighton Road, Clifton, New Jersey 07015-5214.

GET
FOUR
FREE
BOOKS

(AN $18.00 VALUE)

rhythm increasing with the pace and volume of their song.

Serena found herself becoming slowly entranced by the hypnotic movements of feather and cloth. The world around her with all of the day's anguish, the pain of her past, of the sorrow she shared with Gage over his family's deaths, the lives lost today, seemed to fade further and further into the background like the last pink streaks of daylight before dusk. "It can't be real. It can't be . . ."

The old man moved close to her, and though one part of her longed to flee, her feet refused to budge despite her mind's ardent plea to move away. He stood so near she could trace every deep crevice in his leathery skin. His black eyes bore into hers, holding her an unwilling captive to the strange, frightening power he emanated.

Looking intensely at her face, he whirled the feather and handkerchief rapidly in front of her eyes, moving in communion with the dancers at the same time, never flinching his constant focus on her.

"Hu! Hu! Hu!" he exclaimed over and over like the rapid beat of a drum, low and pounding in her mind.

She felt Gage holding her firmly by her shoulders. Did he sense the strength draining from her into the ground beneath them? Did he feel it too? It was as though every pour in her skin had opened to release her pain, drop by drop, like bad blood. The anguish poured forth from her back into nature's waiting pool.

Older now than time, the man waved his hands before her face, fanning her with a spirit's breath, drawing his hand slowly, deliberately from the level of her eyes away to one side, then upward into the air. Unconsciously, she followed his every movement, her gaze belonging to him.

Somewhere behind her, all around her, she remained

vaguely aware the song and dance continued on and on without pause.

"Gage—" she heard the sound of her own voice.

"Give yourself up to it, Serena, don't be afraid. Let it take you away from this. Tonight. Now. We'll go together."

Serena blinked, her eyes suddenly burning, her vision blurred. Was the thick mist in the air smoke? Was it her imagination? "Such a strange, sweet smell . . ."

"It's all right. I'm here with you."

She heard Gage's soothing voice, then the repeated words of the dancers, and the old Indian, "Hu! Hu! Hu!" But the voices melded together; Gage's, the others, her own.

She heard herself repeat words she didn't understand in a slurred, almost drunken fashion. Her knees turned to water, her head began to float. She drifted beyond, away, to a place of safety and beauty, softness and light. A cloud high above the troubled earth. She didn't realize her body existed until she staggered against Gage's hard chest.

"Give yourself to it," he murmured close beside her. "Stay here with me. This is one place we can always be together."

She had no choice left but to yield, to him, to the ancient one, to the song. Her will flew away on the wings of night owls. The old man held her transfixed by his movements. Her body began to sway, then slowly turn, out of Gage's arms and into the center of the circle.

She merged with the other shadowy figures whirling there. She spun and twirled with them, apart from them, next to them, one with them, yet alone with her own spirit and the spirits of her dead loved ones. Faster and faster they danced, lost in their solitude, yet not alone. Never, never alone.

They swooped and spun, wilder and more furiously, dancing out the pain and anger, the regrets and desires unfulfilled, possessed by the music, the throbbing beat of their own feet and voices.

She gave way completely to her body's whims, for in the dance was freedom, peace, blessed escape. Again and again Gage's face flashed before her, beautiful, serene. His lips formed the words of the song, though now her ears heard only the music of a night wind.

She sang with the starlings at dawn, bayed with the wolves beneath the stars at midnight. She became the ripples in a bubbling brook, a fallen leaf caught by the autumn winds, a cluster of cool moss hidden in a canyon crevice. She was all and she was nothing.

And then she was not.

Chapter Ten

As she watched him approach, a bewitching sense of unreality swept over Serena, taking her mind back to those first mysterious encounters with Gage. Traveling the edge of the heat devil, the horse and rider seemed to skim the earth as they moved through the shimmering air, the dust shifting and swirling up behind them in a golden-brown cloud. She lifted her hand to shade her eyes against the sun's glare, watching him come to her. Hot wind flattened the thin cotton of her dress against her body. It wailed a weak song off into the Vermillion Cliffs, a song no one else heard, reminding her how alone she was.

He never came in the full light of day. Yet at a distance, the image of a spirit rider visited Serena so strongly, she half-believed she'd finally succumbed to madness and had truly resurrected Gage Tanner from the heat and wind and rock and the lone cry of a restless wolf.

She stood by the chicken coop, unable to move or react, waiting, her breath trapped, her heart racing.

When the rider neared enough for her to see color and detail, Serena let go her breath in a long, ragged sigh. The white face of the palomino and the wide-brimmed hat introduced a man other than the one she hoped to see. Ross Brady slowed, then stopped his horse a few feet short of the front gates.

"Afternoon," he said, slowly swinging out of the saddle. The large shadow cast by his hat left half his face in darkness.

"Good afternoon," Serena answered, still trying to shake free of the lingering disorientation. After the otherworldly events of last night, waking up to apparent normalcy this morning, then seeing a haunting reflection of the Spirit in the Wind on the horizon, she struggled to ground herself in reality again. Except what was real? If she hadn't awakened to Nathan's coos and gurgles, seen him in the morning light, all of it might have seemed a dream—or nightmare.

If Ross noticed her strange silence, he said nothing. "I was on my way to the post, and I promised Mandy the next time I was out your way, I'd stop in and deliver a message for her." He turned his head a little, his gaze sliding quickly around them. "She said to tell you your supplies are in."

"My supplies . . . yes—yes thank you." Dragging a hand over her face, Serena forced herself to concentrate. "I'm sorry, I—I'm not thinking clearly. We had some trouble, last night . . ." She glanced vaguely across the yard to the gates, finding it hard to believe herself. The ranch looked exactly as it had yesterday morning and the morning before.

"Trouble?" Ross moved a step closer and Serena could feel his eyes on her. Startled out of its roost, a chicken flew out of one of the stalls behind them, its wings clumsily beating the air. The palomino snorted, pawing nervously at the dirt. "What kind of trouble?"

Briefly, keeping at bay the memories of fear and horror, she told him, mentioning Nathan, but deliberately leaving out Gage's part in coming to her aid.

When she'd finished, Ross pushed his hat up a little, eyeing her up and down. "Tragedy," he said shaking his head. "You seem to have come out of it all right, though. Must've been quite a job, shootin' off what—five, six men?—then buryin' four dead."

"Pete helped me," Serena said cooly. "And I don't care whether you believe me or not, Mister Brady. It happened."

"Didn't say otherwise. Have any idea who did it?"

Frustration and leftover fear spilled over into Serena's voice. "I wish more than anything in this world right now that I did. But it was dark. And with all of the sudden commotion, the gunfire, the damned horses and dust. It all happened in a few short minutes. Lives ended, just like that. And the killers—they seemed to come from nowhere, then vanish back to nowhere."

"Funny thing though," Ross went on, heedless of her outburst. "They kill four Mormons and miss the chance to take the ranch. Wouldn't have been too hard, seein' as you were outnumbered and the gates were open."

"That's what—" *That's what Gage said.* Serena sucked back the words on a sharply drawn breath. A prickling sensation crawled up her neck. She resisted the sudden urge to look around. Was he was out there, watching her now? "That's what my uncle said," she finished quickly to cover her near slip. "Something must have scared them off."

"The Spirit in the Wind, maybe."

She started, her eyes widening before she caught herself. "I don't believe in that nonsense."

"Don't you?" Ross shrugged. "A lot of folks do.

You're lucky you're not the superstitious kind. Bein' out here alone . . . it can play with a person's mind."

"Can it?" Outwardly, Serena tried to sound unconcerned. But her eyes strayed to the plateau outlined on the horizon beyond Ross. If she looked hard enough, she could almost see Gage, watching her from somewhere atop the sheerest point of the cliff. The wind curled around her and she felt him, his hands embracing her under the midnight shadow of Heaven's Window, his breath on her neck.

"What does Pete think?"

"Pete . . . ?" Serena's gaze gradually focused again on Ross's face. "About—?"

"The shooting."

"Very little that makes sense . . . rustlers maybe, outlaws. I thought at first it was Reed's bunch. But he wouldn't have left. Not when he could have gotten inside."

"I agree. But that leaves you with outlaws who kill Mormons and leave water behind." He was looking away from her, toward the slope where she and Gage had buried the Mormons beside the graves of his family.

For the first time, Serena studied him closely. His voice was slow and thoughtful; he stood stiffly, one hand straying to rest on the saddle sheath that held his rifle. "If it wasn't Birk or his cowboys, then it had to be outlaws. Didn't it?"

"There are all sorts of outlaws," Ross said, almost under his breath. Without an explanation, he started walking toward the slope.

Without hesitation, Serena followed. She didn't know what to make of Ross Brady, but she had a half-formed feeling he was probing for a clue she had, whether she knew it or not. Did he know more than he was saying? If so, how could she make him tell her? Somehow, with

Nathan here only a few short hours, finding out who was responsible for the killings seemed all that mattered any more.

She caught up with Ross at the edge of the grave sites. He stood staring down at the newly turned earth, his face creased in thought.

"You knew them, didn't you? Gage Tanner and his adopted family, I mean," she said when he quickly glanced up at her.

"Most folks 'round here did."

"It was horrible, the massacre." She looked once at the graves, seeing the faces that asked her for sanctuary yesterday. Shutting her eyes to the vision, she turned away. "It's hard, to survive here, let alone with children." Glancing back at the ranch house, she thought of Nathan sleeping in the makeshift cradle by her bed, a small life so resilient, yet so fragile. "They must have been close to each other."

Ross eyed her curiously. "That might have come. Later. In the beginning, they were together because Gage made Libby, her sister, and her sons his responsibility. He thought he owed his friend Jon, and instead of makin' sure his widow was provided for then movin' on like most men would've done, he devoted himself to her and her family." He shook his head, frowning at the horizon.

"I thought—" Serena stopped, biting at her lower lip. "I assumed he intended to marry her."

"No. Gage never settled on a life of his own so he kept borrowin' from other people who needed him for a time. When they no longer needed him, he moved on, owing no one, owning nothing."

"You sound as if you knew him well."

Ross' gaze rested for a long moment on the horizon. Serena fidgeted with the folds of her skirts. She opened her mouth to break the silence, stopped. A gust of wind slammed closed the gate to the chicken coop and she jumped.

Ross made an abrupt motion, as if shaking off some uneasy burden. He turned and looked down at the grave marked with Gage's name, then to Serena. "Maybe he still can't stop gettin' tangled up with people who ought to be solvin' their own problems."

"You make it seem like he's still here."

"Some say he is. Especially women who know he's a soft touch for a bird with a broken wing," he said pointedly.

"Meaning me, I suppose. I've managed well enough on my own so far. And I don't think a ghost would be much use to me in rebuilding the ranch," she added half mocking, half challenging. She'd begun to wonder how much he knew about Gage's odd, shadowy existence. Enough to know he was still alive?

"I'd give that idea some extra thought," Ross said, starting to walk back toward his horse. "You got to have more crust than an armadillo to survive out here, especially with a baby on your hands. But you also got to be willin' to unbend enough to help out when it's needed. No tellin' when you might need to call on help in return."

"I can take care of myself."

"We all got somethin' we can't take care of. Admitting it is the best way to stay alive." Reaching his palomino, he took up the reins and nudged the horse around so he could fit his boot into the stirrup and heft himself into the saddle. "And I'd keep in mind not everyone shares your notion to settle in one spot. When a man's born to wanderin', he keeps wanderin', even after the grass is wavin' over him."

With a tug of his hat, Ross wheeled the palomino

around and into a canter over the plain in the direction of the plateau.

Serena stared after him, trying to decide if he'd come to warn her away from the ranch. Or away from Gage Tanner.

Ross guided the palomino's path at an angle away from the ranch, keeping one eye on Serena. She looked after him for several moments, then turned and walked back inside the gates. He waited until they closed behind her before turning his horse back in the direction of the ranch, riding the ridge next to the cattle corral.

Circling behind the stables, he walked the palomino to the back of a rocky outcropping. As he entered the shadow of the cliffs, Gage stepped into his path. Ross' horse skidded to a stop, rearing back a little.

"The way you come and go, you deserve the reputation I give you in all my storytellin'," Ross said, climbing down from the saddle. He looked at Gage's face, haggard from lack of sleep, set with cold determination. "You're lookin' more and more like a ghost every day. I take it you been here since last night."

"Last night . . ." Old memories, new fears haunted his expression. "How did you know?"

"I could feel your eyes on me every time I turned around while I was talkin' to her." Ross propped his foot up on a rock, pushing his hat back. "You borrowed yourself some more trouble, friend. You plannin' on keeping it this time?"

Gage's quick tensing, the flick of hot emotion across his face, told Ross more than his words. "She won't leave. And there's the boy now."

"She mentioned him."

"Four more people are dead. If I don't stop it, I'll be digging two more graves."

"Or I'll be fillin' yours," Ross said bluntly. "They

say when a man sets out on revenge, he better first dig two graves."

"I've already done that." There was no humor in his mocking half smile.

"The lady told me you don't think last night was any of Birk's boys' doing."

"She told you—"

"Not in so many words. But I heard your name just the same."

For the first time Gage's straight stare wavered. Ross noticed it with a curious satisfaction. He'd been right. There was more to it than just finding out who was bent on killing anyone who stayed at the ranch. And damned if it didn't make everything more complicated.

"You got an idea who it was," Ross prodded, not asking.

"An idea. That's all. I'm going to spend a few days with the Paiute. They see more of the territory. They might have heard rumors."

"Maybe. I'll keep an ear open just the same." Straightening, he pulled his hat back down. "One more thing—if things at the ranch start lookin' better, Birk Reed won't be the only one askin' why."

"I know."

The terse answer surprised him. Ross stared at Gage for a moment. Suddenly he saw a flash of the conflict in Gage's eyes and understood. "It's a risk. Not just for you."

Gage nodded. "I want it done with. If my idea is right . . . Serena and Nathan can't end up like—"

Like Libby and her sons. There was nothing he could say to counter that. Nothing that would make any difference.

"You can back out of this now," Gage said, looking at him squarely.

"That I could," Ross returned. Walking to his horse, he picked up the palomino's reins and tossed them over the horse's neck before climbing back into the saddle. "But I won't. Hell'd be a spring house before you'd quit on me. So I'm returnin' the favor." He smiled grimly. "Let's just hope she doesn't end up buryin' the both of us."

Balancing the lantern carefully, Serena trudged down to the cattle stable, alternately cursing and asking herself why it should matter if Whiskey Pete missed another supper. He was crazy, and he would have some insane reason for spending the better part of the last three days at the stable. He wasn't worth risking her life to walk outside the gates at night! Cursing herself and the old coot with equal fury, she kept a steady pace to the stable door.

Serena had nearly convinced herself to ignore him. But after last night's killings, she couldn't shake the image of the Mormon party standing outside the gates in the gathering darkness, trusting her to lead them to safety inside the walls. If it meant threatening him with her own gun, she had to get him back inside.

She felt a surge of apprehension and a stronger pang of guilt leaving Nathan tucked in his bed, though he was warm, fed, and soundly asleep, inside the locked gates. But it was nearly fully dark now. And Pete, damn him, was still at the stable.

He met her at the stable door. Before she could say anything, he folded his arms over his skinny chest, and glared at her defiantly. "I ain't goin'."

"I didn't ask you to," Serena snapped. "I only came to see—"

"I ain't leavin' Deacon Mather."

"Deacon Mather?"

"He's ailin' and I ain't leavin' him."

"But—you shouldn't be outside the gates after dark. That's what you're always telling me," Serena pointed out. "He's only a bull—"

"Not to me." Pete's arms dropped to his side and his shoulders slumped. The blue of his eyes clouded over. "After the tree devils come and gone, Deacon Mather and Lucky Joe and Last Chance, they was the only ones left to listen to me. No one else wanted the lot of us. He didn't leave me; I ain't leavin' him."

Swallowing hard, Serena walked around Pete to Deacon Mather's stall. The bull lay on the stall floor, breathing heavily, his eyes dull and half-closed. She looked up from Deacon Mather to Pete. His eyes were fixed on his friend, worry mixed with despair on his face.

"What's wrong with him?" Serena asked, kneeling down by the bull's side, holding the lantern aloft to peer more closely at him.

"Don't know," Pete said mournfully. "He took sick 'bout three days back, actin' worn out and walkin' like he took too much whiskey. Since then, it's all I kin do to git him to take even water."

Serena stared at Deacon Mather, biting at her lower lip. She didn't know a damned thing about caring for animals, let alone nursing them. "Amanda might know," she murmured half to herself, "or one of the ranchers. But we can't go to Vulture Creek tonight . . ." She glanced quickly at Whiskey Pete. "Why don't you go get some supper? I left it for you on the stove. I'll stay with him while you eat and get a few hours' rest. You can check on Nathan for me, too." She held up a hand as he started to protest. "You won't do Deacon Mather any good if you get sick yourself. Tomorrow, I'll go to the trading post and maybe I can find someone who can tell us what's wrong with him."

The quick spurt of hope in Pete's eyes made her glad she'd offered to help. Nodding, he bent to Deacon Mather and gently patted the bull's massive head before leaving Serena alone in the stall.

Serena set the lantern on the stall railing, then sat down in the straw beside Deacon Mather again. The night seemed to be borne on the cooling air, drifting gently down to scatter over the desert. A soft breeze wafted through the open stable door bringing with it the attar of pine and grass, mingling with the smell of straw and cattle. Idly stroking her hand over Deacon Mather's smooth hair, she let the desert's evening chorus lull her into a sense of peace. The bull's massive head lolled, resting against her leg while she smoothed her hand up and down his neck and shoulder in a soothing caress.

She waited, listening, watching moths dance in and out of the nimbus of lamp fire. When a tall shadow melted into the pool of light, Serena slowly looked up, locking gazes with Gage, knowing before she saw his face he would come.

His intent stare probed inside her, searching. She met it fully. In that one look, deep in his eyes, Serena saw he belonged to the danger, mystery, and raw strength of the wilderness territory. She had determined to take part of that territory for herself, but only now was she beginning to understand the courage and tenacity it would take to hold onto it.

"You're making a bad habit of going outside the gates at night," Gage said at last, his voice low and rough.

He moved a few steps into the stall. The dim light stole the initial impression of otherworldliness from him, and Serena saw the lines of tension and exhaustion etched around his mouth and eyes. She put aside any cutting response and instead said quietly, "Pete gave me little choice but to come out after him."

"I would have thought after last night—" His hand flexed into a tight fist at his side.

"I survived. I always do." She turned to Deacon Mather. "Do you know anything about nursing bulls?" she asked, changing the subject. "I told Pete I would sit with Deacon Mather, but I'm not doing him much good. Pete says he's been sick for nearly three days. I don't know what's wrong with him. I thought you might."

Flicking her a scowl, Gage dropped down on one knee beside her, running deft hands over the bull, checking inside its mouth, pressing his ear to its chest. "It's loco disease," he said tersely, sitting back on his heels.

"Loco disease?"

"Livestock get it from eating locoweed with the browse. It's poison. He didn't get a lot of it, or he'd be dead by now. But a little's enough to partly paralyze a full-grown bull."

Serena was surprised at the painful worry that stabbed at her. "There must be something you can do for him. He can't just die!" She touched a hand to Deacon Mather's face. "He's Pete's friend."

She looked up at Gage to find him staring at her with something close to wonder. "Woman," he said softly, "I'll never figure you out." He shook his head. "Wait here." Swiftly and silently, he stood up and left the stable, returning a short while later with a pail half-full of water and a handful of what looked to Serena like crushed leaves.

"Dandelion," he said in answer to her questioning glance. Setting down the bucket and leaves, he rolled up his sleeves and knelt back down. With a little water, he worked the leaves into a mash in the hollow of his palm. "It may help purge some of the poison. But I'll need your help. Can you do it?"

"Guide me," Serena said, adding with a mocking smile, "I'm not as helpless as I seem."

Gage said nothing, only rolled his eyes at her before turning to Deacon Mather.

Holding Deacon Mather's head in her lap, Serena watched with admiration as Gage skillfully coaxed the mash and several handfuls of water down the bull's throat. He talked soothingly to Deacon Mather the whole time, his hands gentle and sure. When he'd finally finished, he sat back, dragging his forearm across his sweat-dampened face.

"Will he be all right now?" Serena asked. Deacon Mather's head still rested in her lap and, if anything, the bull seemed stiller than before.

"Hard to say. There's nothing to do but wait it out. Come on—" Getting to his feet, Gage sluiced off his hands in the bucket, slid them down his thighs, then held out a hand to her. "He needs rest, and I need a drink."

Serena carefully lifted Deacon Mather's head and laid it on the straw before sliding her fingers into his. Gage drew her to her feet, dousing the lantern before he led her out into the cool evening. They walked to the ranch house and Serena let them inside the gates. She followed Gage to the oasis and sat down beside him at the edge of the silver pool to scoop up handfuls of water. Her thirst sated, Serena slanted a glance at Gage, her eyes following the flexing of muscle in his shoulders and arms under the shadowed light of the moon, the motion his hands made as he cupped the water and brought it to his mouth. He looked so serious, so focused on the task, just as he had when he was tending to Deacon Mather.

Then, it had inspired an appreciation of his knowledge and skill, the balance between his strength and tenderness. Now, it inspired her to mischief.

Plunging her hands into the water, she scooped up the largest handful she could and flung it at him, catching him squarely in the chest and face. He looked at her in total disbelief and Serena started to laugh.

"I'm sorry," she said, pressing a hand to her mouth in a vain attempt to stop the giggles. "B-but you looked so—so intent . . . I just couldn't resist." Giving in to the merriment bubbling up inside, she laughed up at him.

"I'm glad you find that funny," Gage said, shaking water from his face. He made a quick turn toward the pool and Serena caught the flash of devilment in his eyes a split second before he doused her with an enormous shower.

Gage laughed with her as Serena plucked at the wet cotton of her dress, scrunching her nose at him in mock affront. "I suppose I deserved that," she said, flicking droplets from her fingertips at him. Her face alive with delight in the game, she raised her arms to thread her fingers through her damp hair, combing errant strands from her neck and throat.

And suddenly for Gage, enchantment took the place of laughter.

The clouded moon bathed her in melted pearl, making her the image of his dreams. Catching his gaze, she slowly lowered her arms and smiled at him. It was at once bold and innocent, demanding and inviting, confident and uncertain. All the things that were Serena. All the things that made her the most provoking and irritating woman he'd ever known; the things that made her the most intriguing and captivating.

He leaned toward her, not knowing his intention until his mouth brushed hers. Then he knew only her.

The moment she lifted her hands to his shoulders and kissed him back without hesitation or qualm, demands of desire, of need, swept aside any thought to tenderly seduce her with his caress.

It felt like everything, all at once. So much promise, coupled with so many fears and questions. The best and the worst of everything he had ever felt, becoming something he had never felt. Something strong and hard, soft and forgiving, without boundaries or definition.

Serena fell into him, losing herself in the feeling that they were together, and would always be together. She tasted the wildness in his kiss, felt the strength in him that couldn't be moved by her demands or her pleas, only by surrendering part of herself.

She leaned closer, wanting to give, to take more, but Gage dragged his mouth from hers, pulling way. Resisting her attempt to move back into his embrace, he gently shackled her forearms, holding her from him, gazing into her eyes with an expression so intent and heated it stole her breath.

Serena searched for words and found only feelings. They defied language, could only be spoken through a touch.

Slowly, his eyes never leaving hers, Gage pushed her back until she lay beneath him. He slid his palms flat against her arms, brushing them up to cover hers, lacing their fingers together.

"I can't stop thinking about you," he said, his voice low and rough, the edges shaky. "You're always with me." His fingers tightened on hers. "I don't want it. It's impossible."

"I can't stop it," she echoed his thoughts before he spoke them. "No matter where I go, you're still here."

Watching her face, Gage grazed a kiss over her parted lips. Serena strained toward him, but he took an eternity, tasting the corner of her mouth, kissing first her upper lip, then the lower, savoring each motion. Finally, he kissed her fully, probing deeply, branding her soul with the mark of his possession.

When he moved his hands to pull her to his side, one palm cradling her face, Serena held to him like a fallen angel to a last chance at salvation. She would never feel this way again, she knew it would be impossible with anyone but Gage Tanner. Greedily, desperately, she ached to keep him always near her.

Pressed close to him, every sensation seemed vivid and magnified. She clutched at each one, stored it in her heart. The rise and fall of his chest with each breath he took; the cool dampness of his shirt clinging to warm flesh; the smell and the taste of him, familiar yet radiantly new.

Lost to her, Gage gave up trying to reason the feelings away. He slid his hand over her throat, to her shoulder, rocked by a tremor of urgency. In some far part of his mind, he heard the rip of cotton as he jerked down the shoulder of her dress. His mouth followed the path of his hand, pressing hot, fast kisses on her neck, her shoulder, the curve of her breast. Serena's fingers fumbled at his shirt, tugging free buttons until she could lay a trembling, caressing hand against his heart.

Part of him rebelled at the desperate, avid haste in which they touched each other. He should be loving her slowly, learning tenderness with time. But she seemed to share his feeling this was the first, the last, the only time they would have this moment. Tomorrow, danger or disagreement or simply the first light might steal it, and he would be left with only his emptiness and his obsession.

If it was impossible, if he was illusion, Serena decided she preferred midnight fantasy to the cold light of reality. Except Gage was no dream. Warm and hard where she touched him; the roughness of his hand a provocative contrast to the softness of her skin where he touched her. She ached, as if something coiled deep inside her, tighter and tighter. It made her moan softly when his fingers flirted at her waist, then grazed her breast, the thin cotton feeling painful on her sensitive skin.

"Serena . . ." Gage's voice whispered hotly in her ear. "Do you want this?" He pulled back enough to look at her squarely, leaving no room for hesitation. "Do you want me?" he whispered harshly.

The echoes of doubt and past hurts threaded in his voice stabbed straight at her heart. "Yes," she told him, drawing him close again. "Only this. Only you."

The truth of her words sent a shudder through her. She did want him. To stay with her, protect her, fill her with the wild, sweet feelings only his touch could evoke. There was no doubt in her. Only need, avid and urgent.

She spread her fingers over his bared chest, touching her lips to the ragged pulse in the hollow of his throat.

The surety of her response should have torn away all the barriers between them and left him free to love her without reservation. Instead, Gage felt his focus, his sense of balance, unraveling, coming dangerously close to chaos. He was being drawn in to someone else's life again, except this time, part of him wasn't content to give her what she needed and then move on. This time he wanted something for himself.

The feeling was so new it startled him with its intensity. He wanted to believe her, wanted to believe she did want him—not merely need him. But he couldn't afford to want, to need. It would only end like it had every other time. With him walking away, empty, leaving behind a piece of himself and taking nothing with him.

And if he allowed himself to care, and she ended up like Libby . . .

With a wrenching effort, Gage jerked himself out of Serena's embrace and to his feet. He took a few steps away from her then stopped, astonished to find himself shaking with reaction. It felt like something inside had torn away and left a raw wound.

Serena sat up, not trusting her voice, not looking at him. He wanted her, he didn't want her. She hated him, hated herself. She wanted to rage and scream at him to come back, to give her what she craved, to keep her safe. She wanted to cry until there were no more tears for a loss she couldn't name.

"Serena . . ."

Squeezing her eyes closed to stop the tears from spilling over, Serena got to her feet, trying to ignore his voice. She swallowed hard, her fingers fumbling blindly with the torn shoulder of her dress.

For Gage, the trembling of her lower lip and her hand nearly tipped the scale in favor of chaos and to hell with the consequences. He moved back within a hand's length of her, hesitated, then reached out a hand to her. Gently, he touched a fingertip to the single tear that slid down her face.

"I'm sorry," he said softly. "I can't give you what you want. Not now. Maybe not ever."

Very slowly, Serena lifted her eyes to his. "What do you want? What can I give you?" When he stayed silent, she shook her head impatiently. "You can't answer because you don't know. You never take anything for yourself, so you don't know."

Uncertainty chased across his face. In the dim moonlight, he looked ravaged, his shirt hanging open, a heavy lock of hair falling over his forehead, his eyes haunted. Seeing him, Serena knew, deep inside, he wasn't unmoved and she seized on the advantage.

Drawing in a shaky breath she swiped a tear from her cheek before staring him straight in the eye. "Let me tell you what I know. We belong together, Gage Tanner. Tell me it isn't true and I won't ask for anything from you again."

"Serena—"

"Give me your word it isn't true. Then I'll have to believe it, won't I?"

Gage stared at her for long minutes. Then, letting his breath go in a long sigh, he opened his mouth to tell her what she wanted to hear. What she didn't want to hear.

But before the words came, he stiffened, every muscle taut. Swiftly scanning the darkness around them, he suddenly grasped her arm, stepping up to shield her with his body.

"What is it?" Serena whispered, remembering the time in the courtyard Gage had known they were being watched. She looked from side to side, seeing nothing.

"Riders. Close."

The tenseness in his voice raced through her. She thought of last night's raid, knew he was thinking of it too. Her stomach clenched. They rushed up the stairs to the lookout. Serena peered out over the wall, expecting the worst.

She wasn't disappointed.

Below, in the front yard, at least a dozen horses formed a shadowy half circle, both riders and their mounts black, phantom figures.

Standing at her side, Gage glanced to Serena, his expression unreadable. He took her hand, holding hard. From the corner of her eye, Serena saw his free hand slide to the gun on his hip in a smooth, almost imperceptible motion.

She squeezed his hand tightly in return and lifted her chin, determined not to show the fear screaming inside.

As Serena looked up, the lead rider in the circle moved in their direction, slowly inexorably. And in the split second before she saw his face, her mind showed her a vivid image of the graves on the slope.

Chapter Eleven

Trembling, her hand gripped so tightly in Gage's she couldn't feel her fingers any longer, Serena held her breath as a horse and rider moved out of the shadow and into the revealing moonlight. A somber, fathomless face from her nightmares emerged from the gloom. His skin leathery, eyes ancient, a long mane of wispy hair shone like silvery light, as though made of the moon and stars above.

Indians. Serena swallowed the residual fear rising up in the back of her throat. She tried to calm herself with the remembrance of that face the night he came to help Gage and her bury the dead. Still, desperation, hunger, thirst might make them turn on Gage and her at any time.

Looking to Gage, she expected to him to stiffen with resistance, to be ready to take action to protect them if need be. Instead he relaxed, his hand slipping from his gun. "Damn," he muttered. "You scared me out of ten years of life, brother," he called down to the lead rider. Glancing over to Serena, he gave her a twisted half smile. "It's all right. Come on, let's go downstairs so we can talk to them without shouting."

"All right?" She gaped at him. "But what if . . . they're still—"

"Friends." Pulling her with him, Gage led her downstairs through the courtyard and outside to greet several men. They climbed down from their horses, stopping at the side of the lead rider. "I didn't expect you here, Kwion," Gage said to the old man. "Not at night."

"Night is the only time you live," Kwion said. He spoke to Gage, but his eyes rested on Serena. "We would not be welcome in the day."

"Not welcome?" Gage glanced back at Serena, a frown between his eyes.

"You fear us," Kwion said, still gazing directly at her. "And yet we have met before. In peace."

Acutely aware of Gage's intent scrutiny, Serena avoided looking at him. "Yes. But I do not know you, only those like you. My parents and all the people traveling with us were murdered by Indians whose camp they had passed by in peace. They came back later to our wagons to torture and burn and kill . . ." She stopped, putting a shaking hand to her mouth, feeling sick inside as the horrors of the past crowded in on her.

"It was not our people."

Serena heard the bite of offended pride in Kwion's voice. If he was a man of peace, she mused to herself, he had been inordinately patient with her accusations. "I want to believe you—" the words died on her lips as she wrestled inwardly with a flood of conflicting emotions. "But I can't forget."

Kwion slowly nodded. "I grieve with you. But you live too much with your ghosts and so you hate all because of a few." His gaze traveled slowly from Serena to Gage and back again. "There is no life for you in the past."

"I'm not living with the past. I'm making a future—here."

"This is your past. A past you returned to."

"How can you know anything of my past!" Serena said defiantly. "I came to this place for safety. It is secure—at least it was. It should have been." The rancor in her voice faded, replaced by bewilderment. She didn't owe him any explanation. What made her try to give him one? "Why won't you leave me alone?"

"Our people need your help." Kwion gestured behind him and the men at his back shifted the horses to open a path for others who herded forward a dozen cows and a steer. "We bring you these in trade for use of the oasis again. Your herd is even smaller than ours, and our animals, our people, will die without the water. Will you trade for this?"

Serena hesitated, her eyes of their own volition sliding to Gage. The expression on his face made her wince.

"Are you saying—" he began. He raked a hand through his hair, staring at her with a mixture of disbelief and anger. "Are you saying you've turned them away from the water?"

"I was afraid!"

"Afraid of what? Of sharing?"

"Of—of them! You can't expect me to just forget what happened. Especially now, with Nathan here!"

"The Paiute didn't kill your parents," Gage said harshly. "Saying you hate them is like saying you hate cows because you got kicked by a horse once. It doesn't make any sense."

"Not to you! You weren't there. You didn't see—" Serena stopped, catching her breath on a sob.

A light flickered in Kwion's eyes before he spoke. "I

understand," Kwion said quietly, his richly-textured voice coming between them.

"No!" Serena closed her eyes, steadying herself. When she opened them again, she met Kwion's expressionless gaze with a level one of her own. "No," she said firmly. "I accept the trade. I need the stock and you need the water. There is a dry pool outside near the horse corral. I've kept the pipe that feeds it closed. We have so few animals to water, we simply let them come into the courtyard to drink from the oasis. But I'll open the gate so the spring will feed the outer pool. You can bring your animals to drink from the water there until you find another watering hole."

Not giving him time to reply, she whipped around and rushed through the gates into the haven of the ranch house, not allowing the tears to fall until she was hidden behind her barriers to the world outside.

Gage watched her leave without making a move to stop her. He didn't trust anything he felt toward her now, not the anger, nor the frustration, nor the poignant empathy that made him want to take her in his arms and offer her his comfort. All of it and none of it made sense.

Standing near, Kwion said nothing, simply waited in silence. The other men prodded the cattle into the nearest corral. "Perhaps you should go to her," Kwion said at last.

"No ..." Gage flexed and unflexed a hand at his side. "No. I need to speak with you."

"Yes. But now is not the time."

"Why not now? I have an idea who might be responsible for the killings here. I want to ask you—"

"This is not the place," Kwion said softly. "There are too many ghosts. Come to us when you are able. Then we will talk." Motioning to his companions, he climbed back on his horse, waiting for the others to follow suit before guiding his mount back in the direction of the plain.

Gage stood where they left him and watched them retreat into the blackness. Even when the night took away the sight and sound of them, he stayed rooted to the place between the open horizon and the gates, torn between desires. To move on. To stay with her.

Go, he told himself. There were a few fleeting hours until dawn. And he'd already risked more than he should by staying the day, guarding her from afar.

Go while you've got the will to choose.

I can't leave her alone. Not like this.

She's selfish and stubborn. She would let them die.

She's afraid.

Never troubled before by indecision, Gage wrestled with the demons in his mind. In the end, his heart made the choice.

He found her in Libby's room, sitting on the bed, her arms wrapped around her knees. The lamp was unlit and the fireplace black, the only light coming from the moon, a misty argent gleam scattered on the darkness. In the muted light he traced the edges of the drawer they'd used for Nathan's cradle, positioned close to the bed.

Serena glanced up when he pushed the door open and stepped inside, then looked away.

"What do you want?"

"They're gone. They left the cattle."

"Fine. I'll thank them tomorrow when they come back for the water," she added with a mocking tone.

Gage crossed his arms over his chest and leaned back against the door frame, eyeing her dispassionately. "Are you going to sulk the rest of the night?"

Her head shot up. "I'm not sulking!"

"Yes, you are."

"No, I'm not!" Serena got to her feet and jerked down her rumpled skirts, glaring at him. "I just don't like it when—"

"—you don't get your own way," Gage finished for her. "I know."

"You never listen to anything I say. That isn't the reason—this time. I don't—I just don't . . ."

"You don't like to be reminded of what happened to your parents." Straightening, he walked to her side and slipped his fingertips under her chin, lifting her face to his. "You want someone to blame. Because then maybe the nightmares will leave you alone."

His gentleness was her undoing. All her anger and animosity fell away, leaving behind an exhausted numbness. "I left them," she said, so low she barely heard her own voice. She shut her eyes because she couldn't bear to see the censure in his. "My father told me to run and I did. I ran and hid and . . . and watched." The tears squeezed out and ran unheeded down her face. "I saved myself. That's what they told me to do. I saved myself and they died."

"Serena—" Gage's fingers tightened on her chin. A single tear slid down her cheek and into the hollow of his hand. "Look at me."

Serena reluctantly complied, not expecting him to understand or condone, but not willing to let him see how much his empathy would mean to her.

"There was nothing you could have done," Gage said softly.

"I could have stayed with them."

"And died with them."

The bitter edge to his voice distracted Serena from her own misery. She looked at him fully, seeing the lines of tension, the places where the soft light forgave the harshness of his expression. "Yes . . . like you, if you had been here with Libby. You want someone to blame too."

"I want justice."

"For them? You must have loved her very much."

"No . . ." For the first time, Serena saw him falter. He released her, but didn't move away. "She was my responsibility. I suppose we liked each other well enough. Gets awful lonely out here . . . but she buried her heart with her husband. I'd promised Jon I'd take care of her, her sister, and the boys." He looked to where Nathan slept, his tiny body tucked in the voluminous folds of a woolly blanket. "I should have been back in time."

"You planned to be home earlier?"

"Several days earlier. But after Ross and I finished the cattle drive we'd originally left for, I decided to chance chasing out over the north rim after some mustangs I thought the boys would like. My horse lost his footing on a rocky hillside when a boulder slid out from under him. He fell, and I ended up having to shoot him. I was thrown free, but hurt my right shoulder badly enough not to have a shooting arm for weeks. Ross and I managed to get one of the mustangs and break him for me to ride back. But it all took precious time."

"But you couldn't have foreseen any of that. Still, you want revenge for them."

"And what do you want after last night? It could have been Nathan we buried."

His ruthless reminder of the truth raked up the guilt she tried to bury with justifications for survival. Four people were dead because she had chosen to deceive them in order to guard her own safety, pretending she was Gage's wife and the ranch was still a refuge for Mormon pilgrims. She had come with a simple plan to save herself, ill thought out, and the more she tried to make it work, the more complicated, the more deadly it became.

She glanced down at Nathan, Gage's words circling in her head, and something swayed inside her, giving her a glimpse of the burden he carried in accepting responsibility for a dead friend's family. Just as she now had accepted the care of Nathan.

"Yes, I want justice," she said at last, feeling the link between them strengthened by a new common goal. Now the reasons to help him find the killers were more than hers alone. "For all of us." Holding his eyes with hers, Serena touched his face. "But what about you? What do you want? After you have revenge, when you're not a ghost in the wind any more, then what?"

"Then—I move on."

"To what?"

His shoulders shifted in an uneasy motion. "To whatever comes."

"So you don't know," Serena said, hearing the truth he left unspoken. "You never had anything and you never take the time to want anything. You just keep moving." Her touch gentled into a caress. "It must be a very lonely life, Gage Tanner."

Reaching up, Gage covered her hand with his, pressing a lingering kiss into her palm. He guided her hand from his face and curled her fingers around the brand of his lips as if it were something rare and precious she might never hold again. "No more than wanting so much for yourself you have nothing to share with others."

"I just want to be safe," Serena whispered. "I'm so tired of being afraid. I'm tried of never having a true home, of always moving, always—running."

Gage's eyes searched her face. Then, with a sigh, he drew her unresisting, into his arms. His face rested on her hair and she listened to the strong, steady beat of his heart as he slowly stroked his hand up and down her spine in a soothing motion.

He held her forever, until Serena felt a part of him again, more what they were together than what she was by herself. He lent her his strength, filling her with it until she could fight back the fear and uncertainty on her own.

"Stay with me," she murmured.

"I can't," Gage said, the words forced out of him. Right now, like this, he wanted nothing more. "It's nearly light."

Serena pulled back enough to look into his face. "I want to see you in the light. To know it's real."

"Maybe it's not." A faint smile, sad and mocking, touched his mouth. "I don't exist any more, remember?"

"Not to me," Serena said, curving her hands around his neck. She moved close enough for each word to brush his mouth, for her breath to be his. "Not with me."

Bending to his strength, she kissed him, her lips and tongue making love to his. She let go of all the pent-up passion and longing inside, giving it to him freely.

Gage held to her shoulders, returning her kiss with a wild, desperate hunger. But Serena felt the wavering in him, the struggle to keep from being consumed by the emotion between them, a feeling both savage and tender, rousing raw desire and moving her to tears. Despite his hesitation, she wanted to keep him with her and she knew she could exploit those feelings, his need to satisfy her own.

She wanted to. Yet she couldn't.

Softening her kiss, she gently withdrew, stepping out of his embrace. "It's almost dawn."

Silently, Gage watched her, searching. "Yes," he said

finally, glancing his fingertips against her cheek. "It is."
He paused, then said, "I would have stayed, if night
could last longer."

Serena shook her head. "Because I wanted you to."
She gave him a wry smile. "You won't believe me, but
somehow that's not good enough for me any more."
Walking past him to the doorway, she stepped outside
the room into the charcoal dimness of the predawn. "I'll
see you to the gates."

He followed her without a word down the stairs, but
when Serena turned toward the gates, he took her hand
and silently led her beyond the oasis trees into the shadows near the back corner of the courtyard, in the direction of the spring house.

"Where are we going?" she asked, glancing over her
shoulder. "The gates . . ."

"I don't need the gates," he answered enigmatically,
saying nothing else until they moved inside the cool
gloom of the spring house. There, he moved to the
hinged door in the floor that led to the cellar, lifting it
open.

"There's nothing down there but some cheese and
milk," Serena protested when he lighted one of the
lamps sitting on a low shelf and started down the narrow stairs. "What are you looking for?"

"You'll see."

"Unless . . . The pipes from the spring that lead to the
oasis in the courtyard and the watering hole out by the
corral—the spigot that controls where the water flows is
down here. Is that it? Are you going to do something
with the water?"

"Not this time. But I'm glad you figured that out."

Exasperated, but curious, Serena followed him into
the blackness of the dusty cellar space, her eyes straining to see beyond the pale nimbus of lamplight. "I've

been here dozens of times," she said. "I don't see what—Gage?" The faint light suddenly disappeared, as if blotted out by a swift hand. "Where are you?" She'd heard the sound of wood creaking, but as she tried to find him, to see anything, it was so dark she saw nothing, not even her own hands stretched in front of her, groping for a familiar object, for him. "Damn you, this isn't funny—"

"But it is a good way to disappear quickly if you have to," his voice whispered in her ear.

Serena whirled around and found herself snagged in the curve of his arm. He held the lamp aloft, smiling down at her in the soft light. "Where have you been?" she demanded. "You were here . . . and then you were—"

"Gone? A good trick, especially if you're a ghost, don't you think?"

"Very funny. How did you do it?"

He took her hand again, leading her to the back of the cellar room, behind one of the freestanding storage shelves that held a few scattered rounds of cheese. "When the Mormons settled here, they weren't any more welcome than they are now to most," he said, stopping at the wall. "They built the walls to withstand repeated attack, but they also planned another way outside, in case they couldn't open the front doors. A back door, so to speak. Only a handful of the most highly trusted elders ever knew it existed, only those who were given charge of the ranch. One of them, the man who entrusted the ranch to me, told me about it, probably without the others' consent. But we understood each other, and I swore to guard the secret." His voice fell to a smooth whisper, "I'm making an exception for you." Positioning the lamp so she could see, Gage showed her a slight recess in the stone wall. He gave it a small shove and a part of the wall seemed to shift.

"It's a door," Serena said, staring at it in amazement. She peered into the opening. "Steps ... do they lead outside?"

Gage nodded. "They go under the main wall and outside. You can be in and out of the walls in a minute or two, if you hurry. I'll show you."

He guided her up the gentle incline to another overhead door. Pushing it open, he stepped up over the edge, helping her up and out.

"The back of the ranch house," Serena said, looking around her at the narrow path separating the wall and the rocky out cropping that ran behind the rear of the ranch property. "I never knew this was here." She nudged the closed door with her foot.

"It's tucked under this overhang of boulders. You have to be careful climbing out. With the boulders for cover, and the layers of sand and rocks, no one's ever suspected it's here," Gage said, dousing the lamp and handing it to her. "And you should know about it. You may need to make a quick exit one day."

"Like you. That's how you were able to get inside locked gates. You almost had me convinced you were a spirit."

"Not quite." Watching her for a moment, Gage turned and started walking away from the hidden door, to the corner of the wall.

A heavy gray mist had settled over the ground, and Serena shivered as they stepped into it, feeling cold inside, as she followed him into the front yard. "Will you come back?" *Tonight?* she wanted to add. *Will you come to me tonight?*

"I'll be back," Gage said. She felt the warmth of his

gaze on her as sure as a touch. "Stay out of trouble until then."

Without waiting for her reply, he swiftly turned and strode away. The mist gathered around him, then stole his substance, gradually transforming him into the Spirit in the Wind once more. Only his presence lingered behind with her, an echo of promise in the darkness.

Serena tugged off her wide leather hat and tossed it on the bar, brushing the dampness from her forehead. She'd left for Vulture Creek a few hours past dawn, but the morning had turned hot as soon as the sun inched its way over the edge of the horizon, making the trip from the ranch seem longer and dustier than usual. And her reluctance to leave Nathan with Pete for the better part of the day hadn't make the trip any shorter.

She hefted herself on one of the stools, leaning her elbows on the bar, feeling the dull weight of exhaustion more strongly than before.

"You look like you could use several drinks," Amanda said, smiling a greeting as she came out of the back room, wiping her hands on a towel. "Ross must've finally given you my message about your supplies."

Serena accepted the glass of lemonade Amanda poured for her with an answering smile. "A few days ago, actually. But I haven't had the time to make the trip until now. I wouldn't have come today except we're running pretty low on just about everything."

"Ross said you had some trouble. He also said you had you a new ranch hand," Amanda added with a grin.

"Until I can find him a new home."

Amanda gave a derisive snort. "A baby ain't a mongrel dog that you give away to the first taker. And believe me, you won't find you too many takers 'round here anyways."

"I'll think of something," Serena said, trying to shrug off the uncomfortable feeling that settled on her shoulders. "In the meantime, I need to add a few things for him to my supplies. I didn't have a baby in mind when I ordered them."

"Don't worry, we'll rig you up. I just hope you don't have no more trouble out there now that you've got yourself a baby. Not that I'd lay any bets on it. Rustlers, Ross tried to tell me, but I'd put my money on Zeke and that bunch. It's no secret they've no love lost for Mormons. And everyone knows Birk's had his eye on that place since he come out west."

"Maybe," Serena said with a shrug, sliding her hand up and down the cool dewy glass.

"Who else could it have been?"

"I don't know. Indians."

Amanda, in the middle of polishing a mug, stopped in mid-motion. "Indians? Apache?"

"It could be, but it's the Paiute who keep coming back to the ranch all the time. Gage—" Amanda gave her a sharp glance and Serena took a quick swallow of lemonade, nearly choking on it. "Gage Tanner apparently trusted them and let them use the spring's water from what I've heard," she said, trying to cover her slip. "But I don't trust any Indian. What if they're responsible for the massacre? Until the Paiute, the only Indians I had the misfortune to deal with were uncivilized savages, violent men who, if they wanted the water badly enough, they would have—" Her sentence snapped and broke as the sudden appalling realization of Amanda's daughter flooded in on her. Hot color rushed to her face. "I'm sorry. I didn't mean—"

"Sure you did," Amanda said, returning to her polishing with a vigor.

"No . . . it's just—Tallie is a beautiful child. I'm sure you—you . . ." Serena faltered to a stop, not sure what she meant to say.

Amanda looked up, staring her squarely in the eye. "I'm not ashamed of my daughter, no matter what folks around here may think or say. Her pa was no savage and neither are the Paiute. Fact is, I'd rather have them on four sides as neighbors than the likes of Birk Reed's bunch."

Serena fidgeted with the brim of her hat, feeling uncomfortable. Amanda had been more than kind to her from the first day she'd walked into the trading post and she didn't want to offend her. But she also longed to satisfy her curiosity. For so many years, she'd feared and hated the Indians who murdered her parents, it was hard to understand how Amanda could not only defend them, but have a child by one as well.

"Go ahead and ask." When Serena glanced up, startled, Amanda smiled broadly. "You want to know about Tallie's pa. Don't bother," she said, waving a hand as Serena started to protest. "It's all over your face."

"You're right. I do want to ask," Serena said bluntly. "My parents were killed by Indians."

"Apache?"

"I never knew. But it's hard for me to think of them as anything but savages."

To her surprise, Amanda started to laugh, a rich, strident sound that made bright places in the dim, dusty saloon. "I wish you could've met Marukats. He was gentler'n any man I've known, and believe it, I've known more than most. I used to wonder how he survived in this godforsaken country." Her face softened and her eyes clouded as she looked beyond Serena to a place in the past. "But side by side to it, there was somethin' strong in him, somethin' that wouldn't break. I never understood it, but I loved him and nothin' else mattered. When Tallie came along, I couldn't have wanted for anythin' else."

"What happened to him?" Serena asked quietly.

Amanda became abruptly matter-of-fact again. "He got in the way of a couple of cowhands full of whiskey and bad feelin's 'bout the Paiute. I found him dead on my doorstep. Tallie was only a week in the cradle."

"My God!"

"So you see, I've got me a different idea of who's the savages 'round these parts."

"But—you stayed. By yourself. Aren't you afraid, because of Tallie and what happened to her father, of what people think?"

"If I was afraid it would be the same as bein' ashamed," Amanda said. "I'm not. And a reputation's a small thing to give up for the love I had with Marukats. I'd give a helluva lot more to have it back again."

Serena looked at Amanda, seeing a different woman, one driven by a kind of passion and determination she hadn't seen before. The story had both confused and touched her; she sensed there were things left unsaid she had yet to understand.

The door of the saloon banged open, turning both her and Amanda around.

Ross pushed his way into the saloon, carrying a grinning Tallie on his shoulders. The little girl clutched at his hat with both hands, her big dark eyes alight with laughter. "Look what the cat dragged in," he said.

"You're not a cat," Tallie said, giggling. "You're a bear. A big cinnamon bear!"

"He sure can be as grouchy as one." Amanda, with a wink for Ross, came out from behind the bar and reached up to lift her daughter down. "You go and wash the dust off your face, and maybe I'll let you have a little piece of that licorice I've been hidin'."

"Red licorice?" Tallie asked hopefully.

"The very same."

Tallie darted a mischievous glance at Ross. "And can the bear have some too? He wasn't at all grouchy."

"If he behaves. Now git," Amanda said, giving her daughter a gentle push in the direction of the back rooms. Turning back to Ross, Amanda grinned. "I could be wrong, but I think the bear has a likin' for sarsparilla."

Ross laid his hand on her shoulder, giving it a quick squeeze. "You'd make a fine wife, Mandy."

"The very day you give up wanderin' the woods and become a husband," she shot back, moving back behind the bar to fetch his drink.

They both laughed and Serena caught the warm, intimate quality of it, as if their exchange were a long-standing private joke that both appreciated the irony of. Sighing, she turned back to her half-empty glass. She envied them their easy rapport. It reminded her of the way her mother and father had been, always teasing and laughing, indulgent with their love. How come it came so simply for some people and not for her?

Serena picked up her glass, raising it to her lips to finish off the last of her lemonade. The door to the saloon opened again and a rush of hot, dusty air swept through the room. Absorbed in her own dark thoughts, she didn't look up until Amanda's voice penetrated the daze she'd locked herself in.

". . . didn't hear 'bout another pilgrimage through here," Amanda was saying. "Most of you folks avoid Vulture Creek and go straight to the ranch."

"We are traveling through the territory to find others

of our brethren still living here who wish to join us and return to a less hostile land," a rich, even voice said, each word slowly and beautifully formed. "The day is hot and we wished to rest the horses."

Serena was too busy trying to carefully and unobtrusively retrieve her hat and jam it fast and low on her head to realize the man had neatly sidestepped Amanda's implied question. Seated two stools down from her, Ross' bulk hid Serena from the view of the three men who stood at the end of the bar. But she could see half the figure of the man who had spoken.

Not imposing in stature, nonetheless, he had an aura of authority about him, a cold self-possession that brought a chill into the heated room. He was dressed all in black, his silver and ash beard halfway to his waist, his eyes narrow and piercing.

He wasn't a man that once seen, was easily forgotten. But Serena only needed his voice to recognize him.

Sliding off her stool, she attempted to move casually toward the back of the saloon, praying the murky light and her wide-brimmed hat would hide her. Ross slanted her a curious glance as she edged her way in the direction of Amanda's back rooms.

Serena saw him lean forward and murmur something to Amanda, and they both looked her way.

Her heart gave an agitated skip. If they gave her away. . . . She felt a bead of sweat trickle down her spine. The room seemed too hot, her breath too short and hurried.

At the end of the bar, the man was reaching for the glass Amanda had set in front of him. As he did, his eyes fell on her. Stopped, crawled all over her. A slight scowl puckered his forehead, drew lines around his mouth.

Serena bolted around the corner of the bar and into the back room, flinging the door closed behind her.

"Is the bear after you?"

The small voice nearly jerked her out of her skin.

Tallie stood a few feet to her left, holding a limp stick of licorice, her hand and mouth sticky and red.

"No—yes." Squatting down, Serena chewed at her lower lip for a moment, exchanging wide-eyed gazes with Tallie. "Yes he is. We're playing hide and seek. Do you know how to play?" Tallie nodded, her dark eyes lit up with curiosity and fascination. "Then if someone comes looking for me, will you promise not to tell them where I am? Please?"

"Sure." Walking to Serena's side, Tallie sat down next on the floor next to her. "I'll guard the door. I did that for Mama before."

"Thank you, Tallie," Serena said, impulsively reaching out to give the little girl a quick hug before scrambling to her feet and tugging her hat down low again. She hurried into the back room Amanda obviously used as a sitting room, figuring there must be a rear door to the saloon.

Rounding a corner and finding herself in a small kitchen, Serena's eyes pounced on the door at the opposite end of the room. She had her hand on the knob ready to turn, when a low voice spun her around.

"You seem to be runnin' into trouble every place you turn." Amanda came into the kitchen, shaking her head. "Tallie's guard duties don't extend to her mama. I'm sure you got a good reason for wantin' to avoid those Mormons."

"Amanda—"

"Don't worry, Ross'll keep 'em busy for a spell. I figure you owe me at least a word or to for me lettin' you sneak out like a rustler avoidin' the posse." She paused.

"Are you Mormon? Is that why you're runnin'? Look, I can understand it. Maybe you just wanted a little adventure, or maybe they wanted to marry you to—"

"No!" The word shot out of Serena's mouth before she could stop it. "No," she said, pushing back her fear and fury. "No, I'm not Mormon. But I lived with them for a time after my parents were killed. And yes—" Hesitating a moment, she plunged ahead. "They wanted me to be someone's fifth wife. I couldn't, I wouldn't do it. So I ran."

Amanda raised a brow. "I can see why, but now that you're here, they can't force you to wed someone you don't want."

"I know it sounds foolish, but you don't know the man who wanted to marry me." Her voice trembled a little. "Once he decided he wanted something, he got it. Or he destroyed it. He's—different from the Mormons who make the pilgrimages here."

"I've seen a few who are," Amanda said, glancing back in the direction of the saloon. "They aren't the kind I feel comfortable bein' around. Well . . ." She rapped her fingertips in an impatient rhythm against her thigh, her face thoughtful. "Well, it won't do you no good to go runnin' off without those supplies, particularly with that little one about. I'll get Ross to bring your wagon 'round back and we'll get you loaded and gone before anyone knows different."

Knowing Pete and Nathan needed the supplies, Serena paused, then with a long sigh, nodded.

After Amanda had left to rope Ross into her plan, Serena ducked out into the backyard of the saloon. Quietly closing the door behind her, she leaned against the roughened wall of the building, willing her heart to slow its furious pace. She had run, but apparently not far enough.

Jerel Webster had found her.

Chapter Twelve

Serena restlessly paced the yard behind Amanda's place, her stomach churning, her heart racing.

What now? Where else can I run?

Her mind frantically scanned every possibility. She was fairly certain Jerel hadn't recognized her. Yet. If she hurried back to the ranch and locked herself inside the walls, letting him believe only Pete was there, he couldn't get in. At least she hoped he couldn't.

But what then? More suspicions, more questions, from him or other Mormon travelers seeking refuge at the ranch. And sooner or later Jerel would ask the right person the right questions and learn the whole story. He would pick up her trail; one way or another he'd hunt her down. To his thinking, making her his wife meant the fulfillment of his divinely decreed destiny. And Jerel refused to let go of what he considered his holy right.

When she had dared to oppose him, he swore he would make certain she regretted every moment of her defiant decision. Even the support for her stance from Elder Caltrop and others of the Mormon leaders hadn't shaken his resolve. Jerel thought Silas Caltrop and the elders of his clan were weak, accusing them of scorning the rigidity and discipline of the old ways in favor of retreat in the face of intolerance. And so Serena had fled, determined to shape her own destiny.

Except Jerel had found her.

A sudden chill pierced the scorching midday heat and Serena wrapped her arms around herself tightly. Each day her past crept closer to the present, forcing her into a tighter and tighter corner. No one would believe her, but she knew Jerel wouldn't hesitate to drag her back to the Utah territory, kicking and screaming. He never doubted it was his right to take her. Fate had led Serena to him, to bear his children one day, to help secure his place in the hierarchy of the hereafter. She was meant to belong to him.

Unless she married someone else first.

Gage, Nathan . . . husband and child.

The idea sounded more perfect than ever. Would he do this for her? Would he rescue her the way he had Libby? Did she want him like that, no matter how tempting the notion?

"No!" She whirled around and marched across the yard. *What's taking Ross so long? I've got to get away from here!*

Conflicting alternatives hammered away at her mind, none of them offering any hope. Marriage to Jerel, accepting the role of his wife, bearing his children, sharing husband and home with four other wives . . . for some women the arrangement worked out ideally. An ordered life, clear-cut responsibilities, a secure place in the family with a devoted husband, the kinship of sisterhood, raising children in an atmosphere of caring and strong faith.

Large, close-knit families, all willing to work for the good of each other, had helped the Mormon clans survive prejudice and hardship, to make the hazardous journeys from Missouri, Kansas, Oklahoma, across the unsettled plains, to build new lives in the harsh Utah territory.

Serena admired their tenacity and devotion. But she knew in her heart she needed much, much more, in every way, than their way of life could ever offer her. She could never share marriage, a husband, a lover with other women. To her, marriage was too intimate a relationship, a communion of two, not of many. Compared to the reality of that sort of destiny, a future with Gage, on any terms, seemed like salvation.

What choice do I have? I have to convince him to stay with me. Now, before Jerel finds me.

Before she could argue herself out of the idea, Ross, driving the cart like a madman, flew out from around the west side of the building, yanking the horse to a stop a few feet from her. "It's all loaded and ready. Mandy lent you her pony for the ride back," he said, gesturing to the mare now hitched to the cart as he jumped down from the driver's bench. "She said to tell you she'll hold on to your mule in trade." He gave her a teasing wink. "You best get on your way."

"Thank you," Serena said, touching his arm in gratitude. She hiked up her skirts, climbed up on the bench, and took the reins. "Can you keep them here long enough for me to get a safe lead?"

"I imagine so. Mandy's talkin' up a storm in there now, showin' 'em every new trinket she's taken in over the last month's tradin'."

"Tell her she'll never know how much this means to me."

"She already does. Now go on." He slapped the mare smartly on the rear, setting the horse off into a fast trot.

"I'll get word to you," Serena called back over her shoulder, gripping tight to the reins with one hand and trying to keep her hat on her head with the other.

"We're countin' on it." Ross waved her off, then grabbing a pile of wood for the kitchen stove, strode back to the rear of the store and kicked the door open. He shuffled through the bar with an easy manner, whistling a light tune.

Amanda glared up at him from the holster she was showing the Mormons. "Well, it's about time," she said tartly. "The fire's near to ashes."

Ross heard the edge of tension in her voice, a sound he'd heard only on rare occasions over the years. Despite the roustabouts she dealt with almost daily, though many riled her temper, few men ever shook her stoic courage. But these three frightened her; he'd keep an eye on them. Amanda didn't scare easy. He trusted her gut instincts about people the way he trusted his own about animals.

He dropped the wood in the corner of the saloon next to the breezeway into the store. "Findin' everything you need, friends? Mandy keeps a fine stock, don't she?"

"We didn't come for supplies," the ashen-haired man answered, his tone cool and clipped. Lean, almost to the point of gaunt, his features looking as if they'd been chiseled from flinty stone, the man didn't at first glance give the appearance of an awe-inspiring leader. But something in the manner in which he carried himself, in the way his companions deferred to him, gave Ross the impression of a man most would think twice about crossing.

"Well, can't blame a woman for tryin' to make a livin', can you?" he said, laughing heartily and slapping the other on the back.

The Mormon's eyes turned to stone. "We stopped for refreshment only."

"Well then, I'm wasting my time here tryin' to sell these to you, aren't I?" Amanda said, turning aside a lit-

tle too eagerly from the men to hang the holsters back
on their hooks.

"Mama, mama!" Dark hair flying, Tallie came running out of the back rooms, heading straight for her
mother. "Where is she? We were playing hide and go
seek and Se—"

Ross bent down and swept Tallie off her feet and
whirled her around until her giggles swallowed her
words. He avoided the dark stares he sensed boring into
him from the Mormon group. "Your Mama's busy with
customers, girl. You ought to be in the kitchen where
you belong."

"I'm finished Ross," Amanda put in quickly. "I'll
take her back with me. Come on Tallie, grab some of
that wood and we'll stoke up the fire so we can fix you
some supper."

"But she disappeared! She was here and she said she
wanted to play hide and seek. Our game's not over till
I find Ser—"

"Sissy's been playin' longer than you have, now,"
Amanda interrupted. She lifted her daughter in her arms
and discreetly covered the child's mouth with her hand
as she ducked out of the store into the next room.

But Tallie's squawks and wriggling drew the three
visitors' rapt attention until the two vanished into the
back. Ross immediately changed the topic, drumming
up the first subject to cross his mind. "Best be on guard
during your travels, there's talk of a band of renegade
Apache in these parts. A lot of killin' 'round here these
past months. Especially at the Tanner ranch," he added,
not sure why, yet interested to see the elder Mormon's
reaction.

The silver-haired Mormon slowly turned from eyeing
Amanda and Tallie back to Ross. "We had heard the last

of the Apache were rounded up after Geronimo's capture."

"Not from what I hear. Ain't seen 'em myself, but I've heard tell of sightings up north of here toward the canyon. Good chance there's still a handful of 'em hidin' out up there."

"We will not be traveling that way."

"I'd imagine not." Ross rubbed his beard, thoughtfully. "You got your own reasons for stayin' as far from anywhere a U.S. marshall might be, don't you now?" For an instant Ross almost regretted the veiled threat, but found he couldn't. His hunter's instincts told him the man was a predator, Serena his prey.

Ross prided himself on the fact he'd never courted trouble. Unlike his friend Gage Tanner, who seemed to go out in search of it, riding a trail that would make the devil himself nervous. Ross avoided people and their problems, content on his own. He didn't need the fuss any more than a steer needed a saddle blanket.

Mandy understood that about him, so he could love her. She set him completely free, making it safe to keep coming back. Not like Gage and the women he had got himself hogtied to. Gage never met a woman who didn't end up being more trouble than any human was worth. And from the way things were heading with Serena Lark, Ross decided his friend's luck had somehow unbelievably taken a turn for the worse.

"We have our own reasons for being in the territory," his Mormon opponent was saying. "And our own rights." There was no trace of menace in the man's voice, but Ross felt it just the same.

"Well friend, the law might not see it that way." He shrugged. "Still, it's your business far as I'm concerned."

"Yes. It is. And now we'll be about that business."

He turned to walk out, followed by his two silent shadows.

"I ought to tell you if that business of yours includes a visit to the Tanner ranch, we put the last group of pilgrims who stopped off there to bed with a pick an' shovel," Ross said. "Someone didn't care for the notion of them stoppin' for a visit. Can't say it was Apache for certain or not. All I know is that they won't be finishin' that journey of theirs."

The Mormon eyed Ross a long, heavy moment. "We know the risks."

"Just bein' neighborly," Ross shrugged again as the men brushed past him.

He waited until the door shut behind them, then moved to the window, rubbing a clean spot on the glass with the edge of his sleeve to look outside. The trio had been joined by several other men, also dressed in black, coming from the direction of the blacksmith's shop. After a brief conversation, during which the silver-haired Mormon gestured once toward the trading post, the group mounted their horses and rode off in a whirl of dust.

Ross watched them leave before calling for Amanda. He found her already waiting in the breezeway.

"What are we going to do?"

"We? Now Mandy you know how I feel about buttin' in—"

"It's different this time. You're already involved, and don't try tellin' me you're not. I can see you know somethin' I don't, and probably a helluva lot more than you've told me." She waved a long, slender finger at him. "Don't you lie to *me,* Ross Brady. I'm not just another faint-hearted female and you damned well know that by now."

Ross backed away from her accusatory approach.

"Hold up there, Mandy." He lifted his hands in front of his face in mock defense. When she relaxed slightly, he took advantage of the reprieve and swept a huge arm around her waist, shackling her against his chest. "Where's Tallie?"

Amanda smiled. "Just finishing her supper . . ."

"Did you straighten things out with her about Serena?"

"She understands just fine. She learned early on how to keep secrets."

Ross rocked Amanda in his arm. "Doesn't she still take a nap after lunch?"

"Mmmm."

"It's blistering out there today." He bent to graze her lips with a kiss. "Good afternoon to close the store down for an hour's rest, wouldn't you say?"

"What about Serena?"

"Ah, Mandy, I don't want to get into this any more than I already am. Whatever mess that girl's into, she's done it to herself."

"You could say the same about me and Tallie. But you don't."

"That's different."

Amanda arched a brow. "Oh, is it now? She can't help that her folks died and left her easy bait for some man who's got the idea he'd like to have hisself half a dozen women."

Running his fingers through his heavy hair, Ross sighed, knowing arguing with Mandy meant either giving in or walking out and waiting for a year or so 'til her temper cooled. "You want me to go after her?"

Amanda sidled into him, brushing her breasts against his chest enticingly. "If you'll just see to it she gets through those gates safely, I promise when you come back I'll make it worth your time." She smoothed her hands down his back and over his hard buttocks.

Ross groaned. "I swear you are the *only* woman on earth who can get away with this kind of blackmail."

She whirled out of his arms, her long golden braid slapping her back behind her. "I wouldn't care if there were a hundred others," she flipped. Hips swaying gracefully inside her tight pants, she pulled the leather tie from her hair and released the long, shining waves. Sauntering out of the store back into the bar, she tossed her tresses over one shoulder and looked back. "I'll be waiting up."

"You better be," Ross grumbled and stomped out into the dusty heat.

Riding furiously against time, Ross caught up with Serena abut a mile from the ranch. Pulling his palomino up beside her, he was met with the point of a rifle at his ribs.

"Ross!" Serena slowly lowered her gun. "I nearly shot you. I heard a horse and thought—"

"You thought right. No tellin' where your friends are right now. I took a short cut. Mandy wanted to make sure you got inside the gates in one piece."

"They didn't see me, did they?"

Ross kept his horse at a trot next to the cart. "Don't think so, but Tallie nearly slipped and as much as said your name. Serena is your real name, isn't it?"

"Yes," Serena mumbled into the rippling heat.

"Do they know about the first massacre? And the recent killings? Did you send a telegram to Utah to tell 'em?"

"No." *And I wouldn't have. Not now. Not ever.* The lie, even of omission, though, came hard with him. "I still can't figure the telegraph machine out. A few pilgrims came through shortly after I got here, though." Serena avoided his eyes. "I told them I was Gage's wife and that he was out on a cattle drive with the rest of the hands. I said Libby and her family were in Vulture Creek with friends."

Ross shook his head. "And they believed that?"

"Yes. And no." Serena sighed. "There were questions I guessed at the answers to. One of them must have had suspicions and passed them along to the elders. There was one man—he didn't seem as if he believed my story about where Gage had gone. I don't even know if he believed I was Gage's wife. And now . . . after the last killings. Someone will be waiting for those people. I've only made things a hundred times worse." She bowed her head in shame, in sorrow.

"It's a fine mess, that's for sure. Your luck seems to be runnin' muddy." Ross mulled over her words then said, "I don't care for the looks of those three you ran from at Mandy's. Somethin's different 'bout 'em. You know all three of 'em?"

"No. Only Jerel Webster, the leader. I'm—I was betrothed to him. He's a very powerful elder. He believes very strongly in the old ways. He thinks the church is being led astray by those that are weakening it with a tolerance for new ideas, peaceful alternatives. Jerel isn't above forcibly taking what he thinks belongs to him and he doesn't like to be crossed. That's why he's come looking for me. I refused to be his fifth wife."

The cart rumbled into the front yard of the ranch and Serena pulled the mare to a halt. Climbing down from the seat, she fished in her pocket for the key and started to unlock the gates. "Go on, I'll be fine now, Ross."

"It's gettin' dark out."

"I'll lock up as soon as I get the cart inside. Pete'll

be waiting for me," Serena said with more bravado than she felt. "I've got supplies now. I can out wait them. It's too dangerous for them to stay here too long, with all the bad feeling in the territory over the Mormons. They'll have to move on."

"You need someone besides Pete to keep watch." Ross heaved a worried sigh and glanced out over the dusky pink horizon. "Somethin' more than a Spirit in the Wind."

A small smile touched Serena's mouth. "It's enough. He's enough. But I think you already know that."

Ross settled back into his saddle. "You're crazier'n Pete, you know that? But I got to admit I admire your spunk. You're a lot like Mandy in that way." He whirled his stallion around. "You can take that as a compliment."

"I will. Get on back to her. I'll be fine."

"Expect a visit tomorrow. I got a feelin' Mandy isn't gonna let me rest easy if I don't."

"Fair enough," Serena said, waving him off into the twilight as she stepped inside the walls of her sanctuary.

She found Gage pacing the courtyard, a wailing Nathan stuck to his shoulder like an extra appendage. Still, Serena couldn't help but smile. Gage, a large man by any standards, looked positively massive next to the tiny, clinging bundle. The baby was all but lost in his powerful arms and the broad expanse of his chest.

"You did come back," she said as she closed and locked the gates behind her.

"I said I would," Gage muttered, exasperation edging his tone. "Here, do something with him. All he seems to do is cry."

Serena laughed aloud. "You'd think you'd never held a hungry baby before."

He practically shoved the child into Serena's arms as soon as she was within reach. "I haven't."

She frowned, questioning, then took Nathan and cradled him against her. "You weren't doing so badly. He's just hungry. There, there, now," she crooned softly to the baby. "I've brought you something else to try."

Whiskey Pete meandered over to the cart, Lucky Joe jumping up on Serena's leg, straining to sniff at the tiny newcomer. Pete slapped the dog down. "Behave yourself, Joe. I know it's a loud little bugger, but the sooner we git his food out of the cart, the sooner he'll quit his squallin'." Taking up the reins, he led the mare to a trough at the other end of the courtyard.

"There's a crate with more milk and a few things Amanda thought I could use. If you'll bring it into the kitchen, I'll try to quiet him down," she said to Gage.

"Gladly."

An hour later, at the kitchen table, fire blazing behind them, Nathan slept contentedly in Serena's arms, sated by the warm milk she'd managed to get into him. She'd avoided telling Gage all that had transpired at the trading post over dinner, and now she was reluctant to disturb their peaceful silence.

"At least Nathan took a little more in than he did yesterday," Gage said over his shoulder as he wiped dry the last of the dinner dishes.

Serena watched him as he carefully replaced the dishes in the cabinet, his hair falling in boyish waves down over his collar, his shirt unbuttoned nearly to his waist from the heat of cooking, his sleeves rolled to his elbows. She saw him as ideal in every way. Strong, caring, passionate, disconcertingly straightforward, with a gritty courage that made him a survivor, and a touch of the wild and untamed that set him apart from any man she'd ever known. A perfect husband and father in her eyes.

"Did you help Libby this much with the boys?" she asked, admiring his willingness to pitch in whenever needed, but curious. "The men I've known never did women's work."

Instead of bristling at the comment as she imagined he might, Gage shot her a crooked smile that made him look impossibly attractive. "That's because the men you know have more than enough women to handle their needs."

"So you don't mind?"

He tossed the towel over a drying rack and set the last dish on the shelf. "I can certainly think of better ways to spend my time," he murmured, lowering himself to straddle the bench close to her. "Can't you?"

She smiled back. "Countless."

With an intent expression in his eyes, Gage lightly rested his hands on her thighs and leaned over Nathan's sleeping form to kiss her. His lips took hers in a long, slow exchange of the quiet, surprisingly domestic passions they'd somehow wound up sharing during the past two days. An easy feeling wrapped her in warmth and contentment, and the kiss went deeper. She met his soft probes with her own, the child in her arms oblivious to the enchantment of love developing around it.

Gage moved closer, sliding his hands back and forth over her thighs, inching her skirts up with each touch. Serena moaned softly, the heat of his hands through her skirts exciting her senses. She leaned back and his lips took her throat on an excursion of delight, flicking small kisses across her neck, to suckle her ear, then down to taste the tender curve of her shoulder.

At the same time his hands continued to move over

the tops and sides of her thighs, easing under her skirts to brush bare skin. She craved the touch of his finger-tips, wanted more, so much more. Second by second, his hands enticed pleasure, suggested magic.

She longed to touch him in return, to explore him as well. It was impossible with the baby in her arms. Yet somehow, knowing she could do nothing but let him have his way added to the excitement of it. Unable to move, she could only concentrate on the primitive long-ing, the ache of desire he made her feel.

"I can't touch you," she said breathlessly when his hands brushed her bottom.

"I know," he whispered, his breath hot in her ear.

"Shame on you, an innocent child in my arms."

"And how do you think that innocent child came into this world?"

"I can't say that I know. Exactly." She teased the cor-ners of his mouth with her tongue and lips. "But I'm willing to learn . . ." Carefully, she shifted Nathan in her arms enough to free one hand. Reaching down, she pressed the top two buttons of her dress open. "Is this the right way to begin?"

Gage's eyes riveted on her movements, on the swell of her breasts she uncovered, not completely, just enough to tempt him to madness. Gently, he reached over to touch the taut nipple straining against the thin cotton of her dress. "You're beautiful, Serena. A man would be a fool to resist what you're offering."

"You're not a fool. Are you?" Her eyes, dark with longing, sought his.

"Serena . . ." Gage buried his face in the sweet hol-low between her breasts, tasting her soft skin until the savor of it threatened to strip his control. He pulled back, feeling more lost each moment he held her. "I'm afraid all you really want is for me to belong to you."

His words struck deep, slicing through the sensual haze they'd fallen into. For a long moment Serena sat in numb silence, unable to contradict him or defend herself.

Abruptly, Gage jerked to his feet, breaking what remained of their impassioned interlude. "I can't do that," he said roughly. "Not even for you."

"I—" Serena started to ask him anyway, to beg him, cajole, threaten, demand he give her what she ached for, what she needed. The words stuck in her throat.

"Don't say it. I won't—" He stopped, tensing.

Serena glanced at the door, feeling a ripple of uneasiness. "What is it?"

"Listen."

"All I hear are the cattle."

"Exactly." Gage strode to the door and flung it open. "All of them. Something's wrong."

"Gage—" She nearly blurted out the whole story to warn him, but Lucky Joe's agitated barking interrupted her.

Whiskey Pete appeared at Gage's side. "That ole excuse fer a fence ain't gonna hold 'em. I warned you it weren't ready for that many cows yet. We don't got the men to pasture 'em. But oh no—"

"They were a gift, we could hardly have turned them away," Gage said shortly. "I'll go out and make sure it holds for tonight."

Serena stood up, being careful not to disturb the baby. "Why don't you let me help you in the morning?" she said swallowing the impulse to tell Gage about Jerel. "It'll go much faster in the daylight, with all of us working. There's no need to risk it at night."

Gage's brows pulled together in consternation. He drifted in thought a long minute then turned to Pete. "You keep watch. You can see, even at night, through the wall better than we can out in the yard. And, you're a better shot than she is."

"Well!"

"It's true. Be realistic for once. If you lend me a hand, I'll have the fence fixed in short time. Pete can warn us, and let us back in quickly if he has to. We can't afford to lose the stock."

"To say nothing of our lives."

"I'm already dead, remember?" he flipped back, his tone rich with sarcasm.

"Well, I'm not," Serena said sharply, causing Nathan to squirm a little in her arms. "And I don't intend to risk my life foolishly. We can get more cattle."

"Oh? With what? Your savings? Mine? Serena, face it, we have almost nothing left. Mandy's generous with her credit, but she is in business. One day she's going to have to cut you off."

"Cut me off? It was we before."

Gage shifted uncomfortably. "Only because we agreed to help each other. Now, I'm ready to keep my end of the bargain, if you're willing to do your share."

"I always do my share," Serena said, stiffening. "I'll put Nathan to bed and be right out."

"Bring your revolver," Gage told her, turning toward the door. "Just in case."

Biting back her growing fear, Serena nodded and rushed upstairs to her room to carefully put Nathan in his makeshift crib. When she had him settled, she took time to stir up the embers in the fireplace and to braid her hair before hurrying down to the corral.

Twenty minutes later, beneath the starry black carpet, she found Gage hard at work in the corral, battling back cattle made restless by the close smell of freedom, while he drove several slender spikes of wood into the ground with a mallet, strengthening the roughly constructed fence.

Serena slipped inside the badly listing gate, being careful not to catch her skirts on the thin strands of barbed wire strung between the wooden posts. "What can I do?"

Gage looked up to her and brushed the sweat from his brow. He'd tossed his shirt aside, and his dark skin glistened with sweat under the gold harvest moon. Serena's finger itched to rub the dampness and soreness from the muscles that flexed with every motion.

"Can you carry some of those posts from that pile over there—" He indicated it with a nod of his head. "I'm nearly out."

"These arms have carried plenty more than a few measly tree limbs!"

"Good. Prove it."

Serena stomped off. How could he be so warmly tender one minute and so cool and annoying the next? "It must be the prerogative of men to change moods like a top spins!" she muttered, heaving post after splintered, knobby post onto her bare arms. Silently she cursed her lack of foresight in not changing out of her dress into something more practical.

Gage eyed her up and down when she dropped the posts at his feet. "I have to admit you're a hell of a lot stronger than you look," he said with a grin guaranteed to inflame her temper. "Now, if you can keep the cattle off my back while I get these in the ground and wired together, it would be about the best help you could give me."

"I'll see what I can do." While she struggled with the stubborn animals, enticing them with food, whipping them with a crop, then finally herding them one by one into the barn with Deacon Mather, Gage wrestled rotting, weather-stripped posts out of the ground and pounded and wired better ones into place.

They toiled well into the night, to the brink of exhaustion, saying little, barely glancing at each other.

"At least there's no sign of Indians or Birk Reed and his men," Serena said after several hours labor, thoughts of Jerel Webster creeping insidiously into her mind. She dumped a new pile of wood beside another weak spot in the fence, stopping to catch her breath, the effort causing a dull pain deep in her chest. Blinking, she tried to clear a gray haze that threatened to obscure her vision.

"You sound winded," Gage said, looking up at her with a frown from where he knelt by a post, tacking a wire end to the wood. "Sit down. We've been at this for hours, and I know Nathan kept you up the better part of last night. You need to rest. We're almost done."

"No. I'll quit when you do. Here." She set her lantern down, feeling more tired than she had in weeks. "I found some more nails out in the shed."

Taking her offering, Gage caught her hand in his, lightly caressing her fingers. "Thanks."

"Thank you—for not letting me lose the cattle," Serena said softly, wondering at the tremor in her heart so simple a touch could provoke. "I was afraid. I would have stayed hidden behind the gates while the only hope for a future here wandered off into the night."

Gage gave a short laugh and let go her hand. "A dead man doesn't have to worry about dying twice."

"No." She touched his shoulder, drawing his eyes to her again. "But do you feel dead? Now? Can you tell me you've felt nothing for the past two days? Nothing for me? For Nathan?"

"We have a bargain, Serena," he said, his face hardening. "That's all."

"I see." Ire and frustration rose in her in equal measures. She whipped away from him, the movement somehow exacting a heavy toll on the all too small reserve of strength left in her body. She should have heeded the signs long before now. The emotional, mental, and physical stresses of the day combined to bring on the sickness she'd managed to stave off all these weeks. Now, her heart began a wild throbbing. A warning.

No not now, please. I have to be strong.

Clutching at a fence post, she tried to walk away from him, to hide the mad drumming that seemed to steal the muscles from her body, to melt her limbs away to naught. With every faltering step her head felt heavier, her mind thicker.

"Serena," she heard Gage's voice somewhere far away, echoing. "Are you all right?" The words reached her ears in a dull, slow motion slur.

Serena clutched at her chest, afraid her wildly pulsing heart was breaking through her skin. "Nathan," she whispered, a moment before the world went black.

Her eyes fluttered open to darkness that seemed unending. She had the sense that time had passed and yet with it the vague memory that when she had fainted it had been nighttime. Rubbing her eyes awake, she found herself tucked comfortably into her own bed, her room dimly lit with the fire of a single candle. The air smelled of milk and soap. Of baby things. And indefinably of Gage, as if somehow he had imbued the very walls with his decidedly masculine presence.

Rolling over to check the bedside for the drawer, Serena's heart nearly stopped. Nathan's blankets were heaped there, but he was missing. She shot up out of bed, the effort shooting a roaring pain through her head. "Nathan! Gage!" she cried out.

"Settle down," Gage said from somewhere behind her head. "He's here with me. And he isn't making my life easier."

Serena sank back into her bed. "What happened? What time is it?"

"I think it's time we talked." Gage brought a freshly, if awkwardly diapered Nathan over to her. Sitting on the edge of her bed, he held the baby in his lap, looking a little more at ease than the last time she had seen him with the infant.

"Gggg," Nathan cooed as he looked up at Serena.

She laughed lightly and brushed a hand down his soft cheek. "You do have the biggest blue eyes." Then to Gage, "Has he eaten anything else?"

"A few sips. He's looking pale. And his hands . . . Watch." Gage lifted the tiny hand that had at first clutched anything within its grasp. It went limp in Gage's palm. "He's losing strength. Just like you. What's wrong with you, Serena? I want to know."

Serena refused to look at him. "I'm not sure. It just— happens sometimes. Not very often. But sometimes. That's why I mostly worked in the kitchen or cleaning inside when I lived with the Mormons. It was easier work. If I worked outside, especially when I was upset or angry about something—which was often," she added with a rueful grimace, "I risked collapsing. Like tonight."

"And you wanted to run this ranch single-handedly?"

Nathan squirmed and Serena reached out for him. Propping herself up against her pillow in a half-seated position, she settled him against her shoulder and rocked him evenly. "When I decided to come here, I thought the ranch was thriving and occupied. By you—

and the family you had taken in. I thought if you were willing to look after them, you would be willing to offer me refuge, for a little while, at least."

Gage looked away. "Well, at least I know you're not completely crazy. You did have some sort of plan."

"Not really," she admitted, though the confession made her feel foolish. "This was the only place that ever felt like a home to me, I remembered it as a haven, the only one I'd ever had. And the way Elder Caltrop described you, it sounded even more the perfect sanctuary. That's why I came back. When I got here and found it all but deserted, I decided to make it a home again. I didn't—I don't have anywhere else to go. I just never expected everything to get so complicated. It seems the more I try to make it work out, the worse things become."

Gage said nothing for a long space of time, simply studying her. Finally, without commenting on what she had told him, he slapped his hands to his thighs and stood up. "Do you feel up to a meal?"

Serena didn't try to force the conversation, knowing with Gage, it was useless. If he didn't want to tell her what he thought, no amount of wheedling or pressuring from her would change his mind. "Yes, I'm starving," she said wriggling out of bed, Nathan resting against her chest. As she stood she realized she wore only a filmy shift. She cocked her head suspiciously at him.

He shrugged. "I had to make you comfortable."

"Here, take him while I throw a dress on," she said, handing the baby to Gage.

"I like you in that."

"Oh, do you?" She turned back and brushed against him. "Well, I dare say you'd like me a whole lot better out of it." Gage sucked in his breath, and Serena laughed aloud. Spinning away from him, she yanked a dress from the chest at the end of the bed and donned it with painstaking slowness, accentuating each movement of her hips, bending and twisting suggestively, deliberately dropping the comb for her hair just so she could bend down in front of him, her dress still unbuttoned, to retrieve it.

"It's obvious none of that religion wore off on you," he said dryly.

"How would you know?" she taunted, flipping her glistening mane of hair across his face to wind it into a prim bun at her nape. "You've never really tempted me."

With that she took Nathan from his arms and strode outside into the cool, dark air. She turned toward the kitchen, but stopped short, for at the center of the courtyard she was met by a picnic table set with a bright tablecloth, napkins and plates and dishes of food. She turned to Gage, unable to hide her amazement. "What's this?"

"I thought you might like to have supper outside tonight," he said, his voice casual, not quite meeting her eyes. "The heat's not so bad, and I figured you'd be starving after sleeping the day away."

"The day away," she repeated, confused. "I thought it was morning."

"It was. About twelve hours ago."

"Oh. Did you stay all day?"

"Of course I did. Someone had to look after Nathan. I stayed inside. Pete did some cooking and I made a few repairs around here." He hesitated. "I hope you're pleased."

"I am. Thank you," Serena said, dumbfounded. She didn't quite know what to make of his gesture. He'd taken the time to do this for her, just to please her, and while uncomfortable with her gratitude, she could see her approval meant something to him. "It's the nicest thing anyone's done for me in a long time," she added, letting the warmth in her heart overflow into her words.

Gage said nothing, but the satisfaction on his face was enough for Serena.

The makeshift family ate heartily, all but the smallest, who sat quietly in Serena's lap, staring up at her. The pleading look in his eyes turned her heart over. "We've got to do something for him, Gage. He can't live on so little nourishment," she said, setting her empty plate aside.

"I've been thinking about it," he began, but before he finished his sentence a spate of loud, angry shouts and a flurry of pounding at the gates cut him short.

"Jerel!" Serena cried out before she could stop herself. Clutching Nathan tighter.

Gage glared at her. "What?"

"Naw, it's Reed, or some of his boys more likely," Whiskey Pete put in. "I seen Zeke prowlin' 'round the corral when I went out t' the barn to check on the Deacon couple of hours ago."

"Did he say anything?" Gage asked.

"Wanted to know where I got the cattle."

Gage and Serena exchanged an exasperated glance.

"Why didn't you tell us?" Serena snapped.

"What's more important," Gage intervened, "did you tell him Serena traded with the Paiute for them?"

Pete shrugged. "Didn't seem no point in lyin'. They was gonna find out 'bout it sooner or later." He scratched thoughtfully at his beard. "Old Zeke didn't seem to like it too much. Cain't tell what'll set a man off, now cin you?"

"I knew it!" Serena shot out. "I just knew sharing the water would cause more trouble." Getting to her feet, she gave a heartfelt sigh. "Get your gun, Pete."

Gage took Nathan from Serena. "Go to the gate but don't open it. Tell him that if he wants to talk to you, he'll have to do it through the gate."

"All right," Serena said doubtfully. "I'll try."

"Open up these damned gates you bitch," Birk Reed's voice slammed through the thick oak.

Hurrying over to the gates, Serena called back, "What do you want, Reed?"

"I know all about you sharin' your precious water with them damned Indians."

"That's none of your business."

"The hell is ain't!" The sound of gunfire cracked just outside the gates, frighteningly close by. Only the walls and the wood divided her from it, from Birk Reed's desperate rage. From death.

"Are you going to kill for it? Again? The way you killed Gage Tanner and all the people here?"

Gage slipped up behind her. "Thanks for keeping your part of the deal."

Serena bristled. "It's my battle too, remember?" She winced as the dull thud of bullets battered the gates.

After several rounds of scattered shots, the gunfire briefly faded. "I didn't kill them," Birk shouted. "But you ain't gonna be so lucky, lady."

"Maybe not with your own hands, but your orders are as good as if you had."

"My boys got their own minds. Now open up!"

"Damn," Serena cursed softly. "He just won't give up." She looked to Gage for help.

Just then Nathan gave a loud wail, holding his arms out to her, his cries competing with Birk's angry yells.

"What the hell—?" Serena could almost see the engaged confusion on Birk's face. "You got a baby in there? Who else you hidin'? More pilgrims?"

Again gunfire hailed all around the ranch, mingled

with the shouting and cursing of the men outside. Silently, Serena thanked the Mormons for their stubborn determination to protect all that belonged to them. The ranch walls would hold, she didn't doubt it for an instant. If she could just convince Reed there was nothing for him here.

Her efforts failed miserably. There was nothing she could say, short of offering him the ranch, that he wanted to hear.

Fed by the ranchers' frustrations and, Serena guessed, a fair amount of whiskey, the rampage continued for nearly two hours. Gage was able to wound several of them and frighten off a few of their horses by aiming out of the slit in the wall. He insisted Serena keep Nathan with her in the upstairs bedroom, out of his way and out of earshot of Birk and his men.

Serena waited, pacing the floor, furious and worried by turns. She did her best to comfort Nathan and had finally succeeded in lulling him to sleep when the commotion outside waned, then stopped altogether.

Giving one last look at the sleeping baby, she hurried out, meeting Gage at the bottom of the stairs.

"What's going on now? Are they out of ammunition? Did they leave?"

"They're camping out over near the corral. Most of them have drunk themselves into a few hours hard sleep."

"Including Reed?"

He nodded, then reached out and took her shoulders in his hands, his face grim. "They killed what little stock you did have. I'm sorry, but there wasn't much we could do about it."

The stabbing hurt and disappointment she felt surprised her with its force. Freeing herself, Serena slowly walked to the picnic table and sank down onto one of the benches. The red and white cloth still lay atop it, its festive colors hiding the aging, splintered wood beneath.

Gage followed, standing close, but making no move to touch her again.

"We've got to get Nathan out of here," she said, voicing the first thought that came into her head. It surprised her, and from the brief flicker of expression that crossed Gage's face she could see he hadn't expected her to put Nathan before her loss. "I want him away from Reed. Somewhere where he can be safe and where someone can tell me how to nurse him back to health. I can't do it by myself." Tears flooded her eyes. She lifted her face to his. "We have to keep him alive. If nothing else lives, he has to survive."

"I know. That's why I've decided to take him to the Paiute until things settle down here."

"What! When? And how—?"

"Now. While I can. As to how . . ." He gave her a faint, lopsided smile. "I'm pretty good at vanishing."

Serena hesitated, searching his face, weighing the resolve she saw there. She trusted him, completely and without a shade of doubt, knowing even if he couldn't give her his heart, he would protect her and Nathan with his life. It was a quality that made her realize just how deeply she had come to care for him. But the idea of leaving Nathan with strangers after everything that had happened—"Fine. I'll have our things ready in a few minutes."

"*Our* things?" He shook his head. "No. Only his. Taking him is dangerous enough. You're safer here with Pete."

"No. No, I'm not." She couldn't let him leave her behind. What if Jerel came? He might even have a key. He'd have no cause to harm Pete, but she'd be at his mercy. "You can't take him away from me and leave him with people I don't know," she said. "I'll spend the whole time worrying over the both of you." It was true. Not the whole truth, but true nonetheless.

Pitting her determination against his, Serena squared her jaw and planted her hands on her hips. "If Nathan goes, I go too."

Chapter Thirteen

"You're crazy," Gage said bluntly, shaking his head. "You're not coming. And I'm sure as hell not going to drag a baby through the desert at night."

"Please. I can't stay here now."

"Why not? You've insisted on doing nothing but for over a month."

Serena bit back a surge of temper, knowing it would only serve to make him more determined to leave her behind. "I need help. Nathan isn't doing well. You know he's still young enough to be nursing, and I obviously can't give him that."

"So now you're ready to leave him with the Paiute, even though you've taken every chance to tell me how afraid you are of them?"

"No," Serena said through gritted teeth. "I need advice on how to care for him. There's no doctor in Vulture Creek. Where else am I going to get it? Besides, after what happened here today, how can you expect me to feel safe? Birk is obviously furious about my agreement with the Paiute. Those ruffians of his aren't going to leave me alone until I give them water."

Gage's eyes narrowed; he studied her for several moments, not answering. Finally, he dragged a chair around and propped one foot on it, crossing his arms over the back, giving her that direct stare that always both unnerved and compelled her to look back. "Tell me the truth."

"I have! I—"

"No. You haven't," he said flatly. "And unless you do, I'm leaving right now. Without you." When she hesitated, he spoke for her. "This has nothing to do with Nathan or Birk Reed. Mormons show up in Vulture Creek one day and you're ready to leave the next. You're running from them. Why?"

"I'm not. I—" Stopping, Serena asked herself why it mattered if he knew. He realized, from the little she told him, that she carried a resentment for Mormons side-by-side with gratitude and even affection for their generosity in taking her in. If she lied, he would know it and leave her behind. If she told the truth . . .

"I am," she said. "At least from one of them. Jerel Webster. I was supposed to marry him. I left three days before the wedding he'd planned, and I came here because—because it was the only place I remembered that felt safe. We were always moving, I never had a real home. Except here, for several years." She looked around the bedroom. "This was home."

She waited, expecting Gage to ask the same question Amanda had, to ask her to explain why she feared Jerel would somehow try to force her to honor their betrothal. Instead, Gage merely looked at her, searching her face as if weighing her words against what he knew or had guessed.

"He's one of the men who came into Vulture Creek," he said at last. "You recognized him when you saw him at Mandy's."

"Yes," Serena answered, her voice scarcely above a whisper. The old apprehension, gray and forbidding, swarmed over her, attacking all her defenses. Turning away from Gage, she knelt down by Nathan's makeshift cradle to give her hands and eyes something else to focus on. The baby gazed up at her, waving his tiny fists at the air. "I can't tell you why Jerel frightens me. Outwardly, he doesn't seem to act differently, except that he's stricter—much more extreme, unyielding. He refuses to give up the old doctrines, even when the law tells him to. There's no softness in him, no forgiveness." She slid the tip of her forefinger into Nathan's grip, gently wriggling it, trying to divorce herself from her words. "I once saw him with a girl who questioned the choice of husband her family had made for her. Her parents were willing to reconsider, but Jerel was insistent. He took her aside and put his hand on her shoulder and spoke to her. Not shouting or bullying, just that. Except I knew she carried the mark of his hand on her skin for three weeks."

Glancing back at Gage, she saw a muscle jerk along the line of his jaw. "We'll have to take the cart," he said, straightening. "The Paiute camp isn't too far, but it would be a dangerous ride for Nathan on Gusano. We'll use Mandy's pony to pull it, since the mule is still at her place."

"You'll take us with you?" Serena said, hardly believing he'd agreed so swiftly, without any questions.

"Against my better judgment." Nathan turned his head at the sound of Gage's voice, smiling his toothless grin when Gage looked his direction. Walking over to the drawer, Gage picked him up, holding the baby in the curve of his arm.

Serena stayed quiet, unwilling to disturb the hushed tranquility that had settled over the room with the stealth of a predawn mist. Watching them, she marveled at the softly lit image of the big man gently cradling the small boy against his chest. Solitude and the wilderness had shaped a hardness inside him that had been honed by tragedy. And yet, at odd moments like this, Serena saw an awkward tenderness in Gage that elicited a sweet warmth deep inside her.

She wanted to go to save herself from a confrontation with Jerel. And Gage was willing to take her, despite his own contrary feelings, simply because he took it upon himself, without reasoning why, to protect her and Nathan.

She'd always thought it would be impossible to survive if she let herself become a caretaker for others' lives. Until she met Gage Tanner. Now she questioned the fear that drove her to live only for her needs. Could there ever be more than a few moments like this between the two of them? Was there a place where they could join together, despite their separate beliefs, separate lives, blending the best of each other, free of doubt and the ghosts of the past?

"You're quiet," Gage said, his low voice coming into her reverie. In his arms, Nathan's head nodded, his eyes drifting closed. "I can't get used to that."

"I suppose that's your subtle way of saying I talk too much," Serena said with a wry half-smile. She rose to her feet, smoothing out her rumpled skirts. "Nathan's asleep. He never sleeps when I'm holding him. He's usually crying. He must like your stillness. You'd make a good father."

A shadow fell over Gage's face. "Not good enough." Moving slowly, he carefully laid the sleeping baby back in the cradle, tucking the woolen blanket around him. He looked down at him a long moment, his eyes full of old ghosts.

Serena touched his arm so he turned to her. "More

than good enough. I've seen you with Nathan. You won't convince me otherwise."

"I have a hard time convincing you of anything," Gage said, his dark mood shifting. With a last look at Nathan, he took her hand and led her outside to the balcony. "We'll let him get a few hours sleep before we go. If we leave near midnight, we can be there before dawn."

"Isn't it dangerous, traveling at night?" Serena asked.

"It's more dangerous in daylight. For both of us."

Knowing he was right, Serena made no comment. She let him lead her to the back of the house, to the place where the balcony nearly reached the height of the stone wall and they could look out over the muted landscape, to the heaven-reaching shadows of the cliffs.

Tracing his strong features in the moonlight, Serena's thoughts went to the journey ahead and suddenly she shivered.

"What's wrong?" Gage shifted to look at her.

"I'm afraid," she whispered.

"I can't take away the risk. I'll do all I can to keep you and Nathan safe, but—"

"No . . . it's not that."

The familiar perceptiveness came into his eyes. "Then what?"

"I don't know. I just feel—" Serena let go of his hand and moved to the edge of the wall, leaning both her palms against it. The desert wind brushed over her body, warm and soft. "Once we're there, it will be the first time I'll see you, that we'll be together in the light. I've gotten used to the darkness, it seems like a part of us. I'm afraid that . . . that it won't be the same. That it won't be any more a dream, but something too real."

"Maybe," he said quietly. "But it had to happen sometime. I can't be the Spirit in the Wind forever.

Someday, for better or worse, I have to go back to being Gage Tanner."

"I know. I know. But I don't want to lose it." She lowered her head and whispered her words into the darkness. "I don't want to lose you."

"Serena—"

"No." She turned on him, her stance defiant and proud. "No, don't say we're impossible, or that it can never be more than it is now. I won't believe it. I want you to stay. I want it enough for the both of us."

"I don't doubt you do. But wanting isn't always enough. Even for you." With a gentle touch, he brushed a strand of hair from her face. "There are some things that'll never belong to you."

"Or some people."

"I don't even belong to myself. How can I be something you need?"

"I don't know. I don't understand it and I don't want to. I only know you are. And that's all that matters to me. That's all that needs to matter."

Gage stared at her, at the stubborn lift of her chin, the rebellion in her eyes and to Serena's surprise, started to laugh. "Woman, you're stubborn enough to fight a rattler and give him the first bite, if it'd get you something you wanted. Although you'd probably argue him to death before he ever opened his mouth."

"Stubbornness can be a good trait, you know," Serena teased back, her mouth twitching up in a smile. She surrendered to the lighter mood between them because he wanted it, knowing he wouldn't succumb or retreat no matter how hard or far she pushed him. And now, especially now, she wanted him close. "And if I didn't do all the talking, we'd never say more than a dozen words to each other."

"Is that so?" Lacing his fingers with hers, Gage

turned to look out at the cliffs again, avoiding her eyes. "The way I see it," he said, "when two people under-stand each other, there's no need for talking."

The slight hesitant waver in his strong voice made Serena's heart give a queer lurch. "Well, I'm not so sure about that," she murmured. "But, I guess I could try to spend a little more time listening."

She stood there with him in the darkness, hearing words only the touch of his hand and the soft spell of the night could speak, and waited for midnight to start them on a journey toward dawn.

The cart lurched over a rut, jolting Serena out of a light, troubled sleep. She sat leaning awkwardly against Gage with her head against his shoulder, Nathan nap-ping in her lap. "I'm sorry," she mumbled, struggling to sit upright again. "I didn't mean to fall asleep."

Gage stole a look at the woman beside him, smiling a little as she yawned and tried to scrub the sleep out of her eyes with the hand that wasn't supporting the baby. "I'd say you've earned an hour's rest. You and Nathan can get some real sleep at the camp. We're nearly there. It's just at the edge of that ridge. You can see the fires," he said, pointing to a place in the charcoal grayness that was lit with a faint orange glow. "I'll be glad to get there myself."

Stretching a little on the hard oak plank seat, Gage twisted his neck from side to side, trying to work out some of the stiffness. He was used to riding, not sitting, and the plodding hours of driving the pony across the desert were catching up to him. In the darkness, on con-stant guard against predators of both the animal and hu-man sort, and with the rickety cart, the trip had taken twice as long as it usually did. Gusano, tied to the back of the cart, seemed to share his restlessness. Unaccustomed to being tethered, the stallion had spent most of the trip snorting and tossing his head.

"You could use some sleep yourself," Serena said. He suddenly felt her fingers on his neck, sliding under the hair at his nape to massage the taut muscles.

The strong, rhythmic motion of her hand felt good. It took away a piece of his tiredness, leaving him wanting more of her. "I'm used to odd hours," Gage said, trying to distract himself from the feeling. "I've learned to do without when it's needed. Working a ranch, scouting—"

"Being a ghost."

"That too."

Her hand moved to his shoulder, kneading through the thin barrier of his shirt. "It will feel good to lie down," she said, her fingers warm where they pressed.

Not knowing what to answer, Gage tried to concentrate on the bite of the leather between his hands and the subtle chorus of sounds around them. Nothing in the air twitched his senses into alertness until he picked out the sharp cry of a cougar in the distant cliffs. The pony gave a nervous whinny. Behind him, Gusano pawed at the ground, pulling back against the tether.

"What is it?" Serena asked sharply, her fingers clenching on his shoulder. "Are we being followed?'

"Followed? No. It's a cougar, too far away to give us trouble."

"Oh . . . I thought. You said, the risk—"

"I was thinking of outlaws or Apache."

Gage glanced at her, then at Nathan awake and wriggling in her lap as if he sensed her abrupt tension. Serena's hand fell from his shoulder and she shifted the baby to a more comfortable position. She looked tired, her lank hair tousled, her dress rumpled, lack of sleep evident in the violet hollows under her eyes. But when

Nathan grinned up at her, grabbing for a strand of hair, the lines of worry and exhaustion softened.

In a few short days, she had grown protective of him, almost possessive. And in the catch of that moment, Gage saw her not as willful and fiercely jealous of her own security, but as a woman both soft and strong, capable of a tenderness and generosity of spirit he hadn't suspected she possessed.

Serena looked up, caught him watching her and smiled. "I think he's starting to like me. Maybe a little. At least lately he doesn't scrunch up his face and cry every time I come near. That used to happen a lot when I was living with the Mormons and tried to help with the babies."

"Maybe because it didn't mean as much to you. With all that's happened, Nathan is more yours than anyone's. And he knows it."

"Ours," she said firmly. She looked at Nathan than at him. "He's ours."

Shrugging, Gage turned away. Though he shared her feeling, there was no way to tell her without admitting much more.

"Unless ... Oh Gage, what if his relatives, others who must have been expecting him to arrive with his family in Salt Lake—what if they're out looking for him, for them now?"

Gage sat silent a long spell. "There's nothing we can do about that, is there?"

"No, I guess not," she admitted, not allowing herself to dwell on the possibility of losing him. Instead, she forced her mind to focus only on the immediate. "I hope your Paiute friends can tell me how to feed him better," Serena went on as if she hadn't noticed his silence. "I'm worried about him."

"I know. I am too." He nodded toward the front of the cart. "The camp's just ahead."

The leaping scarlet and orange glow from a dozen different fires grew as they neared the camp. Up ahead, shadowy figures of people and horses moved in and out of the cool gray fog, barely illuminated by the dawn light that hovered on the horizon.

Gage sensed Serena stiffen the closer they came to the camp and guessed at the images the fire and her own mind conjured up. "It's all right. There's nothing to be afraid of."

Blindly, Serena's hand groped over the cart seat until she touched his thigh. Not hesitating, Gage gathered up the harness reins in one hand and took hers in the other. She held tight, and he could feel her drawing the comfort and strength she needed from his touch.

"Yes. I know," she said finally. Giving his hand a final press, she let go and cradled up Nathan in her arms. "It will be just fine this time."

The cart rattled slowly over the uneven ground, then gradually pulled to a stop at Gage's command just inside the Paiute camp. Climbing down from the seat to help Serena to her feet, Gage turned as Kwion emerged from the mist, wrapped in a tattered blanket the color of the dawn sky.

"We welcome you, brother," he said. "We have been waiting for you to come to us. It has been many days."

"Too many. I didn't have time to send you a message, but we need shelter for several days." Gage gestured to Serena and Nathan. "The baby was separated from his mother and Serena needs your help in caring for him."

"I'm having trouble feeding him," Serena put in before Gage could say any more. "He's used to being nursed and I can't do it. But there must be some other way I can feed him." She broke off and for the first time looked fully at Kwion, both defiant and pleading. "I ask a favor and you owe me nothing. And I haven't exactly welcomed your people at the ranch. But I'm asking for your help. For Nathan's sake. He has no one else. And I know how it feels to be suddenly alone."

Gage stared at her, unable to hide his surprise. He realized how much it took for her to ask for Kwion's help, and couldn't suppress the rush of admiration knowing she had swallowed her pride and fear for Nathan's benefit.

"We will do all we can to help," Kwion said, a faint smile disturbing the creases on his face.

Letting go a pent-up breath, Serena's shoulders slumped a little. "Thank you," she said. "Now I owe you a debt."

Shaking his head, but not answering, Kwion extended a gnarled hand and guided her forward into the camp. Gage followed behind as Kwion led them to a hut and called to a smiling, round-faced woman sitting just inside the doorway. He spoke to her in his own tongue and after a few moments, the woman turned and grinned broadly at Serena and the baby. "This is Wuri. She has borne many sons. She will also show you where you can rest."

Serena looked at Gage. In her eyes, he saw warring desires and he nodded his encouragement. She watched him for a long moment, then, holding Nathan close, followed Wuri into the hut.

"Much has changed," Kwion said as he started walking toward the opposite end of a camp to where a fire burned brightly at the front of a tepee. He sat down on the ground near the flames and waited for Gage to follow suit before continuing. "You come now at morning. What brings you out of the darkness?"

"The baby needed help, and there was trouble at the

ranch. But I would have come anyway, to talk. I thought I had better bring them along. I didn't want to leave them alone, the way things are . . ." Gage paused, then added, "There's a new group of Mormons in the area."

Kwion glanced up from the fire. "You fear more trouble will follow them? Or that they have brought it with them?"

"I don't know. Maybe both. Some of the ranchers attacked the ranch last night when they heard Serena agreed to let your people as well as the Mormons use the oasis. It could be the reason for the last raid on the ranch."

"Possibly. But I have also heard that the few Apache still hiding in the territory have vowed to take their revenge against cavalry men and their families. Anyone and everyone who helped capture their leader. Perhaps they think the woman at the ranch now is related to the Spirit in the Wind, Gage Tanner. There was a raid, three days past now, at a ranch near Fredonia. Twelve were killed and they took five women and children," Kwion finished, his tone deliberate.

Gage flashed him a hard look. "But you don't think it was Apache, do you? Either time?"

"Both times bear the mark of their brutality. Yet—" Kwion shrugged. "The bitterness of revenge is the most fearsome poison. It can drive sane men to acts of madness."

"I suppose it can." Rubbing a hand over his jaw, Gage felt the weight of responsibility add to his burden of tiredness. "I'm not quite mad yet, although some might argue it. There are times I believe it myself."

"You need rest," Kwion said quietly. "There is time for it here. Perhaps when you can see and hear clearly, you will find your answers." He looked to the other end of the camp. "All of you."

Gage followed his gaze. He couldn't see Serena, but he felt her near, always inside him, as much a part of him as his breath or the beat of his heart.

He wanted answers, and not only to settle the questions he'd carried with him all these weeks. But to questions he hadn't yet asked, those that could only be answered by his heart.

The afternoon sun slanted toward evening when Serena straightened from bending over Nathan's pallet, putting a hand to massage the small in her back. "He's better," she told Wuri, knowing the Indian woman didn't understand the words, but could hear the relief and pleasure in her voice.

Wuri smiled broadly, holding up the makeshift bottle formed from a cow's udder, she'd coaxed Nathan into suckling, then indicating the baby with a wave of her hand. Serena had hoped to find a wet nurse among the Paiute women, but when she described this to Wuri with gestures, Wuri's face grew sad and she merely shook her head.

Serena nodded, returning the smile. It had taken several hours of patient encouragement, but for the first time in days, Nathan was full of milk and contentedly making an attempt to bat at a small hide-covered ball that Wuri had hung over his pallet.

With Nathan cared for, a large measure of Serena's tension and fear had eased. She actually began to relax with Wuri and the other women who came to see the baby. She had sat among them at Nathan's side, strangely soothed by their chatter and exclamations over the tiny boy.

Slowly, before she fully realized she'd allowed it, they had drawn her into a camaraderie that required no language to be spoken or felt. They brought her food, showed her where to bathe, then with much laughter and clapping, finally persuaded her to don a buckskin shift that barely skimmed her knees. It surprised her to find how much more comfortable and practical the shift was compared to her own constricting, heavy cotton skirt and blouse.

Another woman then coaxed Serena into letting her braid her hair into a long thick plait that hung nearly to her waist. When she tied the ends with a soft strip of leather, all of the other women nodded and motioned their approval. All but one, that was. Serena noticed her peeking around from behind a poplar tree a short distance away, a coolly assessing look on her pretty face.

Now, as Wuri urged her outside the hut for the first time that afternoon, Serena thought she ought to feel foolish or self-conscious about wearing the Indian garb. But the supple hide fit her body like a handclasp, warm and smooth. In it she felt free, at ease as she walked bare-foot through the camp, basking in the late-afternoon heat and the gentle brush of the pine-scented wind.

She wondered about Gage. Looking into the deep golden sun that brushed the edge of the cliffs, she realized for all of her heart-fear, she hadn't seen him in day-light. Maybe she wouldn't. Maybe he truly was a dream of the night. Her Spirit in the Wind.

The air fell still and for a heartbeat of time, a hushed silence scattered like falling leaves over the camp.

Serena stopped before the dying embers of a fire and as if her thoughts and desires called him to her, the flap of the tepee in front of her moved aside and Gage stepped out of it into the shadow it cast.

He stood with his back to the waning sun, delving into her eyes the moment their gazes met. Serena stared back, at sea in a wash of feeling with no name, wondering if her vision deceived her.

They joined together in a glance, inexplicably, inexorably bound by ties both fragile and powerful.

Gage couldn't look away. He saw her in the golden wash of sunlight, stripped of her fear and hatred, and thought her more beautiful than any women he'd ever seen or known. Spellbound, he stepped out of the darkness and into the light toward her.

The shock of difference in him left Serena stunned. It was as if suddenly she saw an image from the past, the vision she'd so often imagined of what he must have been, and not the man she knew. A man who lived in the shadowed cavern between death and life.

"You look like you've seen a ghost," Gage said lightly.

He stood near enough for Serena to breath in the clean scent of water and wind, to see clearly the clouded green of the eyes that had searched hers so many times. Tentatively, she reached up and touched his face. "I'm not sure I haven't," she said. "You're—different."

"That doesn't sound like a compliment." He took his time looking at her, all of her, from her face to her bared legs, then back again. "You're different too." A hint of a smile touched the corner of his lips. "And I like it."

A fulgurant heat rushed through her, sparking like lightning up and down her limbs. "I didn't mean it as an insult. It's just, I've gotten used to you being something . . . wild, a part of the night, not quite civilized. Now . . . now, it's as though you've gone back to what you were. As if you've come to life again." She said the last words slowly, like a discovery she'd hoped to make, but imagined impossible.

"Maybe I have. Today. Here. With you." He hadn't intended the words, didn't even know they were inside him until he said them. But he knew they were true. "It might be time to start rejoining the living," he added. "Sorry you're disappointed."

"I'm not disappointed." She smiled, cocking her head to look at him from all angles. "It's an improvement. Except for this—" she added, flicking her fingers at his beard. "Somehow it doesn't fit you any more."

Gage rubbed a hand along the side of his face. "It'll have to wait. I don't trust myself with a razor when I can't see what I'm doing."

"Let me," Serena made the offer on impulse. "I can probably manage without doing too much damage to you." With a mischievous challenge in her eyes she added, "You trust me, don't you?"

Raising a brow, Gage let the question pass. "What have I got to lose?"

Chapter Fourteen

"What the hell do you mean by *gone?*" Ross stared at Whiskey Pete, frustration at the old man's vague babblings rapidly soaking up what little patience he had.

"I mean what I told you," Pete said, squinting with his good eye at Ross as if the other man had gone deaf and stupid. Seated in the straw in Deacon Mather's stall, he turned his attention back to the bull, stroking the animal's massive head with a gentle hand. "Took the youngin' and left afore dawn. All of 'em. They told me t' stay inside the gates, but I couldn't leave the Deacon out here by hisself again, now could I?"

"Serena and Nathan went alone?"

"Alone? Naw, he went with 'em. Took Miss Amanda's pony and the cart and he drove 'em away. Thanks fer bringin' Last Chance home to me by the way."

Silently cursing Gage and his nasty habit of getting tangled up in problems that weren't his to start with, Ross pushed back his hat with his thumb. "What happened here last night? The yard looked like you been slaughterin' every cow between here and Phoenix."

"Was Reed and his boys," Pete said, groping in the straw for the bottle he'd pushed there. "I told Zeke she

was sharin' the water with the Paiute and he got mad
'nough to eat the Devil with his horns on. Must've told
his boss, and they all come out here, aimin' to put holes
in whatever was breathin'." He took a long draught of
whiskey, choking a little over the last swallow. "She
said I shouldn't have told 'em. S'ppose that's true."

"He'd have found out one way or the other," Ross
said, bending down to lay a consoling hand on Pete's
shoulder. "Don't go blamin' yourself over what can't be
changed. Why didn't you go with her? It ain't safe for
you alone. Especially out here."

Pete looked up to him, an expression of utter disbelief
on his unshaven face. Lucky Joe, lying next to him,
perked his ears and glared up at Ross, as if sensing his
friend's agitation. "Why you're as dull-headed as them
two. They tried to git me to leave the Deacon when he's
ailin' and go along on their fool journey. Well, I'll tell
you same as I told them. That'd be like leavin' my own
kin. If I had any."

Ross's anger melted to reluctant pity. "S'ppose it
would. Let's at least get him into the courtyard. Then
you'll all be behind locked gates."

"Won't matter," Pete said, shaking his head sadly.
"Won't matter if we's in there or out here if the tree
devils come back. They'll find us, they will. Gates don't
matter none to 'em. They got their own magic."

"Tree devils . . . you mean the Paiute?"

"Naw." Pete tipped the bottle down his throat for the
last drop. "Not Indian magic. They never hurt no one.
No sir, ain't no one can fight the devils. Just the look of
'em is 'nough to make an icicle feel feverish."

"Friend, I think you need to sleep it off. You've
drunk enough to start seein' things that ain't there."
Ross reached down and latched onto Pete's limp arms.
"I'll get you back inside those gates and—"

"Let me be!" Whiskey Pete shot back, struggling against him. "I ain't leavin' the Deacon, not till he's good as new."

"Dammit, Pete, you ain't even got a gun with you, do you?"

Pete stared blankly at the bull, caressing its neck, mumbling under his breath.

"Take this," Ross said, unholstering his revolver and pushing the gun into Pete's hand. "I'll go on up to the cliffs and check there," he added, thinking aloud. "Can't imagine where else they might've gone."

Reluctantly, he left Whiskey Pete with the bull and headed back to where he'd tethered his palomino near the gates Pete had left open. He started to close them, to at least give the appearance the ranch was protected. But on impulse he decided to have one look around, both inside and out, for any hint of where Serena and Gage might have gone. Pulling his rifle from its saddle sheath, he walked in the direction of the horse corral, feeling jumpier with every crunch his boots made on the hard ground. An odd, eerie silence hung over the ranch; death's still poison spread over the yard, paralyzing time itself.

He found traces of mayhem everywhere. Not only had Reed's boys killed the livestock, but they'd done a through job of ransacking the place, knocking down fencing, shooting up the barns and shed, leaving broken bottles and bullet holes like calling cards of destruction.

Sickened at the waste, Ross walked back to the ranch house and through the gates to hunt the courtyard and rooms. He searched behind each closed door, finding nothing but the signs of a hurried departure—drawers left open, dishes still on the table, dropped clothing left behind.

"What've you gone and done now, Tanner?" Ross

muttered to the silent walls. Finding no answers, he decided to check Gage's cliff dwelling, then go back to the trading post and at least tell Mandy what had happened. Maybe she would have some ideas.

He stopped in the kitchen to make sure the fire in the stove was safely out. As he was about to pull the door closed behind him, he heard voices coming from the courtyard. Not Gage, and definitely not Serena Lark. His hand tight on the rifle, Ross peeled back the curtain and stole a glance. The same trio of Mormons he'd run into at Mandy's, alone with several others, looked to be splitting up for a search.

"Hell and damnation," he muttered thinking all he wanted to do was to get out fast. And alive. More than anything on earth he hated the idea of getting mixed up in other people's messes and he now found himself roped to the center of one as big and mean as the lead bull in a buffalo herd.

"Maybe she was killed, along with the cattle," one of the men was saying to the grim-faced elder. "Although there is one horse, outside the gates, saddled and still alive. It must have been left behind by whoever did this."

"Perhaps . . . There are other possibilities, though. If she did not come back here, then I am right and she has heard of my presence in the territory. She has always been a willful, impulsive child. It is her way to flee without forethought or plan, foolishly believing she can deny destiny."

"But—the animals?"

"I suspect that was not her doing. The water supply here has always been coveted by all living in this area." The ashen-haired man cast a hard look around him, causing Ross to shrink back from the window to avoid being seen. "Tanner convinced the savages they had a right to use the oasis. Perhaps she did the same and brought this upon herself. Or perhaps there is some truth to the stories of Apache raids in this part of the territory."

"Should we look for her, Moroni?"

"Yes. But search for the living as well as the dead. It could be she is merely trying to frighten us into thinking it is unsafe for anyone to stay here. It is unlikely, but with Serena Lark, it is possible." He paused, his eyes sweeping the courtyard again. "And look for signs of others, as well as her. I haven't decided whether or not I believe everything or anything I have heard."

The man at his side nodded. "Brother Abe and I will look upstairs, and the rest can search the grounds."

Nodding, the elder man started toward Whiskey Pete's rooms. "For her sake, she had best be here, alive or in spirit. If I must track her much further, I might find it more rewarding to string her up by her beautiful neck than to make her my wife."

Ross waited for all the men to disappear from view, listening to their footsteps over his head as they looked through the upstairs rooms. He wondered why they didn't expect to find Gage and his adopted family on the ranch and decided they must have talked to someone and heard about the massacre before they arrived. Except, if they had, why did the Mormon leader have doubts about what he'd heard?

Rubbing at his beard, he tried to recall the name Serena had given for the elder. One of his men had called him Moroni; Ross felt certain that wasn't the name Serena mentioned. It was Woerther, or Weston—Webster. Jerel Webster. Mornoi must be some Mormon nickname, he mused, shrugging off the oddity.

At the first opportunity, as noiselessly as the deer he hunted, with circumstances of predator and prey re-

versed, he slipped out onto the front porch and inched
his way along the wall beneath the cover of the balcony
above, toward the open gates.

A few swift strides took him safely outside, where he
made for his palomino. The suddenly missing horse
would cause raised eyebrows among the Mormons, but
at this point, Ross didn't care. Throwing a leg up, he
kicked the horse soundly and headed straight out of
trouble's path. He'd find that cliff dwelling of Gage's,
and if they weren't hiding there, he decided he might
just borrow it for a few days.

Bearing a contented, sleeping Nathan in the pack tied
to her back, Wuri padded up to where Gage and Serena
stood outside the hut, watching the twilight spread over
the camp. Silent and perceptive, her black eyes searched
Serena's, then Gage's face before she spoke.

Serena was learning that among the Paiute it almost
seemed part of an unwritten code of manners that when
one approached a couple or group of others, that person
first paused to sense the mood of the meeting, waiting
and absorbing the atmosphere between them so as not to
interrupt an intimacy or an important discussion or even
an argument. How unlike most people she knew, she
mused, who simply assumed the right to join in, saying
whatever came off the top of their heads, regardless of
the intrusion.

She'd noticed from the start Gage offered this same
consideration, pausing always to listen in silence to the
temperament of her heart and mind before speaking.
Now she understood where he must have learned it, although in him, it seemed more instinctive than a lesson
he had been taught. At first, she'd been irritated with his
habit of watching and saying nothing, thinking it his

way of ignoring her. But she had come to appreciate that quality in him, secure in knowing he truly wanted to know how she felt and what she thought. He made her feel as if her desires and needs were more important than any other, even his own.

The Paiute, also, treated each other with the same consideration. In so many ways she was being forced to admit that these *savages* were turning out to be far more civilized than the self-righteous who condemned them.

Myself included, she wanted to say to Wuri as she looked back into the woman's kind face. Serena longed to ask forgiveness for her unfair judgment of the Paiute, for her groundless hatred. Wuri and Kwion's attentive care had probably saved Nathan's life; if it took the rest of her own life Serena vowed to find a way to repay them.

Tears of gratitude and regret suddenly welled in her eyes, but she lacked the words to express their meaning to Wuri. She turned to Gage. "How can I let her know how sorry I am for the way I treated them, how much what she's done for Nathan means to me?"

Gage smiled and stroked her cheek gently with the back of his knuckles. "Look in her eyes, Serena. She knows already."

Looking from one to the other, Wuri mimicked his action, reaching up with the back of her hand to touch Gage's freshly shaved cheek. A grin curved at the corners of her mouth, making the thin laugh lines at the edges of her eyes more pronounced. Mischief sparked in her eyes she nodded at him. "Good face," she said, turning to Serena for confirmation.

Serena brushed her fingertips down his other cheek, bringing a flush to it. "Oh yes, very good face," she teased. Her eyes drifted over the rest of his body. "Very good everything."

Gage swiped her hand away and kissed it. "How would you know?"

"I have an excellent imagination."

"You do, do you? Well, then it ought to satisfy your curiosity."

"On the contrary, it only arouses it further," she said, dropping her voice low and husky. Certain she'd achieved the desired level of discomfort for Gage, she flung her hair back over her shoulder and turned away from him to check Nathan.

Gage scuffed at the dirt with his boot and cleared his throat, then spoke for some time to Wuri in Paiute. When they'd finished, he moved to touch Nathan's little hand. "Wuri says we're to join the ceremony tonight."

"Oh? What sort of ceremony?"

"It's hard to describe. Something like the night they came to the ranch, but more formal. It's a sort of a Sunday meeting under the stars. But first we have to prepare ourselves."

"How?" Serena asked warily, unsure of the odd combination of devilment and uneasiness she saw in his expression.

"We have to—cleanse ourselves. Then our skin will be painted and we'll dress in the clothes they've prepared for us."

"Well, a bath sounds like heaven itself. But paint on my skin . . . I don't know."

"After all of their generosity toward us and Nathan, is it too much to ask? Consider it an honor to be asked to join them," Gage said. "You wanted to thank them, this is a good start. Part of the ceremony includes stripping themselves of anything made by white hands. Yet they've asked us to be a part of it."

"You belong here," Serena told him, then added quickly before he could chastise her again, "But I suppose it would be an insult to refuse. And I am curious. What about Nathan? Who'll look after him?"

Gage nodded to the sleeping baby. "Wuri said his belly is full and he'll sleep for hours. She said one of the women will stay with him while we're away."

"Is it the same dance they did that night at the ranch? That was so—so strange ... I still don't know what happened to me. To us."

"Magic," Gage said matter-of-factly.

Serena stared at him. "Magic?"

"Yes, magic," he echoed, drawing a finger down her cheek. "Don't you believe in magic?"

"I—I don't know," Serena faltered, the look in his eyes, the softness in his voice, unraveling something inside her.

"You should. And yes," he said, dropping his hand. "It's similar. They'll commune with their dead. But it's never exactly the same. For tonight's dance, the elders have fasted and prayed two days. Tonight they'll see visions that bring past and present together."

Serena shook her head. "It makes me nervous. But whatever happens, right now it almost seems it would be worth enduring just to have a hot bath."

Gage smiled oddly. "Oh, it's hot all right. But I wouldn't exactly call it a bath."

"What are you talking about?"

"Come on," he said, taking her hand in his. "I'll show you."

Wuri walked beside them as far as the edge of the camp, then motioned them toward the mesa beyond the cluster of wickiups and tepees. Before Wuri left them to settle Nathan for the night, Serena lightly kissed the baby's forehead.

She touched a hand to Wuri's shoulder. "Thank you,"

she said, punctuating her words with a smile in hopes Wuri would understand.

Gage repeated their thanks in Paiute, and Wuri nodded, returning a smile, then turned with Nathan to return to the shelter of the hut before night's cool breezes replaced the last of the day's heat.

With no other words of explanation Gage veered off in the direction of the mesa, seemingly heading nowhere. Taking two steps for his every one, Serena followed at his heels. "Where are we going?" She strained to scour the flat barren land in the fading light. "There's nothing out there but rocks and snakes and sagebrush."

Gage pointed to a massive dark mound in the distance. "See that?"

"That boulder? Of course I see it. I see them every day."

"It's not a boulder. It's a sweat-house."

"Oh, a bath-house. What an odd little building." She shrugged off her trepidation. "Who cares what it looks like, it sounds wonderful."

"No. Not bath-house. I said sweat-house. The only water we'll be bathing in is our own sweat."

Serena stopped short. "What?"

Grasping her hand more firmly, Gage tugged her forward. "You'll never feel more refreshed." He grinned, an impish glint in his eye. "Trust me."

"Not likely," Serena retorted, struggling against his iron grip on her hand. "I'm sweaty enough, thank you!"

Gage tolerated the tug-of-war less than it took her to draw a breath before bending down and tossing her over his shoulder. "We can't be late to the ceremony. Kwion won't understand."

Like a stubborn goat, Serena squirmed against him, grumbling and cursing the rest of the walk to the secluded little structure. At the low doorway he sat her on her feet and without preamble, promptly began unbuttoning his shirt.

Serena stared at his fingers. "What—what are you doing?"

"Strip."

"Strip?" Her eyes widened. "Are you serious?"

"Unless you want your clothes drenched in sweat."

"You mean—" She looked from him to the sweathouse and back again. "We're going in there, together? Naked? Just the two of us?" She suddenly smiled. "You didn't tell me that part."

Gage rolled his eyes at her. "It's hotter than Hell in there. I doubt you'll feel much like—like doing that. The most you'll feel is faint after a few minutes."

"We'll see about that." As slowly and seductively as her eager fingers would move, Serena worked at the laces of her shift to remove it. If the promises of her heart couldn't tempt him to stay with her, perhaps she could seduce him into staying with the pleasures she knew her body could give. "Indian women certainly have a much easier time undressing," she said, easing first one shoulder, then the other out of the deerhide dress. "No corsets or petticoats—or anything else." She held the loosened garment against her until Gage looked up from the holster he was unbuckling at his hip—then dropped it. "I think there's something to be said for Indian customs, don't you?"

He stared at her, eyes hot, his hands frozen on his gunbelt. Finally, by obvious force of will, he dragged his gaze down, flinging aside his holster and concentrating on the seemingly insurmountable task of removing his boots.

"Here, let me help you," Serena offered, smiling to herself. Before he could refuse her, she knelt in front of him and lifted his foot in her palms. Inch by inch she tugged first one then the other boot and sock from his feet, taking time to stroke the tops of his feet and toes as she did.

Dumbly, Gage watched her, then his hands moved to fumble at his waistband.

"No." Serena slowly rose, brushing his fingers aside. "Let me."

"I don't think—"

"Don't. It's too late." Forcing her trembling hands to a light, lingering touch, she slid his pants down his long, muscular thighs and calves, her fingertips trailing over the tiny hairs and skin as she eased the covering from his body. "There. Now we're even," she said, looking up at him, a smile playing with her mouth.

For a moment, she thought she had broken his resolve. He stared down at her, every muscle flexed, his breathing fast and hard. "Go inside," he said at last, roughly, the ragged edge to his voice telling her how far she had pushed him. "I'll be there in a minute."

"But it's almost completely dark out. I want to see you as you see me. You're so beautiful, Gage," she murmured, gently reaching out to graze her fingers over his broad shoulders, down his arms.

Gage almost laughed, but the sound caught in his throat. "No one's ever called me *that* before."

Serena stepped closer. Close enough to touch without touching. Too close to turn back. "You're the most perfect man God ever formed, Gage Tanner." He was, and not only in flesh, she mused. The sheer power of his presence, his straightforward way of facing life, the strength in him that neither she nor anyone or anything else could bend or break; the passion and the tenderness she sensed when he touched her, held her, whispered to her in the midnight darkness—all made him the man of her dreams. She leaned into him, her breasts to his chest, and pressed a kiss to the soft matt of hair that covered the spot where his heart would be. "I want to see all of you."

Her bold temptation elicited a deep groan from him. "Woman, you're as brazen as any panther I've tangled with. And twice as dangerous."

"Not to any man. Only you."

Briefly his body melded to hers in surrender and Serena savored the warm, exciting feel of his skin against her own. But as quickly, he pulled back, leaving her cold and bare under a sunless sky.

"We don't have much time. The ceremony's going to start in less than an hour."

Gritting her teeth against the disappointment and frustration his rejection spurred in her, Serena turned away and opened the low door to the sweat-house. A scorching rush of dry heat greeted her as she made her way inside the cramped space to sit down on a bench built around a central heap of searing red coals.

The tiny room was black except for an eerie red glow that radiated a dull light, but the heavy air swelled with the heady scent seeping up from layer upon layer of sage strewn about the dirt floor. Before she'd stepped inside her body burned from within, now the fire spread outward through every fiber, every tender nerve.

By the time Gage found his way inside, she was aflame.

He had to bend at the waist to fit his tall frame into the squat little house. Aching to sit where his leg could brush her thigh, instead he forced himself to sit opposite her, separated from her by the pit of red fire.

He settled onto the bench and found her watching him, her umber eyes aglow and penetrating. Hungry. She stared at him, an avid need on her face, eager to brand him as hers with the all-consuming love she of-

fered. And the terrifying part of it was he half-wanted to
give in, to let her possess him.

Her spirit, her courage, her unflagging stubborn determination to have what she wanted, to survive against
any odds, had breathed warmth and life into the cold
desert of his heart. To hold her, touch her, love her, join
with her in the ancient dance that lured him with its lost,
wild call . . .

The unwanted thoughts crossed his mind as his eyes
slipped from hers to caress her breasts, the soft curve of
her waist and supple bloom of her hips. Flawless, her
skin shimmered with moisture in a crimson and gold
aura that framed her like a sunset halo shining around
the only flower in the desert.

How terrible a fate could it be to belong to a woman
like that, he mused, his eyes drifting lower still, to the
triangle of curls a shade darker than the wild mane of
sienna waves tumbling down her shoulders and back.

He averted his eyes in time to see her lips part to run
her tongue around them. The heat alone would have
brought sweat spilling from every pour in his body, but
watching her, craving one moment of passionate abandon, wanting her more each second, made every drop
feel like blood. He was melting at her feet for want of
her, desperately groping in every corner of his soul for
the will to defy his own damned code of honor and simply take her without thoughts of tomorrow, of yesterday.
It hurt, deep inside, to watch her and not take everything she begged him to make his own.

So many nights he'd come to this place with other
men, other women, but then it was only part of a ritual.
The nakedness seemed natural and benign. Now, his
body found hers, despite the heat, despite the space that
separated them, without a single touch.

Serena lifted her arms to her head and swept her

heavy tresses above her head. The gesture lifted her breasts to his eye level like an offering. Holding her hair up over one arm, she leaned her head back and trailed fingers down her long, slender neck to the damp cleft between her breasts and over her flat belly. "I'm on fire," she murmured. "It's so hot. Isn't it?"

"Too hot." His need throbbing to the brink of explosion, Gage abruptly stood. But he made the swift motion without thinking and his head crashed against an exposed log in the crude ceiling. "Dammit! I'm getting out of here."

Rubbing the pained spot, he caught a smile punctuate Serena's wide-eyed stare and realized her eyes had drifted below his waist, giving her evidence of his need right in front of her face.

"Satisfied?" he asked, moving his hand from his head to his face to rub away the rivulets of sweat.

She eased off of the bench and faced him, her skin shining wet. "No. Are you?" And with that, she brushed by him, leaving him to stare after her, integrity and resolve suddenly feeling like cold companions.

As Serena stepped outside, the coolness of the early evening shocked her burning skin, but as it quickly dried her, she felt something beyond the cleansing power of soap and water. It was a purification, a purging by the elements. She delighted in the tingling renewal that spread over her flesh like a blanket of showering stars.

Unexpectedly, out of the black void that seemed to stretch endlessly across the desert at night, a figure bearing a flaming torch appeared at her side. Serena gasped and instinctively shielded her nudity with her arms. But Gage, stepping out of the sweat-house behind her, had no such reaction. Instead, he nodded a greeting to the newcomer Serena now saw was a young, very beautiful woman.

She stood straight and slender, her smooth features betraying no emotion, approaching them with a solemn grace, heavy garments draped across her free arm. As she drew near and planted the torch in the earth beside them, Serena made out a picture of a bright yellow crescent moon painted on one high-boned cheek.

Serena didn't need to understand Paiute to catch the quick, thorough assessment and dismissal the young woman gave her, for her sharp black eyes spoke her mind perfectly. Nor did she need language other than the silent, universal dialect of intimacy to see that the other woman was entirely comfortable with the appearance of Gage's nude body.

Striding past Serena, she began helping Gage into the clothes she had brought. For a moment Serena stood by, affronted and numb, glaring at the other two, her imagination running amok with pictures of them making love in ways Gage refused to show her.

"Is *that* part of the ceremony too?" she asked tartly.

"Yes," he said with annoying nonchalance, not looking at her.

"Who is she? I have the impression you've met before."

"Her name is Lehi."

Lehi finished smoothing the deerskin shirt over Gage's chest, then with a quick glance over her shoulder to Serena, she murmured something to Gage in Paiute.

Her eyes narrowing in suspicion, Serena asked, "What now?"

"She says your skin is whiter than winter snow."

"Oh. Thank her for me, will you?"

"It was an insult."

Serena clenched her jaw and bent to swipe the dress Lehi had discarded at her feet. The action brought on a spate of angry words from Lehi. "Tell her I just want to get dressed and go back to the camp," Serena said through gritted teeth.

"She'll dress you too. But first she has to rub a special grass oil over your body. It's tradition." Lehi moved to fasten the snug leather pants she'd slipped up his legs, but Gage interrupted her and gestured to Serena.

"I'll bet it is. She isn't going to touch me." Disregarding Serena's tone, Lehi drew a small pot from her dress and took Serena's arm in her hands to rub a strange scratchy substance over it. Serena jerked her arm out of the other woman's grasp, glaring at her.

"It's all right," Gage said. "It's only a special grass the women use as perfume."

Suspicious yet curious, Serena bent to sniff the pot. The scent was unexpectedly intoxicating. "It's . . . fresh," she admitted despite her irritation. "It smells like spring. Tell her to give me the pot. I'll put it on myself."

Again Gage translated, and Lehi, eyes narrowed at Serena, obeyed. When Gage had dressed, Lehi took another smaller pot from a pouch at her waistband and dipped her finger in. She touched paint to Gage's chest where his shirt hung open, then to his face, drawing strange symbols resembling animals, ripples of water and wind, the elements of a storm, then a star and a half-moon.

Deliberately avoiding looking at them, Serena finished perfuming herself and slipped into the dress. The soft leather hugged her every curve as though it had been designed to fit her and no one else. Surprised and pleased, she ran her fingers over her hips to smooth it against her, then ventured a sideways glance to Gage. A sweet sense of victory swelled in her when she found that even though Lehi's fingers touched his skin his eyes were on her alone.

After Lehi completed the drawings on Gage's face, she looked to Serena. Serena shook her head and extended her palm in a gesture that asked for the pot.

"I'll do it," Gage said, taking it from Lehi. He dipped his index finger into the paint. "Close your eyes."

"You'd better not make me look ridiculous," Serena muttered.

Gage tipped her chin upward and stroked the cool mixture over her skin. "Let's see . . . something appropriate. Hmmm. Red paint. That's good. Suits your temperament. But what symbol?" He paused, then laughed to himself. "The paw print of a panther. Perfect. Tonight you're Panther Woman."

"Now wait one minute," Serena said, intending to back out of his reach. But the light, wet touch of his fingertip to the tender skin on her face had an instantly hypnotizing effect. "That feels . . . nice." Standing perfectly still under his spell, she let her mind wander. His finger sent delightful shivers everywhere he dabbed the paint, eyelids, cheeks and throat. What a delicious way to combat the desert heat, letting him trail the cool liquid inch by inch down her arms and legs . . .

"There." He turned her face from side to side in the light of the torch someone had provided before they stepped out of the sweat-house. "Not bad for an amateur."

When Serena opened her eyes, to her relief Lehi had vanished. "What is it between you and that girl?"

Gage wiped his finger on the corner of his discarded shirt. "She's hardly a girl. And what was between us was no more and no less than a few nights she warmed the loneliness out of."

"That's more than I have with you."

"Don't compare what we share with what Lehi and I had," he said, his expression suddenly intent. "You owe us more than that."

"I owe us? What about you? I want everything for us. I've made that plain. But you—" She whirled away from him. "You wouldn't have me if my life depended on it! And, as a matter of fact, it does."

Gage sighed. "Please Serena, not now."

"Then when?" Turning on him, she held up her left hand, splaying her fingers. "I may not have tomorrow. Jerel will find me. No matter what you think. And as long as I don't have a ring on my hand, he'll force me to go back with him and he'll make me his wife. Is that what you want? Why won't you rescue me from him? You'd do it for anyone else, not me. Why won't you keep me safe? I know you can." Her voice softened. "No one else can but you. You're the only man I've ever felt safe with. The only man I've ever wanted, or needed this way."

"You only want me—" He stopped, glanced away from her then back, his expression closed. "You only want me to save you from him."

"No. I want you because I—" Serena stopped just short of admitting to him the truth of the depth of her feelings for him. She couldn't. Not when she wasn't sure he loved her, could ever love her in return. "Because I—care for you, more than I've ever cared for anyone, and I know I could be good for you. We could make a home for Nathan."

Gage said nothing for a long moment. "Listen," he said, cocking his head toward the camp. "The drums have begun." He clasped her hand in his and held it, stroking the back of it with his other palm. "You're terrified of him. I'll protect you, Serena. You have my word." He rubbed his fingers around the spot where a wedding band would go. "But just because you're afraid isn't a good reason to marry, for either of us. And whether you'll admit it or not, you know it too."

Serena's heart pounded out her frustration, her fear to the beat of the distant drums. "There isn't any right and wrong here. We have to make our own rules."

"Some rules have nothing to do with time or place. They just are." He held her hand a moment longer, then let it go. "I'll help you, but I won't got that far. I can't."

"Can't? Or won't?"

"Take it any way you like. Come on," he said, touching her shoulder. He pulled up the torch Lehi had left for them to light their way back. "It's beginning."

The circle had formed and the drums were beating a steady, throbbing rhythm by the time Serena and Gage joined the gathering. The night was clear and cool above, mated in opposing harmony to the fires that reached light into the blackness and showered the earth with their own flaming stars. Above the call of the drums, Kwion's deep, weathered voice muted all others. At once with unquestioned authority he caught and held the tribe's rapt attention. But as Serena and Gage approached, he paused, slowly raising his hand from beneath the heavy deerskin shirt he wore to gesture them to stand in the two vacant spots to his side.

Serena followed Gage, sensing this gathering held a very different tone than the unearthly predawn ceremony she'd been drawn into the night of the massacre. The tribe stood solemn and still now, save for the soft beat of the drummers' fingers on their instruments, all attention focused on the eldest tribesmen of the Paiute.

Kwion spoke to Gage in hushed tones, then Gage turned to Serena. "He says I'm to translate his words to you tonight so you will understand his people and their story. Will you listen?"

Her throat went dry with emotion. She found the only reply she could offer was a nod.

Gage gripped her hand reassuringly and looked to Kwion to continue.

The Paiute elder stretched his arms out to embrace his people and the universe around them. As he spoke, punctuating his story with slow, expressive gestures, Gage whispered his message to Serena.

"We are a people without a home," Kwion's rich voice wove between the night and silver smoke. "And we are few. When the land was ours to roam without fear, our home was a place we could hunt and plant. Food was plentiful and we lived as one people with the *tu-weap,* the earth, and *tu-omp-pi-av,* the world above. The white men came and food grew scarce. We scattered like seeds to the wind. We found food only in the earth, the locusts and ants and cacti and roots. Now we have nowhere left to scatter, for there is no more land to scavenge upon, no more home for us to call our own."

Serena clung to Gage's arm, wishing she didn't have to hear Kwion's words, knowing she had no choice. She stared skyward and wondered how different the night sky might look if for every Indian who had died since white men came to their homelands a star had fallen from *tu-omp-pi-av.*

"Our people died from the sickness brought to this land," Kwion continued. There was a harshness to his tone now, and it gave Serena the sense of a buried outrage and sorrow at a destiny lost. She felt its echo in Gage, began to realize the extent of his compassion for the Paiute, his empathy with their plight, his anger at those that misjudged them without cause. And also realized how much she had come to admire those qualities that had made him a respected brother in the tribe.

"We were a dying people already when the settlers

came to build their ranches on the grasslands that fed us," Kwion continued, Gage telling her the meaning of his words. "Their sheep and cattle grew and took our grasslands and water; our pinons and junipers became their fences and corrals and their fire. And we knew hunger. Our children were born dead."

He turned then to Serena and Gage, his voice now dark and low with the weight of grief. "We pleaded with those who came to our land for mercy; we moved our camps close to their settlements to trade, to work. But they did not need our willing hands. We became a burden to them and they despised us." Kwion reached out and laid a gnarled hand on Gage's shoulder. "Only you showed us compassion, brother, giving of yourself freely. The others demanded we accept their ways before they would give us a share of what we needed. Only when we gave our lives as they wanted, did they keep us strong enough to help them defend their herds against Navajo and Ute raiders. In doing this, we lost ourselves. Many forgot the old ways to pretend something they were not. Many of our people turned against one another and joined the Navajo warriors to survive. Many were killed during raids."

A long hushed silence drifted over the camp, Kwion's words' quiet echoes carried by the smoke and wind. Finally, he turned slowly from Gage to Serena and motioned for her to stand in front of him.

Serena hesitated, looking to Gage. "It's all right," he whispered. "I promise."

Uneasy, she obeyed. When she faced him, her heart trembling in anticipation, Kwion lifted her hand and turned it palm up. In it, he placed a small object, and though the only light came from the flames behind her, Serena could tell it was one of the beautifully woven baskets no other tribe she knew of could match for skill and precision.

"It's beautiful," she murmured. "Thank you. But—why are you giving me such a gift?" She swallowed hard and looked straight into his eyes. "I've been as selfish as the settlers before me. I denied you the water, I didn't listen to your pleas, and yet . . ."

"Yet now you understand where before you only feared. You have listened," Kwion said, this time in her own language. "And this time with your heart." He laid a hand on the delicate basket. "This is for your child, when he is grown, so he will remember our people and the health we gave him. Your child brings a sign to us. If he lives because of our help, perhaps our children will live again also. We are no longer a proud people. We only wish to survive."

Tears welled in Serena's eyes. "I want that for you and more. And as long as I live at the ranch, the land and the water are yours too. I never had the right to deny you."

When he smiled, Kwion's dark face transformed like an Arizona landscape. Out of the dry desert plain arose the jagged cliffs and chasms of the canyon walls that told the history of his people and his land without one word. It happened in an instant, yet spanned time itself.

"Come, join us. Now we dance the *Nanigukwa* with friends to protect us from our enemies."

Enemies. How different the word struck her now. Once men with black hair and dark faces, Indians, all and any, were the word's definition to her. Yet tonight she would dance with those she once feared and despised to ward off the real enemies. People who destroyed others lives, who murdered for land and cattle and water. Men who took whatever they wanted, even at the cost of human life. The fire blazed close by, but there was a cold place in Serena's heart when she thought of men like Birk Reed. And Jerel Webster.

Something between desperation and a deep, indefinable longing prompted her to want to believe in the magic of the dance, to believe she, and Nathan and Gage and the Paiute could be safe from anyone or anything that threatened their fragile existence.

She was staring blindly at the basket in her hand, feeling the heat surround her, the chill of fear inside her, when Gage stepped in front of her and touched her face.

"Tonight you can believe in magic," he murmured, mirroring her thoughts, and suddenly the chill became a slow-burning warmth. "Give yourself to it, Serena. This is my dance." He brushed his lips to her forehead, then drew back, the fire reflected in his eyes. "The Ghost Dance."

Chapter Fifteen

Like the smoke curling from the flames around her, blurred memories of the sounds and scents from that first night she danced with the Paiute wove their way through Serena's mind. But any hesitation she might have had about participating before Kwion spoke had faded with the misty gray column of smoke into the clear midnight sky.

"I'll dance beside you tonight Gage," she murmured, seeing herself merge with the fire in his eyes. "Teach me their ways."

Silhouetted against the starry heavens, the others began the soft rhythmic steps of the dance, pressing moccasined feet into well-worked earth. In the distance behind them, lofty crags and cathedral spires hovered, giant shadows of divine centurions sent to watch over the small gathering of fragile human spirits.

Murmurs of drum beats mingled in harmonious accompaniment with the haunting moan of the wind in the pinions, sounds of man and nature as one in the celebration and the grief of existence. And yet the sounds seemed a part of the vast, endless desert silence, rather than an intruder in its stillness.

Serena let her eyes drift closed, her feet move as they

willed, her body sway and blend with the low pulsing cadence in the air. She felt Gage's warm hand close about hers and smiled to herself. Under this spell of timeless motion and sensation, it was enough to have him near.

She didn't realize Gage didn't share her absorption in the ghost dance. Instead he was falling into her, watching, drinking of her peaceful grace. His feet stepped with hers, his heart longing for the same. One by one the others ceased to be, and only Serena, his wild panther, his proud, free soaring eagle, the other part of his soul, took the night—stole his breath and his life.

Serena what have you done to me? You've taken a part of me and made it yourself. If I leave you, I'll never be whole. And if I stay, I'll lose what's left of me to you. You've given me life, but only to breathe through your lungs . . .

Oblivious to his tormenting thoughts, Serena surrendered to the dance, every sensual dip and sway of her body an innocent seduction. Unknowingly, she cast a sweet, savage spell over Gage's weakening will, drawing him closer to the perilous edge of a passion from which there was no return.

He scarcely noticed a basket being passed from hand to hand until he found it in his. Dipping into the offering of leaves, he drew Serena close. "Here," he said, lifting one of them to her lips. Her mouth parted willingly, for once without question or doubt. Only absolute trust shown in her soft eyes.

He placed the leaf on her tongue, then lifted one to his mouth. But she gently interrupted the motion, taking it from his fingers to her own. She ran the tip of her forefinger around his lips as they parted, but instead of feeding him, she took the end of it between her teeth. Leaning closer, she lifted her chin and invited him to bring his mouth down on hers to take the gift from her lips.

And he knew what she proffered him was far more than a single morsel; it was an offering of sustenance, all that she was, all that he needed to live. Desire, communion, purpose—she would feed him all of these so he would never hunger again.

His insides wrenched with the pains of a starving man. Losing his tremulous hold on resistance, Gage crushed his mouth to hers, and took all she could give. The bitter, intoxicating taste of the leaves mixed with the savor of smoke and sweet temptation on her mouth. Ignoring the mounting tension and excited whoops and cries of the dances that the nadir of the night always brought as the Ghost Dance reached its full height of frenzied illumination, he consumed her, took her inside himself and made her his own.

Serena sank into him, twining her arms about his neck to bring him to her. Gage wrapped his arm about her waist, lifting her from the ground, pressing his hot, urgent kisses deeper still. They fell together into the otherworldly trance the ceremony was meant to bring them to alone. Clinging like lost spirits in the night, their souls joined to explore, from the depths of need to the heights of fulfillment.

Her thoughts, her feelings spinning wildly from the heat of Gage's probing kisses, the heady fire in her blood, Serena rode one surging wave upon another of sensation she could never imagine or describe. He touched her everywhere, body and soul, and the feelings built and flamed. Her face, the curve of her back, her breast, he stroked her inch by inch, his hands slipping easily over the smooth, clinging leather of her dress.

She echoed his every caress, her hands greedily pulling him nearer, absorbing every bit of him he would give her. Her lips molded to his, drinking, tasting, tumbling into passion's embrace, until almost at the same time they found themselves breathless and weak, leaning into each other for support, breathing labored, hearts pounding for release. They parted, in shock, in awe, and stared at each other, unable to speak.

Serena's head swam in a strange, confused, flurry of images. "What is it?" she asked him, not hearing the sound of her own words, not sure if she had even spoken.

Gage opened his mouth, but it was Kwion's voice that answered. With great effort, Serena searched the haze enveloping them. Something in the back of her mind tried to reassure her it was only the scattered dust kicked up from the fury of the dance, and not the magic Gage promised sweeping them into another reality.

"I have seen you in a vision tonight," Kwion said, emerging from the mist to stand before them.

"Serena?" Gage asked, his body swaying against Serena.

"Both of you."

"I don't want to hear it," Gage almost groaned.

Serena protested, "I do. Tell us. What did you see?"

"What you already know, but have not yet come to accept as the truth."

"Truth?" Gage shook his head, and Serena heard the slight slur to his voice. "What truth?"

Kwion laid a hand on his shoulder and took Serena's hand in his. "I saw two cedars at a canyon's edge. Both stood proud and strong. I saw the earth at their trunks, and I saw below, down, far down, to the root."

"Roots," Serena murmured, not certain why the word slipped from her lips. She felt strange, her head light. It was as if the thinking, reasoned part of her stood to the side, watching another manifestation of herself she scarcely recognized.

"No. Only one root. Each tree stood alone, separated by a plain of grass, many bushes, a small pool of water. But beneath, they were joined at the root. One could not survive without the other, for if the root were damaged, both would fall. They were two lives, one being, neither whole without the other because their lives were one."

Serena searched his face. "You saw this tonight?"

"Yes. For the third time. I saw it first when Gage brought you to his dwelling to recover from your fall. Again the night we came to help bury your dead."

"You see the same vision each time we're together."

"It has been so."

Turning to Gage, she looked to his eyes, wanting to read his thoughts. But the late hour and the waning firelight made it difficult to judge his expression. "What do you suppose it means?"

"It means he thinks I'd be a lot more help to you and a lot less trouble to him and his women if I married you," he said, pressing his palms into his eyes, trying to rub the blurriness from them.

He gave her no reason to believe, but an insidious, numbing warmth was spreading through her, and all she felt was the certainty of Kwion's vision. "He's right," she said, sliding her hand up Gage's arm to form the final link between the three of them.

"I don't know," Gage answered, looking from her to Kwion. "I don't know what's right." He held Kwion's gaze for a long moment until the elder man gently nodded, stepping back from them. "I can't make you promises I can't keep, Serena."

"I only want—"

"To be the wife of the man you choose. You deserve that much, at least."

"What are you saying?" Serena asked, not sure if he'd said the words or the Paiute magic spoke to her.

"That I'll marry you. You make a strong point for it where Webster is concerned. And Kwion has given me an idea for a way we can both be satisfied with the arrangement."

"Arrangement?"

"We can marry according to Paiute law. It's real enough for your purposes." He pressed his fingers to his temple, as if ordering his thoughts had become a struggle. "It won't be legal, but Webster won't know that. You'll have a husband in name and you'll never have to worry again about being taken back to the Utah territory against your will."

Serena jerked away. "You'll marry me—but it won't be real?"

"It'll get you what you want. Your safety."

"I want more than just safety! If I do this, when Jerel goes away, you'll have your freedom, but I'll be left with nothing. That's not what I want." She felt suddenly cold inside. "I don't want just to be safe anymore," she said, realizing for the first time that it was true, that somehow her feelings for him had changed her in a way she was only beginning to realize. "I want to be with you."

"It's the best I can offer," Gage said. "It's your decision, Serena."

Serena clenched her hands at her side, looking at him with mingled despair and frustration. He had her backed into a corner. He'd happened upon a way to both rescue her and escape from her, despite her best attempts to persuade him with passion and the feelings she had for him. And he had left her no recourse but to accept his way—or nothing at all. "You don't leave me a choice," she said at last, her voice hard and bitter.

"Yes, I do. Just not the one you want."

She debated and argued silently with herself for several minutes while Gage moved a little away and spoke to Kwion in hushed tones of Paiute. About to resign herself to his terms without hope, a glimmer of opportunity struck her. If they were married, even by Indian law, perhaps she could use her illusionary status as his wife to give him a taste of a husband's privileges. And then, who knows what could happen between them? She might be able to persuade him that a future with her could be Heaven—instead of the Hell he imagined.

"I accept," she told him, hiding the triumph she felt. "I want to be your wife tonight."

Morning broke into Serena's hut with bright yellow slashes of light. She awoke, head throbbing, eyes gritty and swollen.

And alone.

She tugged the discarded blanket at her side back over her shivering limbs. "It was all a dream," she muttered to the dust motes swirling in the streak of sun over her head. Idly, she reached one hand out to run her fingers through them and as she did, she noticed the thin, braided leather band on her wrist. "What? It couldn't have happened . . ." She touched the band, wondering at its significance. "What does it mean? Did he say he would marry me?"

"I did. And we did. Though you were hardly awake long enough to say yes," Gage's deep voice rumbled into her one-sided conversation.

Stunned by his casual announcement, Serena's eyes jerked to where Gage stood at the opening of the hut, looking back at her with faint amusement. "We had a wedding last night?"

"I did. You left me at the altar, in a manner of speaking."

"I fell asleep?"

"Nodded off right against my chest while Kwion was still shaking his feathers over our heads."

"I'm sorry . . . I—"

"Don't worry, I did the same thing about five minutes later."

"Did you—sleep with me?"

"Until you stole the blanket and I half-froze, I tried."

"Some wedding night. It sounds like I've already failed you as a wife," she mumbled, wishing she had the courage to ask him whether he'd wanted to do more than sleep with her. He must have at least undressed her, for beneath the blanket she lay bare. "Gage—" she broke off, couldn't bring herself to ask.

He read her silent question. Stepping inside the shelter, he sat down close to her, stretching his long legs out in front of him. "No. That we didn't do. Wuri kept Nathan with her for the night and I slept here. But that's all."

"Oh." She made no attempt to hide her disappointment.

"You'll be glad you had the rest. We're leaving here this morning."

She stared. "We are? Why? I'm not ready to go back to the ranch and—"

"We're not going back to the ranch. Not yet. I'm going to show you the Grand Canyon. Some of the finest mustangs in the territory are there," he said with something approaching enthusiasm. "We should be able to get at least a dozen if we're lucky. Since the cattle are gone, you have nothing to live on. We both know sooner or later you're going to have to move on, Serena.

The ranch doesn't belong to you. I want to give you something to start a new life with."

"Mustangs? The Grand Canyon? You would do that for me? But . . ." She wanted to thank him; she wanted to tell him it wasn't enough. She wanted to tell him he was all she wanted. . . . "But what about Nathan?" she sputtered at last. "He can't possibly make a journey like that."

"Wuri isn't about to let him out of her sight. You heard Kwion—Nathan's survival has become a symbol to the whole tribe. And we'll only be gone a little while." Some of the animation left his face. "Enough time for your Mormon suitor to either catch up with us and accept me as your husband, or to give up altogether and go back to Utah."

"I know him. He won't give up. And if he finds us—"

Gage shrugged. "Let him come. What does it matter?"

Pulling the blanket around her, Serena sat up, hugging her arms around her knees. "I wish I had your confidence. He can be so—ruthless. Jerel always gets whatever, and whoever, he wants, usually in the name of divine sanction. I don't think he'll give up as easily as you imagine."

"No man has a right to take a woman against her will, Serena. And I've met enough Mormons to know most of them believe that now too." A note of menace threaded into his voice and Serena recognized the hardness in him that had kept him alive, and apart from anyone who tried to come too close. "But if you're right, and he tries, as far as I'm concerned, he gives up his rights as a man. If he wants to behave like an animal, then I'll treat him like one."

"But the ranch—the killers might come back again while we're gone."

"If they do, they'll find my grave and believe the rumor that I'm dead. After Reed's raid, the ranch looks just about as bad as it did the first time the killers came. They'll think it's abandoned, and move right·in. Which is what I'd hoped would happen before—"

"Before I showed up and ruined your plan by fixing up the place. Everyone for miles around must know someone's living there again. Mandy and Ross promised they wouldn't tell it was just a woman and a crazy old man, but there's Reed and his gang, and who can guess what the Mormons have heard and told along their travels."

Gage shrugged. "No telling. But as to ruining my plan, I only did it to begin with because my shooting arm was in a sling, and because I knew they'd wait a good long time before coming back if they thought I was still there. They'd figure I'd have called in backups and the law, that I'd be ready and waiting for them. Now, the more I think about it, you might actually have helped. Why, with all the rumors folks are carrying by now about the goings on at the ranch, the bastards ought to come back out of sheer curiosity . . ." He heaved a deep, labored breath. "Unless all they ever wanted was me."

"You mean they might have killed everyone only to get to you?"

"Might be. After the massacre Whiskey Pete said they were looking for me by name."

"Pete . . . He'll be at their mercy. Or Jerel's, if he comes looking for me."

He took her gently by the shoulders. "Serena, Whiskey Pete is where he wants to be. Remember, we begged him to come with us. At the last minute I even told him he could take his animals to the Paiute, but he refused to leave the ranch. Said he'd rather die at home with his 'family' than live in a strange place with strange folks."

"I suppose you're right." She sat pensively a moment, considering the situation. "But if the killers wanted only you, then once they've found your grave, they'll move on. What will you do then? How will you catch up with them?"

Gage released her shoulders and moved away, a distant look in his eye. "I'm not sure." His voice went hard. "But if I can't lure them to me, than I'll find them if it takes the rest of my life." He was silent a moment, then turned back to Serena. "What I do know is that we had to come here when we did, or we would've lost Nathan. And with the time we've been away already, another week or so will only give them more time to let their guard down and settle in at the ranch."

But if this happens the way you think it might, they'll be there when we get back."

"Exactly."

When he left her, she stayed huddled in the warmth of the blanket for a few minutes longer, trying to dispel the chill inside her. Gage would protect her with his life. Yet the security she once prized above all was beginning to seem like a hollow compensation for the love she wanted.

By the time Gage signaled the small caravan that included him and Serena, two Paiute scouts, and a trio of extra pack horses, the burning western sun sat on the flat horizon, shedding a crimson light that flushed the sky above and the desert below a salmon pink.

Over two long, hard days and one much too short

night, they'd beat a steady trail through gray sage country, where the air was pungent with the sharp scent to the winding trail that led up the limestone ridges of the Buckskin Mountains.

All day the horses sweated and struggled up the forty-five mile crossing over the Kaibab plateau, their feet slipping time and again on the smooth limestone. Gage would have stopped sooner had the spring the Paiute promised on the far side of the Kaibab had water. But finding it dry, surrounded by a pathetic band of lowing cattle nosing the damp earth and chewing the sparse grasses along the dried banks, they'd had no choice but to keep pushing to the next watering hole.

Now, ready to kiss the ground just go be off her saddle-burned bottom, Serena slid off the spotted mare she had borrowed from the Paiute, every joint and muscle cursing Gage for the furious pace he demanded of them. She'd had to stop several times during the journey to rest, fearing an attack of the weakness that would leave her prone and helpless for a good half day. Gage always encouraged the brief reprieves, never showing irritation at the delay. But Serena couldn't help but feel guilty and annoyed at her failing.

She led her mare to where the other horses had already plunged their heads into a pond formed at the base of a jagged crack in the limestone wall. A trickle of water cut the small watering hole out of the red clay. Serena could easily see that after one thorough watering, it would take all of the next day to refill. Tying the mare loosely to a branch, she let her drink her fill.

Gage strode up beside her and swiped his bandanna from his neck. "Here, you've earned this." He plunged the cloth into the pool, then stepped over to wipe her face and arms and neck with the deliciously cold water. "Thanks for not whining all the way," he said with a teasing grin. "You're not half bad to travel with, you know that?"

"Thanks for not cursing me from here to Hell, as Amanda would say, for having to stop so many times," she returned lightly. She whipped the cloth from his hand and doused it a second time for herself. "And I ought to be a good traveler. I spent my childhood in the back of a wagon."

"It's not quite the same," he said, before turning back to the horses. "And the least I can do is stop for you."

Once the horses were secured for the night, Serena could no longer make out where solid land dropped off into the fathomless void of the Grand Canyon. She only knew at last they'd reached the canyon's edge, and tomorrow they would descend into it. Beneath the rising amber crescent moon, the canyon seemed an endless black sea full of mysteries, beauty and danger.

Oddly, as she stared off toward it now, her only impression was one of a boundless void it cut into the land. Emptiness. Isolation. Suddenly she missed Nathan and the easy camaraderie of the Paiute camp to the point of tears.

In the midst of her lonely thoughts, Gage appeared at her side. "Tomorrow, I'll take you there."

"I'm not sure I want to go."

"What's this?" he asked, slipping his fingers over her shoulders to rub the soreness from her neck. "You're tired that's all. And hungry."

"Starving," she said absently.

His fingers fell still at her nape. "I hope Nathan ate today."

Leaning her head on his shoulder, Serena sighed. "You read my mind. I miss him. I didn't realize until now how much."

"Me too."

"But I know Wuri will take the best possible care of him."

"No question about it."

They stayed together, quiet for a timeless span. Serena moved a little against his shoulder, liking the feel of him next to her. "I wish we were near the oasis tonight so I could take a long, cool swim." She lifted the corner of the shirt he'd loaned her to wear with a pair of boys' leather pants the Paiute lent her to travel in lieu of a clumsy dress. "I feel filthy."

"I wouldn't mind taking advantage of that too. But tomorrow night you'll be able to swim in the bluest water you'll ever lay eyes on."

"Really?"

"You can judge for yourself. It's a lake at the bottom of a towering waterfall." He gazed off toward the black hole beyond. "Closest place to Heaven this earth has to offer from what I've seen."

Serena sighed. "Well, right now it looks more like the mouth of Hell. You make it sound so magnificent, I'll take your word for it." She snuggled closer to him. "I can't wait to see it."

Wrapping his arms around her, Gage kissed her hair.

Despite her pleasure at his touch, Serena didn't try to stifle the yawn that betrayed her exhaustion. "I couldn't sleep last night. Did you hear the lobo wolf? He sounded so lonely. He must have bayed until dawn."

Gage shifted behind her, his hands absently moving up and down her hips, the curve of her waist. "I heard. I've felt that way myself a few times, holed up in that cave I've been calling home."

"You don't have to stay there any more, you know," Serena said softly. "You could stay at the ranch. With me. Hiding is just as easy there."

"I'm tired of hiding—or just plain tired tonight."

"You're a tough guide, Gage Tanner, I'll give you that," Serena said, trying to ease his obvious discomfort with the turn of conversation.

He laughed wryly. "And you have more of the same to look forward to tomorrow. We'd better get some food cooking or we'll fall asleep on empty stomachs." He nodded over to the two silent Paiute waiting beside the fire they'd already started. "I think we owe them that much."

Serena reluctantly roused herself from her comfortable pose. "I'll have supper ready in no time. They packed so much food—"

"More than they had to give. They're too generous and gentle for their own good sometimes."

"Like someone else I know," she teased. Then, sobering, she added quietly, "I now can see that about them. I was blinded by my parents' deaths for so long—"

"Sshhh. That's over now. Now we'll be able to help each other."

"When we go back to the ranch, everything will be different. You'll see. They can use the land, the water for their livestock. I will do anything I can to help them," she said, eager to convince him of her sincerity. "After everything they've done for Nathan. They saved his life."

"They're trying. He went without food for so long . . ."

"Kwion knows magic," Serena said firmly. "He'll make Nathan well. I believe it with all my heart."

"So you believe in magic now, do you?" Gage slid his forefinger under her chin and tipped her face to his. "Since when?"

"Since I've known you," Serena whispered, turning

from him and moving quickly toward the fire before he could deny her.

Predawn dew settled on Serena's nose, tickling her awake. At first, her eyes fluttering open, she forgot for a moment where she was. With sleep-blurred vision, she glanced around the grassy meadow where she lay, to a small grove of pines and fir trees where the horses were tethered for the night. It was the deep, rhythmic breathing of the man in the bed roll on the other side of her that reminded her there was nowhere else on earth she'd rather be.

Even so, curiosity over the canyon she'd dreamed of all night tugged at her, leading her to give in to the impulse to slip out from the warmth of the scratchy woolen blankets and walk the hundred yards or so to the canyon's edge for a glimpse of all the wonders Gage had described to her late into the night. As noiselessly as possible, she pulled on her clothing and tiptoed away, careful not to wake him or the other men. She walked barefoot through the dew-slick grass strewn with white-flowered yarrow and daisies blue as the sky overhead. A light wind caught her hair, teased her with its refreshing morning mist that smelled of damp earth and pine and the woody richness of the forest, tempting her to run instead of walk to the canyon's rim.

Serena surrendered to the call of the breeze with abandon, chasing the little puffs of flowers with her toes, racing through them in childish play. In the distance shallow canyons and low-rounded hillsides replaced the razor-edged cliffs and the endless mesas they'd passed along the way, a palette of hues from deepest black to a hundred shades of scarlet and violet to the purest of gold and white.

At a spot where a cliff jutted out over the rim of the canyon she drank in her first glimpse of the treasures below through a mist of pink morning light. Rocky ledges burned and browned into the richest reds and purples plunged into shadowed crevices. Streaks of silver-blue streamed down gaps between distant cliffs shining like liquid crystal through the rosy haze that hung over the entire canyon like a veil hiding a face too beautiful to behold in full light.

How long she stood breathlessly taking in the sight, she couldn't have said. Engrossed with the vision spread at her feet, she didn't hear the footsteps behind her, didn't feel the hands press into her back, pushing her forward to the very edge, until it was too late.

Her toes forced to peak over the rim, she cried out, "No! Please—don't!"

As quickly as the assault began, it stopped. In the next instant, she found herself swept off her feet into Gage's arms, her body his captive. A deep, resonant peal of laughter split the air and he swung her around in his arms.

"You—! You . . . you almost killed me and—and you're laughing!" Serena said, breathless with fear and his sudden appearance. "I ought to push *you* off that cliff. You scared the devil out of me!"

Gage stopped spinning, but held her tightly in his arms. "I did? Finally? Then it was worth dragging myself out of my warm bed to follow you."

"Oohhh," she spat struggling to break free of him. "You're a brute and a bully, and—"

Gage silenced her tirade with his lips. He covered her mouth with his, demanding her response, refusing to retreat until she gave into him.

Shoving at his chest, Serena made a half-hearted attempt to escape. But the power of his persuasive kiss quickly overpowered her wounded pride. As she softened to him, he too gentled his hold on her, his hands caressing her back.

"You're shivering," he whispered, setting her on her feet and moving to rub warmth into her arms. Glancing over her head he added, "That boulder's right in the sun. Sit with me and warm up a little before we head back. We'll feel the sun rise while we watch it."

Serena followed his gaze. "It's awfully near the edge. Will I be risking my life if I follow you?"

"Always." He led her to a spot down a few rocky steps on a small grassy ledge that just caught the sun's bright, warming rays. Sitting down, his back to the smooth boulder he'd pointed out, he splayed his legs, and patted the green earth between them. "Here, I'll make sure you stay warm while you get a look at the prettiest picture you'll ever lay eyes on."

Without hesitation, Serena sat between his thighs, nestling her back against his chest. He wrapped his arms around her and she relaxed, feeling sheltered from the world. Nothing soothed her more than simply to touch him, to give into his embrace. Her hand resting back against one shoulder, they sat together in silent reverence, watching the changing rainbow before them as dawn burgeoned to its fullest peak, striking rock and the river far below with layers of palest yellow to molten gold.

Intense warmth wrapped them in an enchanted intimacy that seemed to contradict the impossibly vast expanse that began where they ended and stretched on seemingly forever. Gage bent to bury his face in her neck. "You smell like morning, fresh and pure as dew. I could waste the day sitting here breathing you in."

"I would let you."

He kneaded his fingers at her waistline. "I know. Except one day wouldn't be enough. I'd have to touch you to breathe you, and touching you might even be better . . ."

Serena reached her arms back and up to wind them about his neck. "I vote for touching," she murmured, twining her fingers in the hair at his nape.

"Maybe you're right." His hands inched upward, his fingers finding the soft bare skin beneath her shirt. "You're so soft," he murmured. Slowly, with the barest hint of a touch, he drew tiny designs on her belly, sliding over and over the tender skin with tortuous deliberation, leaving a trail of desire in his wake.

Serena moaned softly and twisted to graze her lips against his. Her breathing quickened, her breasts rising and falling so close to his hands with every motion she made that she ached for him to touch her there, to take her breasts in his palms, to take what she yearned to give.

Gage answered her lips with his, enticing her with a taste of the honey and temptation unique to him alone. She wanted to intoxicate him, drive him past his reluctance, his rigid resolve, straight into her arms, forever. And yet, she knew if she moved too fast, demanded too much too soon, he would run from her as far and as fast as he could.

Thinking of him, she responded slowly, offered herself without asking in return. It was a feeling new to her, yet all the more seducing for its languor, its heady promise.

And despite the struggle she sensed at his hesitant fingertips, at last, her tender kisses leading him on, he brushed her breasts with his hands. She sucked in a breath, the faint sound stripping another layer of his defenses.

His palms brushed the underside of her breasts as his

fingers slid over the taut tips. She felt him changing everywhere their bodies met, tension gripping him; he was losing his battle for control, his reason being swept aside by the force of sensation and need that drove her to tempt him further, push him farther than she ever dared before. She pressed against him, and feeling him harden where she touched him, repeated the motion, excited by the evidence of his arousal.

"Serena," he rasped, "don't . . ."

She arched back, thrusting her breasts into his hands. His thighs gripped around hers, his calves closed over her ankles, locking her to him. The realization he did need her as she needed him sent a selfish surge of primal need through her, making her ache to force him to admit his want. To act on it. And in that moment, she felt the power to do that much and more. To let loose the panther inside her and seize control of his mind and body, overwhelm him with the pleasure she could create with her touch.

He said her name again, and the harsh edge of agony in his voice cut through her like a dagger of lightning. It wasn't the impassioned plea for love she longed to hear, but the prayer of a drowning man. He was begging for her to take control—to lead him away from, instead of toward, the fulfillment she craved.

In a word, her name, he pleaded with her to think not of herself. Or her needs and desires. But of him. Of his need to preserve his identity. Of his honor. Of his freedom. Of all of the things she didn't, couldn't understand.

In a single furious jerk she was out of his arms and on her feet, leaving him to stare after her.

She ran from him, wildly and without direction, wrenched between what she wanted and the decision made by her heart.

* * *

They scarcely spoke during the descent into the canyon. It had been a long, treacherous downhill ride, winding their way along the often perilously narrow path that led to the paradise Gage described, lying nestled in the dense forest at the bottom of one branch of the gorge.

The zig-zag strip of ground they travelled plunged deeper and deeper by the mile into the cavernous expanse like the paths of their separate thoughts into worlds apart.

After setting up camp in the waning afternoon sun, Gage pointed the way to the promised waterfall and pool. "Take your time," he said shortly. "I know you're sore all over."

"What are you going to do?"

"Look around. We'll split up and scout the area for signs of ponies. There's still plenty of light. You should have time for a long swim before supper."

"Fine. I'll do just that." She whirled away from him to hide the hurt and disappointment nagging at her with the memory of his promise to show her the waterfall himself.

Stomping off into the dense woods in the direction he'd described, she let the sound of rushing water guide her to a sight almost as breathtaking as the beauty of the canyon itself. Crystal waves of white capped waters rushed off the edge of an enormous cliff, tumbling and splashing their way to a pristine, sapphire pool nestled in the center of a lush wooded glen, an oasis in the sheer fortress of stone.

"It is a paradise," she whispered to herself, "except that paradise takes two."

She plopped down at the water's edge, tossed her

boots aside and dangled her feet into the cool water. For a time she sank into lonely melancholy, staring blindly at the magnificence of it all. But the temptation at her toes gradually broke her sad solitude, beckoning her to plunge into the refreshing bath.

Shaking aside the day's misadventures, Serena quickly shed her clothes and tossed them over a branch. Sucking in a deep breath, she dived straight down, relishing the burst of new energy the renewing waters spread over her. She kicked and paddled her way across the length of the pool, dipping under to blow bubbles then tossing her heavy hair back to let the sun tingle against her wet skin. Delightful sensations touched her body, only to remind her of him . . .

She played alone, daring herself to go beneath the powerful surging waters, to dive from higher and higher cliffs that flanked the deep pool. Far from the relaxing swim she'd begun, it escalated into a furious game against her own frustrations, the water teasing her hungry body with the promise of pleasure every time she splashed against it, toying with her like a lover, refusing to give her more than a taste of promised release.

Finally, exhausted, she pulled herself from the pool and swept her shirt down from the tree to lie atop the grass for a bed. She'd only planned to close her eyes long enough to let the sun dry her skin.

Instead she fell into a dream, a dream of herself circling above a sleeping woman like a dove, watching her at rest in paradise, nude, for there was no shame, washed and warmed by the elements. Only in her dream a lover came to her side, bending over her to lightly stroke her clean, shimmering skin. Carefully so as not to wake her, he trailed light kisses up her ankles to her thighs. He touched her the way one touches a fragile flower found blooming in the desert, tenderly, with awe.

His bare bronzed chest glistened in the afternoon sun, his hair striking his shoulders in waves of copper and gold. Like an immortal, he had the beauty to leave her smitten from the mere sight of him and the power to subdue her with a single word. And yet he had something more. His every touch spoke of the force of a will the man within controlled, hard and unshakable, making him all the more desirable.

Strong, gentle, perfection . . .

How real his lips seemed when they met hers. Her body tingled from the vision, bathed in warmth, her eyes fluttered open.

"You—"

"—woman, are determined to bring me to my knees. Seeing you like this . . . my God—you just might have done it this time, Serena." Gage's voice came to her ragged with emotion, husky with desire.

But this time it was Serena who determined to remain unmoved. The hours of empty frustration, his cold treatment all along the trail down into the canyon, his damned, frustrating self-restraint overrode the pleasure of her sensuous dream, trampling any feelings of desire.

"Not this time," she spat, wriggling away from him. Stark naked she stomped out of his reach and plunged back into the cool water to escape him.

"Serena, it's getting dark. Come out of there," Gage called, annoyance fast replacing passion.

"Go away!"

"I'm not leaving you here alone. We need to get a good night's sleep so we can round up the ponies first thing and be on our way back home." She knew he was trying to reason her out of her temper, and not doing a very good job of it. "We found the herd I've been looking for for months."

"Good for you. Why don't you go back and get your horses and leave me in peace?"

"Not without you. Now get out of that water."

"You can just come in and get me, if you want me so badly, Gage Tanner." She dared him only because she knew he wouldn't do it. He'd have to shed his clothes too, and that would be too much temptation for him. Acting deliberately provoking, she dived under the water and swam toward the fall. He'd get mad and leave her after a few minutes. Which was fine with her! She'd had a wonderful afternoon alone. She didn't need him coming around upsetting her all over again.

As she stroked toward the surface for air, her hand hit a hard object. Hard and covered with hair. She stuck her chin out of the water and gasped for air. Before she knew how he'd done it, she found herself crushed against his chest, locked in his arm as he treaded water beside her.

"Didn't think I'd come after you, did you?" Gage said, a self-satisfied smile tugging up the corner of his mouth.

"Let me go!"

"Stop squirming or you'll drown us both."

"Fine. You're already dead, and the way my life is going, I might as well be!"

"Woman, you could tempt a saint to sin." Kicking and swearing all the way, Gage managed to drag her through the water to the edge of the pool. But as soon as he let her go long enough to catch his breath, Serena darted out of his reach, climbing a nearby rocky cliff like a mountain goat. Except that the long, shapely limbs scaling the cliff weren't like any animal he'd ever seen. Except the female animal.

And Serena Lark gave that word new definition. Where on earth did she get the notion she could run around like a wild animal, naked as the day she was born? At best she'd end up with sore muscles and a few scratches. At worst she'd end up pinned to the ground. Under him.

Staring up at her while she continued to climb to dangerous heights, Gage didn't know whether to simply admire the view she presented him, or give into the primitive lust she excited. In short order the latter impulse won. He shot out after her, gaining on her with every leap up toward the rocky ledge she was headed for.

Serena reached her goal first by several steps. And when he looked up, she merely glanced down and laughed. Her mockery prodded Gage to reach her twice as fast and he climbed the last rocks to the ledge in double time. But as he took the first step toward her, she glanced over her shoulder, tossed back her hair and dived straight and poised into the pool below.

"What the hell—"

Gage glanced over the edge, the height twisting his stomach as he watched her plunge into the dark, smooth waters.

With a small spray, she disappeared, then resurfaced, and looked up at him, smiling. He waited atop the cliff, pacing. He could see her clearly, but for the distance of the jump, felt miles away from her. While he wrestled with an unexpected aversion to leaping into something he hadn't first thoroughly scouted out, Serena swam to the water's edge. She climbed out of the pool and began to dress, taking her time with each piece of clothing.

"Lovely view, isn't it?" she called up to him.

"I'll make sure you regret this," he shot back.

"Threats and promises, that's all I ever get from you."

That did it. With a deep breath and a silent prayer

Gage stepped over the edge. He scarcely felt the cool air graze his arms and legs as he fell, but the force of the water when he hit was colder than hell on a stoker's holiday and hard enough to knock the wind out of him in one blow.

Feeling half-drowned from the depth of his plunge, he clawed his way back to the surface and came up shouting, "Damn you, woman. If I get my hands on you—"

Her response was a peal of infuriating laughter. "You won't have the chance, Mister Tanner." She started picking up his clothes, tossing him a glance over her shoulder. "You have to learn how to land. I've been practicing all afternoon. You shouldn't leap before you look, you know. It's not like you," she said, echoing his own thoughts so precisely Gage wanted to ring her neck there and then. "Then again, maybe you ought to try it more often. You might get better at it."

More furious than he could ever remember being, Gage limped through the water to where Serena waited, holding his clothes. But before he could make the stinging muscles in his legs and behind work well enough to drag himself out, she dropped them in a heap on the ground and turned away, heading in the direction of the camp.

Laying on the bank of the pool, trying to get his breath back, Gage decided it was probably a damned good thing she was gone. Right at the moment, he doubted all the willpower he had and then some would be enough to keep him from showing her just how far he had fallen.

Chapter Sixteen

Serena knelt by the tiny stream, tossed her wide-brimmed hat aside, and plunged her hands into the icy water. It was barely two hours into morning, but she felt as if they'd been riding for the better part of the day. Washing the dust down her throat with a long drink of water, she glanced at Gage. Still seated on Gusano, he held the reins wrapped around one fist and looked out over the landscape around them like a hawk sitting prey.

He'd been tense and silent since just before dawn when they'd set out on the last leg of the journey back to the camp. Serena sensed that unlike the day they'd climbed out of the Grand Canyon, his mood now had nothing to do with leaving that isolated sanctuary behind.

"What is it?" she asked, walking over to him, shading her eyes to look into his face. "Something's wrong."

His eyes flicked from their scrutiny of the cliffs to her and back again. "Nothing. Nothing's wrong."

"I thought you didn't lie. I know that look, I've seen it all too often. And you've been driving us hard all morning, harder than usual. Are we being followed?"

"I don't know. I can't see anything out there. It's just . . ."

"Just what?"

"Probably nothing." Swinging down from Gusano, he pulled off his hat and raked a hand through his hair, resting his elbow against the saddle. A ripple of weariness crossed his face.

"Gage—" Serena laid her hand on his arm. "Won't you at least talk to me? You can't take back all that's happened, no matter how much you want to. We're a part of each other, we always have been. I want to know what you're thinking, what you're feeling. I want to understand."

"Maybe you want too much," Gage said brusquely. Shaking off her hand, he brushed past her and strode toward the stream.

Serena stared after him, feeling helpless to bridge the distance between them. The more she asked, demanded of him, the less he was willing to give. Because she wanted protection, he had agreed to become her husband, at least in the eyes of the Paiute. And though they weren't true lovers, in those days at the canyon he had taken her to desire and beyond. She'd tempted and teased and goaded him to make love to her, while he struggled against his own aching needs, in the end each time denying himself to safeguard her innocence.

He was more than her lover, bound to her by a caring that went deeper even than vows. For vows could be broken, but sacrifice was evidence beyond words.

But despite it all, Serena felt she knew less of him now than she did when he was only her midnight visitor, her watching spirit on the horizon.

She didn't know how to bring him close again and she began to fear it was the last thing he wanted.

Retrieving her hat and the spotted mare from the side of the stream, Serena climbed back into the saddle, the brilliance of the morning clouded by a dull hopelessness she couldn't shake. She'd never felt this way before—confused, unsettled, torn between fighting and pleading, beaten down by a sickness in her soul.

If this was love, Serena thought grimly, she would be better off alone and beleaguered by every trouble the territory had to fling at her.

They set off again toward the camp at the same furious pace Gage had set from the beginning, driving the ponies and straggling cows toward the cliffs.

The day had stretched into the long hours of afternoon when Serena finally traced the shape of the camp in the haze of dust and heat. She said a silent prayer of thanks, for during the last hour, her heart had begun its warning rhythm. The sight made her urge the mare into a slightly faster gallop, thinking how ironic it was that less than two weeks past the Paiute camp was the last place in the Arizona territory she would have considered a haven.

Wuri was among the group that met them at the edge of the camp, holding Nathan in her arms and greeting Serena with a broad smile.

"He seems so much bigger," Serena said, a surge of unexpectedly fierce joy rippling through her exhaustion as she reached out for the baby. Tears pricked her eyes when Nathan grinned up at her, his tiny hands stretching out to her face. "You remember me," she murmured to him.

"You're impossible to forget."

Serena glanced up in surprise. Gage held her gaze for a moment, the expression in his own clouded, before turning to Nathan. "He has gotten bigger," he said, brushing the back of his finger over the baby's cheek. "He must be eating." Looking over at Wuri, he spoke briefly to her in Paiute. Wuri nodded vigorously, smiling at Serena and gesturing to the baby. "She said to tell you not to worry, that now you'll be able to care for him on your own." He paused. "If that's what you want."

"It's what I want," Serena said defiantly, startling herself with the resolve she heard in her voice and felt inside. To this moment, she hadn't considered Nathan's future beyond getting him to eat. Now she knew Gage had been right when he said Nathan was more hers than anyone's. They had survived together and the thought of giving him up was incomprehensible. Especially now, when she tried in vain to stop the whisper in her heart that told her she would soon have to give up Gage. "He lost his home, now he has a new one." She looked squarely at Gage. "With me."

"You're young and unmarried." He winced a little over the last word. "And alone. You haven't given much thought to how hard it will be to raise a child by yourself."

She refused to let him see how much it hurt to hear him say alone. "I've given it all the thought I need to. Amanda raises Tallie alone. I can take care of Nathan on my own."

"Mandy is willing to make the sacrifices it takes."

"Meaning I'm too selfish and demanding to devote myself to a child or anyone else, I suppose," Serena said hotly, her face flushing both with anger and the rapid pace of her heart. Gathering Nathan close, she pushed past Gage, ignoring the curious glances of the gathering around them. "You don't know everything about me, Gage Tanner," she flung back over her shoulder. "Maybe I do look out for myself, but at least I don't walk into someone's life, fix everything to my satisfaction, then walk away. At least I have a life!"

Serena stomped across the camp to the hut she shared with Wuri, kicking aside the flap and ducking inside. In her arms, Nathan made little sounds of discontent, obviously upset by the tension between her and Gage.

"I'm sorry," she soothed, sitting down to calm her body's furious call. As she concentrated on slowing her breathing, calming herself, she cradled him in her lap. "I'm sorry. Maybe you're not so glad to see me now," she whispered breathlessly. Touching the tiny fists that waved up at her, she bent and pressed a kiss to his forehead. "But I'm glad to see you. At least you listen. At least you—you . . ."

Love me. She couldn't say the words, couldn't bear to feel the pain that went with them.

Nothing had worked out the way she imagined it the night she made up her mind to flee Utah for the ranch. Then, she had convinced herself she would find a home, and when she found the ranch deserted it seemed the answer to all her prayers and wishes.

She believed tenacity and hard work would give her what she wanted—security, happiness, love—simply because she wanted it. Except that that girl who believed blindly seemed to be someone she didn't know anymore. Now, forced to face the folly of her actions and to make the best of her bad choices, not only for her sake, but for her baby's, she knew what it was to be a woman.

A woman alone.

"Why can't he love me?" she murmured to Nathan, easing down with him to lie on the soft deerskin pallet. "He's willing to give me everything in his power, even his life—everything except his heart."

Nathan made a mournful little sound, his wide eyes gazing up at her almost as if he felt her sorrow. Tears spilling over on her face, Serena cuddled him to her breast and held him as tightly as her weakened arms would allow, feeling at that moment, in the world they had only each other.

Hours later, Gage leaned his arms on the cedar fence, one boot propped on the lower rail, watching the mustangs move restlessly in the confines of the moonlit canyon. He felt like they did, penned up, pushed toward something he didn't understand and couldn't fight.

He'd lived his whole life never expecting to have anything or anyone belong to him. Drifting into other people's lives, he'd done what he could, and when all was said and over, found himself alone again. Now, when he had the chance again, when it would be easy enough to take all Serena offered, he found he wanted much more. Or a lot less.

He wanted something for himself. This time with Serena, unlike with Libby, it wasn't enough to give to her, to look after her. He had to know she wanted more than the protection he could offer, the home he could give her, the adoration she craved. He longed for the assurance that she wanted *him,* not just someone who could fix a fence or shoot a straight shot. He needed her simply to want to be with him—plain and simple. Regardless of what he could or could not *do* for her.

Or he wanted to forget her. Rid himself once and for all of the damned crazy, confused feelings she churned up inside him. She had determined to make him love her. But he didn't want to be made.

The sound of footsteps, light and sure, behind him, pulled Gage out of his thoughts. He made an instinctive start for the gun on his hip, stopped in mid-motion when he sensed the shape and scent of her in the darkness.

"I thought you might be here." Serena walked up to stand a few feet from him. Still dressed in her pants and boots, she'd pulled her shirt out and let it hang nearly to her knees. She didn't look at him, but instead leaned against the fence post to gaze out at the horses.

"I couldn't sleep," he said.

She said nothing, merely nodded, her eyes still on the mustangs.

"Everything all right with Nathan?"

"Yes. Fine."

Gage slanted several glances at her, unsettled by her uncharacteristic quiet. "Serena—" he began, then stopped, not sure what he wanted to say. "Earlier today . . . I'm sorry. I didn't mean—"

"Yes." Serena turned to look at him fully. "You did. But it's all right. You just wanted me to be sure I understood how difficult it would be to raise Nathan on my own. Didn't you? And I do. But you should also know that once I make up my mind to do something, I don't change it. Nathan and I are staying together."

"I don't doubt it. We'll have to see about getting you settled somewhere. You know you can't stay at the ranch."

Serena raised a brow. "Will *we?*" Shaking her head, she glanced back at the horses. "I don't think I've ever seen a corral quite like this one."

"I found this canyon a few years back when I first started scouting the territory," Gage said, sensing her reluctance to talk about her future. Their future. "It forms a natural corral on three sides. When I came to manage the ranch, I fenced in the open side with the idea of having a place to build up a horse stock of my own. There wasn't room for it at the ranch."

"Are you going to do it someday, have that stock of your own?"

Gage shrugged, keeping his tone light. "Doesn't seem much point in it. I'm always moving on."

"To what?"

He couldn't answer the question because he'd never had the answer and his silence roused her temper just like he knew it would.

"I don't think it's selfish to want something for yourself, to have a dream," she said. "And if it is, then it's not wrong! You've got to demand things in life, you've got to take them, because otherwise no one will give them to you."

"Does that include you?" Gage saw the sudden uncertainty in her eyes and exploited it. Slowly, he straightened and began walking toward her, pinning her against the fence with his steady gaze. "Do I have to take what I want from you, or will you give it to me?" He stopped, his body just brushing hers. Taking her chin in his hand, he lifted her face to his. "Maybe it's not wrong, but it doesn't feel right to me if I have to demand it or take it."

Serena's defiance crumbled at his touch. "I'm only . . . I'm afraid of not getting what I want. I'm afraid of being alone," she finished so low he scarcely heard the words.

"Is that the worst that can happen? Being alone?"

"I don't know," she said, pulling away from him and turning to face the horses again. "I used to think it was. I thought if I was alone, I would never have a home, never truly be safe. Now . . . I don't know."

The droop of her shoulders and the bewilderment in her voice roused Gage's protective instincts. Circling around behind her, he linked his arms around her, drawing her to his heart, his face against her hair. She was in his arms before he had time to think of regrets. "I don't know either," he whispered. "And right now, I don't care."

Serena willingly leaned into his embrace, resting her

head back on his shoulder to look up at the sky. The velvety blackness spread over them, sparkling with the light from an infinity of heavenly diamonds, from dust to brilliant jewels. "I remember when you showed me Heaven's Window, and the story you told me about looking through the heart of stone to see the truth. I wish it were that simple."

"Sometimes it is," Gage said. He lifted one hand to caress the curve of her throat, finding the pulse that quickened when his fingers skimmed her soft skin. "Some things you know. Without saying anything . . ." The words, spoken against her temple, tasted like a kiss. "Without being told."

He followed her gaze up to the night sky, as if it would confirm the one truth he'd carried in his heart since the first moment he saw her at the oasis. She was a part of him, and he of her. And no matter how far or fast he traveled, through nights without day, on trails with no end, she would be there.

They stood bound together, not speaking, while the wild splendor of the night played a sweeping symphony of sound and scent and starlit imagery. They shared the silence of lovers breathed in between the midnight music, and for a time they lived in a place with no boundaries, no frontiers, where everything was possible.

"I don't want the sun to rise," Serena said at last, holding fast to his arm around her waist. "I wish it could always be like this. A place without light, only dreams."

Gage turned her to look him, taking her face between his hands. "This is no dream, Serena."

"Then show me," she whispered. Twisting her arms around his neck, she brought his mouth close to hers. "If only tonight, make it last forever."

She would have rushed into the feeling, avid to have

it all at once. But he bent her back into the curve of his arm, his free hand brushing over her face and throat, with a tenderness that held her spellbound. "You make me believe in forever," he said softly before he kissed her, long and slow, making them both breathless with an emotion that went far deeper than passion, flamed hotter than desire.

When he ended it, not trusting himself to succumb to the feeling, Serena looked up at him with a plea in her eyes that nearly made him give her all she asked for, then and there. "I've changed my mind," she said, her voice shaded dark and warm with longing. "Forever isn't long enough."

"No." Gage stole one last lingering kiss from her parted lips. "It isn't." Slowly bringing her upright, he took her hand in his. "I'll take you back into the camp. You should try to sleep if we're going to make the trip to the ranch tomorrow."

"The ranch. Tomorrow . . ." She glanced away from him, then drawing in a breath, looked back up. "Yes, I want to go back. Whatever or whoever we find there, it's time."

They walked in silence to the hut where Nathan and Wuri slept, then hesitated just outside.

"I should at least check on Nathan," Serena said at last. "I wish—" She stopped, catching her lower lip between her teeth.

"Serena, I—"

"I hope you can sleep now," she blurted out before Gage could decide what it was he wanted to tell her. Pulling her hand from his, she ducked inside, leaving him alone in the darkness, sleep the last thing on his mind.

* * *

Several hours later, in the deepest part of the night, a confusion of noise woke Serena with a start. Still dressed, she lay uncomfortably curled up beside Nathan, her head fuzzy from the abrupt disruption of her light, troubled sleep.

Struggling to sit up, she tried to decipher something familiar from the commotion outside. It sounded like a jumble of running feet and shouts and people talking all at once in a language she didn't understand. She was nearly to her feet, half asleep and too tired to feel more than a faint annoyance at the disturbance, when the sharp retort of gunfire cracked the air.

Acting on instinct, Serena bent and swooped up Nathan in her arms, gripping him tightly to her breast. "Not again," she murmured to him. "Not again. I can't face it again."

Wuri's hand suddenly clamped on her arm. The older woman's eyes, wide with terror, sought hers. Serena didn't understand her torrent of words but she understood the fear.

"I don't know what's happening," she said, more to herself than to Wuri. Seeing Wuri's fear, sensing it in Nathan, moved something inside her, gave her a courage she didn't know she possessed. "But I'm going to find out."

Giving Nathan a quick, hard hug, she thrust the whimpering baby at Wuri. "Take him," she urged. "Keep him safe." Wuri clutched the baby, shaking her head slowly, then vigorously as Serena snatched up the revolver she'd kept with her, and edged toward the flap covering the opening to the wickiup.

"No," Wuri said, pointing to the outside. "No."

Another gunshot bellowed over the voices. Serena's eyes whipped toward the flap and back. "I won't sit and wait for them to find us. I can shoot. I have to go help."

She laid her hands on Wuri's shoulder, trying to work reassurance, determination into her tone. "I can't protect Nathan if I don't know what's happening," she said, touching the baby's cheek. Briefly pressing her lips to his forehead, she wheeled around and ducked outside.

Chaos had flung itself over the camp. Several men struggled to control pawing, rearing horses; others ran on foot in the direction of Gage's canyon corral. Mingled between the shouts and calls of the men, Serena heard Paiute children, what few there were, crying; horses spouting agitated snorts and whinnies; gunfire snapping and exploding all around—and the excited bleating of what sounded like a herd of sheep.

Skirting the edge of the turmoil, Serena dodged several errant sheep, and the three youths chasing after them to start toward the corral. She hesitated once, faced with the expanse of darkness between the edge of the camp and the canyon, her fingers molding to the hard butt of her revolver. Shadows, interspersed with streaks of white and brief orange spits of gunfire, churned the blackness.

Two images flashed into her mind. The Apache attack that killed her parents. Gage wounded—or worse—by another band of midnight marauders, perhaps the same ones responsible for the massacres at the ranch.

Serena started to run.

She reached the corral just as Gage, a rifle in one hand, swung onto Gusano's back. Breathless, her heart thudding painfully, Serena dashed up to him, grabbing at Gusano's bridle to get his attention. "What happened?" she demanded. "Are you all right? Who was it? The same people who attacked the ranch?"

"What the hell are you doing here!" Rumpled, his

shirt gaping open, he looked as if he'd been roused out of bed and tossed into the middle of an unfair fight. "Get back to the camp. It's not safe."

"Not until you tell me what's going on!"

Gage jerked the reins up short to keep Gusano from surging forward. The stallion reared back, snorting and shaking his head. "Damn it, woman, just one time can't you do what you're told? There was a raid on the corral," he went on, not giving her time to protest. "They took the mustangs, and they ran sheep through the camp to cover their tracks, but we're going out after them anyhow. Maybe there's something out there we can follow."

"Track them? But you can't—" Seeing the resolve settle on his face, Serena stopped. She wanted to tell him he couldn't leave her unprotected, she needed him to keep her safe. But the memory of his voice telling her his dream for the corral killed her protest. "Be careful," she said instead, touching his thigh, then stepping away from the horse.

He shot her a look compounded of disbelief and admiration. "I will. Take care of Nathan. I'll be back soon." Prodding the stallion's flanks with his heels, he urged Gusano into a gallop, several of the Paiute following in his wake.

Serena watched him disappear into the night, clenching her hand into a tight fist to keep her fear at bay. "You'd better come back, Gage Tanner," she whispered. "That's one promise I expect you to keep."

She ran back to the camp, not wanting to linger any longer than necessary at the corral. Back inside the hut, too winded and light-headed to object, she submitted to Wuri's fussing and admonitions, obvious even in an alien tongue. Even Nathan seemed to chide her for her reckless action, shaking his fists and scrunching up his face when she bent over him to reassure herself he was all right.

Spending a few minutes soothing him, Serena tried to put aside her worry for Gage for a little while. It might be hours before he returned and in the meantime—she left Nathan contentedly sucking his thumb and got to her feet, pacing the small, confined space. Wuri clucked her tongue at Serena's restless movement, gesturing for her to lie down and rest.

"No . . ." Serena shook her head. Sleep would bring dreams. Nightmares. "No, you rest," she said, mimicking Wuri's signals.

Wuri scowled at her, maternal disapproval and concern clear on her face.

"It's all right," Serena said, briefly touching Wuri's arm. She waved a hand at the doorway, then pointed to herself. "I'll be back." Moving quickly before Wuri could resume her protests, Serena picked up her revolver and stepped into the night.

She breathed in a long draught of the cool air, willing her pounding heart to settle to a slower pace. Many of the Paiute still milled about the camp, talking in low hurried voices, some busily calming the jittery horses and cattle that hadn't escaped, others chasing after the few sheep left separated from the herd. It was over. Gage would soon be back, maybe even with a few of their horses. They would return to the ranch in the morning and lock themselves safely inside their fortress again, away from the fear. Away from the killing.

It all sounded so reasonable. All except the gnawing uneasiness that kept her from believing it.

Serena checked and rechecked her ammunition and gun, walked around the wickiup and poked at the fire pit with the toe of her boot. She had nearly convinced herself to go back inside and attempt a few hours sleep when the thunder of riders approaching hard and fast rumbled into the camp.

"He's back soon," she said to herself, turning with several of the men to look toward the sound. A sudden, cold fear grabbed her. "Too soon." Gage wouldn't have given up after less than a half hour of tracking his quarry. He could hunt a whisper in a tempest and once determined to have it, would stay on its trail a lifetime.

And if it wasn't Gage returning. . . . In a split second, Serena dashed back inside the hut. "Wuri—" Frantic to make the other woman understand, she gestured to the outside, then to Nathan. "Someone's coming. Riders. You have to keep him safe. I'll try and protect us, but you—" she pointed to Wuri, "you have to stay with Nathan for me."

The first rifle retort gave Wuri an instant understanding.

She hurried over to the baby and picked him up, cradling him close, her eyes wide with apprehension.

Pressing her fingers to her mouth to warn Wuri to keep quiet, Serena, gripping the revolver, crouched low and lifted the flap just enough to scan the camp.

It was too dark for her to make out how many riders had come. But from the yelling and rapid exchange of gunfire, she guessed the Paiute were at least matched, if not outnumbered. Gage might not be back for hours. And when he returned, he would find her and Nathan—

"No!" Serena fed her courage on the fire of anger and resolve. "Enough of this madness! I won't let that happen to him. Not again. We're going to survive." She threw a look back at Nathan, huddled in Wuri's arms. "All of us. One way or the other."

Crawling outside, Serena inched her way to the closest tepee. She shot a quick glance around it in time to see one of the wickiups at the far end of the camp suddenly catch fire.

The flickering orange glow of the flame illuminated the tangle of bodies and rearing horses. A gray haze snaked through the camp, leaving a trail of acrid-smelling smoke. Sweat beaded on her forehead and trickled down her back. She tasted it, salt mixed with the bitter gall of fear. Somewhere to her left a woman screamed. Rifle fire peppered the air.

Less than a dozen feet from her, a woman came flying out from between two tepees, pursued by a tall bony man. As he caught the woman's shoulder, spinning her around, one arm raised high, Serena caught the flash of a knife blade in the moonlight.

Without thinking, without considering the cost, Serena sprang to her feet, aimed the revolver and squeezed the trigger.

The shot caught the man in the shoulder. Staggering sideways, he dropped the knife. Serena rushed forward, snatched it up and tossed it as far as she could, catching hold of the woman's arm at the same time.

"It's all right," she said, knowing the words wouldn't be understood, but hoping she could at least communicate some reassurance. "It's all right. Come on . . ." Half-dragging the woman, she pushed her toward one of the tepees. When the dazed woman had stumbled inside, Serena whipped back around to face the battle.

Several of the men scuffled in hand-to-hand fights, others taking aim at the riders circling through the camp. The intruders were Indian, probably the Apache Kwion had warned her and Gage of, and memories of the attack on her parent's wagon caravan threatened to burst into panic inside Serena. She fought the urge to turn and run as she had so long ago. Run far and fast.

Instead, as one of the riders galloped down the middle of the camp, bending to snag an arm around a running woman, she fired off another shot. The bullet narrowly missed the man, grazing his horse's neck. The animal reared back in pain, forcing his rider to let go of his prize to keep from being thrown.

He swerved off at an angle away from her, and Serena pressed a hand to her chest, her gun hand sagging as a dull pain swelled inside her, making her catch her breath.

She turned to step back out of the fray for a moment. But the shrill wail of an infant and an angry, frightened shout froze her in mid-step. "Wuri—Nathan!"

A surge of dread and fury swept aside her weakness. Running back toward the wickiup, she had the revolver ready and leveled a second before she saw the two men. The shorter of the two held Nathan while the other, his back to Serena, struggled to hold a kicking, shrieking Wuri.

Her hands trembling, Serena pulled the trigger on the tall man. The shot hit him in the side, lurching him backward. As he fell, he flung Wuri forward and she landed on her hands and knees, stunned.

"I want my baby," Serena said, pointing the gun at the shorter man. She wished her voice were stronger, that the barrel didn't wobble so much. Taking a few steps closer, she nodded to Nathan, whose loud cries nearly drowned out the sounds of the fight behind them. "Give him to me."

The man hesitated then made a motion toward her. Serena tasted the sweetness of relief—a split second before an arm whipped around her from behind, hauling her backward.

"No!" Serena twisted in her captor's hold, trying to keep her grip on the pistol. But his hand clamped on her wrist and yanked her arm down and up behind her back. The gun dropped to the ground at her feet.

Reaching up, she clawed at the man's face and kicked back with the heel of her boot. He grunted and a hot angry voice muttered something unintelligible in her ear. Serena sucked in her breath at the pain as he jerked both her wrists together and swiftly bound them with a hard leather thong.

Then, half-dragging, half carrying her, he started toward his horse. The man holding Nathan trotted after him, leaving his wounded companion and Wuri where they lay in front of the wickiup.

Fear and panic swarmed inside Serena. All her nightmares came together at once. Except this time, they were worse than she ever dared imagine because Nathan was in the middle of the horror.

This time, no Spirit in the Wind would come to her rescue. By the time Gage returned, she and Nathan would be gone.

He would blame himself. But he would have his answer for the massacres at the ranch.

Chapter Seventeen

Nudging Gusano a few steps closer to the edge of the rock overhang, Gage took a long look at the distant riders coming up the narrow path between the cliffs. He'd managed, with hard riding and a familiarity with the terrain, to skirt around the group that had raided the corral and come out in front of them. Shunab, one of the younger Paiute who joined the hunt, had followed the riders more closely to get a better idea of what they faced. Waiting for him to catch up, Gage weighed the odds of getting his horses back without triggering another massacre.

From what he'd seen of the raiders, he guessed they'd only be too happy to oblige if he gave them any chance.

Apache. He'd known it even before he got his first glimpse of them at the corral. Considering their vow to even the score for pointing the Cavalry straight to their leader, Gage figured he was lucky they still thought him dead and had taken only the mustangs.

The crunch of horses' hooves on the rocky ground tightened his hands on the reins.

Shunab weaved his pinto pony between the other riders gathered behind Gage, stopping the pony next to Gusano. "You were right in saying they would take this trail," he said. "But I saw only three riders so far. They must lead to secure the way before the others follow. We will wait. Here, we have the advantage of surprise."

Gage nodded. "They've also got those mustangs to worry about," he answered in Paiute. "If we take the north trail down—" He stopped abruptly, swiveling so sharply in the saddle Gusano snorted and tossed his head. "What did you say?"

Shunab stared at him curiously. "We have the advantage of surprise," he said slowly.

"No. You said—there were three riding apart from the others."

"Yes. But only three." He broke off as Gage wheeled Gusano around and back toward the southern cliff trail in the direction they'd come. "What is wrong?"

"Back at the corral, there were nearly a dozen more."

Gage didn't hear the hasty exchange between Shunab and the other men, nor the sounds of them following him. He only heard the thundering in his head and felt the sick fist of fear in his gut.

Chasing ponies again, he'd left Serena and Nathan unprotected. Had broken his promise to keep them safe. If he didn't get back to the camp in time, if he found them like before. If he didn't find them . . .

As Gage drove Gusano in an all-out gallop over the plain toward the camp, a white lather of sweat foamed on his neck. Up ahead, he could see gold and orange flames leap at the sky. The smell of smoke and gunpowder grew stronger the closer he got until it became a stinging, acrid fog.

He heard rifle shots. The snap of a revolver.

"Serena." Thoughts of her, in a thousand situations he never wanted her to be in, flashed across his mind.

He slowed Gusano at the edge of the camp, bolted

out of the saddle and hit the ground at a dead run, gun drawn, before the stallion pawed to a stop.

The thick haze and the darkness made it nearly impossible to pick out faces from the confusion of bodies and horses. One of the Apache riders galloped by, the rifle raised to his shoulder aimed directly at the fast-approaching Shunab. Skidding to a halt, Gage fired a single shot, hitting the rider in the chest and knocking him off his horse.

Gage didn't take time to acknowledge the whoop of admiration from his friend. Dodging around a woman and two children running for the shelter of a nearby tepee, he sprinted toward the place he'd last left Serena.

His heart stopped, lodging in his throat when he saw the shape of two figures crumpled in front of the tepee. Her revolver lay on the ground, a few feet from them. Frozen in place for a moment, his vision blurred and he saw the bodies of Libby and her family. "Serena . . ."

"No!"

Her voice snapped Gage back. Whipping around to the sound, he spotted her being dragged by one of the Apaches to a waiting horse. A second man followed, carrying Nathan.

He had the space of a heartbeat to act. Neither Serena nor the two men had seen him. Seizing the advantage, Gage moved swiftly alongside them, using the tepees and smoke for cover.

The man holding Serena reached his horse and attempted to lift her into the saddle. As he did, she kicked out and caught the horse squarely in the rump, startling it back a few paces. Cursing viciously, the man caught Serena with a blow to the side of her face that knocked her to the ground.

Gage flinched at her cry of pain, his hand flexing

hard on the butt of his gun. If he shot now, with Nathan still captive . . .

While his companion fought to control his horse, the second man took a few steps away, searching out his own mount.

In one single, noiseless motion, Gage came up behind him, striking him sharply at the vulnerable point between his skull and neck with the butt of the revolver. He slumped, senseless, and Gage scooped up Nathan before the man's body hit the ground.

"You'll be all right now," he murmured to the wailing infant, jamming his revolver back in the holster to gather him closer. Nathan quieted a little at the sound of his voice, whimpering against his shoulder. "And she'll be holding you again soon. I promise. But for now—"

Gage threw a glance around them. Quickly ducking into the tepee nearest them, he startled a huddled group of several women and children. Rattling off a few words of explanation in Paiute, he shoved the baby at one of the women and dashed back outside.

He got there just as the first man put Serena in the saddle. Binding her hands in front of her, he started to lash her wrists to the pommel. At that moment, Serena looked up and Gage's eyes met hers.

Her startled exclamation spun the man around. As he turned, Gage swung a fist into his face.

It was over in less than a minute. Shoving the unconscious man aside, Gage quickly untied Serena's wrists with shaking hands, and pulled her down from the horse and into his arms.

"You came," she said, her voice trembling. "Nathan! Is he—?"

"He's fine. I left him in good hands."

Relief flooded through Serena, stealing her strength. She still couldn't believe he was here, holding her, touching her. A few moments ago, the thought of ever seeing him again had seemed impossible. "I thought—I was so afraid . . . you wouldn't come."

"Don't think about it," Gage said roughly. He moved his hands over her, swiftly, jerkily, reassuring himself she was whole. Nearly losing her had shaken him deep inside, thrown him off center. She lifted her face to him and he grazed his fingertips over the ugly red streak on her cheekbone. "I should have killed him." His expression tightened. "I should have been here to begin with. If I hadn't gotten here in time, you and Nathan would have—"

"No." Serena put her hands on either side of his face, forcing him to look straight into his eyes. Tears shimmered in her own eyes, but behind them he saw her strength. "No, don't say it. Don't ever say it. It didn't happen. And it won't happen again. We're all right. All of us. We're all right."

His devastated expression was almost more than she could bear. Stretching up, she pulled his mouth down to hers, kissing him with a frantic need to convince him he hadn't failed her, that nearly losing all she had gained only made her more desperate to hold to him.

Tears spilled down her face and Gage tasted them, felt them wet his skin. The sounds of fighting raged around them, but this one moment he took for himself, this one moment of heaven in the heart of his own personal hell. Burying his face in her neck, he held her tightly as if this time were the first time, the last time, forever. "I'd give my life if I could take away the memories, if I could change what happened. Serena . . ." Her name was a prayer on his lips. "I know what you must feel—"

"No, you don't!" Suddenly angry, she pulled away from him, facing him with a fire in her eyes. "I feel glad, fiercely, completely glad, that we survived, that we're all together again. How could I blame you! My God! You saved our lives. When I saw you there, all I could think was that you found us! Somehow you found us. You came back for us," she ended, her voice trailing to a whisper as the tears started again.

"I'll always come back for you. Always," Gage said softly, taking her hand. He stared down at her, memorizing each line and curve of her face, until a nearby rifle shot recalled him to the danger around them. "But right now, I'm getting you somewhere safe. You can stay with Nathan—"

"Wuri! She was there when they . . . I have to make sure she's all right."

Before Gage could stop her, Serena dashed off in the direction of the hut. Drawing his gun, he followed after her. Giving a cursory glance at the man lying motionless a few feet from them, he shoved his revolver back in the holster and helped Serena lift a still groggy Wuri to her feet and get her safely inside.

"I think she'll be all right," Gage said as Serena pulled a blanket around Wuri. "Look after her. I'll be back. But right now they need the extra gun."

"You're right." Serena got to feet. "I'm going with you."

"Like hell you are! After what just happened how can you even think of going back into it?"

"After what just happened, I can't think of anything else! You can stay and argue with yourself if you like. I'm going." Darting back outside, Serena ran to the spot where her revolver had fallen.

It was gone.

She whirled around just as Gage came out of the hut and in a blinding flash, realized he had stepped between her and the man holding her gun. The man she had shot to rescue Wuri.

Lying on his side, the blood from his wound black in the moonlight, he raised the gun, his finger on the trigger.

"No! Gage!"

Her warning came simultaneously with the sharp crack of the revolver.

Gage staggered backward, dropped to his knees, and at the same time, jerked his own gun from the holster and fired.

The force of the shot flung the man to his back. His gun slid from his hand.

The rapid hail of events left Serena stunned. "He— you . . ." She stared at the dead man, then her gaze slowly swiveled to Gage. "Oh, my God, no."

Doubled over, one fist still locked around his gun, he gripped his thigh, blood already running between his fingers.

Serena threw herself at him, kneeling on the hard ground, afraid to touch him anywhere. "I'm sorry. It's my fault. I should have listened. I should have stayed inside. Are you—is it . . . ?" She looked down at his leg. A dark stain was rapidly spreading from a point midway above his knee. His hand clenched over it, taut and white.

"I won't deny you're hard-headed," Gage said, grimacing at the pain that washed up his leg when he tried to shift his hand. Moving gingerly, he slowly uncurled his fingers from around his gun and shoved it back into the holster. "But we seem to be spending too much time tonight apologizing to each other. Let's call it even, all right?"

"You got the wrong end of this bargain," Serena muttered. "I need to do something about your leg. How bad is it?"

Gage fought a wave of dizziness. "It missed the bone. It'll keep." He tried to focus on her, on the scene around them to keep from succumbing to it. "It's quieter. Sounds like the worst is over. You should check on Nathan. I left him there," he said, nodding in the direction of the nearby hut and immediately regretting it as the motion knifed his leg with a sharp pain.

"I'm not going to leave you here alone like this!"

"I'm not going anywhere," Gage said with an attempt at a wry smile. "I'll be here when you get back."

Serena cast an agonized glance at the hut, torn between the need to reassure herself Nathan was safe and her fear of leaving Gage. "I can't—"

"Go on," Gage urged her. "I want to know he's safe too."

Feeling ripped in half, Serena got to her feet. "I'm going, but I'll be back. And with help. I know I can't drag you inside alone," she added, reaching far for a lighter tone.

"You mean there is something you can't do?" She scowled at him, then her face collapsed in anguish. "Go on," Gage said. "It'll be all right." Hesitating, she finally turned and ran off in the direction he'd indicated.

When she'd gone, Gage drew in a long breath, steeling himself. Sitting back on his heels, he stretched out his good leg, then gradually straightened out the other. The effort cost him in pain and a good measure of strength.

Cursing under his breath, he waited for the faintness to subside before fishing a rumpled bandanna out of his pocket. He tied it tightly just above the wound in his thigh, feeling it cut into his skin.

The sounds of fighting had faded, and in the murky

predawn light he could see the Paiute milling about the camp, beginning to restore some order in the aftermath of the mayhem. *I should be up and moving.* The thought dog-paddled through his head.

He tried to put action to it by pushing up on his un-injured leg. For a moment, he wavered, unable to stand or move back. Before he could do either, a wall of blackness fell down on him, making his last memory a blinding pain.

Gage woke with the sun in his eyes and Serena bending over him, her face a study in concern.

Her features relaxed into a smile when she saw the awareness in his gaze. "You've finally come back to me," she said softly. "I was wondering if you were going to keep your promise." She put her hand to his forehead. "No fever. I think you're going to live. Again."

"I feel like hell," he rasped. "How many hours have I—?"

"Two days."

"Two *days?*"

Serena nodded. "Kwion said you were lucky the bullet passed through and missed the bone. It could have been much worse." Her voice faltered. "I've been so worried."

Gage groped for her hand, squeezing it tightly, letting the silence between them say all he couldn't. "How's Nathan?" he murmured finally.

"He's fine. He misses you." She stroked her hand against his face. "You should sleep. We'll talk later."

Waiting until he had drifted off again, Serena slowly unbent and got to her feet, putting a hand to her back as she stretched stiff muscles. For the first time since the Apache raid on the camp had ended, she felt she could give in to exhausted relief. She looked down at Gage, watching him for a long moment before quietly moving outside to stand in a patch of late-afternoon sun.

Kwion, seated by the fire pit, glanced up. "He is better."

"Yes. Thanks to you. You know more about healing than any doctor I've known."

"Perhaps in healing the body," Kwion said. "But it is you who has healed his spirit. You have brought him back from the land of the ghosts. Soon, he will be whole again."

"Not until he has his revenge," Serena said, sitting down opposite him and staring into the cold remains of the fire. "I want to believe what you say, but he won't rest until he tracks down the Apache responsible for the raid. They must be the same ones who killed Gage's family and the Mormons. Gage told me they wanted revenge because he was among the scouts who led the Cavalry to Geronimo."

"That is true."

He didn't disagree with her, but something in his bland tone caused Serena to look at him curiously. "Who else could it have been? I can't see Birk Reed and his men murdering two women and two boys for water. Even if they did suspect Gage of managing the ranch for the Mormons, there are easier ways to prove it. Besides, they believe Gage is dead. If they killed Libby and the boys, they would know he was alive."

"It appears so."

"If it wasn't the Apache, who else could it be?" Serena repeated, irritated at the old man's ambiguous answers.

"Coyote comes in many disguises. It would be wise for you to remember that when you return to the ranch and think of opening the gates. Libby did not and she paid with her life."

"I don't understand. If you know who killed them—"

Kwion slowly shook his head. "I do not know for certain. I only see and hear what is around me. And I know Apache revenge would be greater if they had taken the wife and children of their enemy. It is not their way to kill what can be used or traded." He rose to his feet, gathering his tattered blanket closely about his shoulders. "When you leave here, it is my wish that you will carry our friendship with you and leave yours with us. You have risked much for us—"

"And you've risked much for me in return," Serena said. "I can never forget it. You've taken away a fear I carried for a long time and made me see more clearly. If Gage hadn't brought me here . . ." She swallowed hard, lifting her chin. "I don't deserve it, but I want that friendship."

A faint smile creased Kwion's face. "It is said there is grave danger in opening your heart to another. But you have courage. You will not turn from it." He studied her face for a moment, then added, "You have traveled far. Now you can continue your journey, but not alone."

Serena sat by herself for a long while after Kwion left her, thinking of his words and feeling a dawning inside, as if she'd carried a truth for a lifetime but only recognized it now. For the first time, she felt she had found a home.

Not with a family or ranch that didn't belong to her, but in a place she never expected. A wild, harsh place of great strength and beauty that gave to her nothing she asked for, but everything she wanted.

* * *

In the hush of the purple evening, Serena walked through the camp carrying the bowl of stew she'd fixed for Gage. After the raid, it had taken a few days for the Paiute to settle back into the simple, everyday tasks of living. Two of the men had been killed and four more wounded, but none of the women or children had been taken and overall, Serena sensed a feeling of gladness and even jubilation among the tribe.

She'd often heard the Paiute described as uncivilized by settlers in the territory because of their unfamiliar customs and simple, nomadic lifestyle. But in the weeks she'd spent with them, she'd learned to appreciate their tenacity and adaptability; despite almost impossible odds they were surviving. They managed to endure an uncharitable wilderness and eke out an existence on meager sustenance, reaping nature's harvest without disrupting the natural order of growth and renewal. She felt only admiration approaching awe at the resilience of the human spirit they displayed at every turn—without force and violence.

She felt at peace here. Weeks ago, it would have been the last word she would have used to describe her feelings at seeing the camp for the first time. Now it seemed like she had been here for a lifetime.

At the tepee, Serena carefully lifted the flap, not wanting to disturb Gage if he was still sleeping. To her amazement, he was sitting propped against his bed roll, wearing only a rumpled pair of pants, wiggling a rattle, carved in the shape of a jack rabbit's head, at Nathan. The baby laughed, swiping at the toy with delighted shrieks.

"I didn't know you were well enough to make toys or to have visitors," Serena said, moving to sit next to him. "You must be feeling much better."

A lock of hair had fallen over one eye, giving him a

look of boyish charm as he smiled at her. He held the gurgling baby close enough for Nathan to touch his chubby fingers to her face. "Wuri brought him. I'm glad for the company. I don't like being cooped up."

"You'll have to stand it for another day or two. I don't want you to end up like Lucky Joe." Taking Nathan from him, she handed him the bowl. "I thought you might like something more than water."

She held Nathan in her lap, entertaining him with the rattle while Gage made short work of his supper. He was nearly finished when Wuri stuck her head into the tepee, smiling broadly at the three of them. She gestured at Nathan, holding out her arms, and Serena lifted the baby to her.

"She says she'll feed him for you," Gage said, translating Wuri's animated chatter. He pulled a face. "She said you've got enough on your hands feeding a man."

Serena laughed with Wuri, waving to Nathan as the two of them left her alone with Gage. "Soon you won't be needing me any more," she said lightly. "For once, I'm the one taking care of you. Usually, you're picking me up off the ground."

"It's part of you. Why do you hate it so much?"

"Why shouldn't I? It's not fair. It gets in the way of things I want to do."

"We all have something that gets in the way," Gage said, setting his bowl aside. "You have to learn to go around it. At least make peace with it."

Her smile rueful, Serena shook her head. "I'm better at going through it. You should try to get some more rest," she added quickly, not wanting to hear his comeback.

"I don't think so." Wincing at the movement, he settled a little lower against his makeshift pillows and picked up the pocketknife and half-carved piece of wood he'd laid to one side. He began whittling at the wood, turning his head to one side to appraise his progress. "Tell me about your growing up."

Serena stared at him in surprise. "What? Why?"

"I want to know."

She raised a brow. "Just like that?" He shrugged and she gave a sigh. Sitting near him, the soft light of the single lantern flickering between them, watching him work, sharing part of her with him, felt intimate and right. "I've told you most of it. My father's work took us to more places than I can ever name. I always wanted a real home, not just the back of a wagon. I remember . . ." Her vision misted as she looked into the lantern flame, seeing the past. "I remember when I was about seven, we stopped in Oklahoma for a month or so and stayed with a widow lady in a big, rambling farmhouse. It was spring and she had a wonderful garden, with blooming apple trees and roses in a dozen colors. My favorites were silver, and I would go out each day and just sit there and look at them. Those roses, that place, seemed like a dream of everything I ever wanted."

"And then you had to leave."

"Yes. She gave me a rose to take with me, but of course it withered and died. We were never in one place long enough for me to see them grow again . . ." Serena shook herself, giving a self-conscious laugh. "I suppose that sounds silly."

Glancing up, she caught Gage studying her with the deep, still look that always made her hot and uneasy.

"Didn't you ever have something you wanted badly when you were young?" she rushed out, feeling embarrassed at her confession.

"I wanted to ride and keep riding." He turned back to his carving, his hands making long deft strokes with the blade against the wood. "My father always told me I would never have anything, that everything worthwhile you got was taken away sooner or later. I thought—" He held the carving to the light, then brought it down again and shaved a tiny sliver from the side of it. "I thought if I kept going I could outrun it. I would never be in one place long enough to have anything someone could take."

"You just make sure other people have it. You borrow their lives. And you stay lonely."

"Maybe lonely is all I can be."

"Maybe it's all you want to be." She didn't give him time to deny her. "And now you're going to have your revenge for Libby."

His shoulders shifted and he drew another long cut on the wood. "Maybe."

"Don't you think the Apache were responsible for the killings?"

"Not entirely. When we rode out the night they raided this camp, though the sheep they brought scattered their tracks, we managed to guess the trail they'd take. Only three riders actually left the raid. The others, the Apache, held back, hiding out to attack again after most of the Paiute men rode away from the camp to follow the raiders."

"Three riders separated from the others? Jerel rode into Mandy's with two others ... That's what you're thinking, isn't it? That Jerel is that close to finding me? When you went out after the Apache raiders, you ended up finding Jerel skulking around the area instead?"

"What I think is that the answers I need are back at the ranch."

Serena wanted to press him, but she was afraid to hear his answers. If he did get his revenge, he would be gone. Yet if he didn't, he would always be a spirit in the wind, beyond her reach. Was there no answer for them?

As though he read her mind, he drew close and whispered reassuringly, "It'll soon be over."

"Will it? For you, maybe." She looked straight in his eyes. "Nathan needs a home. I want a home. If we can't stay at the ranch—"

"I won't let you wander in the wilderness alone with a baby," Gage said lightly. He made a final cut on the carving, studied it for a moment, then handed it to her with a diffident shrug. "I thought you should bring at least one pony back with you," he said, not meeting her eyes as she gazed in wonder at the tiny replica of a galloping mustang. "We should be going soon. A day or two maybe. We'll make better time in the light."

"The light?" Serena's eyes shot up in astonishment. "We can't go during the day. Someone might see you."

"It seems to *someone* we're easier prey at night. I won't risk it. Not again." Gage held up a hand when she opened her mouth to protest. "Don't bother arguing. It won't do you any good."

Serena started to debate him despite the finality in his tone, warning her away. The weary look on his face stopped her. He obviously expected a quarrel. "I won't," she said, half to herself. Without waiting for him to respond, she moved closer and laid her cheek against his heart, her hand caressing his shoulder. "I won't argue. But I also won't forget what you're doing for me, for Nathan. I want—I wish . . ."

Stroking his hand over her hair, he asked softly, "You wish what?"

"I wish I could give something to you." Serena raised her head, spreading her fingers over his chest. Her eyes sought his, searching, probing. "But to receive a gift you have to accept it." She leaned toward him until her mouth hovered a whisper from his; her breath was his. His heart quickened under her palm and she lightly ran her hands downward, grazing his damp skin, just brushing the edge of his thighs with her fingertips. "You can have something, everything. You just have to take what I can give."

Serena waited, not moving, feeling the struggle in him, seeing it in his eyes. She waited an eternity, until they were both ravaged by opposing desires, the strengths of their passions and his resolve not to surrender.

It hurt, deeply and endlessly, when she forced herself to pull away, unable to bear it any longer. "I used to get everything I wanted," she said, her voice hoarse, barely above a whisper. "But there never used to be you." Maneuvering to her feet, Serena walked slowly to the threshold of the tepee, feeling stripped and pale. She looked back only once. "Maybe I'm crazy for believing we're a part of each other. Maybe I'm possessed by a spirit that doesn't exist except in my heart. All I know is I can't, I won't let go. Even if you do."

She turned away, leaving the flap open, letting the night inside.

Tossing her pack into the back of the cart, Serena took one last look around the camp. For the past three days, knowing she would be leaving, she had spent nearly all her waking time with the people she had come to consider friends.

During the light, she shared in the daily tasks of foraging and cooking and caring and playing with Nathan and the few other children who were too young to be put to help around the camp. In the silence of the night, she sat by the fires, listening to songs and stories translated for her by Kwion, and it was then she most strongly felt the

Paiute's mystical link with the elements, felt it bind her to them and to the wilderness around her.

Gage had been able to stand on his injured leg, but she saw the pain in his face along with his resolve to master it. She had continued to tend to him during his recovery. But since the night of their conversation, they had said little to each other beyond the mundane.

Now, looking toward the journey back to the ranch, Serena felt a foreboding. They had to go back. Yet she wished, more than ever, they could stay.

A familiar delighted shriek drew her out of her dark thoughts. Wuri, carrying Nathan and accompanied by many of the women and children, gathered around her to say their goodbyes. Behind them, Kwion walked alongside Gage, who moved slowly, hampered by a limp.

Giving Nathan a fierce hug, Wuri handed the baby to Serena. The older woman's eyes dimmed with tears as she touched Nathan's cheek, then Serena's hand. She said something, gesturing to the baby, her expression speaking more clearly than words.

"It is difficult for her to see you and the child leave," Kwion said. "She wishes for you to return, when you are able."

"I will," Serena said, looking at Wuri and nodding. She cradled Nathan into her embrace and reached out to hug her friend with her free arm. "I'm going to miss you too." She looked around at all the gathering. "All of you."

She said her goodbyes to them, giving and receiving warm embraces. When she was finally ready to leave, Wuri stopped her just as she was about to step up onto the cart seat. Smiling through her tears, she pressed a small pouch into Serena's hand. Serena glanced questioningly at Kwion.

"It is a gift of the heart," he said. "When it is time, when you are truly ready to explore the places in your soul that have no boundaries, burn the contents in a fire that equals your passion. The smoke is said to carry the essence of all you are in the wind and bring your heart to you, wherever you may be."

Serena shared a long look with Wuri. "Thank you," she whispered. "Maybe some day, I will find my heart again."

Hugging Wuri one last time, Serena climbed up on the seat with Nathan in her arms and waited for Gage to take up the reins. He turned the pony in the direction of the ranch and Serena twisted in her seat, the sun in her eyes, to watch the camp grow smaller and smaller, until it was only a mirage on the endless plain.

She left Gage to his silence during the journey back, too uneasy to voice her feelings, too uncertain about where they were together. Was it forever? Or would it end today, or tomorrow, or in a moment she wouldn't expect until it was too late? When she could finally see the image of the ranch sharpen in the distance, anxiety washed over her.

"You hold back here. I'm going ahead to look things over," he said shortly. "If I'm not back in a few minutes, take Nathan and go to my cave." He swung off Gusano and handed his reins to Serena. "Take Gusano. He's fast and he knows the way. I'll take Amanda's horse for now," he said, unhitching the horse from the cart.

"But—"

"Not this time, Serena."

She nodded in silent retreat. As she watched him ride

away, the sun sliding down the horizon, day giving way to twilight, she breathed out a prayer.

The minutes stretched on like hours as she waited, watching for a signal from him. "How could he have done this day after day?" she murmured to Nathan. "I can't bear the waiting!" To her utter relief, at last he emerged on the plateau again, waving a hand out against the backdrop of a clear, salmon-colored sky.

Pulling to a stop at her side, he looked drawn and serious instead of grateful, as she'd expected. "It's safe," he said curtly. He hitched Amanda's horse back to the cart and climbed back up on Gusano, then led them to the foot of the gates. "I'll take Mandy's horse and Gusano down to the corral. You can take Nathan inside."

"Fine." Not looking at him, Serena shifted Nathan to a one-arm hold and unlocked the gates, slipping inside. "Pete?" she called out into the stillness. "We're back." No voice answered. "Pete?" She glanced inside his room, finding it empty. Not even Lucky Joe was in residence. "Where can he be?"

Walking from room to room, downstairs and up, her uneasiness began to blossom into a feeling of dread. "He can't just have disappeared," she told herself, standing in the middle of the dining area.

"What's wrong?"

Serena's heart gave a lurch as Gage appeared without warning in the doorway. She sucked in a breath, letting it out slowly. "Pete. He's not here. Where could he be?"

"He's not in the kitchen, either? I called for him in the stables, Last Chance, Deacon Mather and the dog were there, but I didn't get an answer from Pete. Still, he might be sleeping one off in some corner."

"Do you think—?" She couldn't say it.

"I'll check every stall."

"I'm coming with you. I'm not staying here alone," she said when his expression hardened. "I'd rather be with you. At least I'll know what's happening."

A muscle jerked along his jaw. "You'd better bring Nathan too," he said at last. "This time we're all staying together."

Nodding, Serena rushed out through the open gates after him to the cattle corral. It was empty. The few chickens left in the coop squawked noisily, startling her. Gage didn't flinch, but Serena noticed his hand flex on the butt of his gun.

Inside the stalls, she walked behind him, hardly daring to breathe. Her gaze fixed on Gage's back, she brushed the handle of a pitchfork left leaning against one of the stall doors. It hit the wood with a loud whack, spinning Gage around.

"Sorry," Serena whispered when he glowered at her.

They neared the end stall, where Deacon Mather resided, and suddenly a slight whimper slipped into the silence. Extending an arm, Gage motioned for her to stay still.

With the stealth of a jaguar, he drew his gun and eased up to the stall, then stepped quickly in front of it.

"No! Don't come in here! You can't come in here." Whiskey Pete's graveled voice raised from the murky depths of the stall.

"My God . . ." Serena came up behind Gage, holding Nathan tightly to her chest. Huddled up under a pile of hay behind Deacon Mather, Whiskey Pete hunched in a corner, Lucky Joe and one of the goats at his side. "What's wrong? Pete—"

"Tell us what happened," Gage said quietly. Holstering his gun, he carefully opened the stall door and knelt down, reaching out his hand as if he approached a frightened, wounded animal. "Whoever was here is gone now. It's only Serena and me. Can you tell us what happened? Who was here?"

"They was here. Them." Whiskey Pete's head shook slowly back and forth. "They came back."

"Who? Who came back?"

Shrinking back further behind Deacon Mather's bulk, Pete twisted his hands together, his eyes wild, filled with never-forgotten terrors. "The tree devils," he said, his voice trembling. "The tree devils are back."

Chapter Eighteen

For a moment they both stared at Whiskey Pete, an uneasy feeling between them.

"Gage—" Serena held Nathan a little tighter. "Do you think he—?"

Gage shook his head. "It's the loneliness—and his tree devils. He's been this way since the massacre. The killers tried to hang him—lucky for Pete they didn't do a good enough job of it. Ross and I found him alive, but he'd been strung up for a while. It left him like this." He gave Pete a despairing look. "Damned stubborn old man. Refused to leave this place since he set foot on it, even after what happened. I threatened him to within an inch of his life to come with me to stay at Mandy's after the massacre, but he refused me square in the eye every time. He wouldn't leave his animals. Now . . ."

"It's not your fault," Serena said softly. She came up behind him, laying a hand on his arm. "Everything wrong that happens to people you care for isn't your fault."

"It's got to be somebody's fault." His face grim, Gage bent down and sat back on his heels next to Pete. Still huddled behind Deacon Mather, the old man stared past him, his eyes clouded. "I was responsible for him, for everyone here."

Shifting Nathan over her shoulder, Serena knelt beside him. "We're all responsible for ourselves. That's all. Only you, Gage Tanner, take care of everyone but yourself."

"And I've been thinking all along that you were the one who had a lesson to learn."

Serena smiled. "I've learned more lessons from you these past weeks about giving and sharing and surviving and facing life straight on than I learned in a lifetime from my mama and papa and the Mormons combined." She dropped her eyes. "And if I were honest, I'd have to say I have a lot more to learn. That's the hardest part, and I'll probably fight it every inch of the way, despite what good sense tries to tell me. That's the way I am. And you too. We both have to be forced into a thing before we'll admit it's good for us."

"Some things can't be forced."

Serena looked up at him. "Some things have to be."

Gage held her gaze for a long, silent moment. "Well, right now," he said finally, "Pete's going to have to be forced out of this barn before he starves or freezes to death."

"You're right." She took a deep breath, reluctantly deciding to drop the discussion for the time being. "If you can get him back inside the walls, I'll get a fire going and put something tempting on the stove. That'll bring Lucky Joe running and maybe Pete will follow."

"Deal."

Serena turned and left them, gently bouncing Nathan in her arms as she walked back to the ranch house, deliberately distracting herself with musings over whether scrapple or shepherd's pie would entice Whiskey Pete's appetite more. Turning recipes over in her mind, her hand busy patting Nathan's back, she lost herself in her musings. At the gate, Serena chided herself on inadvertently leaving the barrier open as she pushed a hand against the rough wood. She didn't have time to regret the lapse.

Inside the courtyard, without warning, she found herself face to face with a grim-faced Birk Reed, flanked by several of his men.

Though Serena's first impulse was to protect Nathan, her second and almost simultaneous thought was of Gage. She couldn't warn him. He might be right behind her, about to walk through the gates into the line of fire of nearly a dozen angry, armed men.

Birk glared at the child in her arms. "You been gone a while, girl. But you ain't been gone that long," he snarled, pointing the tip of his revolver toward Nathan. "I know that kid ain't your flesh 'n blood. But then I s'ppose you Mormons don't care which mama takes care of which youngin' since they all got the same papa."

Her heart throbbing beneath the child she treasured as much as if he were flesh of her flesh, Serena clutched Nathan to her breast. Although fear lay cold and coiled inside her, the snickers and guffaws from the men roused the hot anger Serena needed to combat it.

"Get off of my ranch, Reed," she shouted at the top of her lungs, praying Gage would hear her and stay away.

The unnaturally shrill sound of her voice stopped Gage cold as he came out of the stable and started toward the gates. Beside him, supported by Gage's arm around his waist, Whiskey Pete continued to mutter until Gage silenced him with a hand over his mouth, dragging him back into the stable.

"Reed's inside with Serena and Nathan," he whispered. Slowly, making certain Pete wouldn't call out, Gage withdrew his hand, shifting to face the other man. He gripped Pete firmly by the shoulders, giving him a shake. "I need you. All Serena and the boy have is me and you."

"And Lucky Joe," Whiskey Pete said, bending to pat the dog sitting at his heels.

"That's right. The three of us against them. Are you ready to help?"

Whiskey Pete nodded. "My niece's in danger."

Gage tightened his grip. "That's right. and we're all she's got."

"She's a mighty good cook," Pete said, scratching at his jaw, appearing to mull over the matter. "Me 'n Joe'd miss that, 'specially her molasses pie. Cain't let Reed take that away from us, now cin we?"

"No," Gage said, fighting images of Serena and Nathan alone and helpless against Reed's men. "We can't let him take either of them away. Now—you're going to help me get them out of the courtyard. If we can lure them back outside the gates, Serena can lock herself and Nathan inside. We need a distraction . . . something that'll bring Reed running."

"Devils! Tree devils, now they'd scare 'em right outta there."

Gage's first reaction was to dismiss Whiskey Pete's notion as insane and to send the old man back to Deacon Mather's stall just to get him out of the way. But the half-witted suggestion sparked an idea. "We might not be able to get those tree devils to cooperate." he told Pete, a determined glint in his eyes. "But I think we can rustle up a ghost."

* * *

With a wild flurry of arm waving, Whiskey Pete shoved wide the heavy gate and came running straight at Birk and his men.

"He's out there! I seen him!" Pete zig-zagged through the middle of the men whooping and hollering out warnings about the Spirit in the Wind, while Lucky Joe barked madly, limping along at his master's side. The whirl of chaos sent horses pawing and rearing back, and men scrambling to gain control of them. "I seen him in the day! Ain't never seen him in the day afore! It's a bad sign. A bad sign!"

Serena gaped, certain Pete's outrageous and inexplicable stunt might set Birk off once and for all. But an odd restlessness attacked the group, and many actually listened to Pete's rantings, growing more agitated by the minute.

What are you up to, Gage Tanner? He'd obviously put Pete up to this—performance, but what good could it do? Surely he didn't expect Birk and his men would believe in Pete's ghost tales.

"Outside! He's there, waitin' fer you Reed. He's lookin' fer you. Mad 'nough to kick a hog barefooted."

"You're crazy, old man," Birk muttered. Serena noticed his hand stray to the revolver on his hip.

"No, no I ain't," Pete shouted. "He blames you—all of you—" He swung his arm at the men. "Fer killin' the widow and her children and all the rest of 'em. I ain't gonna go tell him you don't want t' talk to him. I'd just as soon tangle with a rattler naked as a babe as I would a ghost."

Birk shifted from foot to foot, throwing glances at the men. A few of them exchanged low-spoken remarks, looking at the half-open gate. "Spirit in the Wind, eh?" Birk scoffed, assuming an air of bravado. "I been lookin' out for him for a long time, but I ain't never seen nothin' but a shadow on the horizon. That story's all bunk. Could've been anyone. Gage Tanner is dead."

"He's dead all right. And he's callin' fer you, Reed. Says he wants his revenge."

Serena frowned to herself. *No. Surely Gage doesn't mean to—he can't! There are too many of them. He can't do it!*

She wished she could read his thoughts, but feared they might only echo what her gut reaction told her. Gage would go to any lengths to get Birk outside the walls and away from the ranch so she and Nathan would be safe. She knew it as surely as she breathed.

"I ain't facin' off against no ghost," one of the men grumbled.

A few of the others sneered at their companion's superstitious fears, but Serena could see some of them were uneasy about what exactly Pete had seen outside the protective walls.

"You all better go huntin' somthin' you can use for a backbone," Birk snapped as a few of his men made sounds about leaving. "And you, old man—" He stepped up in front of Pete. "You tell me what you really seen out there."

Pete started off again on his story of the Spirit in the Wind's revenge, and while Birk was arguing with him and the men distracted, Serena seized the chance to edge her way toward the oasis, using the trees for shelter. She hurried to the spring house, praying Nathan would stay silent long enough for her to reach the hidden cellar passage Gage had shown her.

When her fingers closed on the handle of the cellar door, Serena let go the breath she'd been holding. Jerking it open, she stepped down inside, clutching Nathan tightly. With a little searching, she found the door to the outside and in less than a minute was standing against the back wall.

The wall shielded her from Birk's men as she looked around the corner in the direction of the stable where Gage had left Gusano.

She didn't dare search for Gage. He was there though. She sensed his presence somewhere near, but not close enough to reach out to, to warn him not to give himself away. But she knew in her heart he meant to do precisely that. He'd stall them, toy with them, lure them away from the ranch, and sacrifice his guise—and his life—for her and Nathan.

And now they had to risk the same for him.

"We can do it," she whispered to Nathan. "We have to." Taking one last look around, Serena wrapped her arms around the baby, blew a kiss into the wind over the horizon, and started to run.

Outside the ranch walls, Gage had positioned himself beside a small grove of trees near the cattle corral, hidden, his back pressed to the trunk of the oldest cottonwood that became his only guard from Reed and his men. He slanted a look to the orange fire on the western horizon, deciding if he didn't hear signs of movement soon, he'd go in and drag Reed out himself. He'd thought about using the back entrance, but decided he'd have less chance of reaching the gates—and Serena and Nathan—in time.

Instead, he gambled on Pete enticing the lot of them outside, then locking Serena and Nathan inside before the shooting started.

Finally, after the longest minutes of his life, he heard Reed and his men ride out into the yard, cursing and shouting to each other. He breathed again. Even if Reed left a few of his men inside, Serena had guns stashed in places inside the ranch house they'd never guess at, and Pete knew as well as she did where each one was hidden. And if the worst happened, she knew about the cellar door. When it came to surviving Serena was as sharp and ruthless as any man he'd met, and with Nathan in her arms she truly became his Panther Woman.

The slam of the gate told him at least part of the plan was a success.

"I don't see no ghost," Zeke's thick voice sawed through the air like a dull knife to old bread.

"Oh, shut up Zeke. Don't you think I know that crazy coot might be thinkin' he can get rid of us by gettin' us out here and lockin' the gate behind us? That's why I left Jake and Clint inside. They'll let us back in, even if they have to put a bullet through his scrawny hide to do it."

"Yeah, but what about the bitch and that brat? Where'd they go? They was right there with us, then soon as you turned yer back, they was gone."

"It's a damned good thing I only need you to use your six-shooter and not your brain, 'cause it's so far up your ass you'd never find it if I did," Birk growled. "What the ever lovin' hell is a skinny girl totin' a sucklin' baby gonna do to us?"

"Well—er—don't s'ppose as I can say, exactly, but all I know is she's mean as any bobcat I ever seen, and shoots afore she knows what she's shootin' at. She's near as crazy as that uncle of hers."

Birk jerked back on the reins of his horse, yanking his gun from the holster. "I don't give a damn where she's run off to. It ain't her I'm worryin' about. And this time she ain't gonna have no place to come back to anyways. I've fooled around long enough over this place. I'm layin' claim to it today."

"But what about the deal you made with—"

"I ain't waitin' for no one or nothing to give me what I want," Birk snapped out. "The deal's been changed. I never planned on keepin' that bargain anyhow."

While Zeke and the others cheered their boss with a loud spate of shouting, Gage scrambled mentally for a clue to Serena's disappearance. She must have escaped using the cellar entrance. But what wild impulse drove her to take Nathan and leave the security of the ranch house before he'd had the chance to take action? She had to have at least guessed at Pete's motives. And his. More importantly, where would she go?

And what did Reed mean by a deal he'd made? The only deal he could have made to claim the ranch would have been with the Mormons. Gage knew Silas Caltrop would never make such a bargain. That meant Birk's deal had to be with—

"So where the hell is this Spirit in the Wind?" Zeke's voice barged into his troubled thoughts. "I ain't seen no ghost and he was s'pposed to be lookin' for you, Reed. Looks like the old man got the better of you."

"Not yet, he don't," Birk said. "And if I do get a look at his ghost—"

"Here's your chance." The hollow sound of Gage's voice penetrated their lively argument, the invisible power of his presence invasive, yet detached from their reality. "I'm right here, Reed. I've been waiting for you."

One by one, each jerked around to follow the haunting sound of a dead man's threat. Gage stepped out from behind the tree, the dusky purple haze of twilight settling around him like a shroud.

"What the hell—it is him," Zeke managed to spit out. "The dead guy. I didn't figure on this, Reed. I ain't paid well enough to tangle with no ghost." He turned his horse away from the yard in the direction of the plain and several other of the men followed suit.

"Stay put! All of you!" Birk shot out. He shaded his eyes against the setting sun, squinting into the last brilliant burst of light. "Listen, whoever you are, I ain't got no fight with you. I only come to get what's mine."

"Yours?" Gage braved a step forward. "The ranch is mine."

Birk gave an uneasy laugh. "What's a ghost need a ranch for?"

"I'm no ghost. And you know it."

A ripple of murmurs coursed through the men.

Birk turned a few shades paler, and Gage saw the hand holding his gun shudder. It took several moments for him to find his voice. "You're dead," he said hoarsely. "Everyone 'round here knows it. There's a grave—on the slope."

"A grave I dug."

"Yeah? Well, if that is you, then somebody's been lyin' to me. And men don't lie to me Tanner. Not more'n once, anyway. So, maybe I ought to put a bullet through you right now to prove you're no a ghost." Raising the revolver, Birk aimed it directly at Gage's heart, cocking back the hammer. " 'Cause if you ain't, after what I been through to get this ranch, you're gonna be."

Gage jerked a six shooter from either hip. "If we end it this way, you'll never get what you want."

"I'll get it. I need this water to keep my herd alive and ain't no one gonna keep me from it."

"No matter who has to die in the process?"

"No matter who."

His aim steady, Gage stared hard into the other man's eyes. "Including Libby and her two boys?"

"If you're accusin' me of killin' 'em, you better say

so straight out," Birk snapped. "I'll tell you just as straight I didn't have nothin' to do with it."

"Didn't you?"

"No. I want the water, but I didn't kill for it. I tried bein' reasonable. I tried everything, dammit! And I lost near everything. I even came down to dealin' with the damn Mormons to get this place."

"You expect me to believe you tried to cut a bargain with Mormons?" Gage said with a derisive twist of his mouth. "You've tried just about everything you could think of to run them out of the territory. Now you're telling me you were willing to manage the ranch for them?"

"I might have been," Birk shot back, a ruddy flush staining his neck and face. "But they're only interested in keepin' it all for themselves. They tried to cut me out. So, to hell with them and with you. I'm takin' what should've been mine from the start." He kept his gun steady. "You gonna try and stop me?"

"Maybe." Gage weighed Birk's expression, his reactions, and all he believed about Reed, the lengths he would go to for the water, and considered what kind of Mormons would be willing to make a deal with a man who wanted to permanently drive them out of the territory. After a long pause, he slowly lowered his guns, his action slapping a look of surprise on Birk's face. "And maybe I can help."

"We heard you comin' a mile away," Amanda said when Serena jerked Gusano to a stop at the doorstep of the trading post.

For a moment, all Serena could do was nod. Nathan had screamed the last thirty minutes of the ride, but at least he was still tucked safely against her body.

Winded, exhausted, her heart hammering against her chest, she glanced over the gathering of questioning faces. Amanda, holding Tallie's hand, and a few others of the local folk Serena had met during one visit or another to the post stood waiting to see what the commotion was about, staring at the breathless woman toting the squalling child.

Serena slid off Gusano's back, her heart paining her with each beat. She could feel the faintness creeping over her, growing stronger with each breath she took. "Help me . . . please," she whimpered. Her knees began to buckle; the ground under her feet wavered like water. "Nathan . . ."

"He's fine," Amanda's gentle voice soothed her, easing her tortured mind. "I got you. Lean against me and let me take you inside."

"Please take him. I—I can't walk and I don't want him to fall." Serena's voice was less than a whisper. "Birk and his men are at the ranch. I've got to get back. But I need help. And we have to hurry—"

"Shhh. Don't you worry none." She supported Serena with one arm, turning to her daughter. "Tallie get on down to the smithy's and find Ross. Good thing you got here when you did," she said to Serena when the little girl scampered off in search of Ross. "Ross was just fixin' to head out toward Kaibab for a spell."

"I'm sorry," Serena said, fighting back angry tears. Infuriated beyond reason by her body's betrayal in her moment of desperate need for strength, she had no choice but to accept help. She hated the shame of her weakness more in that instant than she could ever remember. Strength survived. But despite the force of her tenacious will, this one frailty persisted, held a power over her, no demands, no amount of perseverance could control.

Her head reeling, she felt detached from reality, heard voices, but no words. Someone lifted her and she felt herself being carried up a flight of stairs, then laid down upon a soft mattress. A cool cloth touched her brow and she drifted away to a memory.

She rode Gusano with Gage under the stars. He held her in front of him in the saddle, talking softly in her ear as he pointed to a line of rocky walls. Beyond them he was saying, the Grand Canyon stretched in all its wonder. But because of the huge rock formation in her way, she had only her imagination and his description to envision it. Frustration gripped her; she wanted more, all the experience at once, to look down into it, to see everything he described with her own eyes.

"It sounds so beautiful," she told him in her mind's remembrance, "but those rocks are in the way. I'd move them if I could, right here and now."

Gage laughed, the low, rich sound she loved to hear. "I don't doubt it. But sometimes even you, Serena Lark, can't move mountains," he murmured in her ear, then kissed her hair, gently, with a touch that told her he cared. Yet there was no passion in his touch, and she knew in her heart there was part of him he held back, part of him he refused to let her reach. "You'll never find any peace until you accept what can't be along with what can."

"Never," she swore.

Never. Now, through the razor-edged pain in her chest, through the raging torment of her thoughts, Serena understood at last what he meant. *Never is now.*

I can't will him to love me any more than I can will myself free of this damned illness. I finally have to accept what can't be.

* * *

When she came to herself again, Serena found Amanda in the rocker next to the bed where she lay, holding Nathan in her lap. Tallie toyed with his little fingers, giggling when Nathan laughed up at her.

"Welcome back," Amanda said, catching her eye.

"How long was I—"

"Only half an hour or so."

Serena dragged herself to a sitting position, the fog slowly clearing from her mind. Suddenly her eyes flew wide. "Birk—the ranch! I have to get back to the ranch!"

"Oh no you don't. Everything's fine. Ross is roundin' up a few friends to help get Reed and his boys off your land. Don't you worry none, Ross could handle Birk Reed blindfolded."

"You don't understand," Serena said, feeling fear well up stronger and harder than before. "Amanda, there's much more to it—"

"I'm sure there is. But it won't do you no good to get riled up about it. How 'bout I fix you somethin' to eat? You're still lookin' pale as a ghost."

Wincing a little at Amanda's unconscious choice of words, Serena debated what to do. If Amanda left the room, she might be able to slip out and get back to the ranch. Lord only knew how Ross and the others might react when they found out Gage was alive, although she suspected Ross already knew as much or more than she herself did. But the others—what if they felt as betrayed, as angry, as she suspected the ranchers would? How could Gage justify why he'd done what he'd done in the midst of the inevitable confrontation? Even if he could, she had to get back and help him, or at least be there to support him.

"I am hungry," she murmured, not quite able to meet Amanda's eyes. "If it's not too much trouble."

"Not a bit," Amanda said with a grin. "I was just fixin' to get somethin' for Tallie and Nathan anyhow. You lie back down and behave yourself. We'll have a plate up here for you in no time. Won't we Tallie?"

Tallie clasped her hands behind her back and stuck her chin in the air. Twisting at her waist from side to side she announced proudly, "I'm baking biscuits for Nathan."

Serena smiled. "You'll help your mama take care of him for me, won't you?"

"Yep. I'm kinda like his big sister, you know."

"I know. He's a lucky boy. We're both lucky to have you and your mama," Serena said, a lump forming in her throat for what she was about to do. She prayed Amanda wouldn't hate her for sneaking off, but she couldn't let Gage face everything alone. Not again.

After she could no longer hear Amanda and the children, Serena, knees shaking, crept downstairs and out into the store. Wiping a sheen of sweat from her forehead, she reached out for the front door handle.

In the same instant, the door flung open, thrusting her into a stack of canned goods and bringing Amanda running. She was still carrying Nathan, Tallie hovering behind her. "What the—"

Serena never heard her. Looking up, her eyes were fixed on the man towering over her. "Jerel," she whispered, her fear burgeoning into terror.

A faint smile creased his face as he held out a hand to her. There was no mirth in the gesture, only the satisfaction of a predator. "The Lord smiles on me. I had nearly given up hope of finding you. And now, I discover you here, waiting for me to carry you to your rightful home."

"No, I'm not going." Pushing back against the cans,

Serena glared at him. "You can't take me against my will."

"There you are mistaken." Before Serena could react, Jerel lunged forward, ignoring Amanda's protest, and grabbed her wrist, jerking her to her feet. "You are mine to do with as I please. There will be no more argument."

"I am not yours! I'm married!" She heard Amanda's gasp of surprise, silently begged her to keep quiet.

Jarel's eyes narrowed. "I know of your so-called marriage. It means nothing. There is nothing legal about a wedding performed by savages."

"Or a polygamous one."

He slapped her hard across the jaw. Tallie screamed. "You make me question whether you have been worth pursuing."

Amanda shifted Nathan to her hip and whipped her knife from the sheath on the opposite side. She strode over to Serena's side. "I'm tellin' you this once, and once only. Get out of my store before I slit your throat and use your hide for my winter coat."

"I will have what is rightfully mine," Jerel said coldly, his gaze never leaving Serena. "Neither you nor anyone else will keep it from me."

Serena feared for Amanda and the children. Alone, Amanda could handle any man she met, but with Tallie and Nathan to protect, up against Jerel and the companions he surely had with him, even Amanda didn't stand a chance in twenty of coming out alive.

"If you leave them be," she said quickly. "I'll go with you back to the ranch."

"Serena, no!"

"It's all right, Amanda." Serena swallowed hard to find the courage to say what she must. "Jerel will either have to deal with my husband there, or with the marshall when he tracks him down for kidnapping and polygamy."

Amanda frowned, her eyes questioning. "What husband?"

Serena winced as Jerel's hand tightened on the tender skin of her wrist. Yet his voice and face stayed smooth and easy. "Haven't you told her you have been pretending to be Gage Tanner's wife all these weeks to the pilgrims who visited the ranch?"

"What good would that do her?" Amanda asked sharply. "Gage Tanner was murdered with his family."

Jerel's eyes went hard. "No. He wasn't. Was he Serena?"

"I—" Serena looked helplessly at Amanda.

"No matter. I will soon remedy that and his ghost story will become truth rather than fiction. We are wasting time." Not giving Serena a chance to explain, he turned and pulled her with him out of the store, Serena kicking and struggling all the way. She knew Amanda wanted to help her, but there was little she could do without endangering the children. At least she knew Nathan was safe . . .

They rode hard and fast against the falling darkness, she in front of Jerel in the saddle. Seven men, draped as he was in solemn black dusters, flanked them like raven's wings.

"We will leave at dawn," he was saying as they finally slowed near the cattle barn at the ranch. "It should be safe for us here. The ranch is abandoned save for the old man, and we can help ourselves to the oasis and whatever food there is." He dismounted, yanking Serena with him and pushing her into another rider's grasp. "Still, we will go ahead while you wait here with her and ensure there is no danger, Brother Samuel."

The man he called Samuel held Serena closer. "As you wish, Moroni."

With a short nod, Jerel got back up on his horse and with the others disappeared around the side of the barn.

Just as he did, Serena caught a glimpse of Birk Reed, riding alone up past the barn, near the corrals. She made an instinctive start forward—Birk didn't have any love for her, but he despised the Mormons, surely he would help. But Samuel dragged her backward, clapping a hand over her mouth, shackling both hands behind her back.

Serena strained to at least listen, overhearing only vague greetings between Jerel and the rancher, wondering at Birk's easy acceptance of the Mormon elder. Then Jerel led Birk far enough away that she could no longer make anything of their conversation. They rode off together back toward the ranch, leaving her still a prisoner, filled with more questions than answers.

Suddenly, a wave of dread rippled strongly through her. Birk was still here, seemingly alone. Where was Gage? Had Birk's men—Serena quickly cut off the thought.

Maybe Gage had managed to make some sort of peace with Reed. But how? It seemed impossible. Yet the alternative was unthinkable.

The questions drove her to the brink of madness. What had happened? Where were the rest of Birk's men? What was going on now? She struggled like a wildcat against her captor, driven to find Gage. She had to know if he'd survived a confrontation with Reed and his men. And only he had the answers to what was happening at the ranch. But, in the end, the fight only led to ropes about her wrists, a gag in her mouth, and the cold fear of uncertainty in her heart.

* * *

At the sound of approaching riders, Gage glanced out the opening in the wall. He didn't need an introduction to know the man riding beside Birk Reed was Jerel Webster.

Serena, dammit woman, where are you? Wherever it is, it better be far from here.

"Just let me go on inside for a minute to tell my boys what's goin' on," Birk was saying to Jerel as the men stopped their horses several yards from the gates. "They ain't as willin' to deal with Mormons as I am."

"Tell them to open the gates," Jerel said, his tone a command.

Birk pushed back his hat, his eyes narrowing. "You don't want 'em thinkin' this is less than a friendly visit, now do you? They got the advantage. They're inside those walls. And if they get the idea you're usin' me to make 'em unlock the gates, they're gonna be inclined to start using you and your boys as targets. My bein' out here won't make no difference. Now—" He shifted a little straighter in the saddle. "You gonna let me do it my way?"

Jerel stared a him a long moment, his expression flat and unfathomable. Finally, he gave an almost imperceptible nod.

"Fine." Giving his horse a slight kick, Birk rode up to the gates.

Gage gestured to Pete and Jake, Birk's man stationed near the gate, to let Birk inside. He'd already sent Clint, another of Birk's hands to stand guard at the cellar entrance, just in case Webster knew of its existence. At the same time Pete opened the gate, he moved further up the stairs, to where the balcony met the wall. Stepping over the balcony rail, he straightened, propping one boot on the wall's edge. "Welcome back, Webster."

He locked gazes with the Mormon leader. Nothing registered on the other man's face. No surprise, no fear. Only a cold, impenetrable mask.

"Tanner." The name was a curse on Jerel's lips. His hand flexed on the saddle horn. "How long have you been back?"

"How do you know I ever left?" Gage said, resisting the urge to draw both guns and send Jerel Webster to Hell where he belonged. "We've never met face to face and no one from Salt Lake ever dares to come down here any more. Only pilgrims pass through."

"And one of those pilgrims was surprised to learn you had taken a wife. A wife who knew little about the widow, or you, or anyone supposedly living here. And he mentioned to me how odd it was the women and children were in town for days on end, and you had taken all of the hands, cattle and horses and left a strange woman and a half-witted old man in charge of the ranch." Jerel stroked a thoughtful hand over his beard. "Oddly, Silas Caltrop never mentioned your marriage . . . although it seems you have taken a husband's privileges with what is rightfully mine."

"You seem to know a lot about what's been happened here. When was the last time you came down to check on the ranch, Webster?" Gage asked between gritted teeth. His hand slipped to his holster. His hand grazed the smooth butt of his revolver.

But before he could make another move, a sudden burst of rifle shot whizzed into the yard in the direction of the Mormon group.

"I got you this time!" Whiskey Pete shouted through the slot in the wall. "You're gonna be dead tree devils this time. Deader 'n a beaver hat. I ain't lettin' you in, not like her. You're goin' to Hell where you belong!" He let go another shot, narrowly missing one of Jerel's companions. The man's horse snorted and reared back, kicking up a whirl of dust.

Gage jumped down from the wall as a hail of gunfire assaulted the stone and wood surrounding the ranch house.

"Somebody's gone and stole the old man's rudder for good this time," Birk muttered as Gage jogged down the stairs to join him by the gates.

"Webster. He and his men tried to hang Pete when they attacked the ranch. But I can't say much for Pete's timing." He took another quick look outside through one of the rifle slits, pulling back as more gunfire careened off the wall near the opening. Jake and Pete returned the fire, shooting through the wall slits, managing to wound two of the Mormon riders.

"Damn Mormons," Birk said. "I always knew they were trouble. I should've never tried to deal with 'em."

"You should've never tried to deal with Jerel Webster. He's nothing like any of the Mormons I've come to know."

"I know he's different. That's why I tried to bargain with him. He said the ranch belonged to him, not the church, and with you gone, he planned on takin' it back over and keepin' the Indians and pilgrims and everyone else away from it. But he needed a gentile to manage it."

Gage flashed a scowl his direction. "And you were willing to do what you always accused me of—break the law so you could hoard the water for your own herd."

"I sure didn't intend to share it with everyone who came knockin' at the gates like you got in the habit of doing," Birk snapped. "It would've worked out fine, if

Webster hadn't tried to change the deal his way. He wanted me to be nothin' more than a damn ranch hand, followin' his orders. So I decided I'd take over this place before he showed up again. Law says he can't own it anyhow."

Several rifle shots punctuated the end of Birk's explanation. The firing continued for several minutes. Then, abruptly, the world outside the walled-in ranch house fell deadly silent.

"It's a stalemate, at best. He won't leave until he has some satisfaction for me getting the ranch over him. And for what he thinks I've done to Serena," Gage said, more to himself than to Birk and his man, and to Pete, who had come down the stairs into the courtyard, drawn by the commotion. *I just hope you're far enough away from here, woman, so he can't get it from you.* He tried to shake off a growing sense of instinctive apprehension that told him she wasn't far enough. "We need to get the marshall out here," he added, his mind racing to come up with a fast plan.

"You got a damned telegraph here," Birk said. "Use it."

"I don't know how to operate it," Gage shot back, his temper fraying at the edges. "Hell for all I know it doesn't work."

Cocking his head, Whiskey Pete looked at Gage with his one good eye. "Works fine," he said, strangely calm.

Gage and Birk exchanged a glance. "How do you know?"

"Weren't never broke. Just takes some know-how to use it."

"Are you telling me you can work it?" Gage asked, dumbfounded.

"Sure. I was here when they set it up. I watched 'em every day fer weeks. It ain't so hard to use. The widow used to let me send word up to Utah fer her every now and again."

Gage shook his head in disbelief. "All these months . . . can you wire the marshall?"

"Long as he's willin' to get rid of them tree devils."

"They'll pay for what they've done, I promise you that." He didn't add that he intended to have that satisfaction himself. He just needed a marshall to clean up the leftovers.

Webster wouldn't leave now, he was sure of it. Not when he was so close to getting what he'd come after. *Too close. He's too close.*

"Pete, where's Serena?" Gage asked, not sure he wanted to hear the answer.

Halfway up the stairs on his way to the telegraph room, Whiskey Pete shrugged. "Don't know."

"She's long gone from here if she's got any sense," Birk broke in. "She took the kid and disappeared 'bout the time you showed up tryin' to scare ten years off of my life."

The vague feeling of trouble focused into full-blown fear. "Gone where?"

"How the hell should I know?"

Gage turned and strode toward the staircase, taking the stairs two at a time. Minutes later, he came trotting back down to the courtyard, jamming the extra ammunition he'd found in his pocket.

"Where you goin'?" Birk demanded as Gage headed for the gates.

"After her."

"You're crazy! If you open those gates—"

"Gage!"

The strangled cry from just outside the gates stopped Gage cold. *Serena!*

"Don't come—" Abruptly, her voice cut off.

"It seems I have something you want," Jerel's raised voice thundered through the closed barriers. "Something else that once belonged to me."

"She never belonged to you," Gage yelled back.

"She was mine, just as this ranch was mine. Destiny deemed it so. But those elders weak in mind and spirit, who turn their backs on the old ways, refused to see it. Like the fools they are, they let those outside the clans take over our lands and push us into a corner of Hell in the Utah territory. You took both this ranch and this woman, and ruined her in the bargain. Now she's less than worthless to me."

"Then let her go. What's left is between you and me."

"There will be nothing left for you once I am finished," Jerel said.

A scuffling sounded, then Serena shouted, "Don't listen to him, Gage! Don't let him—"

Gage heard a loud smack and a muffled cry. He started for the gates.

"You can't let 'em in here," Birk insisted. "He's usin' her to make you lose your head."

Birk's assessment gave Gage a moment's pause. Until Serena screamed his name.

Ignoring Birk's cursing and Jake's startled glance, he took off running toward the spring house. He pushed past Clint, leaning against the door, ignoring his protest.

"Where are you goin' now?" Birk called after him, fast on his heels. "What's the use of hidin' in the cellar—"

"There's another way outside through here," Gage said, already down the stairs and at the wall. Shoving open the hidden door, he glanced back at Birk. "Very few of the Mormons know about it. Odds are Webster doesn't. If I can surprise them, Serena will have a chance to get back inside the walls."

"You got a better chance of gettin' yourself shot full of holes."

"That's my business. I didn't ask for your help."

"Well, you got it, like it or not," Birk said gruffly, following Gage up the incline to the door leading to the outside. At Gage's look of disbelief he added, "If you go and get yourself killed, I'm never gonna have the chance of getting this place. The Mormons won't deal with me, not after this. And if I wait for the marshall, I'll end up gettin' blamed for puttin' the bodies in all those graves you dug. Besides," he added with a grim smile. "I got somethin' of my own to settle with Webster."

Hesitating a moment, Gage gave Birk a sharp nod, of acceptance and in some measure, understanding. Then, drawing his revolver, he shoved open the door.

They had barely set foot on the rocky ground when, without warning, they were suddenly surrounded by eight of Jerel's men, faced by the muzzles of as many guns.

"You made a mistake in thinking you were the only one of us who knew about this way outside," Webster said, guiding his horse to where his men gathered around Gage and Birk, taking their guns. Jerel looked down at them with barely disguised hatred. "And saved me the considerable trouble of coming inside to get you. Get the others," he ordered several of his men. "I want *no* witnesses."

He motioned to the remaining men and they forced Gage and Birk around the wall, into the yard at the front of the ranch house.

"Are we leaving tonight, Moroni?" one of the Mormons asked as Jerel neared.

"Yes. Soon, there will no longer be a reason to stay." He looked down to where Serena lay on the ground near the wall.

She flung one anguished glance at Gage, then glared up at him, her hand pressed to the thin slash across her middle he had made with the tip of his knife. "Moroni? Is that what they call you now?"

Jerel said nothing, only watched, his eyes burning, as his men dragged her, beside Birk and Gage through the now open gates to the oasis.

"Serena . . ." Gage, struggling against the three men holding him, swept her with a look compounded of relief at seeing her alive, and a grim determination to see her safely away from Jerel. His face darkened when he saw the angry red palm print on her cheek, the ripped dress.

"I tried to get help," she said. "I'm sorry—"

Just then, Whiskey Pete, squirming and hollering terror-stricken protests, was jerked alongside them, a spitting and cursing Jake and Clint behind him.

"I have been waiting a long time for this day," Jerel said, taking a thick length of rope offered by one of his men. He tossed it over a high branch of one of the cottonwoods.

"Tree devils!" Pete screamed. "Jus' like the last time. They had me swingin' in the trees, holding me there. But I got loose. I got away from 'em. And now they're back! I told you they was tree devils! I told you!"

Serena gasped. "Tree devils—Jerel . . . you—"

"He was after me," Gage said, the hardness in his tone daring Jerel to refute him. "He rounded up a few renegade Apache to make it look like the Apache had taken their revenge against me. But I wasn't here. Libby thought he and his men were Mormon pilgrims so she let them inside the gates. And then Webster killed her, the boys, all of them, because Silas Caltrop had given me the ranch to run instead of letting him have it." He stared directly at Jerel. "You killed them so you could have what you wanted. For your own revenge."

"Except I did not get it," Jerel said, a slight smile touching his mouth. "Now, I will finish what I started. And this time I will have the pleasure of first letting you watch your lover and your friends die."

At his gesture, one of the men picked up Serena and put her on the back of his horse, tying her wrists behind her back before settling the noose around her neck.

Into the deepening darkness, Serena strained to look for the last time into Gage's eyes. "I can't think of the words, to tell you . . ." She stopped, overcome with a flood of sorrow and regret and anger at what they had gained and were about to lose.

She waited for him to say something. Instead, he stared, motionless, into the black vista beyond the open gates.

"Gage?"

"Listen," he said at last.

For several seconds, Serena heard nothing. Then a familiar, once terrifying sound reached her ears.

The voices of the Paiute, so low and haunting, they could have been spirit whispers as easily as human chants, began to weave a circle around the oasis. Growing louder, repeating over and over the same drumming beat, echoing from all directions.

Jerel's men began looking around in increasing agitation. Horses shuffled nervously, kicking up dust.

"Moroni—it sounds like Indians."

"I can see nothing—"

"They sound as if they are everywhere, many of them. We are surrounded!"

Serena closed her eyes tightly shut, daring to hope against hope.

"Kwion," Gage murmured like a prayer of thanks.

Jerel called for his men to close the gates, but before any of them could act on the command, the space between the gates and the yard beyond them, and then the courtyard were suddenly filled with silent-moving figures.

The full moon illuminating the ebon sky above them, the shadows of the Paiute appeared from the heart of a silver mist. Garbed in the sacred leather and white of the Ghost Dance, their faces, painted with stars and moons and the mystical symbols of life, reflected the night's magic, terrifying and magnificent.

The lone bay of a coyote hailed their coming. Another, then another joined, their wild, mournful howls a primitive orchestra for the ceremony, rebounding off the canyon walls to fill the air with the voices of an unearthly choir.

As the night music swelled, the dance began. Dark figures, streaked with light, moving into a tighter and tighter circle around the Mormons, pressing nearer and nearer, their wail and song and snakelike movements gripping the men in a paroxysm of fear.

Gage seized his chance. Breaking free, he ran up to Serena and knocked aside the man holding the reins of the horse, jerking her down and into his arms. He hugged her close for a split second, then hurried to untie her wrists.

He'd flung the ropes aside and turned slightly to get a better look at the gash on her middle, when from the corner of his eye he saw Jerel slide a hand under his duster toward his hip.

Whirling about, Gage bent and snatched up the revolver of the man he'd hit, aiming it at a point between Jerel's eyes. "Not this time, *Moroni.*"

Standing at Gage's side, Serena knew in that moment he intended to kill Jerel. She could see it in his eyes. He would have his revenge.

"Gage . . ." Trembling, the blood thundering in her ears, Serena stretched out a hand to him. "Not like this—"

She hesitated, suddenly realizing the thundering was growing louder, stronger. It became the sound of horses' hooves, blending with the chants, and as the riders neared, Serena recognized the man at the lead.

"Ross! Thank God!"

Hearing his friend's name, Gage slowly forced his finger off the trigger. He and Jerel exchanged a long stare.

Ross pushed his way into the center of the circle to where Gage and Serena stood. "You may not thank me, friend," he said, drawing Gage's attention from the Mormon leader. "But I told everyone I could lay a hand on the truth about you bein' the Spirit in the Wind. Every man among them said he'd have helped you all along if you'd only asked. Mandy especially. She's none too happy with either you or me right about now."

"Did anyone get a message to the marshall?" Serena asked.

"A rider came by Mandy's just as we were gettin' ready to leave. Said the sheriff up at Lee's Ferry got a telegram from here and he's roundin' up the nearest one he can find. Seems your friend there—" He motioned to Jerel. "—has a few other killin's to his name. He and his group call themselves the Avenging Angels. They used Apache to help cover their tracks. God's special messengers of death for anyone who don't see things their way," Ross added with a twist of sarcasm. "We'll get 'em rounded up and hold 'em for the marshall. They'll get a fair trial at least, before they're strung up."

"He doesn't deserve to wait that long," Gage said, stepping up to Jerel, pressing the point of his gun against his throat. "He killed Libby, all of them . . ." His finger rubbed the trigger.

Serena would have rushed up to him, but Ross' hand on her shoulder stopped her. "It's up to you. But you'll be lettin' him die easy."

Each passing second seemed to last an eternity. Finally Gage jerked the gun down, spinning away from Jerel. He shoved his gun back in his holster. "Get him out of here before I change my mind," he told Ross.

Ross and his companions finished freeing Pete, Birk, and his men, and then rounded up the Avenging Angels, ushering them into the yard, Serena and Gage stood side by side at the edge of the oasis, not speaking, not touching. Around them, the Paiute continued their low chants, now a gentler, more tristful song, as compared with the frenzied dancing of before.

"Libby, her sons, my men died here," Gage said at last, his eyes fixed on the black void of the plain. "For what? For land and water? Life means nothing if it means less than the elements."

Serena touched a tentative hand to his shoulder. "Their deaths were brutal and senseless, and there's nothing that can take away the sorrow of that. But this water has also saved the lives of the Paiute. And the Mormons whose faith is pure. It saved my life."

Gage slowly turned to face her. "It's taken mine. I don't have anything left to give it. Or anyone."

The blunt meaning of his words tore at Serena's heart. She was losing him. And worse yet, she had to let him go.

Straightening her shoulders, she drew in a long

breath. "You're like this ranch to me, Gage," she said softly. "I thought if I wanted you badly enough, if it were the best thing for you as well as for me, if I poured my love and my soul into you, that sooner or later, like the ranch, you would belong to me. That I could will things to be and not to be. But I was wrong. It never was mine to take." She brushed a hand over his cheek then stepped away. "And neither were you."

Chapter Nineteen

Late afternoon sun slanted through violet-gray clouds shifting shadow and light on the plain as Serena slowly walked through the whispering grasses back to the ranch. She hugged her knitted shawl loosely about her, closing out the wind that carried the first chill suggestion of autumn.

Many of the Paiute, their cattle and horses, were gathered around the pool near the corral, nodding or speaking a few words of greeting to her as she passed. Each day as she opened the pipe to let the water flow freely from the sheltered oasis, outside the walls and gates to fill the watering hole for them, she felt a sense of satisfaction. They came nearly every afternoon now, sometimes accompanied by the women and children, and this day in particular, Serena was glad of their company. She hadn't been able to stay inside the ranch house to watch Gage gather his few stray belongings and say his final goodbyes to Whiskey Pete, Kwion and others of his Paiute friends, and especially to Nathan. It seemed impossible, unthinkable he would actually leave. Yet he had made it clear he wouldn't stay.

And now she had to say goodbye too. For the last time.

He was standing near the gates, giving a last tug to the rope tying his bedroll at the rear of Gusano's saddle, his expression closed, his gaze intent on his task. Watching him, it seemed he had already left her, in mind and heart, if not in body and spirit.

At the sound of her footsteps, though, he looked up, and in that moment, Serena saw a conflict of emotion cross his face. Regret, indecision, pain, all replaced by his familiar, immovable resolve.

She stopped several feet from him, the sun in her eyes, shadow on his face. "It looks like you're ready," she said, the words coming hard. "Did you say goodbye to everyone?"

"Everyone except you."

"I wanted to be the last." Serena wrapped her arms around herself, the ache of loss inside her already almost too strong to bear. "I hope . . . I hope you find everything you're looking for. And more."

Walking around Gusano, Gage closed the distance between them. He half reached out as if to touch her face, then let his hand fall back. "What will you do?"

"I'll survive," she said, lifting her chin, forcing a smile, determined not to let him guess at her crumbling strength. "I'll find work, something I can do. Maybe in Albuquerque, or Taos. For now, Nathan and I are going to stay with Amanda until I can find us a home. A real home. And I will. You can count on that."

"I never doubted it." Gage paused, glanced down, then at her again. "Serena—"

"No." Hot tears stung her eyes. "Don't say you're sorry. Don't say it'll be all right, that I'll forget. Because it isn't, and I won't. I can't."

"Neither can I." Before she could react, Gage pulled her into his arms. "God help me, neither can I," he muttered, just as his mouth covered hers. His kiss was hungry and hard, as if he wanted to brand her with his essence, and take the memory of her touch deep inside himself for the long days and nights he would be alone.

It was a forbidden taste of all she had gained and all she had lost, and a last selfish indulgence she should never have allowed. Paradise at the gates of Hell. Yet Serena couldn't deny it, though it left her torn and bleeding inside. She finally summoned the last of her courage and wrenched out of his arms, tears running down her face. "Please ... you should go."

Gage said nothing, only stared at her for what seemed like forever. At last, moving stiffly, he turned and walked back to Gusano. In the saddle, his hat pulled low, he slowly picked up the reins. The stallion tossed his head, whinnying low.

Serena stood trembling, her hands clenched at her sides. Her shawl slipped to the ground at her feet. Then, as Gage's hand moved to turn Gusano in the direction of the plain, she gave into desperation. Running up to him, she laid a hesitating hand on his thigh. The muscle under her fingers flinched. His fist tightened on the reins.

"I have to tell you—before you leave ..." She drew in a steadying breath. The words rushed out, carried by a deep-running river of emotion. "It sounds ... meaningless to say I love you. It doesn't begin to describe my feelings because they're so much more than that. I've known for a long time I would never find words to tell you how I feel about you. It's nothing I've ever felt before or ever will again. I never dreamed I would love someone like you." Her voice caught on a sob. "Or lose someone like you."

Not giving him time to respond, Serena spun around and ran, full out and recklessly, in the direction of the cliffs. She kept running, headlong into the wind, no

longer rational or thinking, but a wild, anguished crea-
ture driven to escape the pain.

At the border of the cliffs, she chose an upward rocky
trail, climbing until she arrived breathless, her heart
pounding, at the edge of a sheer bluff. She walked to the
very brink of the rock, to the edge of her world. From
her vantage point, she could see out over the plain, to
the plateau where she had first caught a glimpse of the
image of the Spirit in the Wind, watching and waiting.

She waited now, watching.

Endless minutes passed, until at last she saw him, riding toward the plateau.

At the same time, the sound of footsteps, light and
sure, came up behind her. Serena glanced once at the
ancient face of Kwion before fixing her eyes again on
Gage's retreating figure.

"You have chosen wisely," Kwion said, following her
gaze. "You can never demand all, only give all—"

"Only to lose everything," Serena finished. Around
them, the long wail of a zephyr echoed through the canyons, an ageless lament in a timeless place. But it
sounded faraway compared to the weeping of her heart
as Gage carried it away with him to a place she could
never go. "It must be wrong to love him like this. But
I don't know how to stop it. You know how to heal. Can
you cure me of a feeling that I've waited a lifetime to
find?"

Kwion said nothing, only watched with her until there
was nothing to see but earth and sky.

When the dust and fading light had stolen him from
her, Serena let the tears slide down her face once more,
unheeded. "He's gone," she said softly, so low the
sound was nearly lost.

"No." Kwion turned to her and the quiet force of his
voice compelled Serena to look at him. "He will always

be with you. Here—" He stretched out his hand and touched his fingertips to her heart. "In a place with no boundaries, no frontiers."

Serena nodded, knowing he spoke the truth. Yet looking back at the empty plateau, all she could believe was that she had lost Gage Tanner forever.

"I think that's the last of it." Amanda picked up the canvas sack and carpetbag that held the clothing and other items she and Serena had packed. "I'll haul these on down to the cart. Can you handle that one?" she added, nodding to the crate Serena was finishing piling with blankets and other odds and ends.

Serena nodded. "There's just these few things from the washstand," she said, wondering why such a small task felt so hard to do. It had been six weeks since Gage had left her, and though she'd had that time to prepare for this day, her last day at the ranch, she wasn't ready. Maybe she would never be ready. She felt drained inside, colorless, as if some strange, insidious illness afflicted her and he had taken the cure. It was useless not to think of him. She had no choice. He was the ghost in every face, haunting her dreams each night, a relentless spirit, always near.

Sighing, she pushed aside her melancholy, determined not to let it rule her, and began pulling out the few squares of linen she found in the washstand drawer. "I'll tuck these in here and then—" Serena's voice suddenly deserted her as her fingers closed over a small, deerskin pouch. The scent of fire, the desert and midnight incense rose up around her, blotting out the nearly barren bedroom. She closed her eyes, feeling the soft hide, filled with the images of ancient dances and dark, warm embraces, and she could almost sense Gage's touch, taste the honey and temptation of his kiss.

". . . You all right? Serena?"

Serena opened her eyes, brought back to the present by the sharp note of concern in Amanda's tone. "Fine," she said, hurriedly tucking the pouch in the pocket of her dress. "I was just—thinking."

"About Gage."

"About what I'm going to do to earn my way." She avoided Amanda's eyes and kept her hands busy stuffing soaps and linens in the crate. "I'm glad Pete will be able to stay on at the ranch. I don't know where else he'd go with all those animal misfits of his. Since Nathan and I can't stay, I was thinking about trying one of the bigger hotels in Albuquerque. I can cook and I should be able to—"

"You should be able to do all sorts of things," Amanda interrupted. Tossing the bag and sack on the stripped bed, she stared hard at Serena. "All sorts of things except forget about that man."

Serena looked back at her friend, her gaze steady. "I don't have much choice, do I? He's gone, Birk Reed's bought the ranch and he's anxious to move in. And, I've got Nathan to take care of. It . . . hurts," she added, her voice trembling at the edges. "Maybe it always will. But I couldn't force him to stay. Now—" She took one last look around the empty room, taking all the images of the past to secret away inside her, then picked up the crate. "Now, Nathan and I have to move on."

"The man's a damned fool," Amanda muttered as she followed Serena out and down the stairs to the courtyard, where Ross waited with the cart. He was bouncing Nathan in one arm, Whiskey Pete beside him making faces at the laughing baby.

"You 'bout ready?" Ross asked, shifting Nathan in his

grip as the baby made a grab at the brim of his hat. "Evenin's comin' in fast and we got a good ride ahead of us."

Serena's fingers brushed the shape of the pouch in her pocket. She glanced up at the cliffs, then to Amanda and Ross. "Yes. Except—I have a favor to ask. Could you go on ahead with Nathan, just for tonight? There's something I have to do before I leave. I have my horse," she said quickly, gesturing to the blue-gray stallion that had been a gift from Kwion. "I can get back to the post on my own. Please. Just tonight."

"I don't think that's a good idea—" Ross started to protest. Amanda elbowed him in the ribs and he shut up in answer to the warning scowl she shot his direction.

" 'Course we can take Nathan," Amanda said. "You go on, do what you have to. Best take a pack with you, though," she added, fishing it out of the cart and thrusting it to Serena. "You never know what you might need."

"Thank you," Serena said, taking the pack and giving Amanda's hand a quick squeeze. She watched her take Nathan and climb into the cart beside Ross, waiting until they'd disappeared through the gates before catching up the reins of the stallion.

Whiskey Pete, his head cocked to one side, scratched at his jaw as Serena tied on her pack and hoisted herself into the saddle. "S'ppose there ain't no need in sayin' goodbye now. You'll be comin' back."

"I don't know. I—"

"You will. No matter where you ride to, you belong in this territory. C'mon, Lucky Joe." The dog, stretched out near the stairs, raised his head to give Pete a bored glance. "Well, c'mon. We'll go and git us some supper. Good night fer a ride," he called over his shoulder to Serena as he stumped off toward his room.

"Don't you let Birk and his ruffians bully you now, Pete. You have to stand up to him, do you hear me?" When he gave no indication that he had, Serena shook her head and guided her horse outside the gates, stopping long enough to close and lock the gates. She paused for a few moments, looking in turn at the ranch, the corrals and stables, and finally the oasis, before kicking her horse into a gallop over the plain.

In the soft purple twilight, her memories easily led her to the trail she wanted, the winding, upward path through the canyons and cliffs that led her to a towering peak. At the top, she slipped off the stallion and took the few steps up to the heart of Heaven's Window.

It seemed a lifetime ago she had first gazed through the stone to the eternity beyond. Then, she looked for the truth Gage promised her, blind to the reality in her heart. She hadn't realized, until too late, the depth of his sacrifices for her, in so many ways. All the things she had greedily tried to grasp, might have been hers if only she had let him come to her willingly instead of trying to force him to love her.

Now, she had only one wistful, foolish hope left to comfort her. Gathering together several scraps of pinewood, Serena built a small fire directly under the stone. When it caught and flared, she pulled out the pouch Wuri had given her, scattering its contents into the flames.

Gold and orange sparks leaped into the ebon air. A curl of smoke started in the core of the fire and, caught by the wind, slowly twined its way to pierce the center of Heaven's Window, misting the first glimmer of starlight.

The sweet, heady scent recalled to Serena every caress of Gage's hands on her body, every whisper of his breath on her skin. Moving in a dream, she unfastened the first buttons of her dress and let the material slip down her shoulders as she knelt by the fire.

An incense born of flame and ancient magic surrounded her in its heated embrace. Tonight, for the first time in her life, she looked into the dancing crimson and gold darts and knew no fear. Desperate with longing for him, love banished the past, drove her to trust the fire to help her cast her incantation.

She thought of him as she slid her hands into the silver smoke, whispered his name as she arched back and spread its scent over her throat and bared shoulders. Her eyes closed to savor the feeling. "Come back to me, Gage, my only love . . ." she whispered into the night.

Bathed in fire and the attar of desire, she heard Kwion's voice echo in her head, speaking to her of a lover's sorcery. *The smoke will carry the essence of all you are in the wind and bring your heart to you.*

Serena wished with all her soul it could be true. Except as she opened her eyes and looked into the flames, the wind died, and in the stillness, she felt her heart was lost forever.

The flames flickered and waned a little and she released a tremulous sigh and lifted her gaze to Heaven's Window, desperate to see the truth of Paiute legend. As she did, a shadow fell across the faint light thrown by the fire on the stone.

Serena caught her breath. She slowly turned and looked up, not daring to believe.

He looked back, the Spirit in the Wind, holding her heart.

"Are you real?"

Her whispered question, a bare, trembling sound, tore away Gage's reserve. "As real as you are," he said, still not quite trusting he had found her.

"You came back," Serena breathed. "You came back.

To me." A single tear slipped down her face, gold in the faint fire glow. "Why?"

Gage forced himself to move slowly as he walked toward her. Reaching her side, he knelt in front of her and touched a fingertip to the damp trail on her skin, feeling her responsive quiver. Gently, savoring the moment of anticipation before he held her again, he took her face between his hands and looked straight into her eyes. "Because I love you," he said, stealing the sweet surprise from her lips with his kiss.

The simple, straightforward confession stunned Serena. In four words, with one touch, he gave her back everything. It seemed impossible, an answer to every prayer she had ever spoken. She clung to him, rocked by a maelstrom of emotions so strong that when he drew apart from her to look into her face, she could only stare back in a bewildered confusion of joy and disbelief.

"You can't be real," she whispered. Her hand shook as she hesitantly touched her fingertips to his cheek. "You left. You said . . . you said you couldn't stay."

"I found out I couldn't leave. I was always here with you." He didn't tell her about the endless string of sleepless nights and the merciless hours of the days when the pain of loneliness was all he knew. But he saw she understood all he left unsaid, and much more. "You were willing to let me, and all we have, go. I didn't believe you meant it until I woke up without you. You gave up everything you wanted for me. When I finally realized that, nothing else mattered."

"I want to give to you, Gage. Everything you want."

"Everything is what I want. Not because I feel I should, or because I have to. Because I want everything for us." Gage struggled to find words to describe to her the feelings he'd never before given a name to. "I thought love was a word I would never feel. Until you. Now I—I don't know how to tell you . . ."

Serena laid her fingers on his lips, the vulnerability in him flooding her heart with emotion. "Yes, you do. Your voice is poetry to me. All you have to do is look at me." She swanned her hand from his face to his throat, slipping her palm lower to press against his heart. "All you have to do is touch me. When I see you, when you touch me, there are no words. Only our sweet communion."

Leaning forward, she brushed his mouth with hers, feeling the throb of his heartbeat quicken under her hand.

With Serena in his arms, holding her, touching her, breathing the essence of her, setting his desire aflame. Gage found an answer to all the emptiness he'd lived with for so long. She filled him, slow and sweet, rain on the desert inside him. "I want to love you," he said softly, looking deep into her eyes, the coupling of flame and incense on her skin. "But if I do, for me, there won't be any turning back. It won't be just for today, or tomorrow. It'll be for always."

"Yes, love me. That's all I want. That's all I'll ever dream of or wish for. Please . . ."

There was nothing left to say as they were swept into each other, no room for doubt or hesitation. Wild and fierce, tender and poignant, depthless and without boundary, the feeling coursed between them, binding them with ties stronger than desire, more lasting than passion.

Serena kindled the embers of the eternal fire between them with her husky words, the temptation of her hands and lips. But it was Gage who made it a slow burning seduction.

Standing, he drew her up with him, so close only a

whisper could slip between them. Barely skimming her body with his, he moved around behind her and lifted her hair from her neck, pressing his mouth to her nape. Serena shivered, sucking in a breath when he unfastened the button of her dress where she'd left off, then the next, pressing a kiss to every inch of her he uncovered.

When he reached the curve of her back, he retraced his path, sliding his hand around her waist to bring her full against him.

Serena felt his need for her and trembled at the power they held over each other. It was sweet torture to let him slowly lead her to love. At the same time, she wanted him to make it last forever. She leaned her head to his shoulder, inviting him to show her the passion his touch promised.

The motion of her body on his stripped away some of Gage's resolve to love her gently, to give her all the dreams and fantasies she cherished, to satisfy her innermost desires. He couldn't touch her without wanting to take and give all of it now.

"Serena . . ." Her name came out as a low, needy whisper.

She turned in his arms, answering his heart's call. Passion flamed inside her, a vivid, hungry ache, bringing fulgurant color to places that had been pale and dim. She lost herself in it, not knowing where he left off and she began. Like the first time, all the times they were together, their spirits were one. And tonight, they both knew at last the time was right to share the rest of their love, for the two halves to make a whole.

They undressed each other slowly, peeling off each layer with delight in the discovery, longing in every caress, a timeless, primal passion in each touch, until they were both breathless with it.

In her eyes, Gage saw the wild, hungry need that

matched his own, fearless and for him alone. He lowered her to the warm earth and she reached for him and the thunder rolled inside him, carrying him toward a place he had never been and would only see in her arms.

His body slid over hers and Serena gave him no space to falter for her sake. He kissed her deeply and then he was inside her, their bodies joined with a shock of feeling that was both pain and naked pleasure. Gage held her close, stroking his hands over her, whispering disjointed words of praise and love in her ear until something inside her drove her to move against him, with him, grasping at every sensation, every feeling.

Each one burst into another, more intense than the last, then another, and again. The stars above her in the heart of Heaven's Window fell inside her and burst into flame. She rode the crest of it, harder, hotter, faster than her mind could see, to the end and the brilliant crash that shattered the darkness and made her light.

Her cry of joy and wonder surrendered Gage to the same heights and left him split asunder and transformed by her love. Shaking from the force of it, he wrapped her tightly in his arms, letting the night gradually enfold them again in its embrace.

They had both come home. Amid the harsh beauty of the wilderness, with all its dangers and uncertainties, she felt safe, secure in a feeling as strong and certain as the ageless stone portal to the heavens. This was her home—their home.

"I love you," she said softly, as Gage lovingly brushed her damp hair from her temple, grazing a kiss against her skin. "I was so afraid, so lost. I thought I would never see you again. I thought I would always be alone."

"Neither of us will ever be alone." Propping up on

one elbow, Gage traced her features with his fingertips. "That is, if you've changed your mind about leaving for Albuquerque," he gently teased. "We belong here."

"I know. Besides, you've already staked your claim with your corral. If we just make one more trip back to the Grand Canyon—"

"I thought you liked security, woman. I'm beginning to think you enjoy living dangerously," Gage said. "Maybe I should think twice about taking you on."

"I won't give you that chance," she returned with an echo of her familiar audacity. "And you're taking both of us on. Nathan belongs here, too. You not only have me, but a son as well."

"Maybe two," he murmured, bending to brush his mouth over her belly, the tenderness in his caress bringing tears to her eyes. He moved to kiss her, taking his time, stirring the ache for him inside her again. "I have something for you," he said at last, breathing the words over her lips.

"Yes," Serena said softly, winding her arms around him. "You do."

"That too. But you'll have to wait a moment for this."

She sat up, looking at him questioningly as he pushed away from her and got to his feet. But he only smiled. Sorting through the pile of clothing they'd scattered over the stones, he retrieved something from one of his shirt pockets and came back to her, kneeling down by her side.

"I want to make it real this time," Gage said, taking her hand in his. "Something we both want for the right reasons. Will you become my wife again, make that promise once more?"

This time, Serena let the tears fall unheeded, full with

the love she felt for him. "If you promise to stay my husband."

"It's all I want." Lifting her hand, he slipped a ring on her finger, a circle of roses, wrought in silver. "And although I can't give you roses, I can promise these flowers, like my love for you, will never wither and die."

Overcome by the emotions cascading from her heart, Serena could only hold him close, telling him with her touch how much it meant to her that he had remembered her childhood dreams. "You always said I did all the talking, but tonight you've been very eloquent in telling me how you feel," she said finally, looking up at him with mischief and love mixed with her tears. Guiding him to lie with her under the midnight sky, she glanced at Heaven's Window, knowing she no longer needed to look beyond to see the truth. "I think I need to hear your promise one more time."